Jane Austen's

PRIDE & PREJUDICE

the graphic novel

KALYANI NAVYUG MEDIA PVT LTD

SCRIPT LAURENCE SACH
ILLUSTRATION RAJESH NAGULAKONDA
COLOR RAJESH NAGULAKONDA, VIJAY SHARMA, DILIP WALIA
EDITS PARAMA MAJUMDER, KOKILA TRIPATHI, SOURAV DUTTA, JASON QUINN
DTP BHAVNATH CHAUDHARY
COVER ART RAJESH NAGULAKONDA

Mission Statement

To entertain and educate young minds by creating unique illustrated books
that recount stories of human values, arouse curiosity in the world around us,
and inspire with tales of great deeds of unforgettable people.

Published by Kalyani Navyug Media Pvt. Ltd.
101 C, Shiv House, Hari Nagar Ashram, New Delhi 110014, India

ISBN: 978-93-80028-74-3

Printed in India

JANE AUSTEN

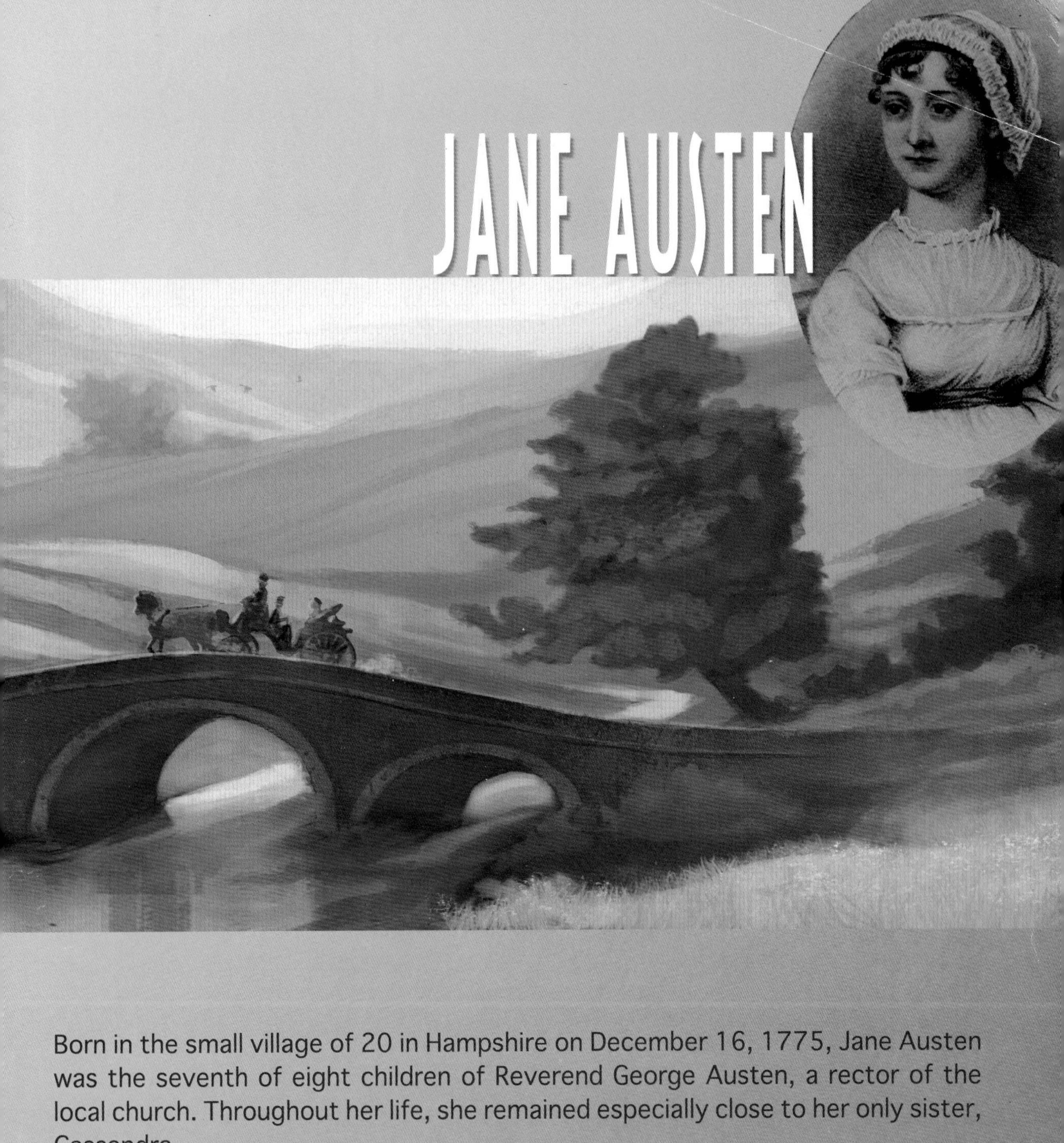

Born in the small village of 20 in Hampshire on December 16, 1775, Jane Austen was the seventh of eight children of Reverend George Austen, a rector of the local church. Throughout her life, she remained especially close to her only sister, Cassandra.

An avid reader, Jane began writing her own stories at the age of ten. She was thirty-six when *Sense and Sensibility* (1811) became her first published novel. Three more followed during her lifetime: *Pride and Prejudice* (1813), *Mansfield Park* (1814), and *Emma* (1816). *Northanger Abbey* and *Persuasion* were published posthumously in 1818.

Jane became ill in 1816 and died in the arms of her sister on July 18, 1817. She was forty-one years old. Jane Austen is buried in Winchester Cathedral.

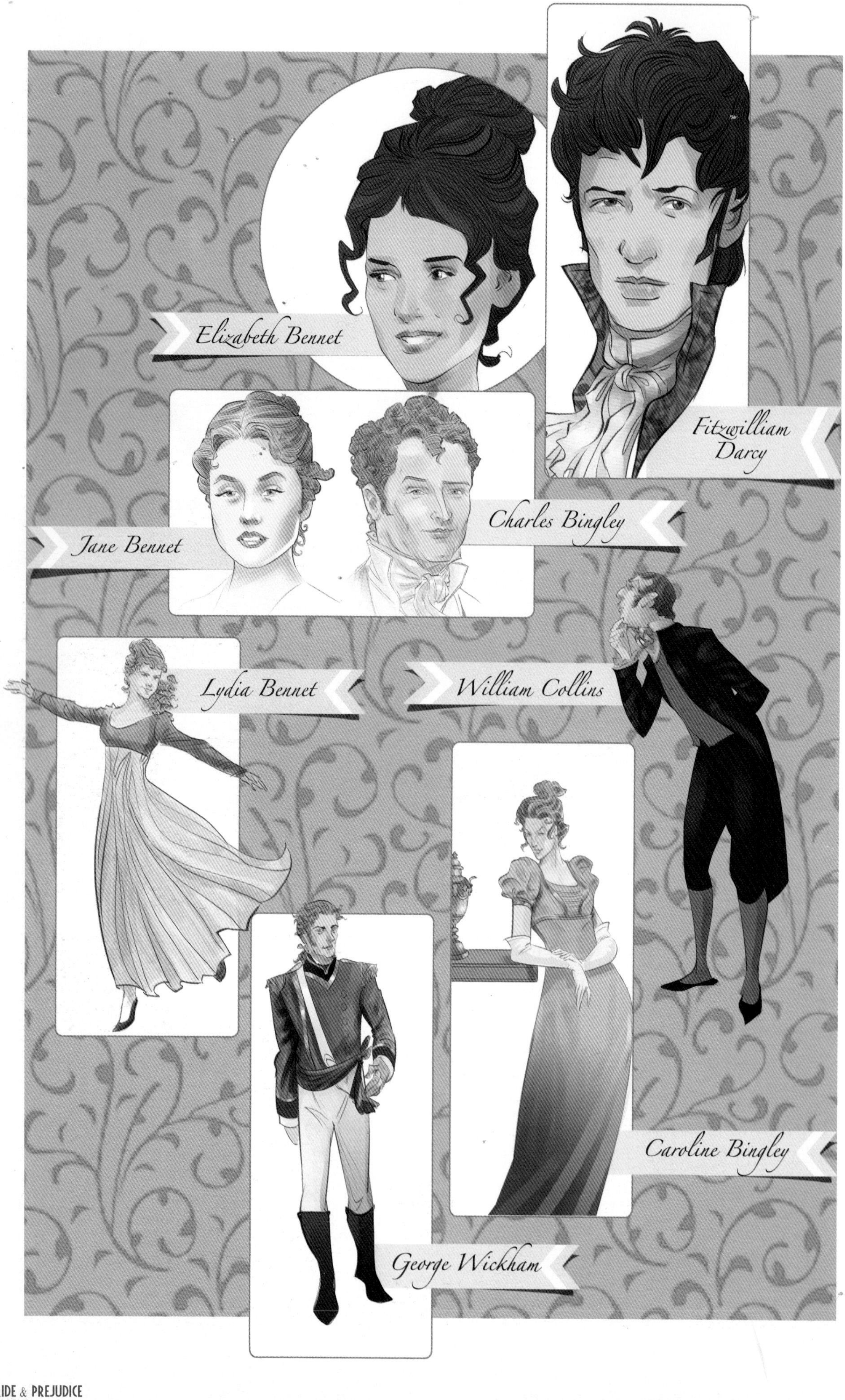
Elizabeth Bennet
Fitzwilliam Darcy
Charles Bingley
Jane Bennet
Lydia Bennet
William Collins
Caroline Bingley
George Wickham

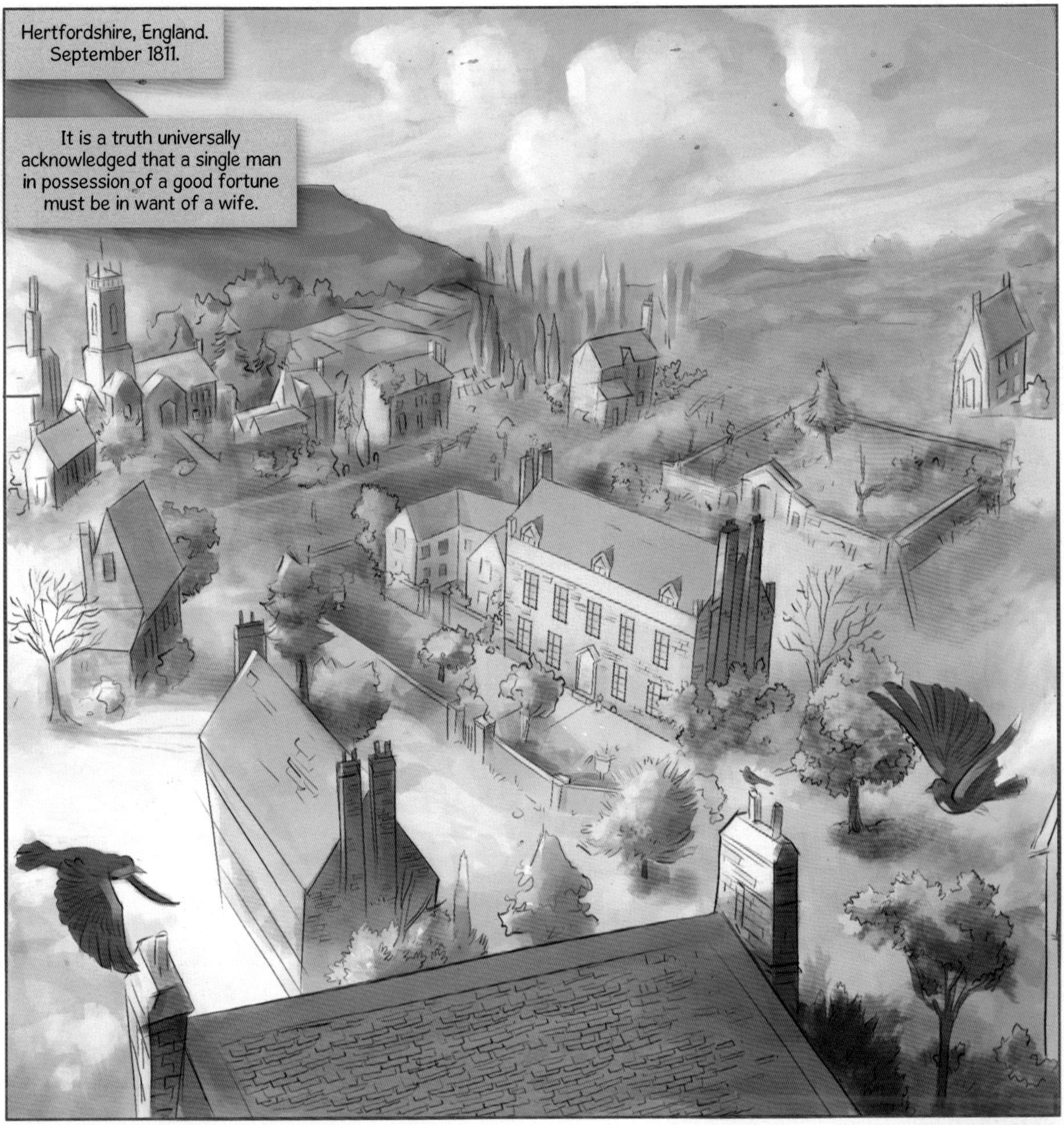
Hertfordshire, England.
September 1811.
It is a truth universally acknowledged that a single man in possession of a good fortune must be in want of a wife.

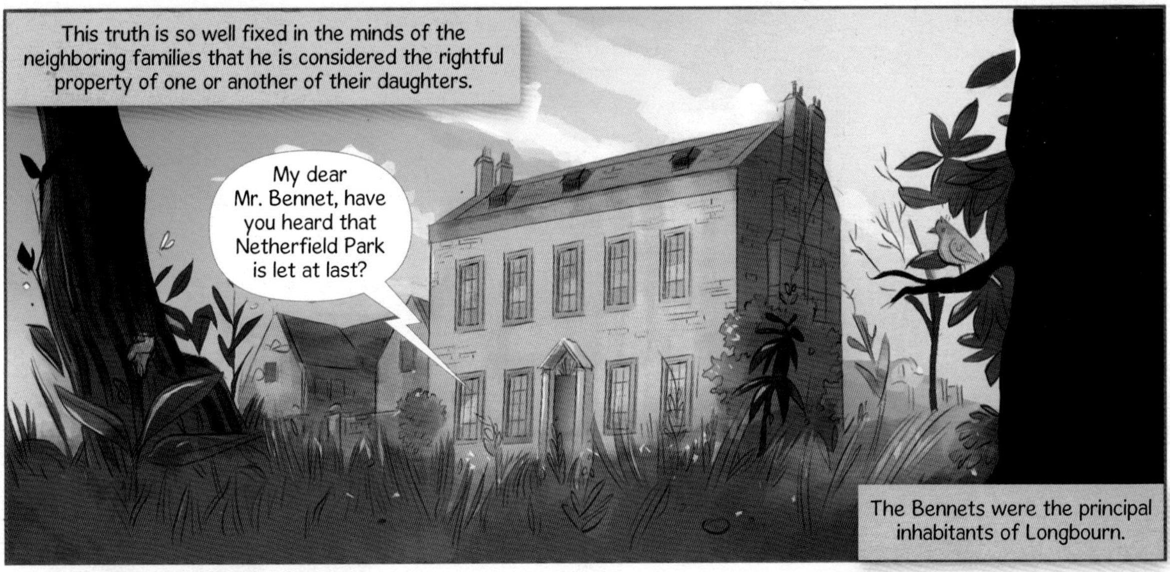
This truth is so well fixed in the minds of the neighboring families that he is considered the rightful property of one or another of their daughters.
My dear Mr. Bennet, have you heard that Netherfield Park is let at last?
The Bennets were the principal inhabitants of Longbourn.

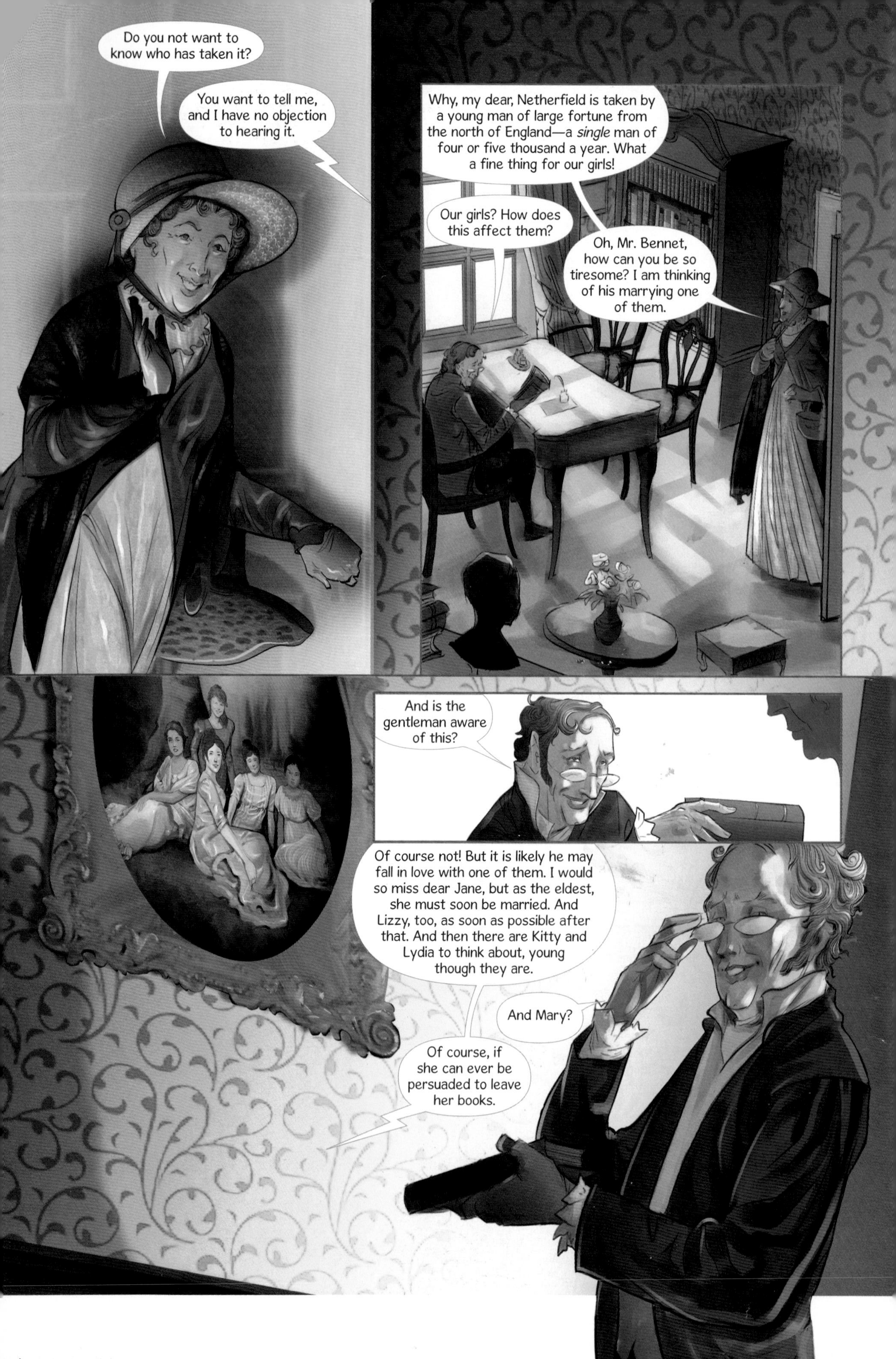
Do you not want to know who has taken it?
You want to tell me, and I have no objection to hearing it.
Why, my dear, Netherfield is taken by a young man of large fortune from the north of England—a *single* man of four or five thousand a year. What a fine thing for our girls!
Our girls? How does this affect them?
Oh, Mr. Bennet, how can you be so tiresome? I am thinking of his marrying one of them.
And is the gentleman aware of this?
Of course not! But it is likely he may fall in love with one of them. I would so miss dear Jane, but as the eldest, she must soon be married. And Lizzy, too, as soon as possible after that. And then there are Kitty and Lydia to think about, young though they are.
And Mary?
Of course, if she can ever be persuaded to leave her books.

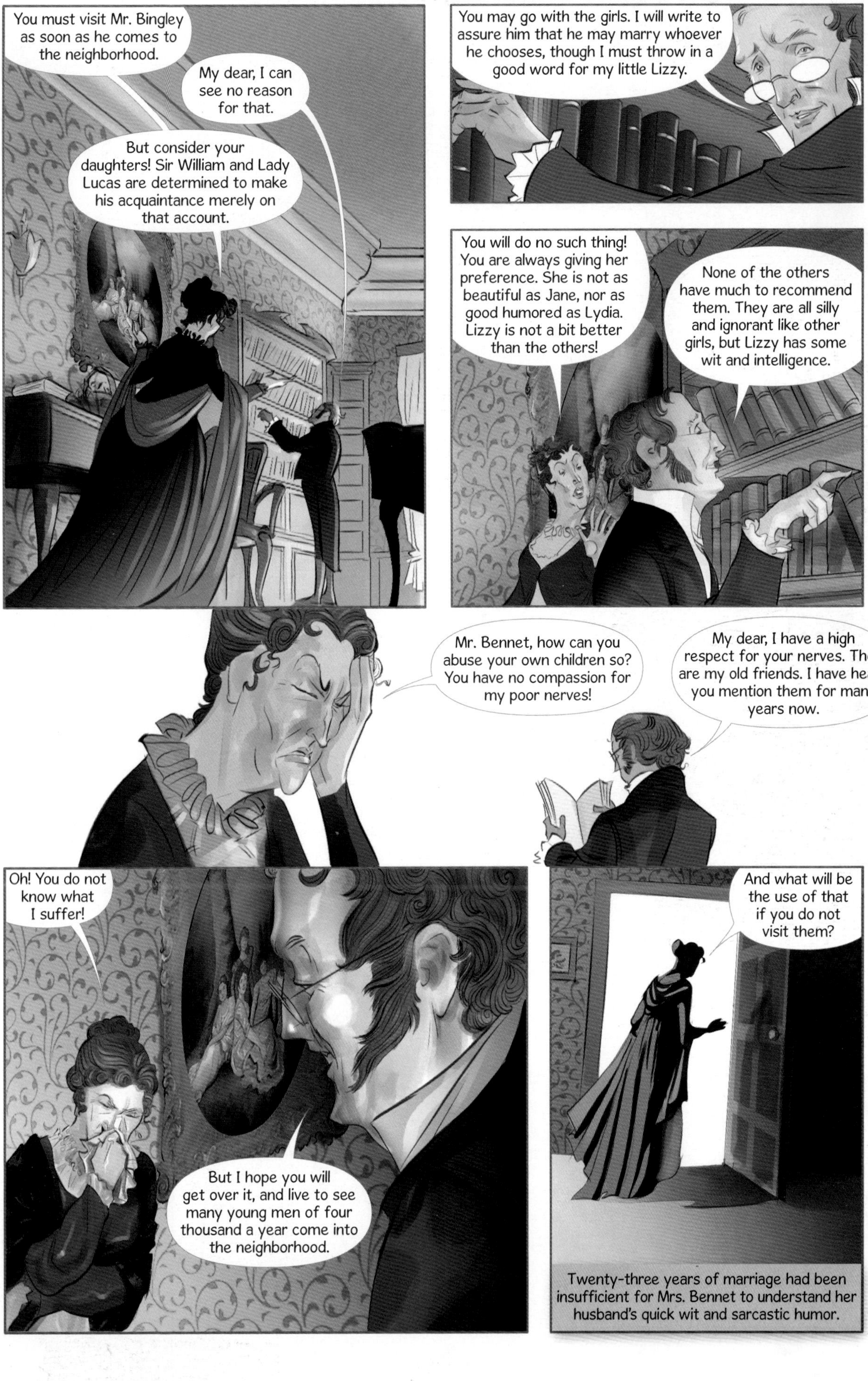

You must visit Mr. Bingley as soon as he comes to the neighborhood.
My dear, I can see no reason for that.
But consider your daughters! Sir William and Lady Lucas are determined to make his acquaintance merely on that account.
You may go with the girls. I will write to assure him that he may marry whoever he chooses, though I must throw in a good word for my little Lizzy.
You will do no such thing! You are always giving her preference. She is not as beautiful as Jane, nor as good humored as Lydia. Lizzy is not a bit better than the others!
None of the others have much to recommend them. They are all silly and ignorant like other girls, but Lizzy has some wit and intelligence.
Mr. Bennet, how can you abuse your own children so? You have no compassion for my poor nerves!
My dear, I have a high respect for your nerves. They are my old friends. I have heard you mention them for many years now.
Oh! You do not know what I suffer!
But I hope you will get over it, and live to see many young men of four thousand a year come into the neighborhood.
And what will be the use of that if you do not visit them?
Twenty-three years of marriage had been insufficient for Mrs. Bennet to understand her husband's quick wit and sarcastic humor.

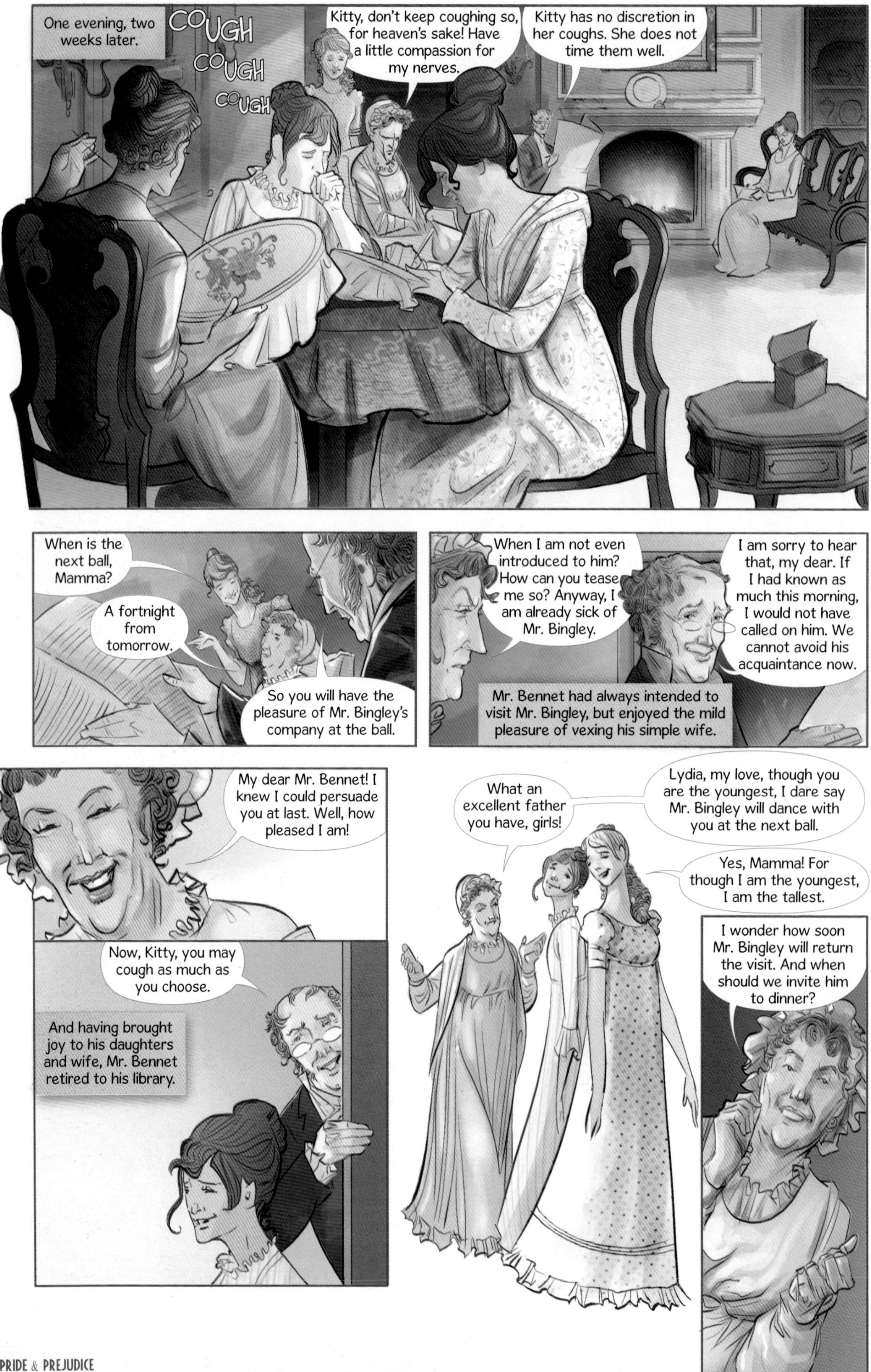
One evening, two weeks later.
COUGH
COUGH
COUGH
Kitty, don't keep coughing so, for heaven's sake! Have a little compassion for my nerves.
Kitty has no discretion in her coughs. She does not time them well.
When is the next ball, Mamma?
A fortnight from tomorrow.
So you will have the pleasure of Mr. Bingley's company at the ball.
When I am not even introduced to him? How can you tease me so? Anyway, I am already sick of Mr. Bingley.
I am sorry to hear that, my dear. If I had known as much this morning, I would not have called on him. We cannot avoid his acquaintance now.
Mr. Bennet had always intended to visit Mr. Bingley, but enjoyed the mild pleasure of vexing his simple wife.
My dear Mr. Bennet! I knew I could persuade you at last. Well, how pleased I am!
Now, Kitty, you may cough as much as you choose.
And having brought joy to his daughters and wife, Mr. Bennet retired to his library.
What an excellent father you have, girls!
Lydia, my love, though you are the youngest, I dare say Mr. Bingley will dance with you at the next ball.
Yes, Mamma! For though I am the youngest, I am the tallest.
I wonder how soon Mr. Bingley will return the visit. And when should we invite him to dinner?

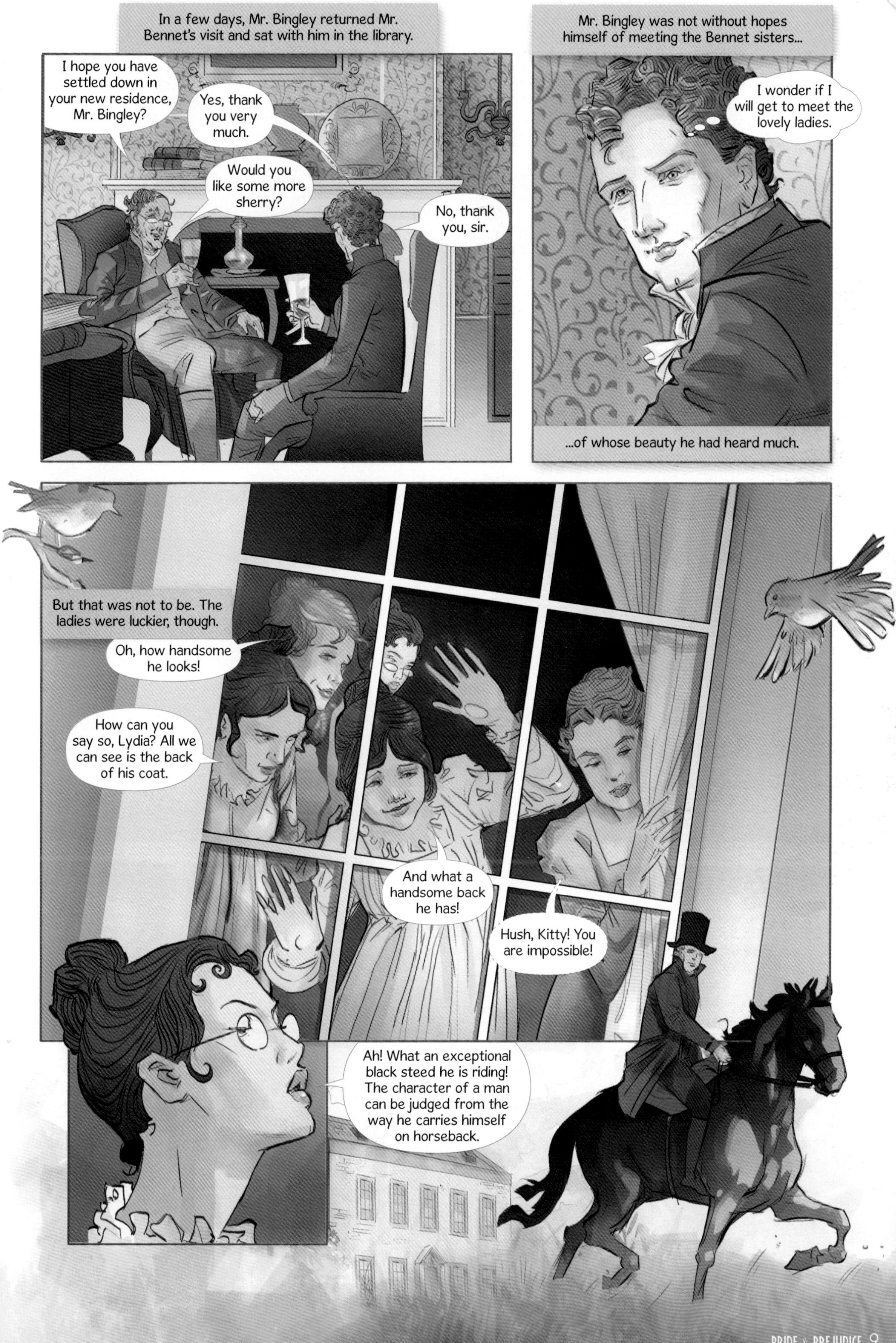
In a few days, Mr. Bingley returned Mr. Bennet's visit and sat with him in the library.
I hope you have settled down in your new residence, Mr. Bingley?
Yes, thank you very much.
Would you like some more sherry?
No, thank you, sir.
Mr. Bingley was not without hopes himself of meeting the Bennet sisters...
I wonder if I will get to meet the lovely ladies.
...of whose beauty he had heard much.
But that was not to be. The ladies were luckier, though.
Oh, how handsome he looks!
How can you say so, Lydia? All we can see is the back of his coat.
And what a handsome back he has!
Hush, Kitty! You are impossible!
Ah! What an exceptional black steed he is riding! The character of a man can be judged from the way he carries himself on horseback.

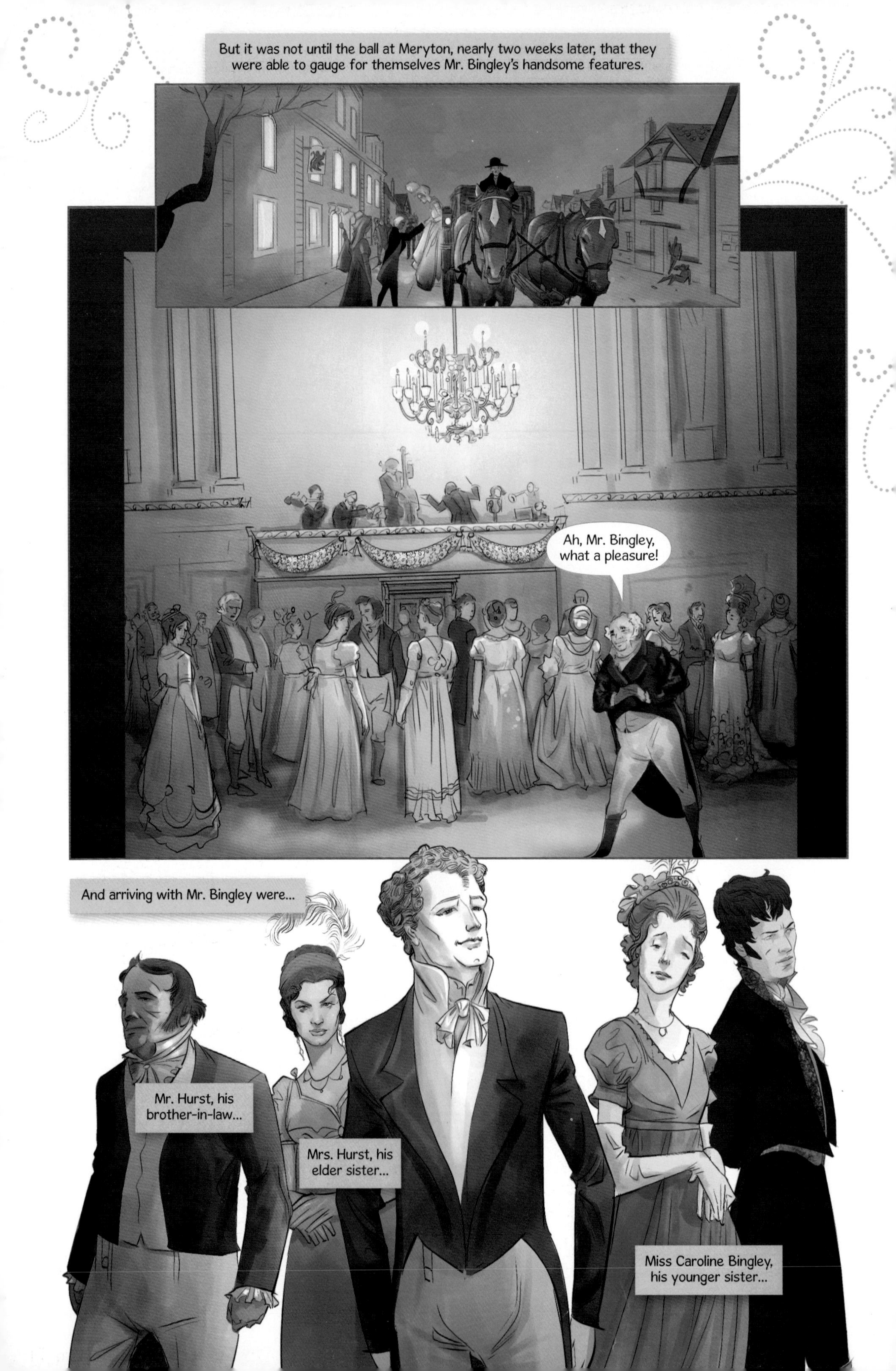
But it was not until the ball at Meryton, nearly two weeks later, that they were able to gauge for themselves Mr. Bingley's handsome features.
Ah, Mr. Bingley, what a pleasure!
And arriving with Mr. Bingley were...
Mr. Hurst, his brother-in-law...
Mrs. Hurst, his elder sister...
Miss Caroline Bingley, his younger sister...

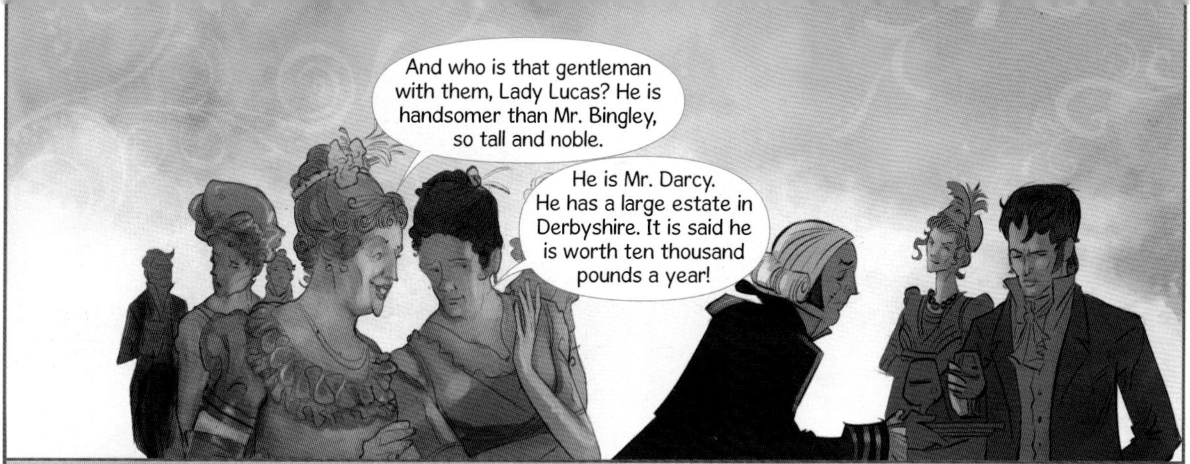
And who is that gentleman with them, Lady Lucas? He is handsomer than Mr. Bingley, so tall and noble.
He is Mr. Darcy. He has a large estate in Derbyshire. It is said he is worth ten thousand pounds a year!

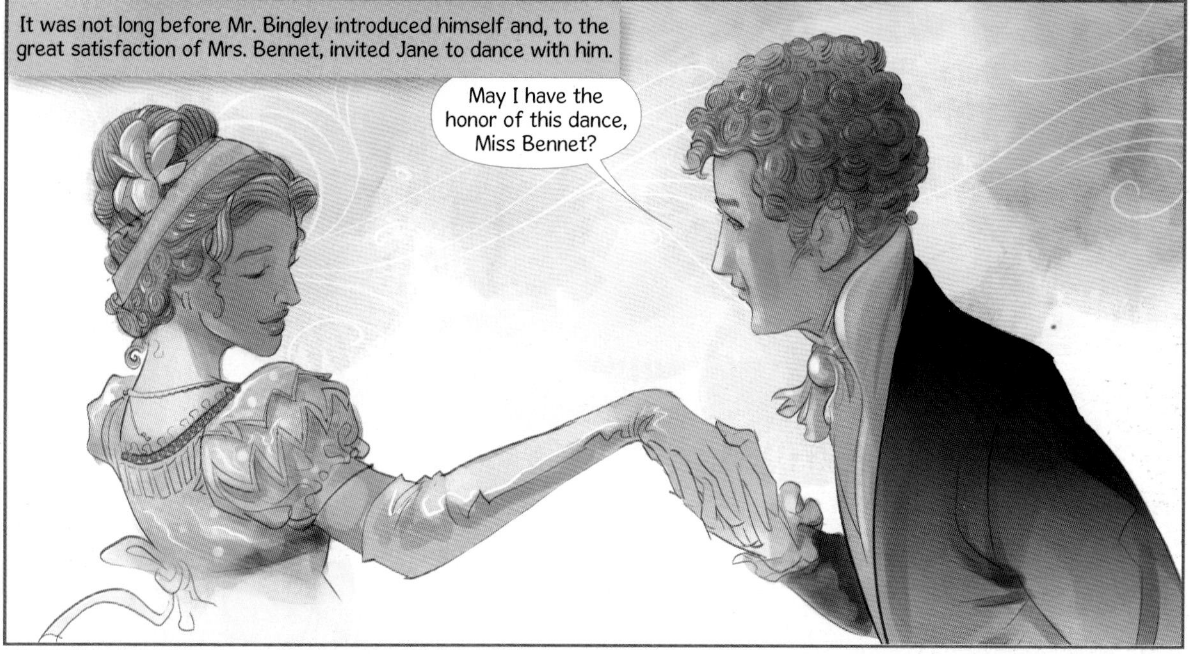
It was not long before Mr. Bingley introduced himself and, to the great satisfaction of Mrs. Bennet, invited Jane to dance with him.
May I have the honor of this dance, Miss Bennet?

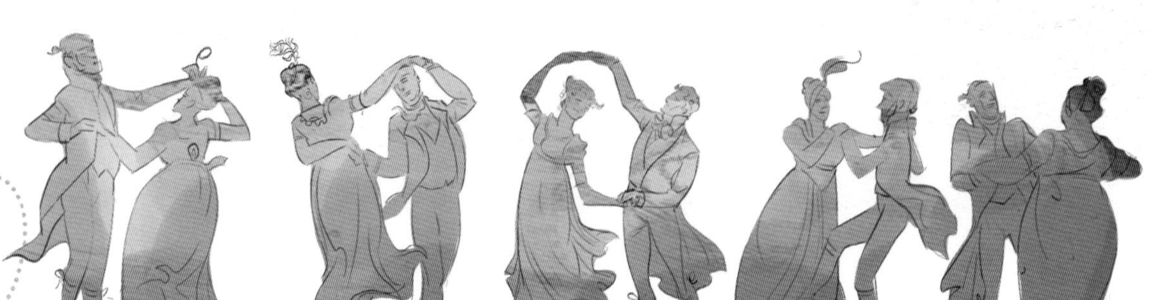

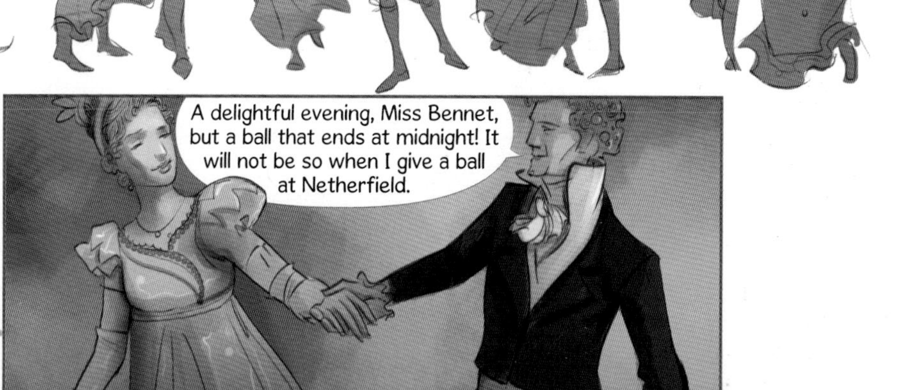
A delightful evening, Miss Bennet, but a ball that ends at midnight! It will not be so when I give a ball at Netherfield.

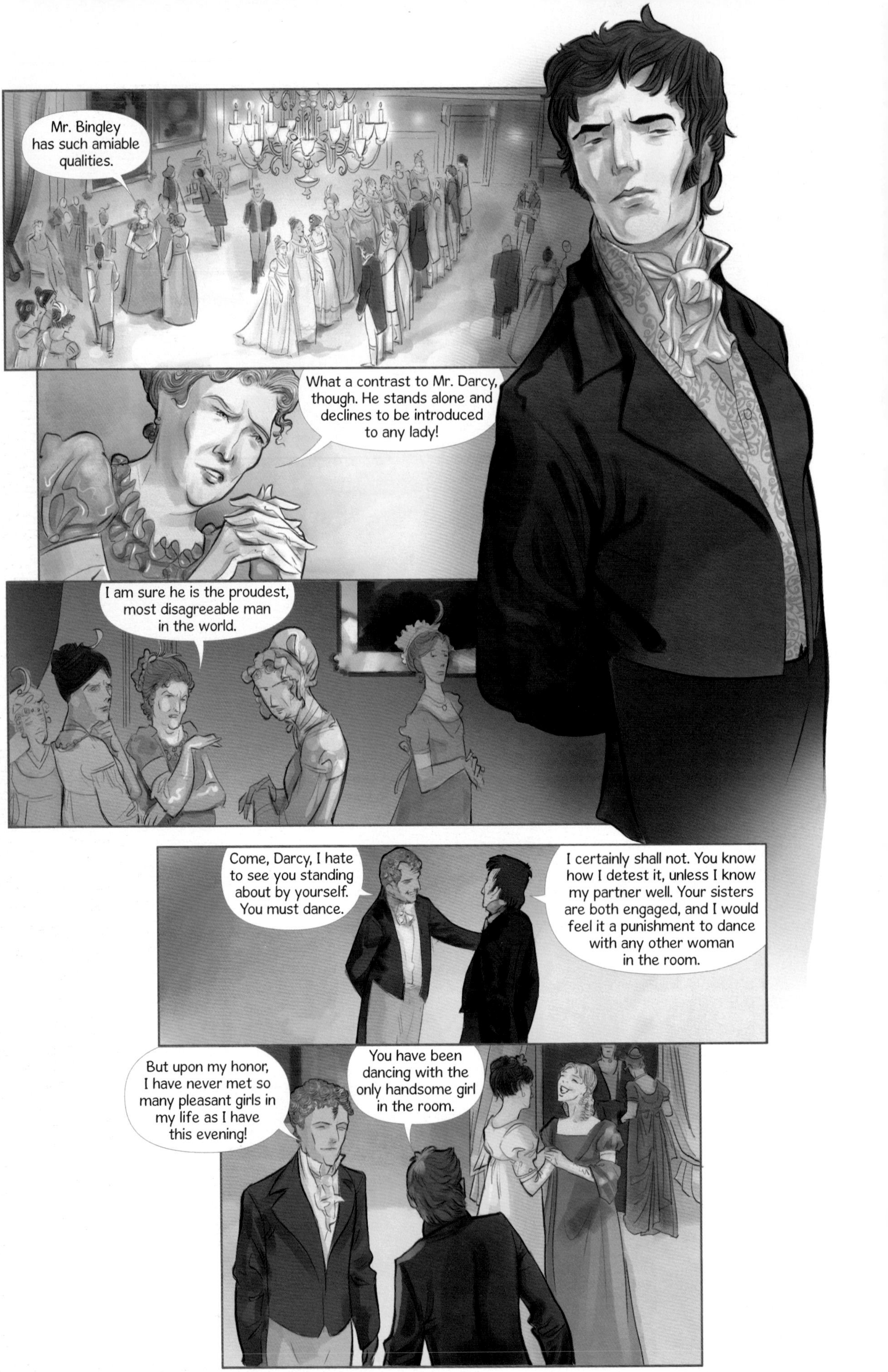
Mr. Bingley has such amiable qualities.
What a contrast to Mr. Darcy, though. He stands alone and declines to be introduced to any lady!
I am sure he is the proudest, most disagreeable man in the world.
Come, Darcy, I hate to see you standing about by yourself. You must dance.
I certainly shall not. You know how I detest it, unless I know my partner well. Your sisters are both engaged, and I would feel it a punishment to dance with any other woman in the room.
You have been dancing with the only handsome girl in the room.
But upon my honor, I have never met so many pleasant girls in my life as I have this evening!

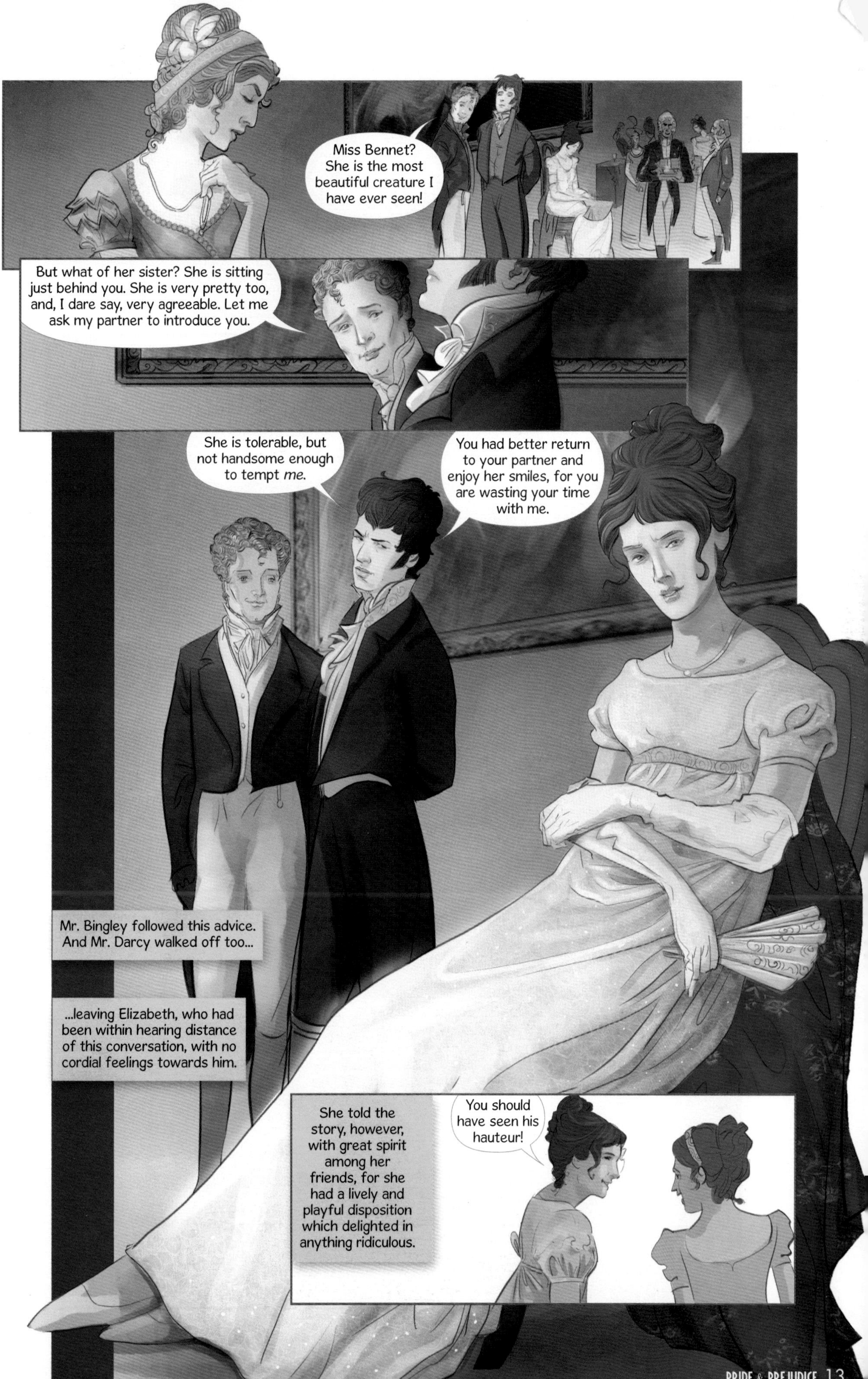
Miss Bennet? She is the most beautiful creature I have ever seen!
But what of her sister? She is sitting just behind you. She is very pretty too, and, I dare say, very agreeable. Let me ask my partner to introduce you.
She is tolerable, but not handsome enough to tempt *me*.
You had better return to your partner and enjoy her smiles, for you are wasting your time with me.
Mr. Bingley followed this advice. And Mr. Darcy walked off too...
...leaving Elizabeth, who had been within hearing distance of this conversation, with no cordial feelings towards him.
She told the story, however, with great spirit among her friends, for she had a lively and playful disposition which delighted in anything ridiculous.
You should have seen his hauteur!

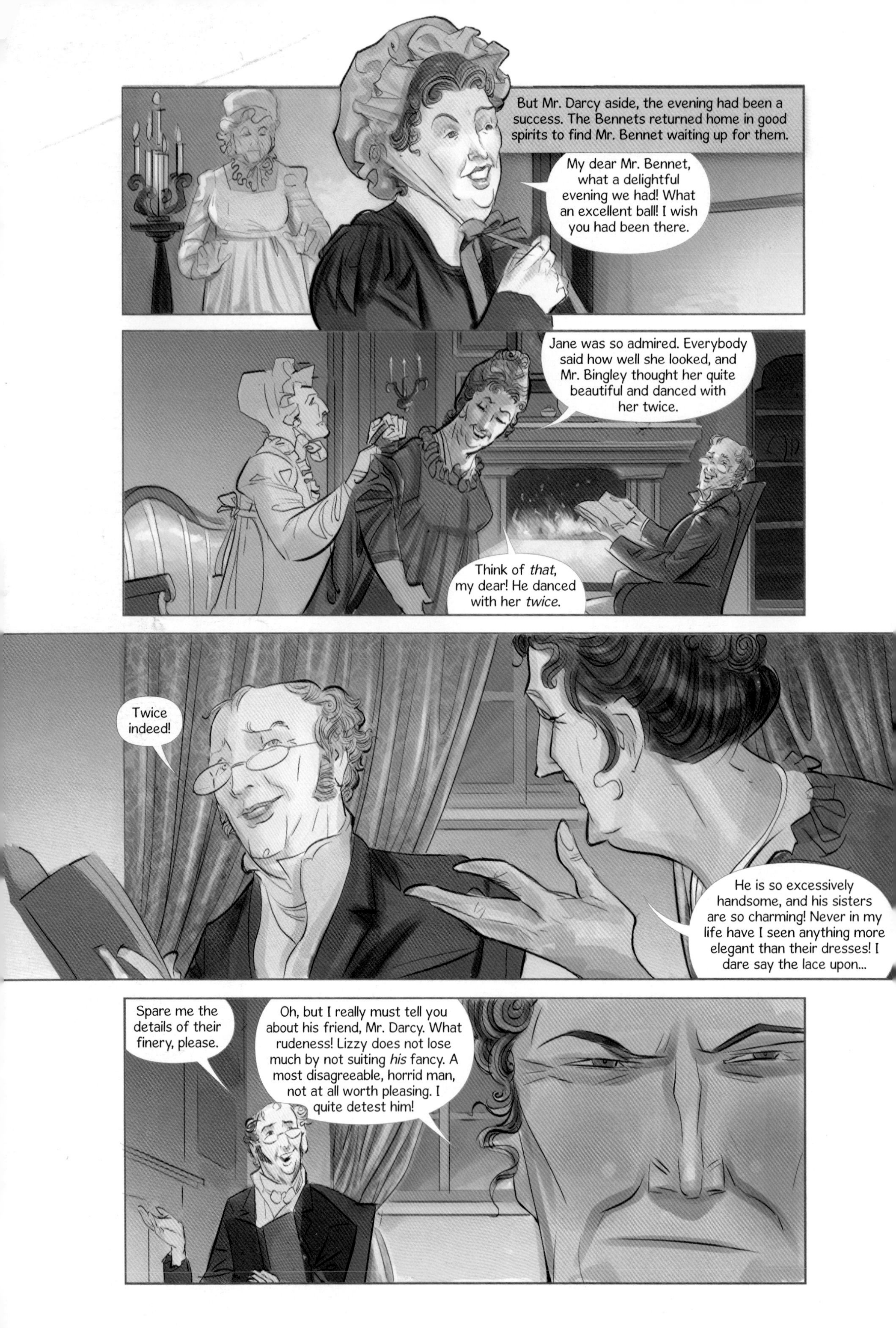
But Mr. Darcy aside, the evening had been a success. The Bennets returned home in good spirits to find Mr. Bennet waiting up for them.
My dear Mr. Bennet, what a delightful evening we had! What an excellent ball! I wish you had been there.
Jane was so admired. Everybody said how well she looked, and Mr. Bingley thought her quite beautiful and danced with her twice.
Think of *that*, my dear! He danced with her *twice*.
Twice indeed!
He is so excessively handsome, and his sisters are so charming! Never in my life have I seen anything more elegant than their dresses! I dare say the lace upon...
Spare me the details of their finery, please.
Oh, but I really must tell you about his friend, Mr. Darcy. What rudeness! Lizzy does not lose much by not suiting *his* fancy. A most disagreeable, horrid man, not at all worth pleasing. I quite detest him!

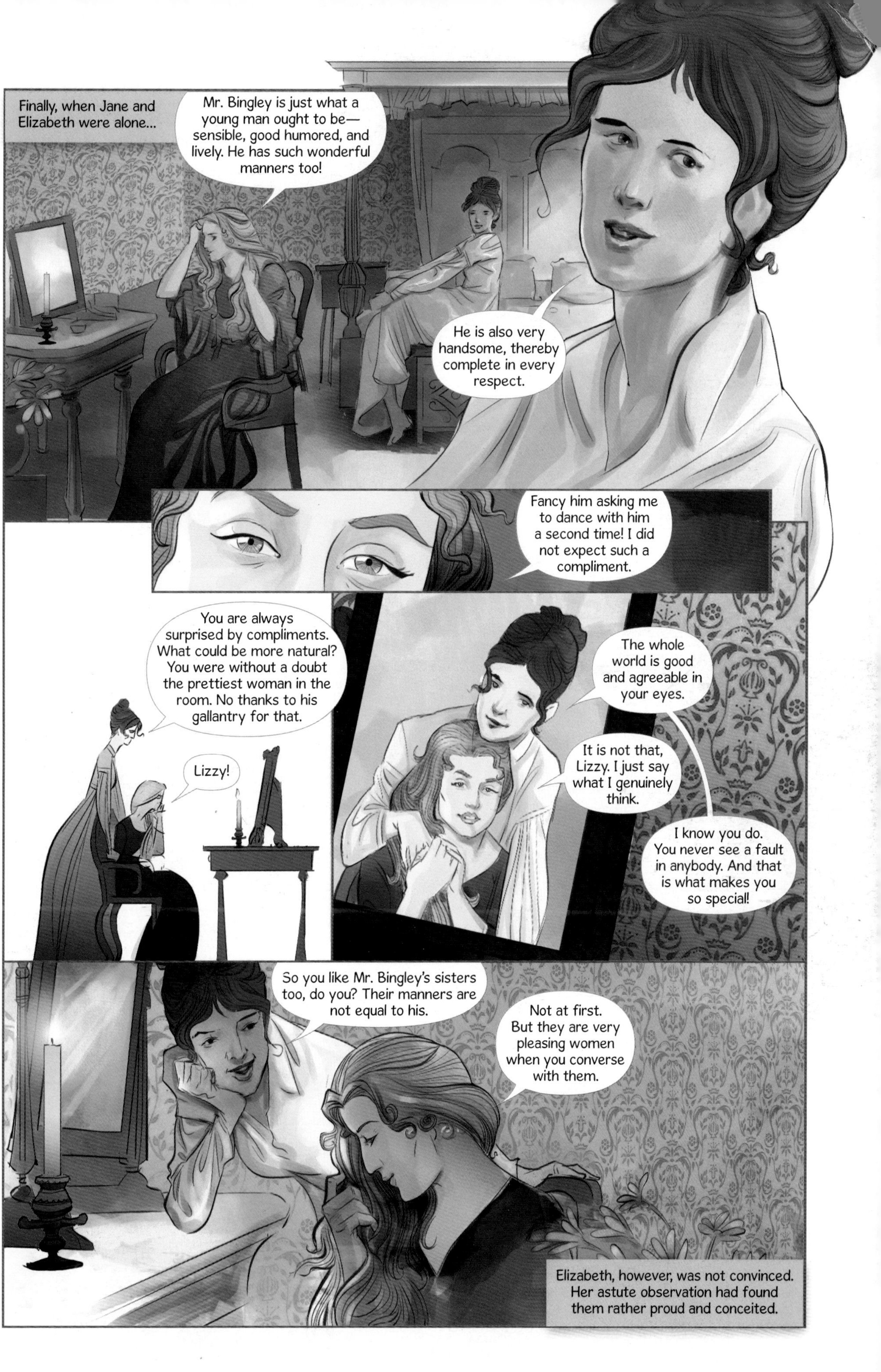

Finally, when Jane and Elizabeth were alone...
Mr. Bingley is just what a young man ought to be—sensible, good humored, and lively. He has such wonderful manners too!
He is also very handsome, thereby complete in every respect.
Fancy him asking me to dance with him a second time! I did not expect such a compliment.
You are always surprised by compliments. What could be more natural? You were without a doubt the prettiest woman in the room. No thanks to his gallantry for that.
Lizzy!
The whole world is good and agreeable in your eyes.
It is not that, Lizzy. I just say what I genuinely think.
I know you do. You never see a fault in anybody. And that is what makes you so special!
So you like Mr. Bingley's sisters too, do you? Their manners are not equal to his.
Not at first. But they are very pleasing women when you converse with them.
Elizabeth, however, was not convinced. Her astute observation had found them rather proud and conceited.

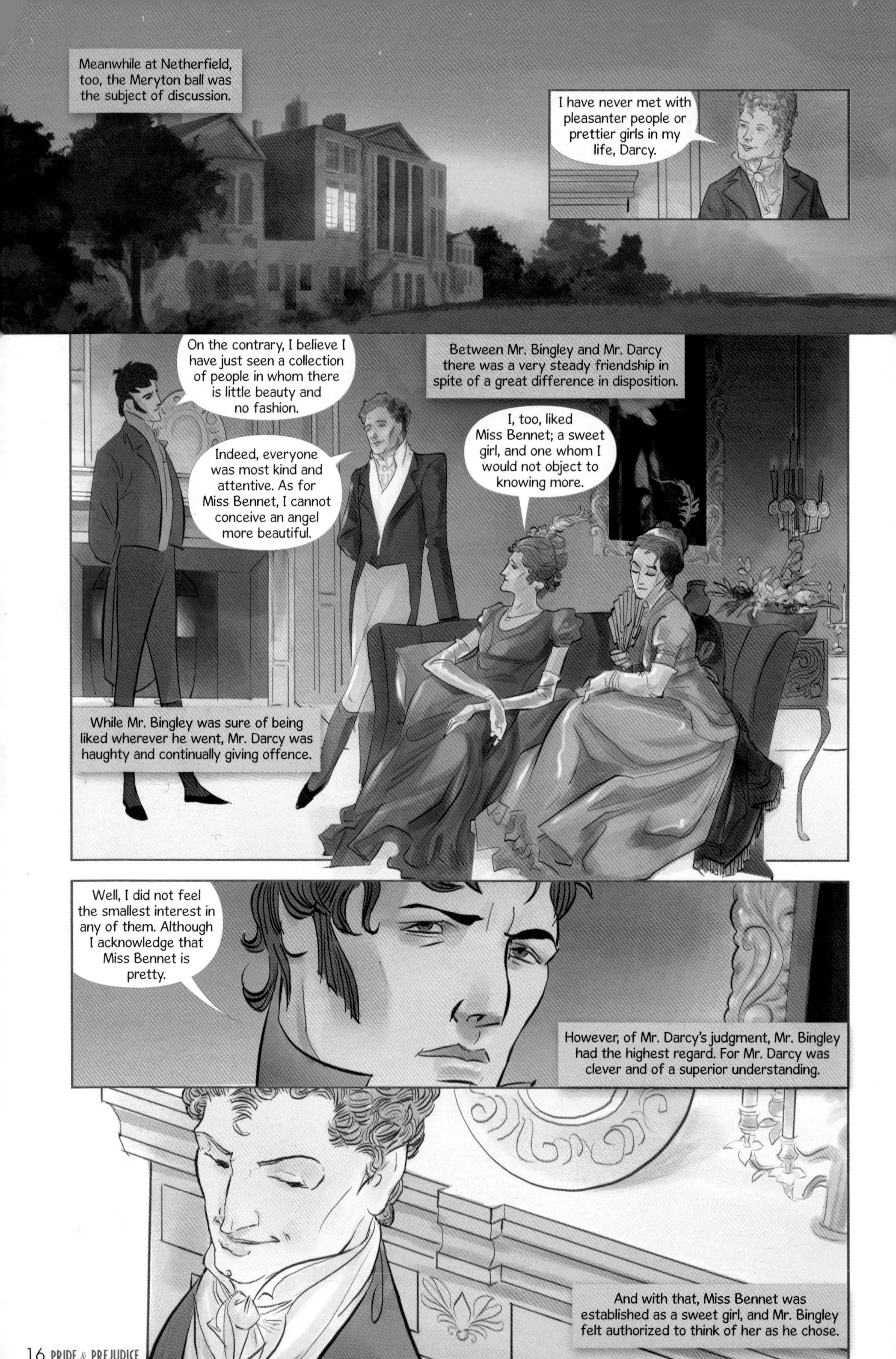

Meanwhile at Netherfield, too, the Meryton ball was the subject of discussion.
I have never met with pleasanter people or prettier girls in my life, Darcy.
On the contrary, I believe I have just seen a collection of people in whom there is little beauty and no fashion.
Between Mr. Bingley and Mr. Darcy there was a very steady friendship in spite of a great difference in disposition.
Indeed, everyone was most kind and attentive. As for Miss Bennet, I cannot conceive an angel more beautiful.
I, too, liked Miss Bennet; a sweet girl, and one whom I would not object to knowing more.
While Mr. Bingley was sure of being liked wherever he went, Mr. Darcy was haughty and continually giving offence.
Well, I did not feel the smallest interest in any of them. Although I acknowledge that Miss Bennet is pretty.
However, of Mr. Darcy's judgment, Mr. Bingley had the highest regard. For Mr. Darcy was clever and of a superior understanding.
And with that, Miss Bennet was established as a sweet girl, and Mr. Bingley felt authorized to think of her as he chose.

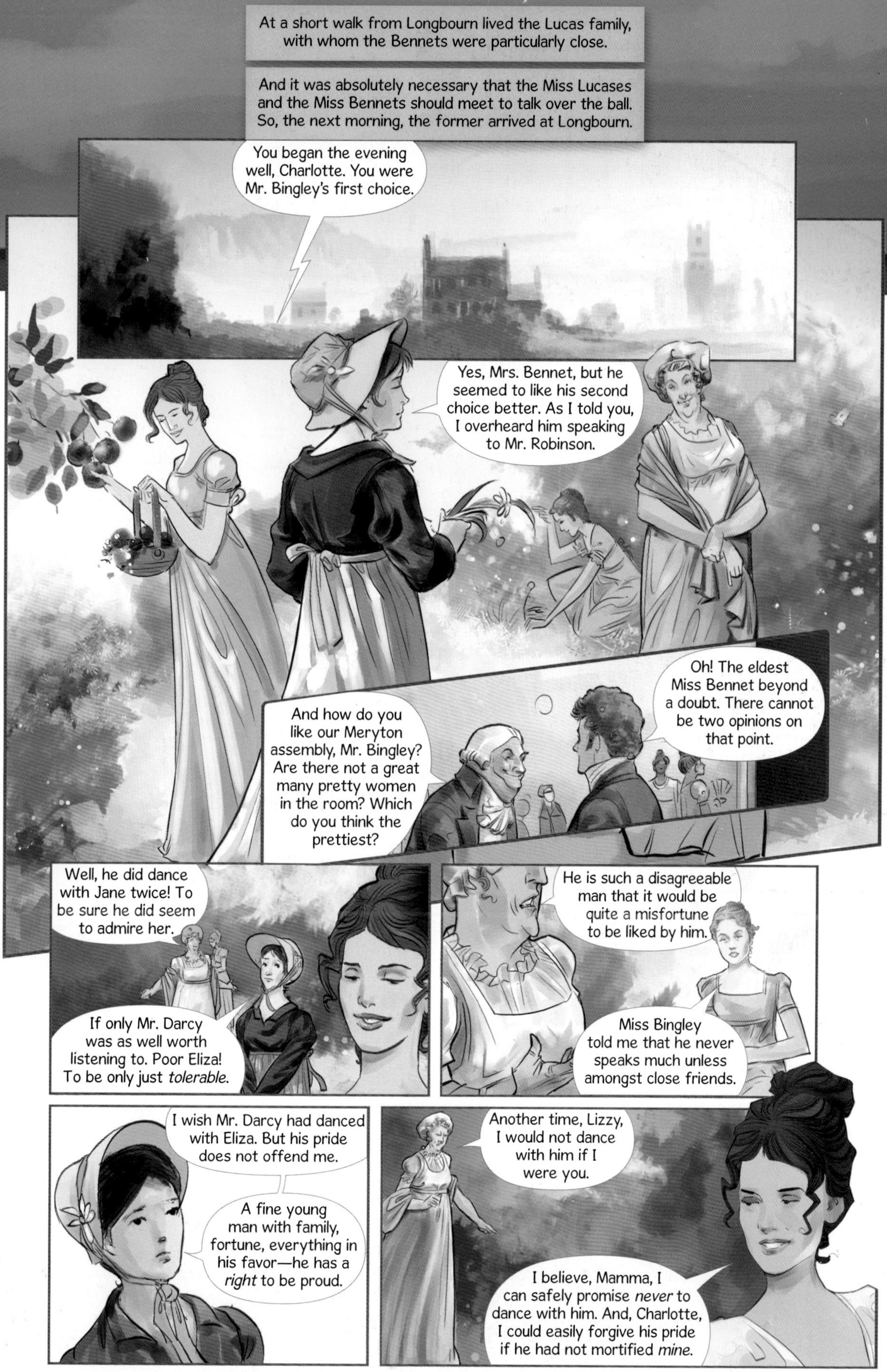
At a short walk from Longbourn lived the Lucas family, with whom the Bennets were particularly close.
And it was absolutely necessary that the Miss Lucases and the Miss Bennets should meet to talk over the ball. So, the next morning, the former arrived at Longbourn.
You began the evening well, Charlotte. You were Mr. Bingley's first choice.
Yes, Mrs. Bennet, but he seemed to like his second choice better. As I told you, I overheard him speaking to Mr. Robinson.
And how do you like our Meryton assembly, Mr. Bingley? Are there not a great many pretty women in the room? Which do you think the prettiest?
Oh! The eldest Miss Bennet beyond a doubt. There cannot be two opinions on that point.
Well, he did dance with Jane twice! To be sure he did seem to admire her.
If only Mr. Darcy was as well worth listening to. Poor Eliza! To be only just *tolerable*.
He is such a disagreeable man that it would be quite a misfortune to be liked by him.
Miss Bingley told me that he never speaks much unless amongst close friends.
I wish Mr. Darcy had danced with Eliza. But his pride does not offend me.
A fine young man with family, fortune, everything in his favor—he has a *right* to be proud.
Another time, Lizzy, I would not dance with him if I were you.
I believe, Mamma, I can safely promise *never* to dance with him. And, Charlotte, I could easily forgive his pride if he had not mortified *mine*.

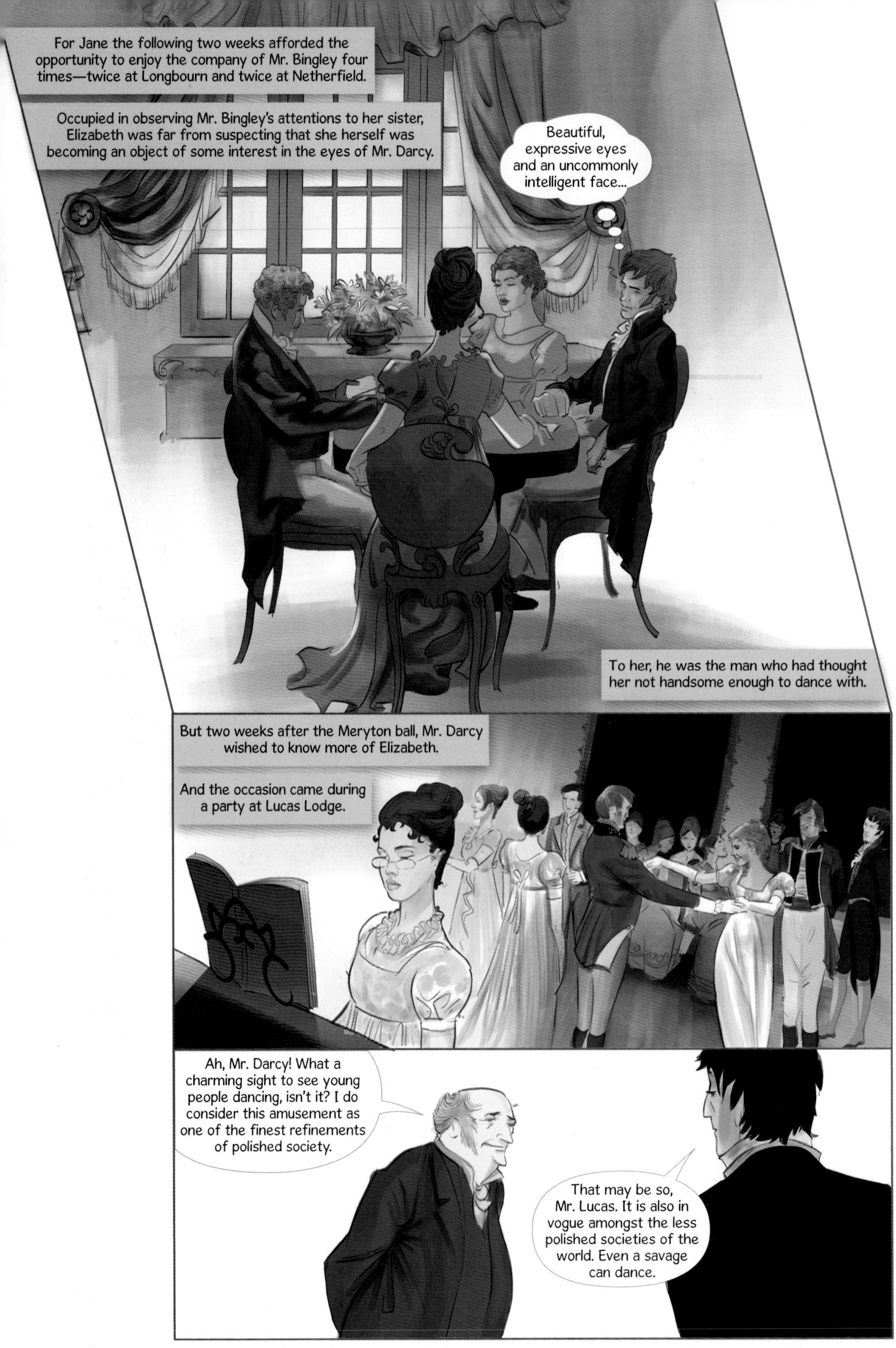
For Jane the following two weeks afforded the opportunity to enjoy the company of Mr. Bingley four times—twice at Longbourn and twice at Netherfield.
Occupied in observing Mr. Bingley's attentions to her sister, Elizabeth was far from suspecting that she herself was becoming an object of some interest in the eyes of Mr. Darcy.
Beautiful, expressive eyes and an uncommonly intelligent face...
To her, he was the man who had thought her not handsome enough to dance with.
But two weeks after the Meryton ball, Mr. Darcy wished to know more of Elizabeth.
And the occasion came during a party at Lucas Lodge.
Ah, Mr. Darcy! What a charming sight to see young people dancing, isn't it? I do consider this amusement as one of the finest refinements of polished society.
That may be so, Mr. Lucas. It is also in vogue amongst the less polished societies of the world. Even a savage can dance.

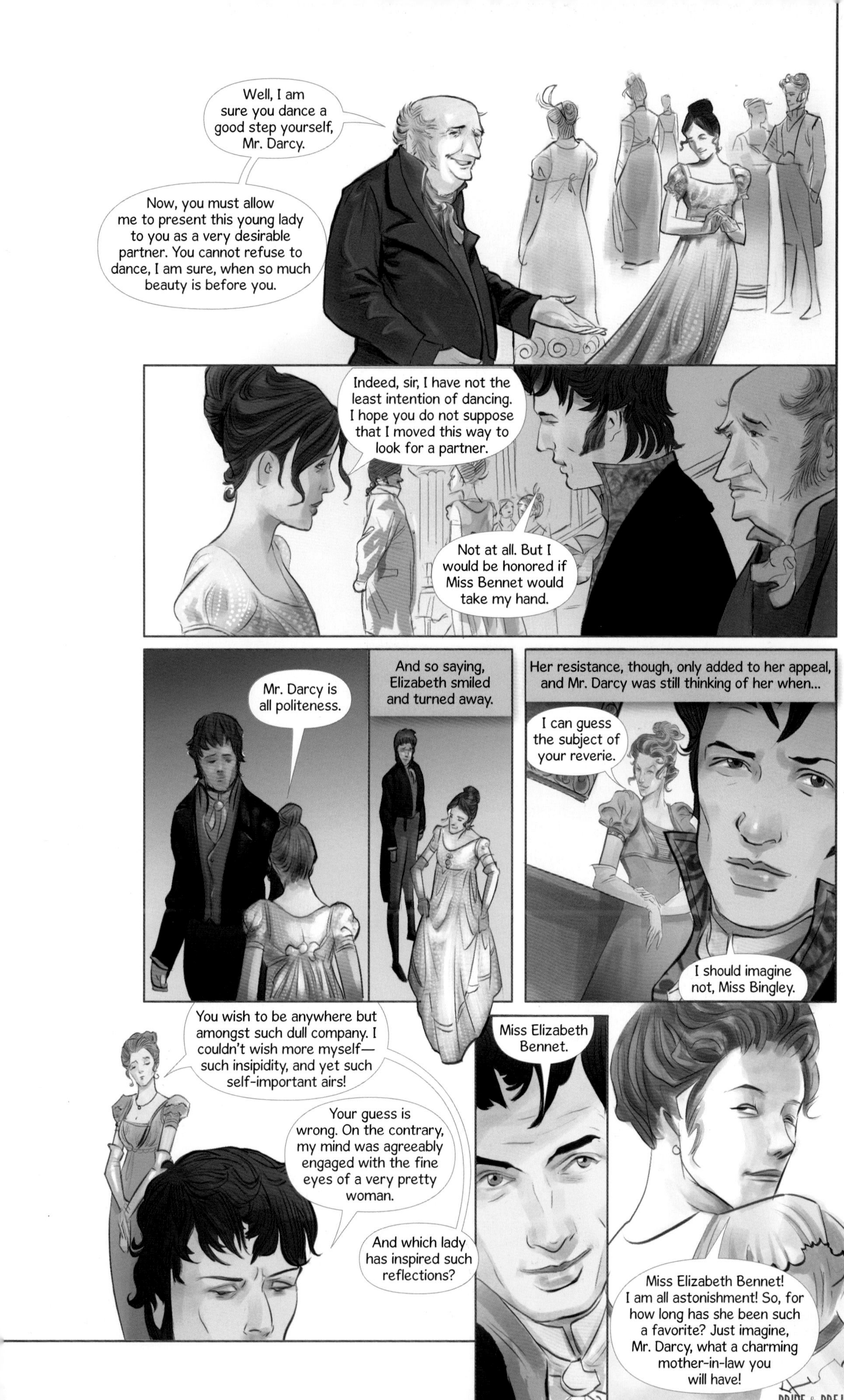
Well, I am sure you dance a good step yourself, Mr. Darcy.
Now, you must allow me to present this young lady to you as a very desirable partner. You cannot refuse to dance, I am sure, when so much beauty is before you.
Indeed, sir, I have not the least intention of dancing. I hope you do not suppose that I moved this way to look for a partner.
Not at all. But I would be honored if Miss Bennet would take my hand.
Mr. Darcy is all politeness.
And so saying, Elizabeth smiled and turned away.
Her resistance, though, only added to her appeal, and Mr. Darcy was still thinking of her when...
I can guess the subject of your reverie.
I should imagine not, Miss Bingley.
You wish to be anywhere but amongst such dull company. I couldn't wish more myself—such insipidity, and yet such self-important airs!
Your guess is wrong. On the contrary, my mind was agreeably engaged with the fine eyes of a very pretty woman.
And which lady has inspired such reflections?
Miss Elizabeth Bennet.
Miss Elizabeth Bennet! I am all astonishment! So, for how long has she been such a favorite? Just imagine, Mr. Darcy, what a charming mother-in-law you will have!

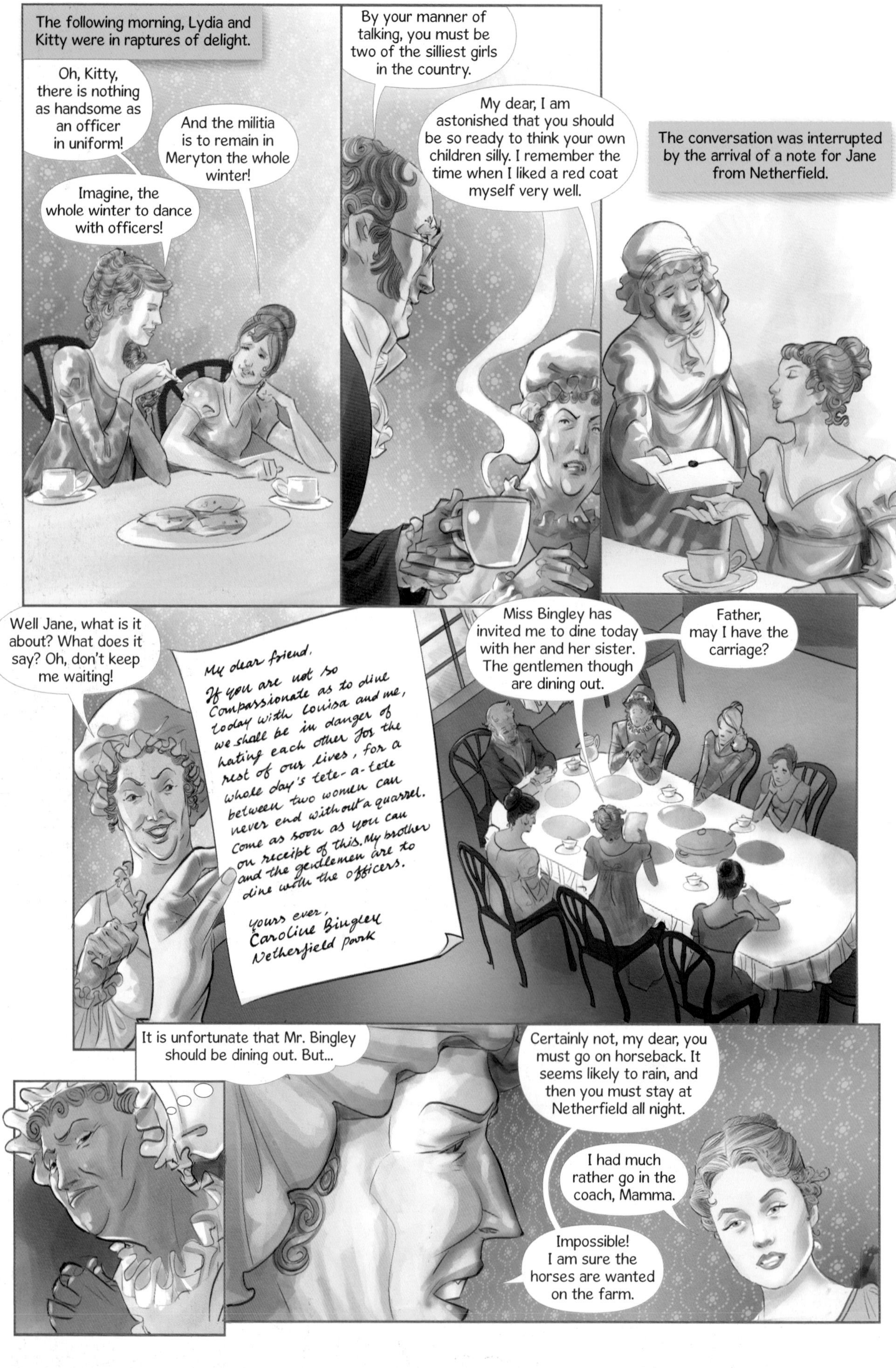

The following morning, Lydia and Kitty were in raptures of delight.
Oh, Kitty, there is nothing as handsome as an officer in uniform!
And the militia is to remain in Meryton the whole winter!
Imagine, the whole winter to dance with officers!
By your manner of talking, you must be two of the silliest girls in the country.
My dear, I am astonished that you should be so ready to think your own children silly. I remember the time when I liked a red coat myself very well.
The conversation was interrupted by the arrival of a note for Jane from Netherfield.
Well Jane, what is it about? What does it say? Oh, don't keep me waiting!
My dear friend,
If you are not so Compassionate as to dine today with Louisa and me, we shall be in danger of hating each other for the rest of our lives, for a whole day's tete-a-tete between two women can never end without a quarrel. Come as soon as you can on receipt of this. My brother and the gentlemen are to dine with the officers.
yours ever,
Caroline Bingley
Netherfield Park
Miss Bingley has invited me to dine today with her and her sister. The gentlemen though are dining out.
Father, may I have the carriage?
It is unfortunate that Mr. Bingley should be dining out. But...
Certainly not, my dear, you must go on horseback. It seems likely to rain, and then you must stay at Netherfield all night.
I had much rather go in the coach, Mamma.
Impossible! I am sure the horses are wanted on the farm.

And so Jane was sent off by Mrs. Bennet with many cheerful prognostics of a bad day. To her utter delight, her hopes were answered.

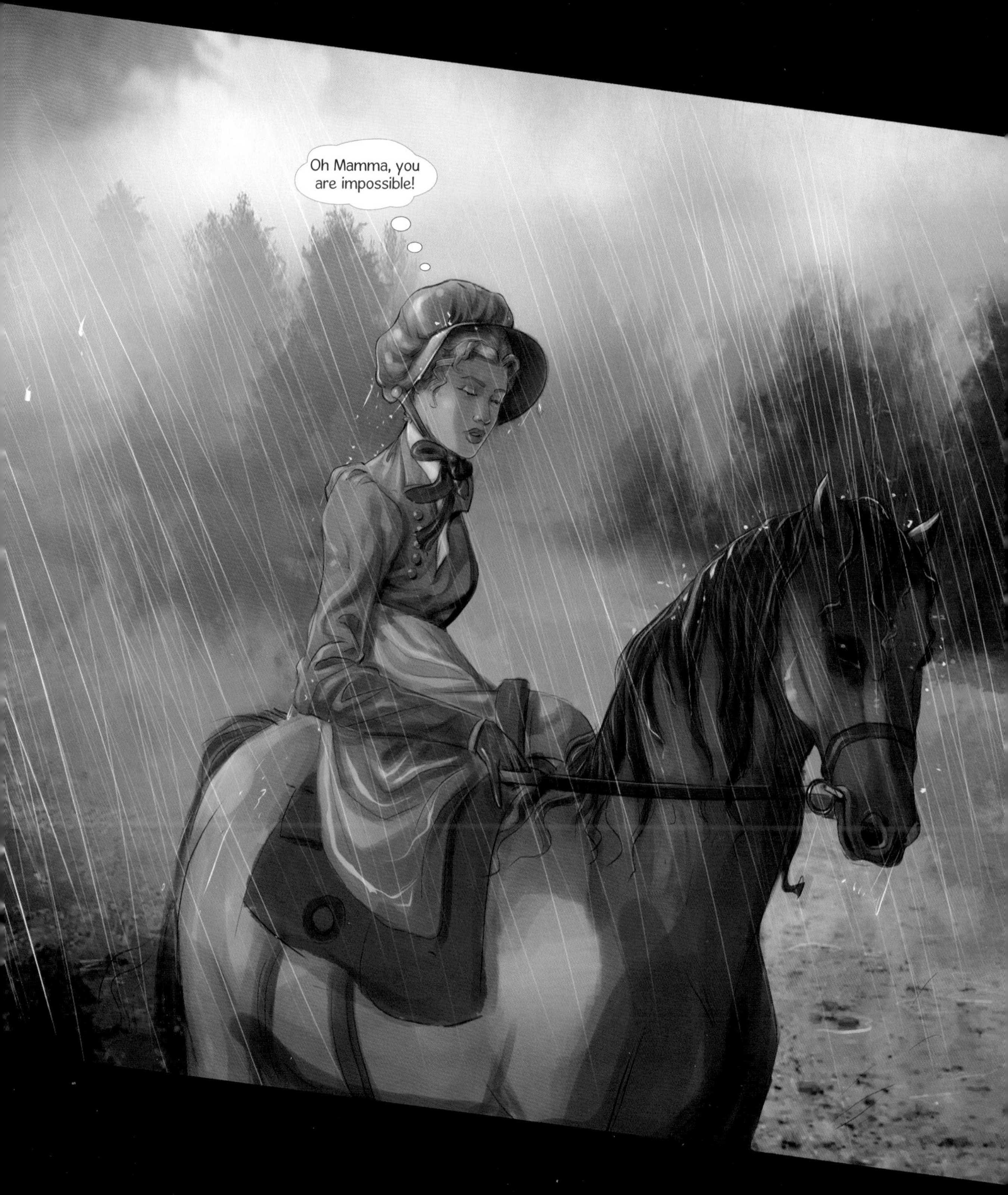
Oh Mamma, you are impossible!

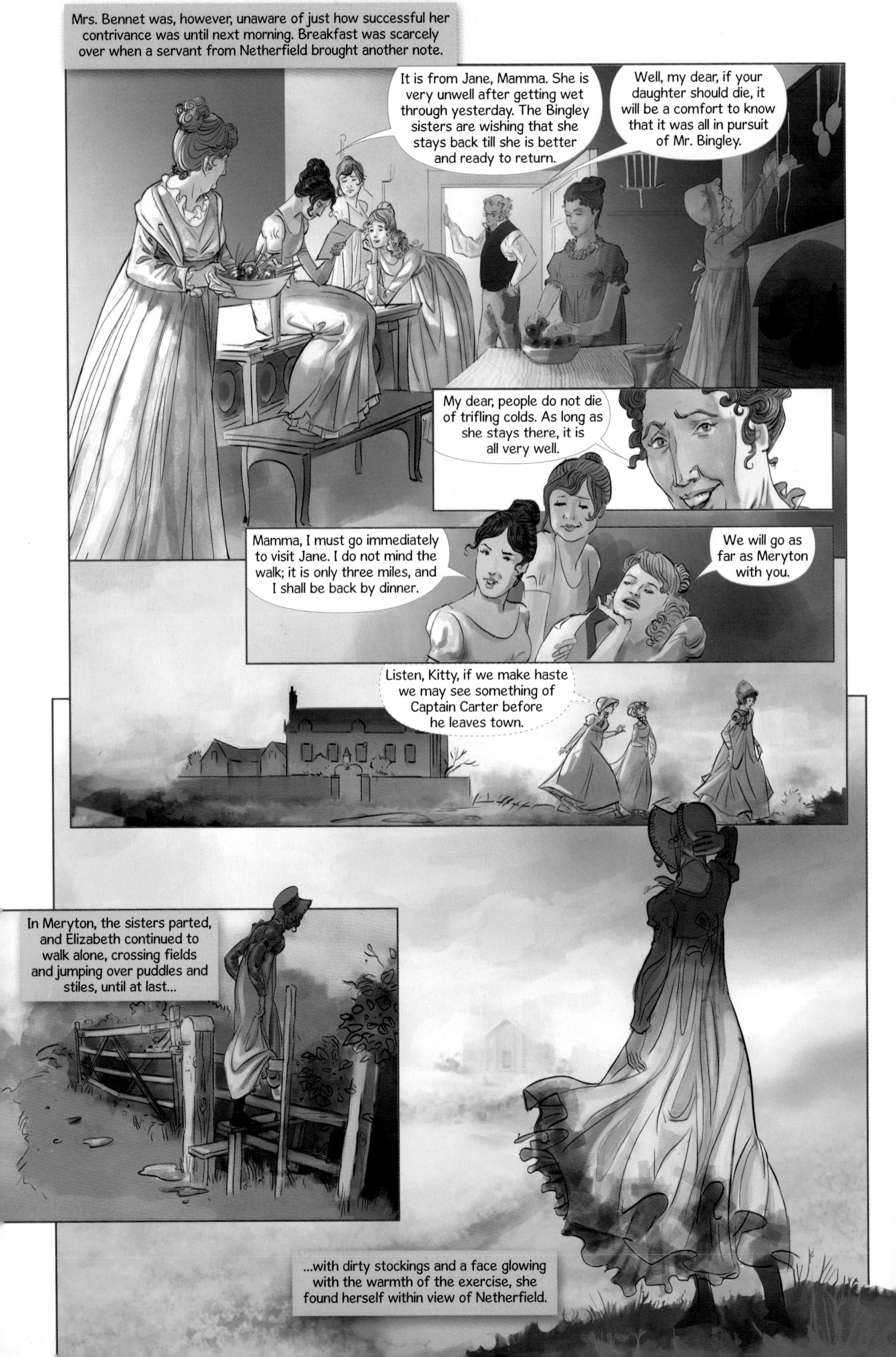

Mrs. Bennet was, however, unaware of just how successful her contrivance was until next morning. Breakfast was scarcely over when a servant from Netherfield brought another note.
It is from Jane, Mamma. She is very unwell after getting wet through yesterday. The Bingley sisters are wishing that she stays back till she is better and ready to return.
Well, my dear, if your daughter should die, it will be a comfort to know that it was all in pursuit of Mr. Bingley.
My dear, people do not die of trifling colds. As long as she stays there, it is all very well.
Mamma, I must go immediately to visit Jane. I do not mind the walk; it is only three miles, and I shall be back by dinner.
We will go as far as Meryton with you.
Listen, Kitty, if we make haste we may see something of Captain Carter before he leaves town.
In Meryton, the sisters parted, and Elizabeth continued to walk alone, crossing fields and jumping over puddles and stiles, until at last...
...with dirty stockings and a face glowing with the warmth of the exercise, she found herself within view of Netherfield.

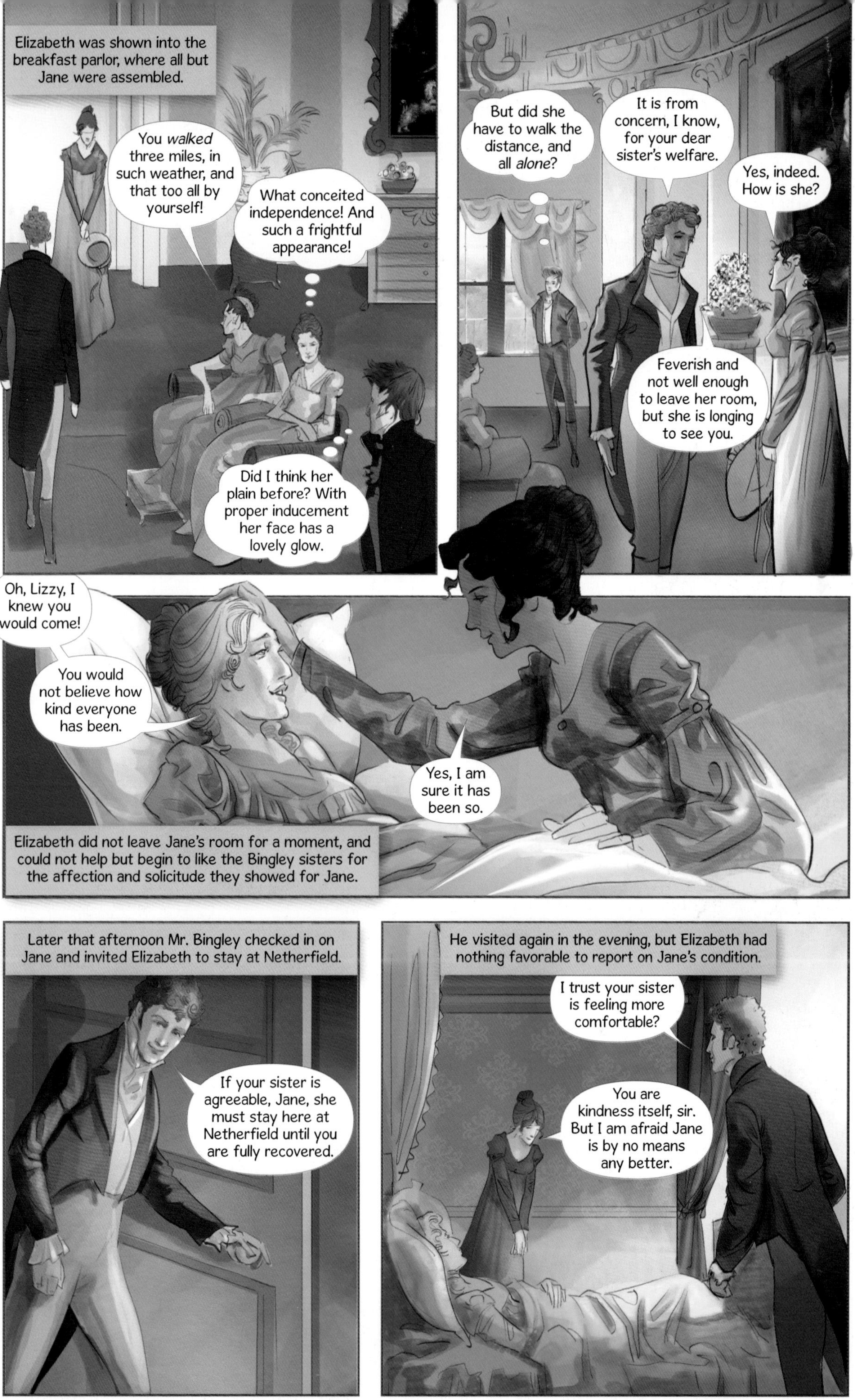
Elizabeth was shown into the breakfast parlor, where all but Jane were assembled.
You *walked* three miles, in such weather, and that too all by yourself!
What conceited independence! And such a frightful appearance!
Did I think her plain before? With proper inducement her face has a lovely glow.
But did she have to walk the distance, and all *alone*?
It is from concern, I know, for your dear sister's welfare.
Yes, indeed. How is she?
Feverish and not well enough to leave her room, but she is longing to see you.
Oh, Lizzy, I knew you would come!
You would not believe how kind everyone has been.
Yes, I am sure it has been so.
Elizabeth did not leave Jane's room for a moment, and could not help but begin to like the Bingley sisters for the affection and solicitude they showed for Jane.
Later that afternoon Mr. Bingley checked in on Jane and invited Elizabeth to stay at Netherfield.
If your sister is agreeable, Jane, she must stay here at Netherfield until you are fully recovered.
He visited again in the evening, but Elizabeth had nothing favorable to report on Jane's condition.
I trust your sister is feeling more comfortable?
You are kindness itself, sir. But I am afraid Jane is by no means any better.

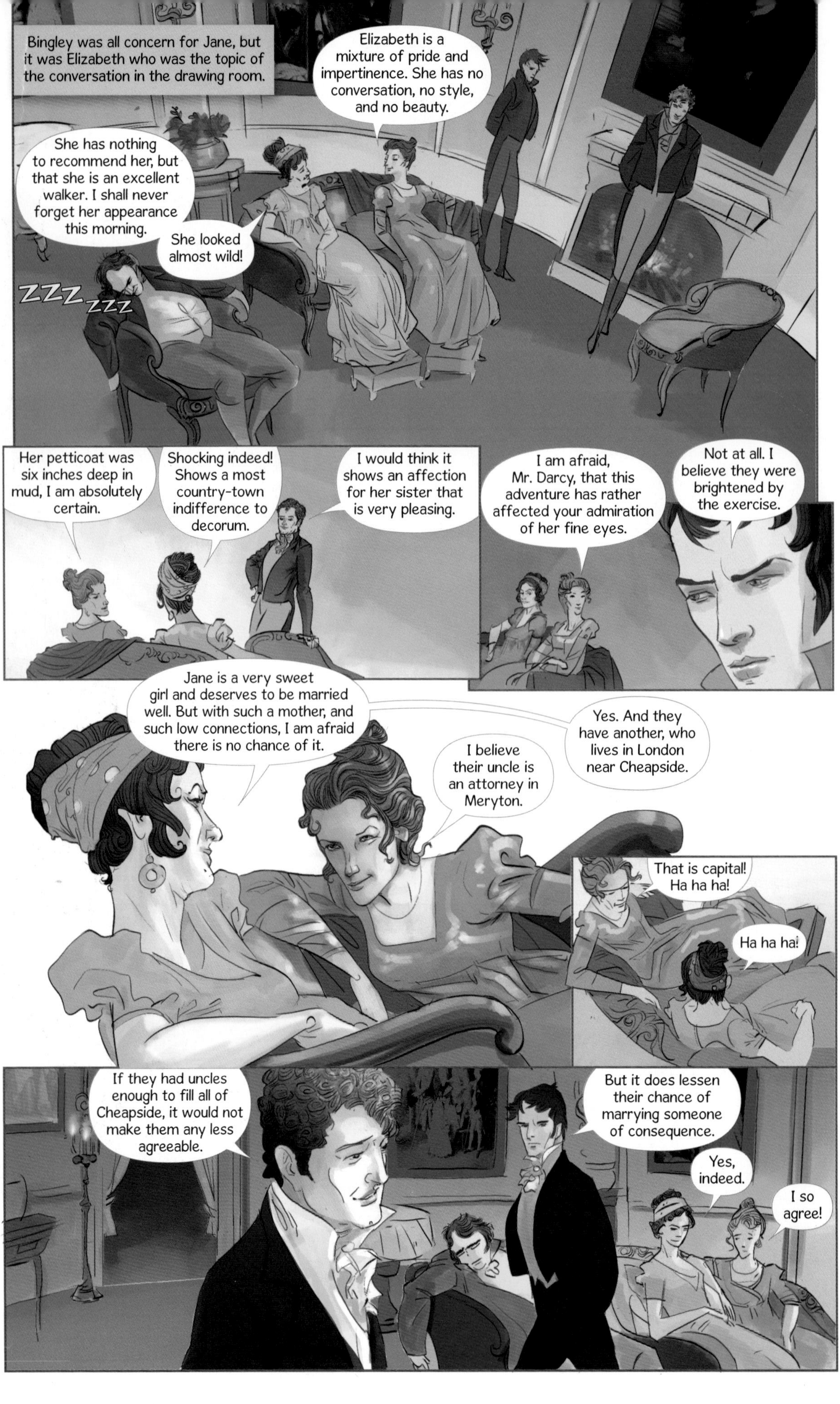

Bingley was all concern for Jane, but it was Elizabeth who was the topic of the conversation in the drawing room.
Elizabeth is a mixture of pride and impertinence. She has no conversation, no style, and no beauty.
She has nothing to recommend her, but that she is an excellent walker. I shall never forget her appearance this morning.
She looked almost wild!
ZZZZZZ
Her petticoat was six inches deep in mud, I am absolutely certain.
Shocking indeed! Shows a most country-town indifference to decorum.
I would think it shows an affection for her sister that is very pleasing.
I am afraid, Mr. Darcy, that this adventure has rather affected your admiration of her fine eyes.
Not at all. I believe they were brightened by the exercise.
Jane is a very sweet girl and deserves to be married well. But with such a mother, and such low connections, I am afraid there is no chance of it.
I believe their uncle is an attorney in Meryton.
Yes. And they have another, who lives in London near Cheapside.
That is capital! Ha ha ha!
Ha ha ha!
If they had uncles enough to fill all of Cheapside, it would not make them any less agreeable.
But it does lessen their chance of marrying someone of consequence.
Yes, indeed.
I so agree!

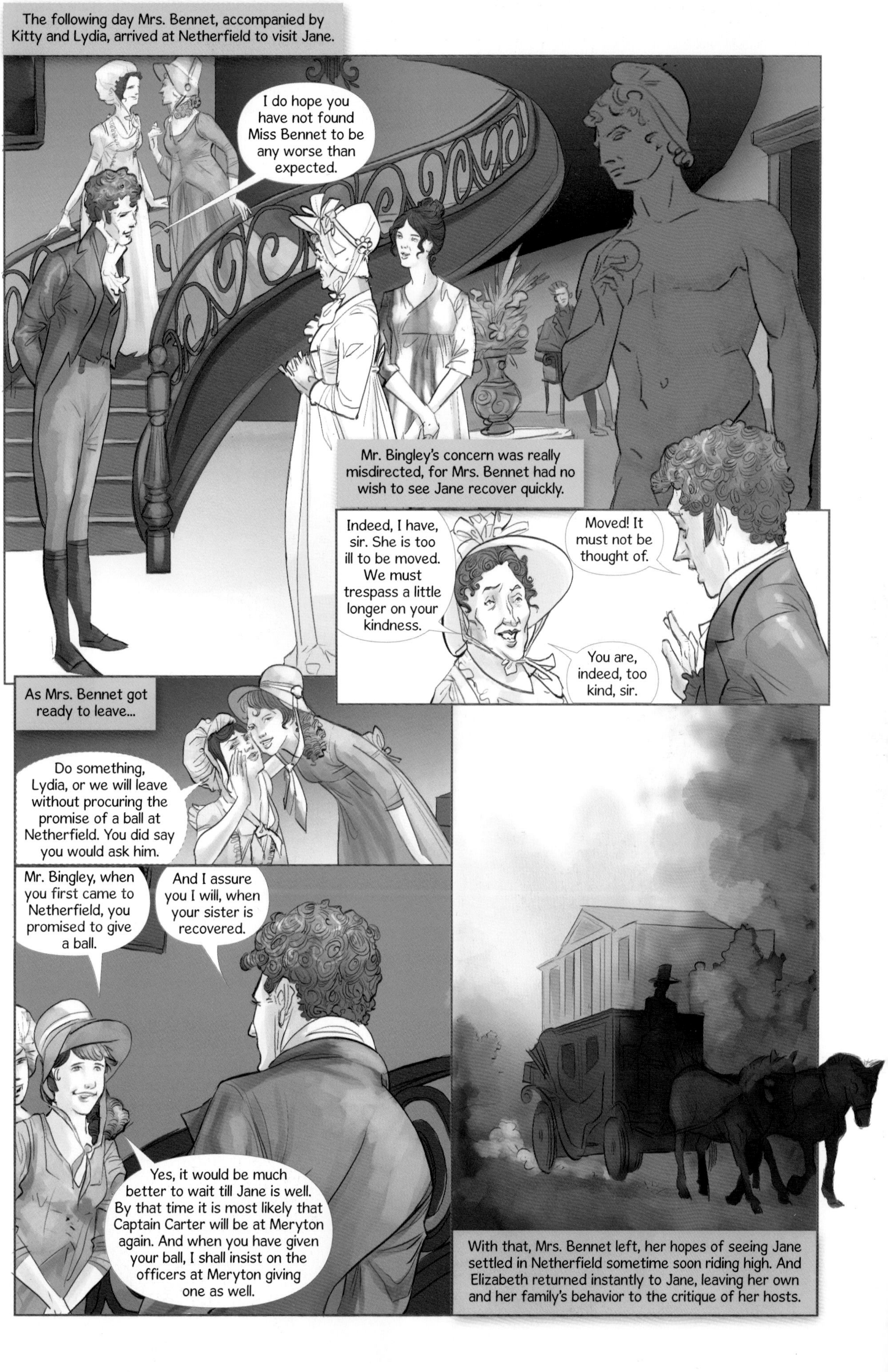
The following day Mrs. Bennet, accompanied by Kitty and Lydia, arrived at Netherfield to visit Jane.
I do hope you have not found Miss Bennet to be any worse than expected.
Mr. Bingley's concern was really misdirected, for Mrs. Bennet had no wish to see Jane recover quickly.
Indeed, I have, sir. She is too ill to be moved. We must trespass a little longer on your kindness.
Moved! It must not be thought of.
You are, indeed, too kind, sir.
As Mrs. Bennet got ready to leave...
Do something, Lydia, or we will leave without procuring the promise of a ball at Netherfield. You did say you would ask him.
Mr. Bingley, when you first came to Netherfield, you promised to give a ball.
And I assure you I will, when your sister is recovered.
Yes, it would be much better to wait till Jane is well. By that time it is most likely that Captain Carter will be at Meryton again. And when you have given your ball, I shall insist on the officers at Meryton giving one as well.
With that, Mrs. Bennet left, her hopes of seeing Jane settled in Netherfield sometime soon riding high. And Elizabeth returned instantly to Jane, leaving her own and her family's behavior to the critique of her hosts.

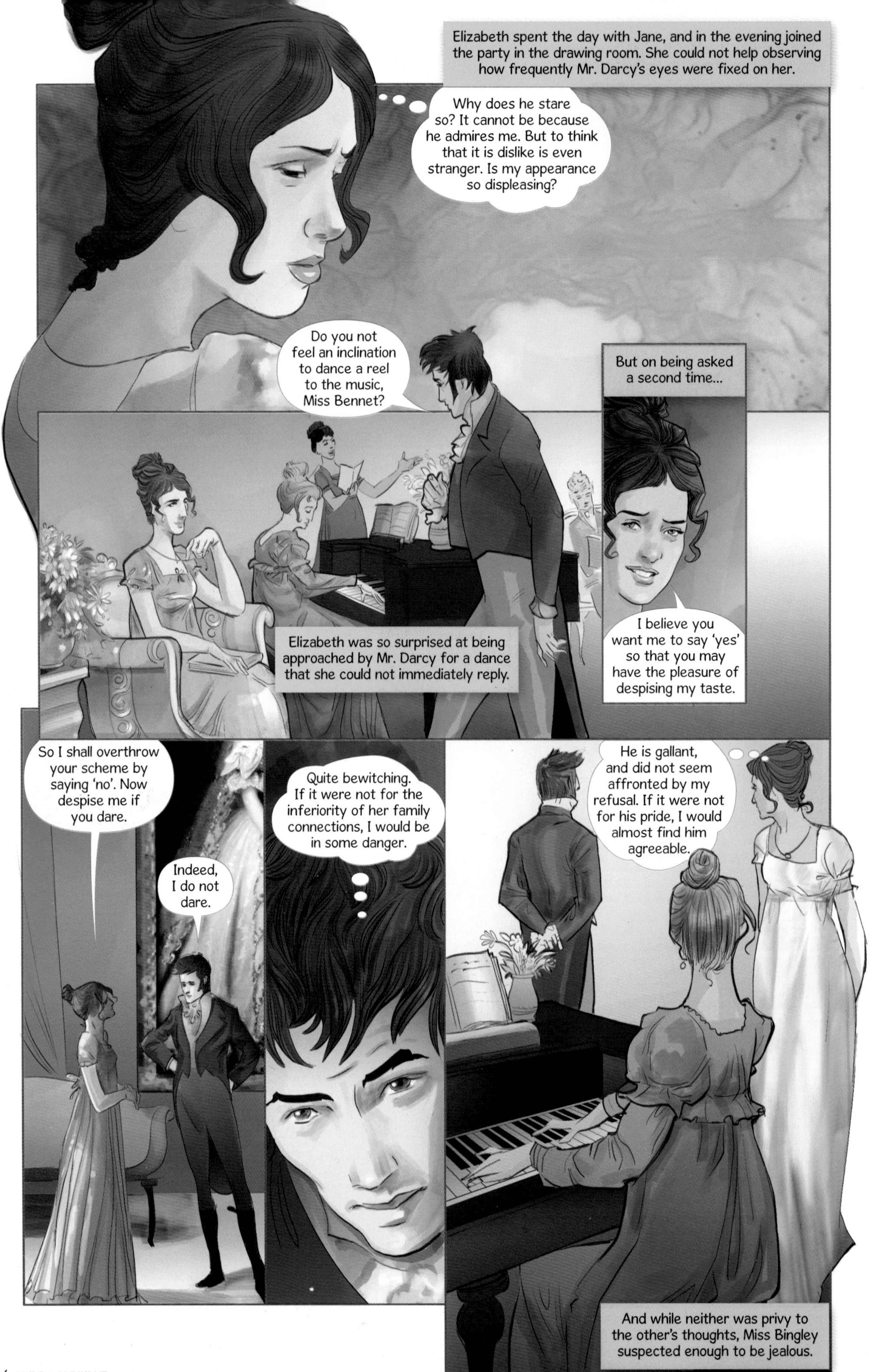
Elizabeth spent the day with Jane, and in the evening joined the party in the drawing room. She could not help observing how frequently Mr. Darcy's eyes were fixed on her.
Why does he stare so? It cannot be because he admires me. But to think that it is dislike is even stranger. Is my appearance so displeasing?
Do you not feel an inclination to dance a reel to the music, Miss Bennet?
Elizabeth was so surprised at being approached by Mr. Darcy for a dance that she could not immediately reply.
But on being asked a second time...
I believe you want me to say 'yes' so that you may have the pleasure of despising my taste.
So I shall overthrow your scheme by saying 'no'. Now despise me if you dare.
Indeed, I do not dare.
Quite bewitching. If it were not for the inferiority of her family connections, I would be in some danger.
He is gallant, and did not seem affronted by my refusal. If it were not for his pride, I would almost find him agreeable.
And while neither was privy to the other's thoughts, Miss Bingley suspected enough to be jealous.

The next day, Jane was well enough to join her friends in the drawing room where she was welcomed with great warmth by Mr. Bingley.

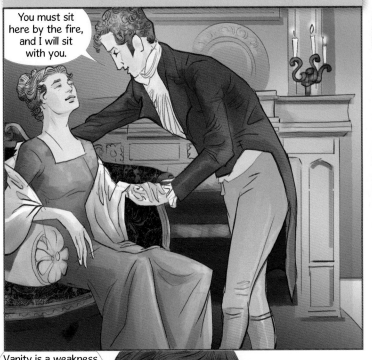

You must sit here by the fire, and I will sit with you.

Meanwhile, Elizabeth had entered into a lively conversation with Mr. Darcy...

I have always endeavored to avoid those weaknesses which can expose one to ridicule.

Such as vanity and pride?

Vanity is a weakness indeed. But pride, where there is a real superiority of mind, will be always under good regulation.

Well then, I am perfectly convinced, Mr. Darcy, that you have no defect.

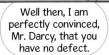

Oh, I have faults enough, but they are not, I hope, of understanding. I cannot forget the follies and vices of others, nor their offences against myself. My good opinion, once lost, is lost forever.

That is a failing indeed! Implacable resentment is a flaw in a character.

There is, I believe, in every disposition a tendency to some natural defect.

And your defect is a propensity to hate everybody.

And yours is to wilfully misunderstand them.

Do let us have a little music.

Miss Bingley's suggestion, stemming from her desire to stop a conversation in which she had no share, offered welcome relief to Mr. Darcy.

I think I run the danger of paying her too much attention.

And till the time when Jane was finally well enough to return to Longbourn, Darcy refrained from paying any attention to Elizabeth at all.

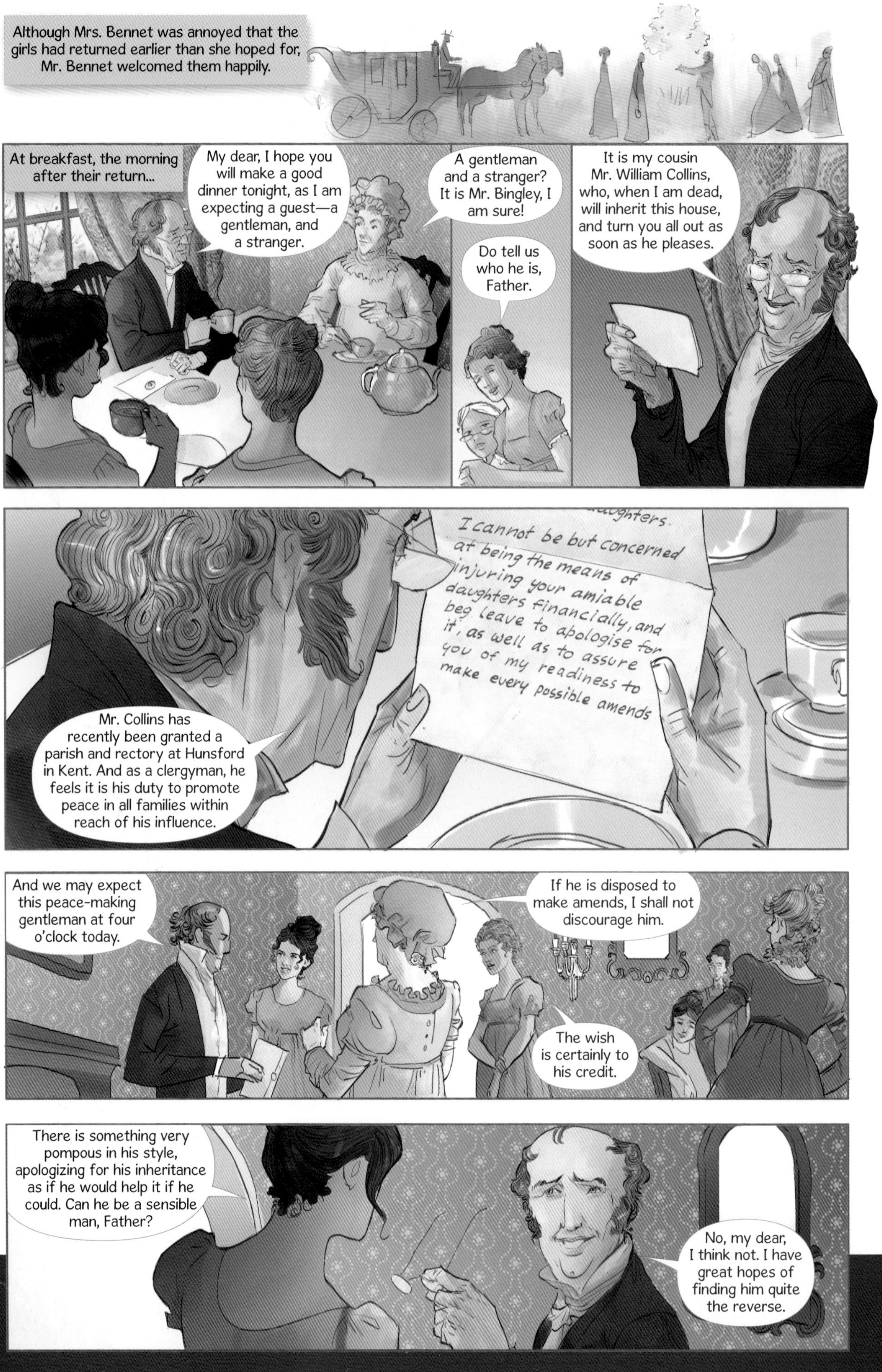
Although Mrs. Bennet was annoyed that the girls had returned earlier than she hoped for, Mr. Bennet welcomed them happily.
At breakfast, the morning after their return...
My dear, I hope you will make a good dinner tonight, as I am expecting a guest—a gentleman, and a stranger.
A gentleman and a stranger? It is Mr. Bingley, I am sure!
Do tell us who he is, Father.
It is my cousin Mr. William Collins, who, when I am dead, will inherit this house, and turn you all out as soon as he pleases.
daughters.
I cannot be but concerned at being the means of injuring your amiable daughters financially, and beg leave to apologise for it, as well as to assure you of my readiness to make every possible amends
Mr. Collins has recently been granted a parish and rectory at Hunsford in Kent. And as a clergyman, he feels it is his duty to promote peace in all families within reach of his influence.
And we may expect this peace-making gentleman at four o'clock today.
If he is disposed to make amends, I shall not discourage him.
The wish is certainly to his credit.
There is something very pompous in his style, apologizing for his inheritance as if he would help it if he could. Can he be a sensible man, Father?
No, my dear, I think not. I have great hopes of finding him quite the reverse.

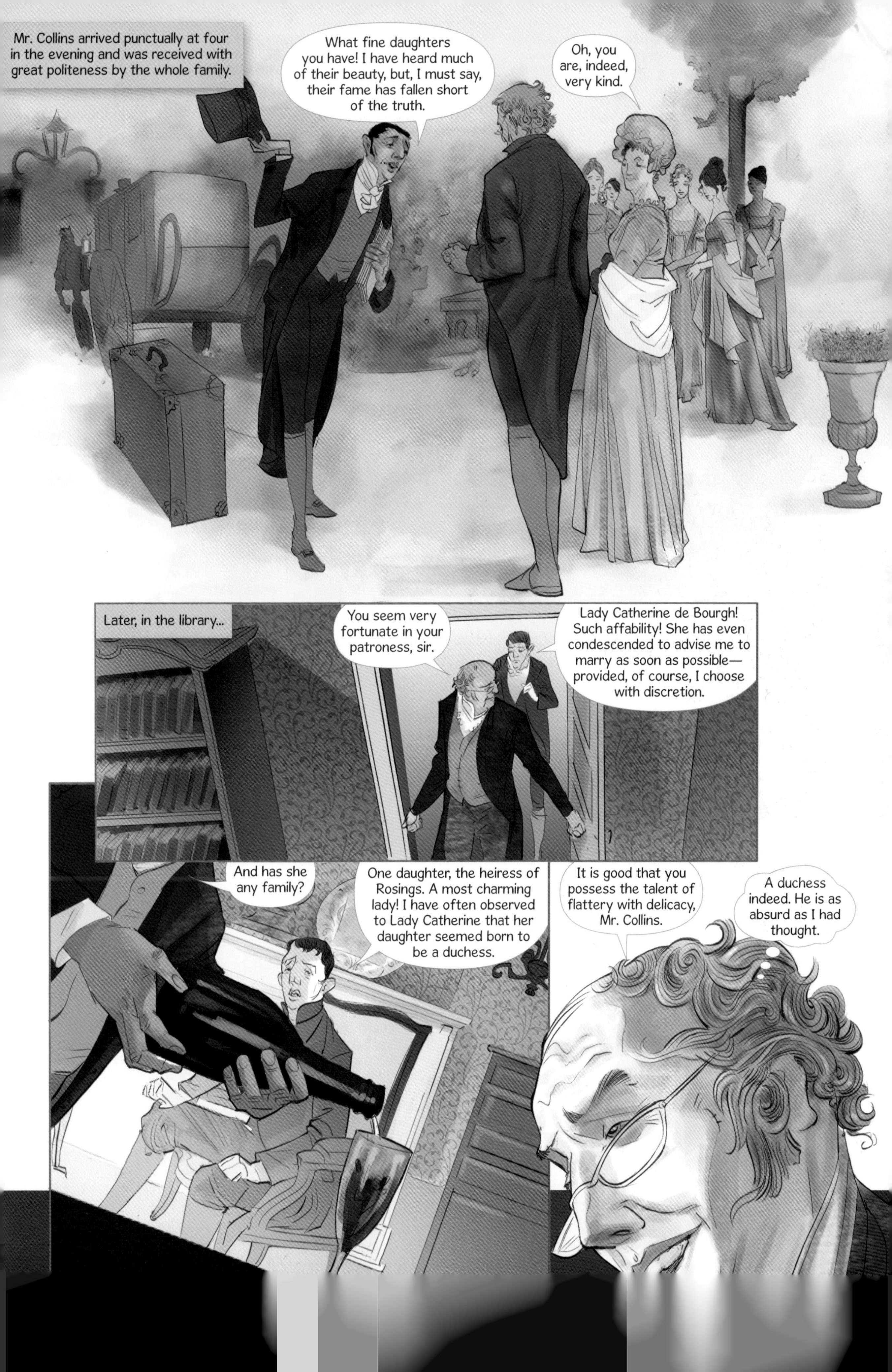
Mr. Collins arrived punctually at four in the evening and was received with great politeness by the whole family.
What fine daughters you have! I have heard much of their beauty, but, I must say, their fame has fallen short of the truth.
Oh, you are, indeed, very kind.
Later, in the library...
You seem very fortunate in your patroness, sir.
Lady Catherine de Bourgh! Such affability! She has even condescended to advise me to marry as soon as possible—provided, of course, I choose with discretion.
And has she any family?
One daughter, the heiress of Rosings. A most charming lady! I have often observed to Lady Catherine that her daughter seemed born to be a duchess.
It is good that you possess the talent of flattery with delicacy, Mr. Collins.
A duchess indeed. He is as absurd as I had thought.

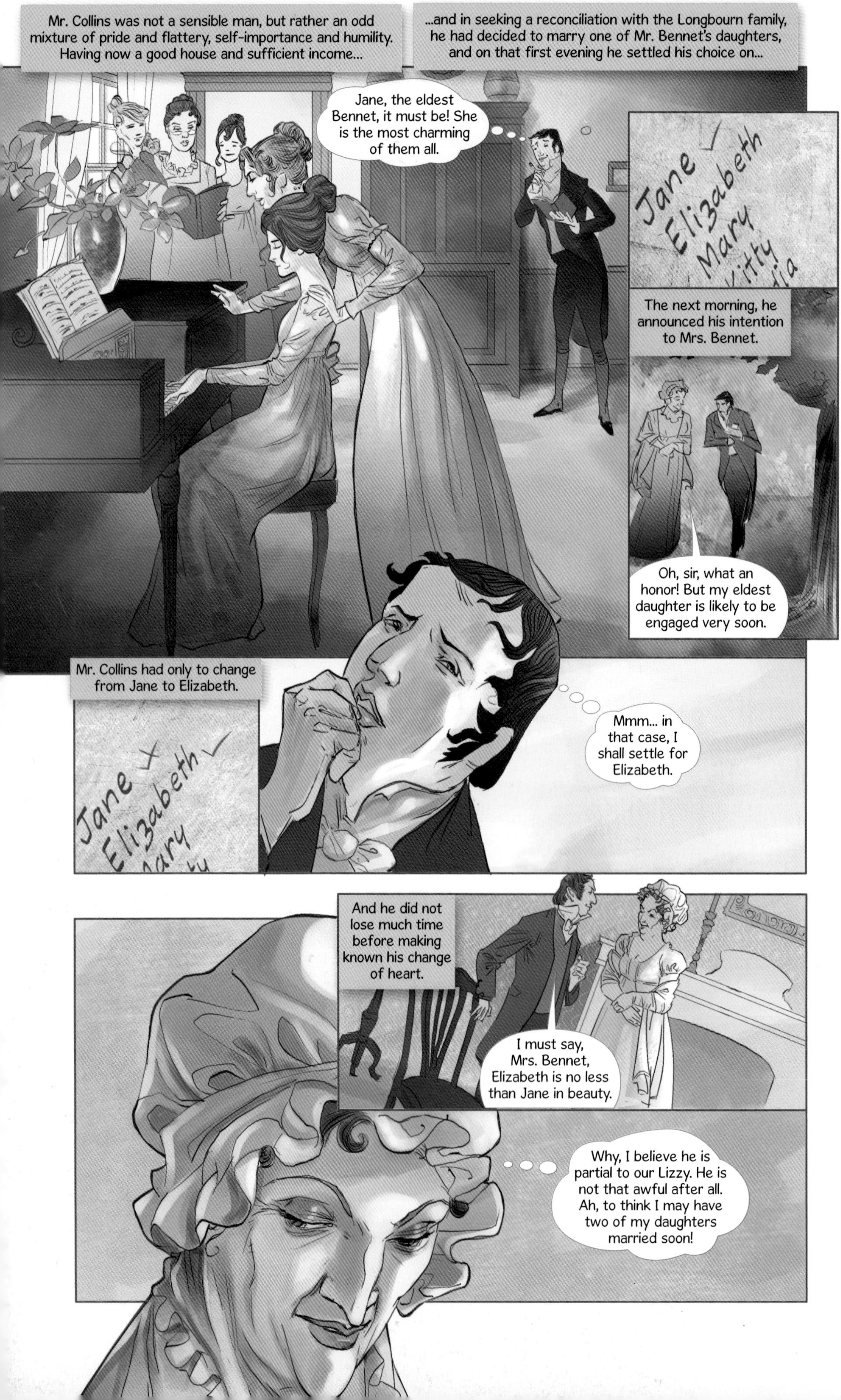
Mr. Collins was not a sensible man, but rather an odd mixture of pride and flattery, self-importance and humility. Having now a good house and sufficient income...
...and in seeking a reconciliation with the Longbourn family, he had decided to marry one of Mr. Bennet's daughters, and on that first evening he settled his choice on...
Jane, the eldest Bennet, it must be! She is the most charming of them all.
Jane
Elizabeth
Mary
The next morning, he announced his intention to Mrs. Bennet.
Oh, sir, what an honor! But my eldest daughter is likely to be engaged very soon.
Mr. Collins had only to change from Jane to Elizabeth.
Jane
Elizabeth
Mmm... in that case, I shall settle for Elizabeth.
And he did not lose much time before making known his change of heart.
I must say, Mrs. Bennet, Elizabeth is no less than Jane in beauty.
Why, I believe he is partial to our Lizzy. He is not that awful after all. Ah, to think I may have two of my daughters married soon!

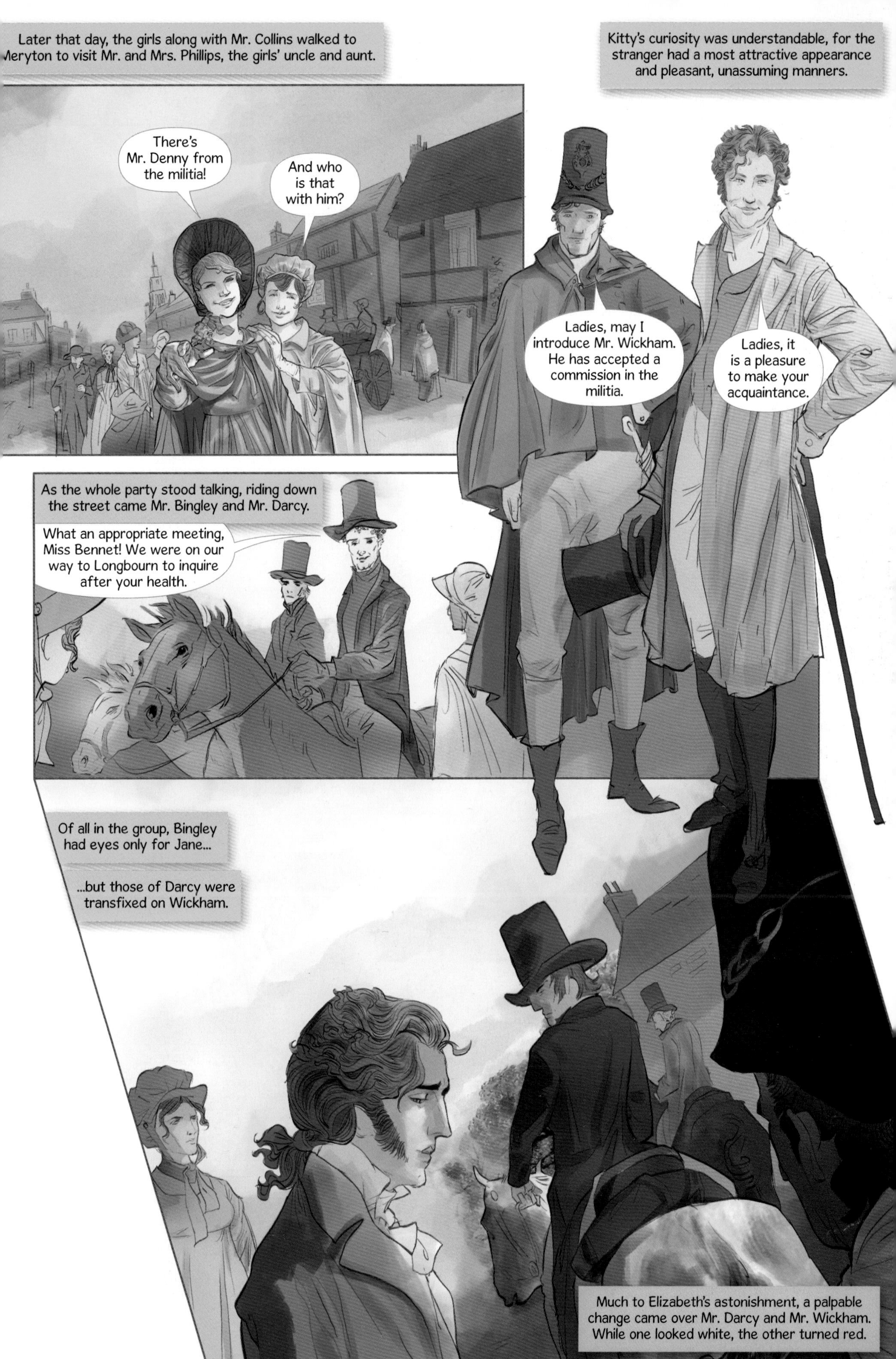

Later that day, the girls along with Mr. Collins walked to Meryton to visit Mr. and Mrs. Phillips, the girls' uncle and aunt.
There's Mr. Denny from the militia!
And who is that with him?
Kitty's curiosity was understandable, for the stranger had a most attractive appearance and pleasant, unassuming manners.
Ladies, may I introduce Mr. Wickham. He has accepted a commission in the militia.
Ladies, it is a pleasure to make your acquaintance.
As the whole party stood talking, riding down the street came Mr. Bingley and Mr. Darcy.
What an appropriate meeting, Miss Bennet! We were on our way to Longbourn to inquire after your health.
Of all in the group, Bingley had eyes only for Jane...
...but those of Darcy were transfixed on Wickham.
Much to Elizabeth's astonishment, a palpable change came over Mr. Darcy and Mr. Wickham. While one looked white, the other turned red.

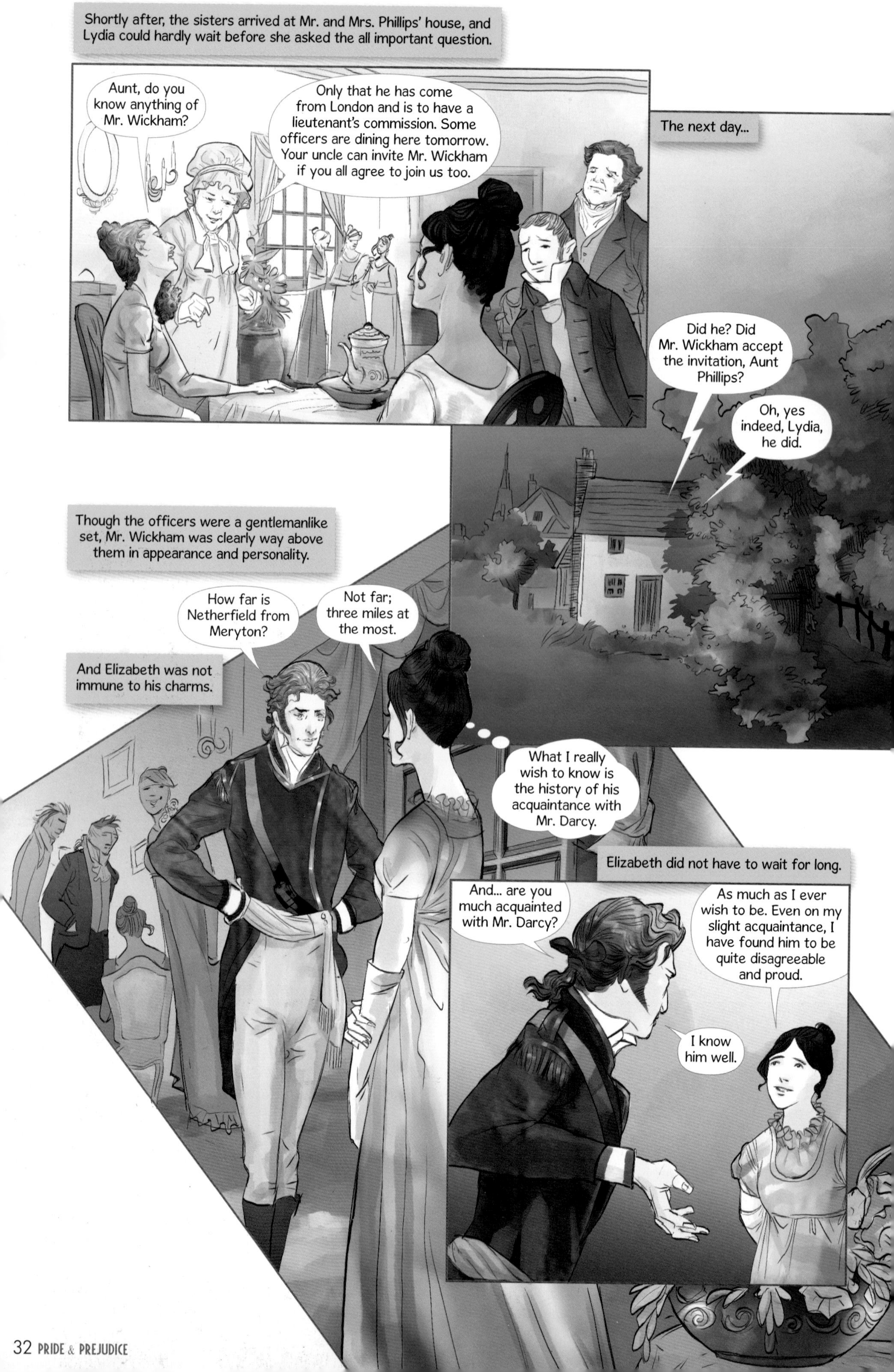
Shortly after, the sisters arrived at Mr. and Mrs. Phillips' house, and Lydia could hardly wait before she asked the all important question.
Aunt, do you know anything of Mr. Wickham?
Only that he has come from London and is to have a lieutenant's commission. Some officers are dining here tomorrow. Your uncle can invite Mr. Wickham if you all agree to join us too.
The next day...
Did he? Did Mr. Wickham accept the invitation, Aunt Phillips?
Oh, yes indeed, Lydia, he did.
Though the officers were a gentlemanlike set, Mr. Wickham was clearly way above them in appearance and personality.
How far is Netherfield from Meryton?
Not far; three miles at the most.
And Elizabeth was not immune to his charms.
What I really wish to know is the history of his acquaintance with Mr. Darcy.
Elizabeth did not have to wait for long.
And... are you much acquainted with Mr. Darcy?
As much as I ever wish to be. Even on my slight acquaintance, I have found him to be quite disagreeable and proud.
I know him well.

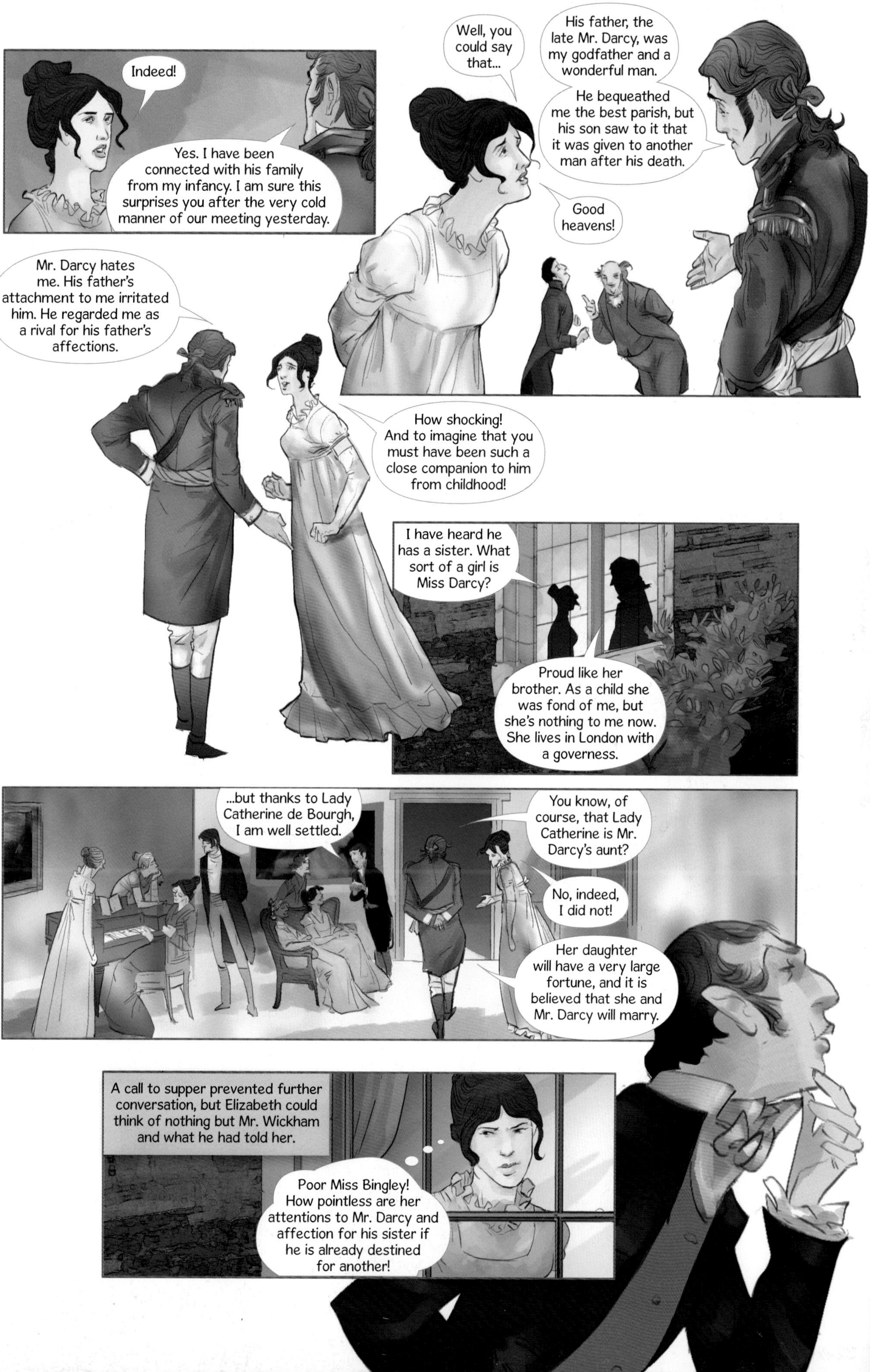

Indeed!
Yes. I have been connected with his family from my infancy. I am sure this surprises you after the very cold manner of our meeting yesterday.
Well, you could say that...
His father, the late Mr. Darcy, was my godfather and a wonderful man.
He bequeathed me the best parish, but his son saw to it that it was given to another man after his death.
Good heavens!
Mr. Darcy hates me. His father's attachment to me irritated him. He regarded me as a rival for his father's affections.
How shocking! And to imagine that you must have been such a close companion to him from childhood!
I have heard he has a sister. What sort of a girl is Miss Darcy?
Proud like her brother. As a child she was fond of me, but she's nothing to me now. She lives in London with a governess.
...but thanks to Lady Catherine de Bourgh, I am well settled.
You know, of course, that Lady Catherine is Mr. Darcy's aunt?
No, indeed, I did not!
Her daughter will have a very large fortune, and it is believed that she and Mr. Darcy will marry.
A call to supper prevented further conversation, but Elizabeth could think of nothing but Mr. Wickham and what he had told her.
Poor Miss Bingley! How pointless are her attentions to Mr. Darcy and affection for his sister if he is already destined for another!

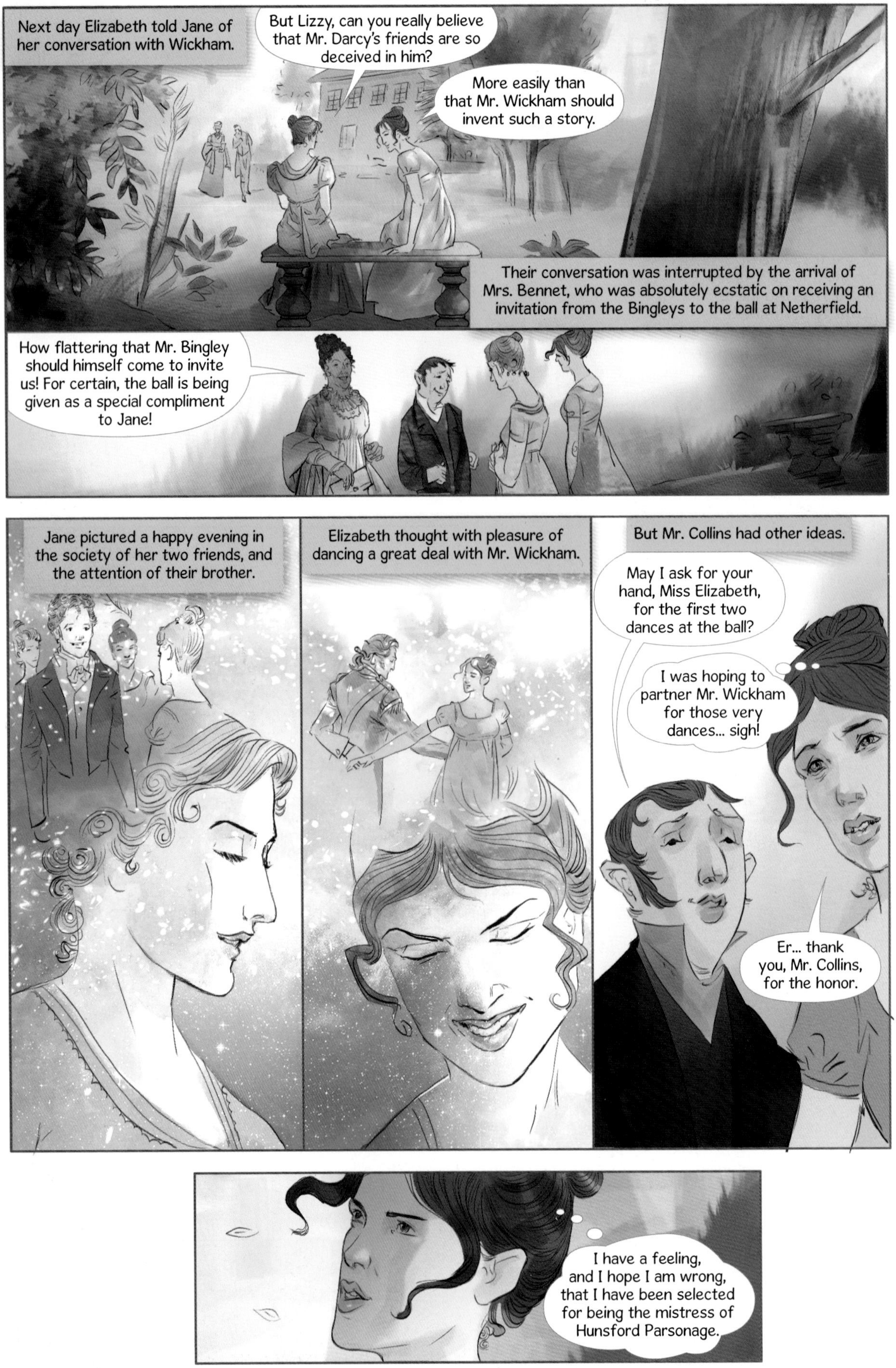
Next day Elizabeth told Jane of her conversation with Wickham.
But Lizzy, can you really believe that Mr. Darcy's friends are so deceived in him?
More easily than that Mr. Wickham should invent such a story.
Their conversation was interrupted by the arrival of Mrs. Bennet, who was absolutely ecstatic on receiving an invitation from the Bingleys to the ball at Netherfield.
How flattering that Mr. Bingley should himself come to invite us! For certain, the ball is being given as a special compliment to Jane!
Jane pictured a happy evening in the society of her two friends, and the attention of their brother.
Elizabeth thought with pleasure of dancing a great deal with Mr. Wickham.
But Mr. Collins had other ideas.
May I ask for your hand, Miss Elizabeth, for the first two dances at the ball?
I was hoping to partner Mr. Wickham for those very dances... sigh!
Er... thank you, Mr. Collins, for the honor.
I have a feeling, and I hope I am wrong, that I have been selected for being the mistress of Hunsford Parsonage.

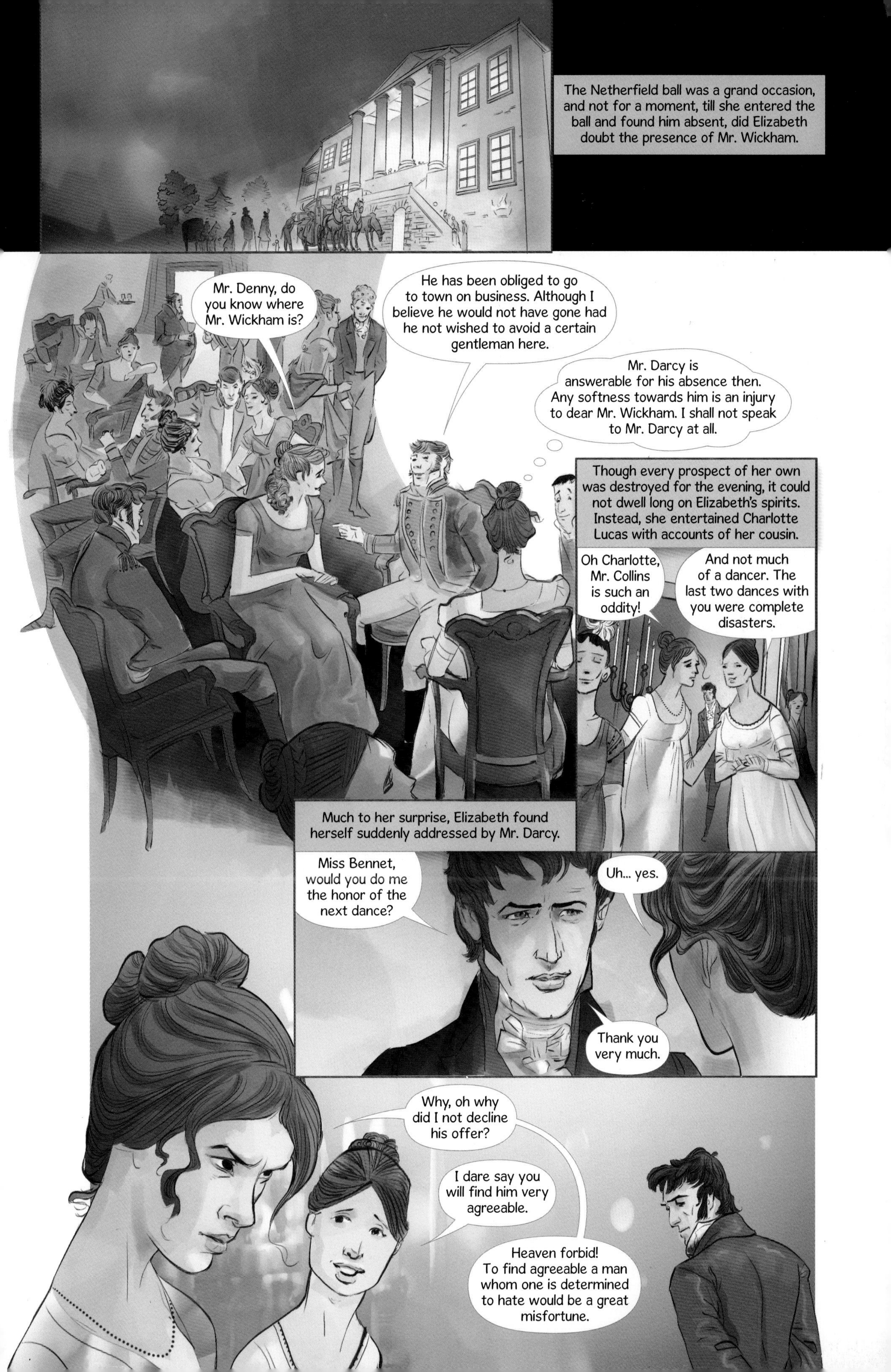

The Netherfield ball was a grand occasion, and not for a moment, till she entered the ball and found him absent, did Elizabeth doubt the presence of Mr. Wickham.
Mr. Denny, do you know where Mr. Wickham is?
He has been obliged to go to town on business. Although I believe he would not have gone had he not wished to avoid a certain gentleman here.
Mr. Darcy is answerable for his absence then. Any softness towards him is an injury to dear Mr. Wickham. I shall not speak to Mr. Darcy at all.
Though every prospect of her own was destroyed for the evening, it could not dwell long on Elizabeth's spirits. Instead, she entertained Charlotte Lucas with accounts of her cousin.
Oh Charlotte, Mr. Collins is such an oddity!
And not much of a dancer. The last two dances with you were complete disasters.
Much to her surprise, Elizabeth found herself suddenly addressed by Mr. Darcy.
Miss Bennet, would you do me the honor of the next dance?
Uh... yes.
Thank you very much.
Why, oh why did I not decline his offer?
I dare say you will find him very agreeable.
Heaven forbid! To find agreeable a man whom one is determined to hate would be a great misfortune.

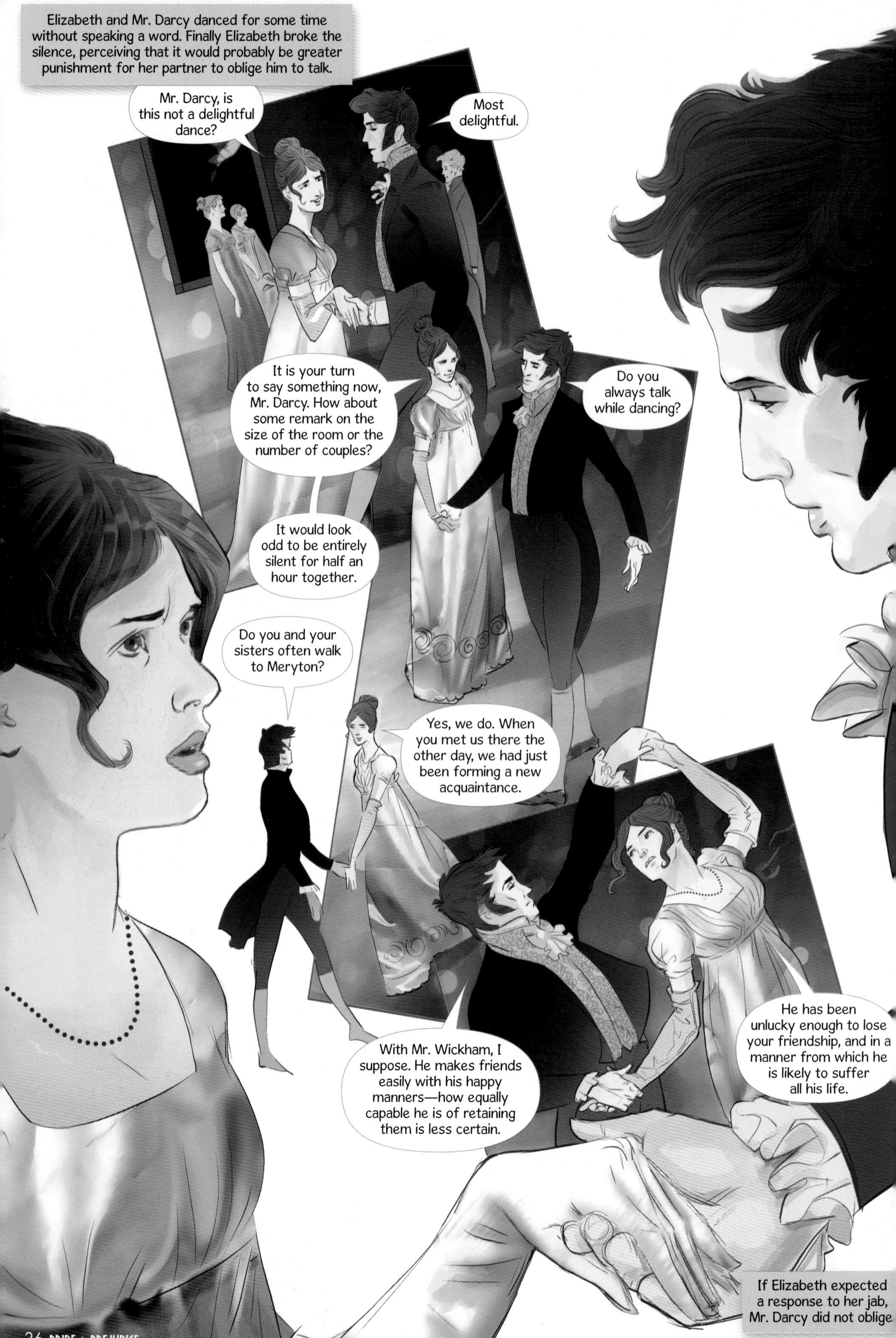
Elizabeth and Mr. Darcy danced for some time without speaking a word. Finally Elizabeth broke the silence, perceiving that it would probably be greater punishment for her partner to oblige him to talk.
Mr. Darcy, is this not a delightful dance?
Most delightful.
It is your turn to say something now, Mr. Darcy. How about some remark on the size of the room or the number of couples?
Do you always talk while dancing?
It would look odd to be entirely silent for half an hour together.
Do you and your sisters often walk to Meryton?
Yes, we do. When you met us there the other day, we had just been forming a new acquaintance.
With Mr. Wickham, I suppose. He makes friends easily with his happy manners—how equally capable he is of retaining them is less certain.
He has been unlucky enough to lose your friendship, and in a manner from which he is likely to suffer all his life.
If Elizabeth expected a response to her jab, Mr. Darcy did not oblige

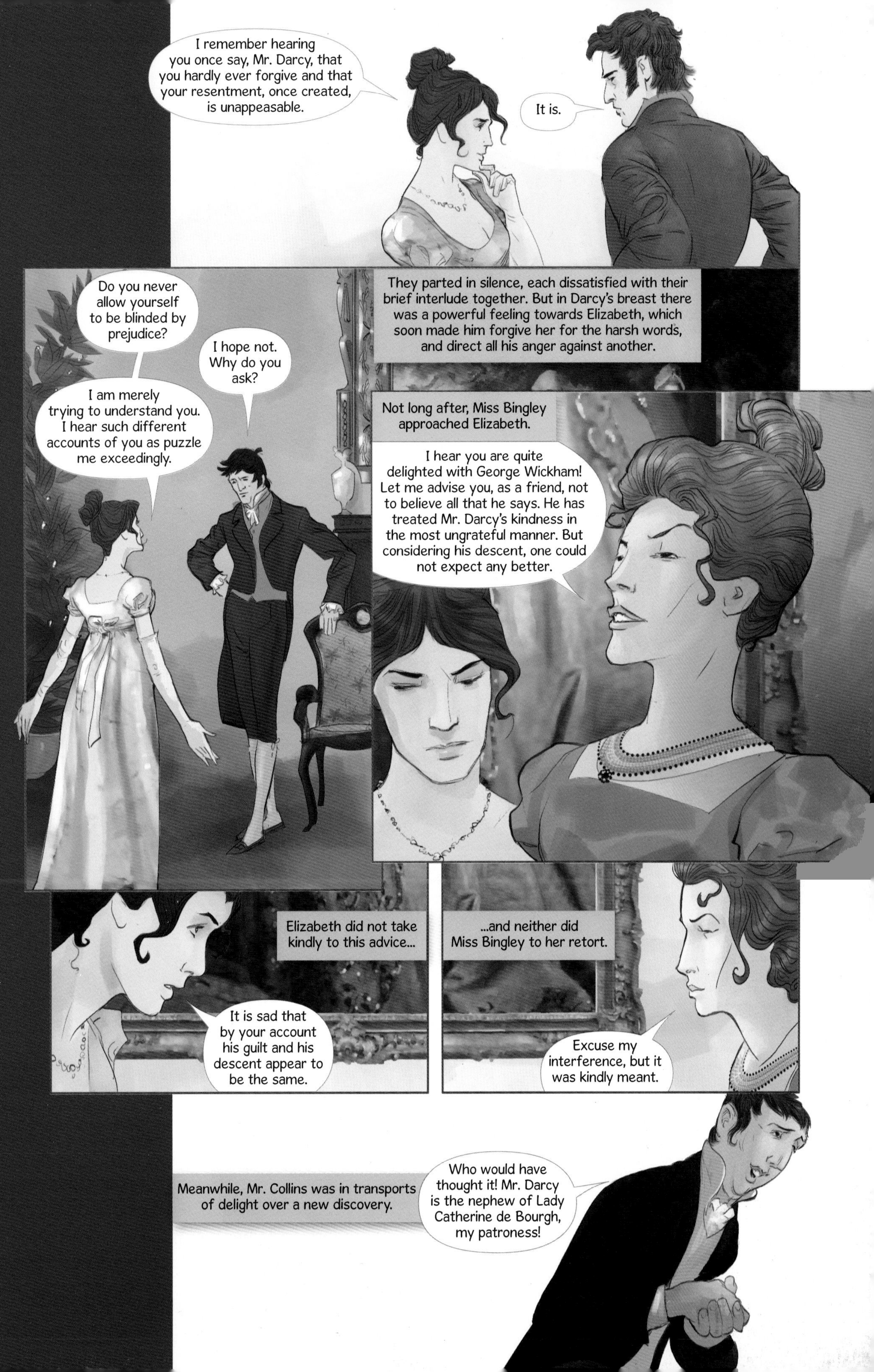
I remember hearing you once say, Mr. Darcy, that you hardly ever forgive and that your resentment, once created, is unappeasable.
It is.
Do you never allow yourself to be blinded by prejudice?
I hope not. Why do you ask?
I am merely trying to understand you. I hear such different accounts of you as puzzle me exceedingly.
They parted in silence, each dissatisfied with their brief interlude together. But in Darcy's breast there was a powerful feeling towards Elizabeth, which soon made him forgive her for the harsh words, and direct all his anger against another.
Not long after, Miss Bingley approached Elizabeth.
I hear you are quite delighted with George Wickham! Let me advise you, as a friend, not to believe all that he says. He has treated Mr. Darcy's kindness in the most ungrateful manner. But considering his descent, one could not expect any better.
Elizabeth did not take kindly to this advice...
It is sad that by your account his guilt and his descent appear to be the same.
...and neither did Miss Bingley to her retort.
Excuse my interference, but it was kindly meant.
Meanwhile, Mr. Collins was in transports of delight over a new discovery.
Who would have thought it! Mr. Darcy is the nephew of Lady Catherine de Bourgh, my patroness!

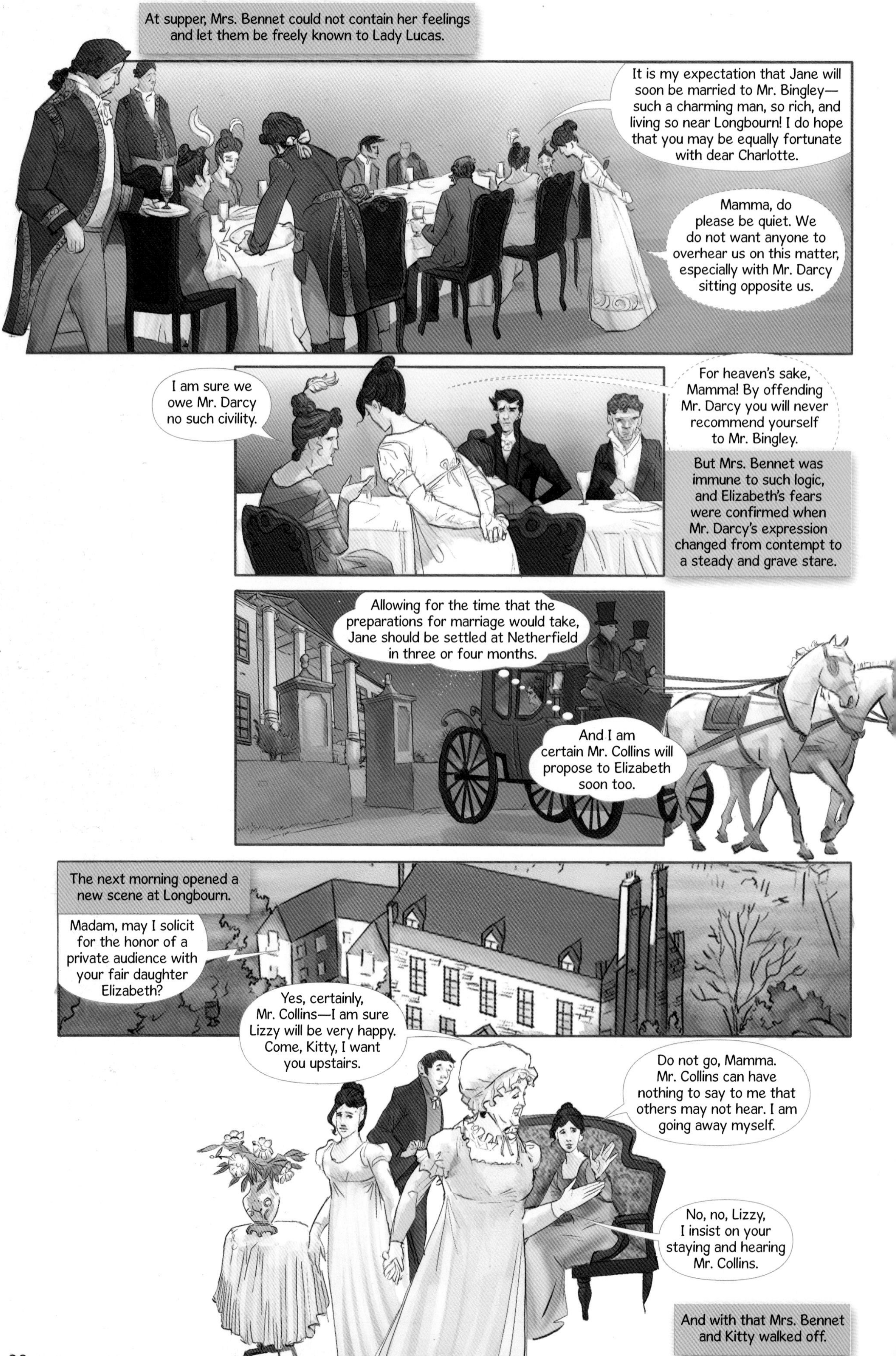
At supper, Mrs. Bennet could not contain her feelings and let them be freely known to Lady Lucas.
It is my expectation that Jane will soon be married to Mr. Bingley—such a charming man, so rich, and living so near Longbourn! I do hope that you may be equally fortunate with dear Charlotte.
Mamma, do please be quiet. We do not want anyone to overhear us on this matter, especially with Mr. Darcy sitting opposite us.
I am sure we owe Mr. Darcy no such civility.
For heaven's sake, Mamma! By offending Mr. Darcy you will never recommend yourself to Mr. Bingley.
But Mrs. Bennet was immune to such logic, and Elizabeth's fears were confirmed when Mr. Darcy's expression changed from contempt to a steady and grave stare.
Allowing for the time that the preparations for marriage would take, Jane should be settled at Netherfield in three or four months.
And I am certain Mr. Collins will propose to Elizabeth soon too.
The next morning opened a new scene at Longbourn.
Madam, may I solicit for the honor of a private audience with your fair daughter Elizabeth?
Yes, certainly, Mr. Collins—I am sure Lizzy will be very happy. Come, Kitty, I want you upstairs.
Do not go, Mamma. Mr. Collins can have nothing to say to me that others may not hear. I am going away myself.
No, no, Lizzy, I insist on your staying and hearing Mr. Collins.
And with that Mrs. Bennet and Kitty walked off.

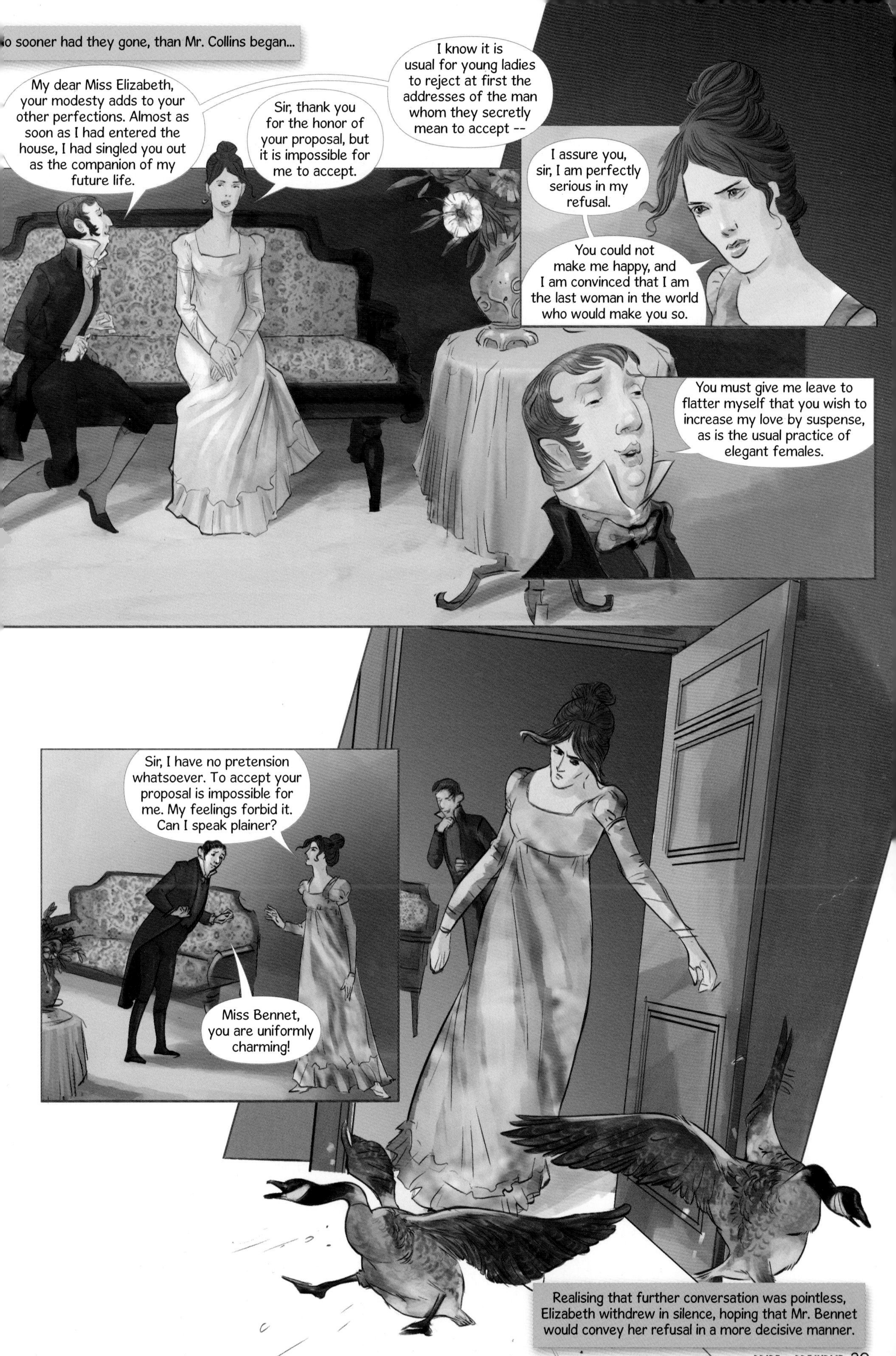

o sooner had they gone, than Mr. Collins began...
My dear Miss Elizabeth, your modesty adds to your other perfections. Almost as soon as I had entered the house, I had singled you out as the companion of my future life.
Sir, thank you for the honor of your proposal, but it is impossible for me to accept.
I know it is usual for young ladies to reject at first the addresses of the man whom they secretly mean to accept --
I assure you, sir, I am perfectly serious in my refusal.
You could not make me happy, and I am convinced that I am the last woman in the world who would make you so.
You must give me leave to flatter myself that you wish to increase my love by suspense, as is the usual practice of elegant females.
Sir, I have no pretension whatsoever. To accept your proposal is impossible for me. My feelings forbid it. Can I speak plainer?
Miss Bennet, you are uniformly charming!
Realising that further conversation was pointless, Elizabeth withdrew in silence, hoping that Mr. Bennet would convey her refusal in a more decisive manner.

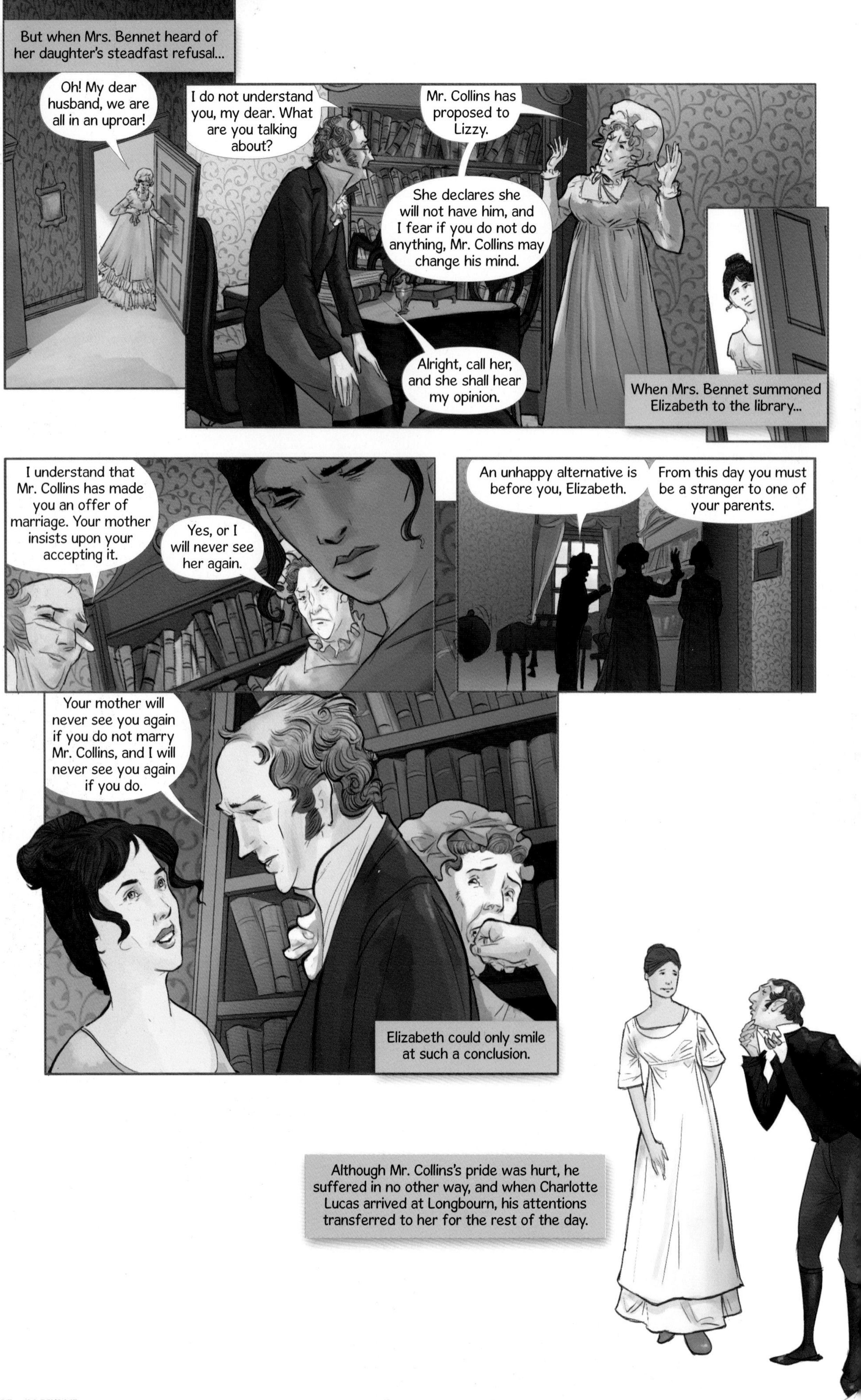
But when Mrs. Bennet heard of her daughter's steadfast refusal...
Oh! My dear husband, we are all in an uproar!
I do not understand you, my dear. What are you talking about?
Mr. Collins has proposed to Lizzy.
She declares she will not have him, and I fear if you do not do anything, Mr. Collins may change his mind.
Alright, call her, and she shall hear my opinion.
When Mrs. Bennet summoned Elizabeth to the library...
I understand that Mr. Collins has made you an offer of marriage. Your mother insists upon your accepting it.
Yes, or I will never see her again.
An unhappy alternative is before you, Elizabeth.
From this day you must be a stranger to one of your parents.
Your mother will never see you again if you do not marry Mr. Collins, and I will never see you again if you do.
Elizabeth could only smile at such a conclusion.
Although Mr. Collins's pride was hurt, he suffered in no other way, and when Charlotte Lucas arrived at Longbourn, his attentions transferred to her for the rest of the day.

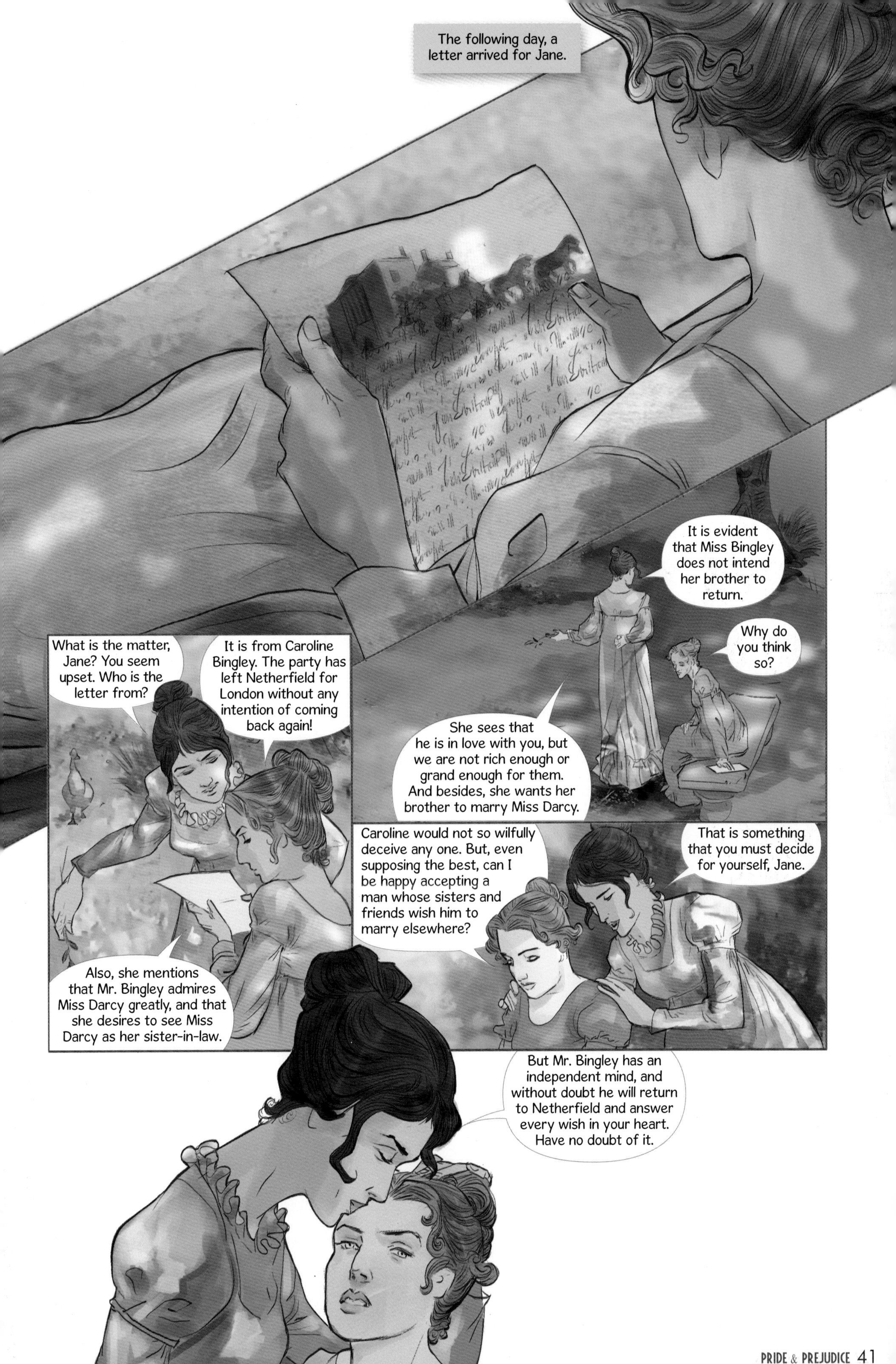
The following day, a letter arrived for Jane.
It is evident that Miss Bingley does not intend her brother to return.
Why do you think so?
What is the matter, Jane? You seem upset. Who is the letter from?
It is from Caroline Bingley. The party has left Netherfield for London without any intention of coming back again!
Also, she mentions that Mr. Bingley admires Miss Darcy greatly, and that she desires to see Miss Darcy as her sister-in-law.
She sees that he is in love with you, but we are not rich enough or grand enough for them. And besides, she wants her brother to marry Miss Darcy.
Caroline would not so wilfully deceive any one. But, even supposing the best, can I be happy accepting a man whose sisters and friends wish him to marry elsewhere?
That is something that you must decide for yourself, Jane.
But Mr. Bingley has an independent mind, and without doubt he will return to Netherfield and answer every wish in your heart. Have no doubt of it.

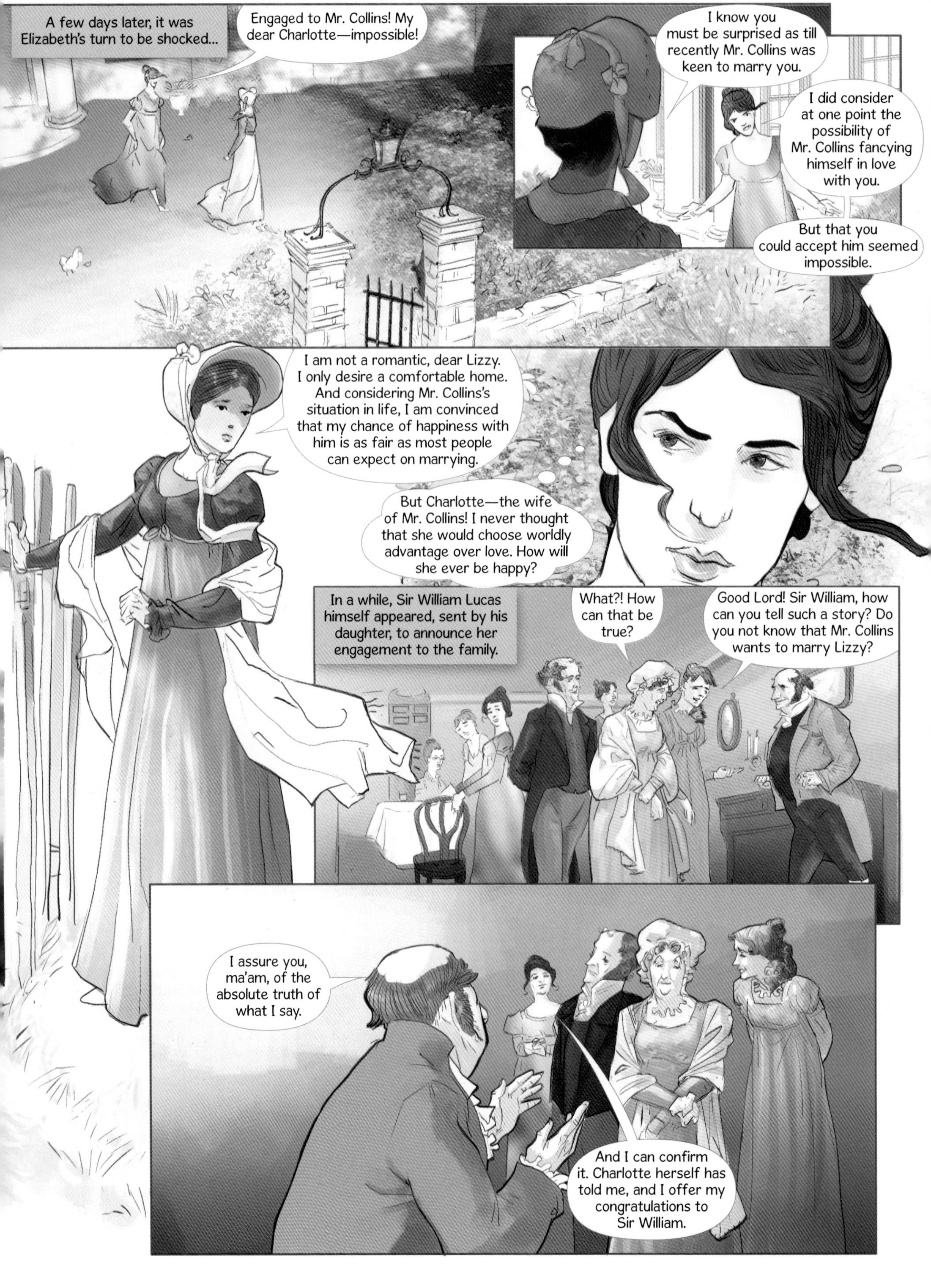
A few days later, it was Elizabeth's turn to be shocked...
Engaged to Mr. Collins! My dear Charlotte—impossible!
I know you must be surprised as till recently Mr. Collins was keen to marry you.
I did consider at one point the possibility of Mr. Collins fancying himself in love with you.
But that you could accept him seemed impossible.
I am not a romantic, dear Lizzy. I only desire a comfortable home. And considering Mr. Collins's situation in life, I am convinced that my chance of happiness with him is as fair as most people can expect on marrying.
But Charlotte—the wife of Mr. Collins! I never thought that she would choose worldly advantage over love. How will she ever be happy?
In a while, Sir William Lucas himself appeared, sent by his daughter, to announce her engagement to the family.
What?! How can that be true?
Good Lord! Sir William, how can you tell such a story? Do you not know that Mr. Collins wants to marry Lizzy?
I assure you, ma'am, of the absolute truth of what I say.
And I can confirm it. Charlotte herself has told me, and I offer my congratulations to Sir William.

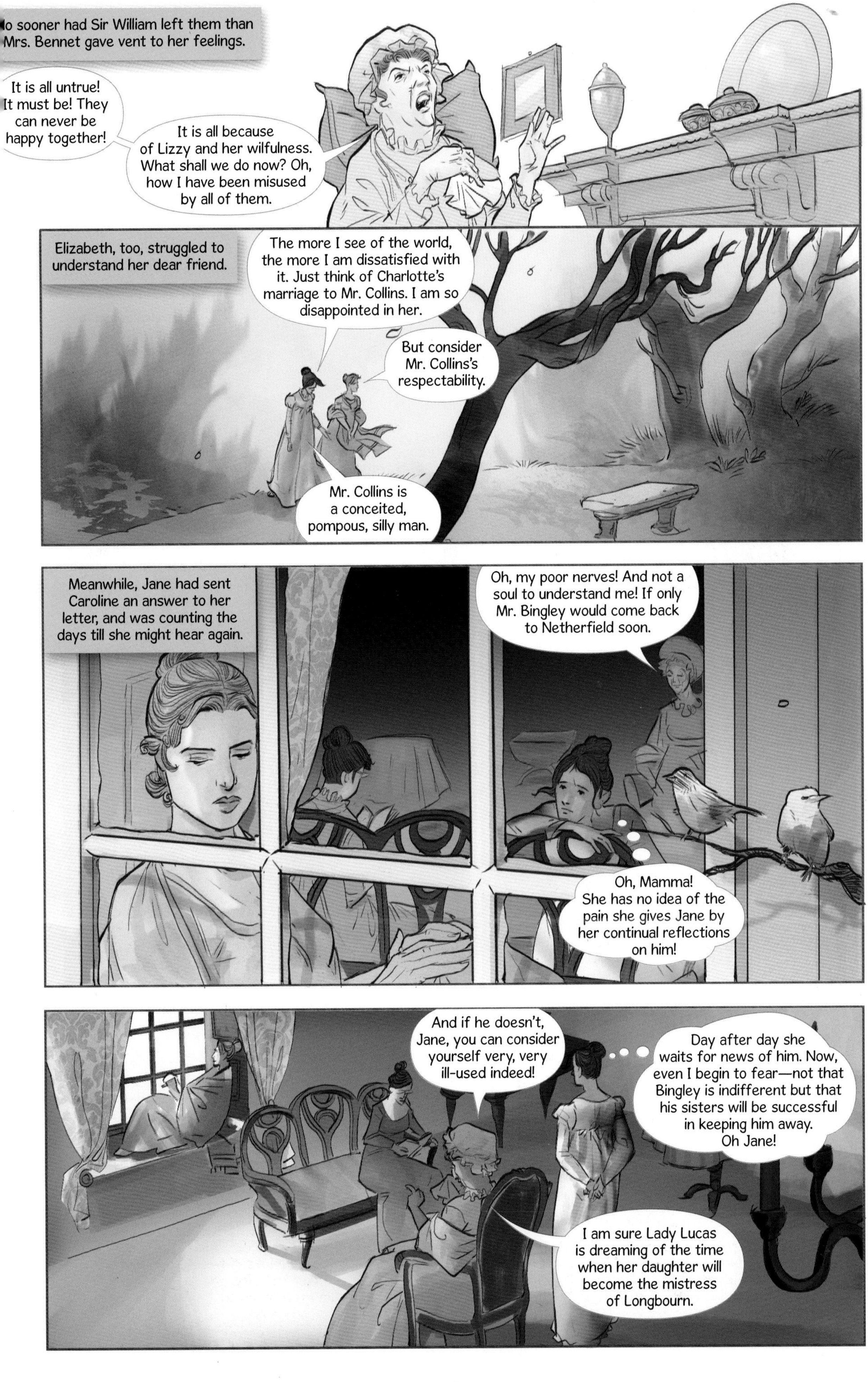
o sooner had Sir William left them than Mrs. Bennet gave vent to her feelings.
It is all untrue! It must be! They can never be happy together!
It is all because of Lizzy and her wilfulness. What shall we do now? Oh, how I have been misused by all of them.
Elizabeth, too, struggled to understand her dear friend.
The more I see of the world, the more I am dissatisfied with it. Just think of Charlotte's marriage to Mr. Collins. I am so disappointed in her.
But consider Mr. Collins's respectability.
Mr. Collins is a conceited, pompous, silly man.
Meanwhile, Jane had sent Caroline an answer to her letter, and was counting the days till she might hear again.
Oh, my poor nerves! And not a soul to understand me! If only Mr. Bingley would come back to Netherfield soon.
Oh, Mamma! She has no idea of the pain she gives Jane by her continual reflections on him!
And if he doesn't, Jane, you can consider yourself very, very ill-used indeed!
Day after day she waits for news of him. Now, even I begin to fear—not that Bingley is indifferent but that his sisters will be successful in keeping him away. Oh Jane!
I am sure Lady Lucas is dreaming of the time when her daughter will become the mistress of Longbourn.

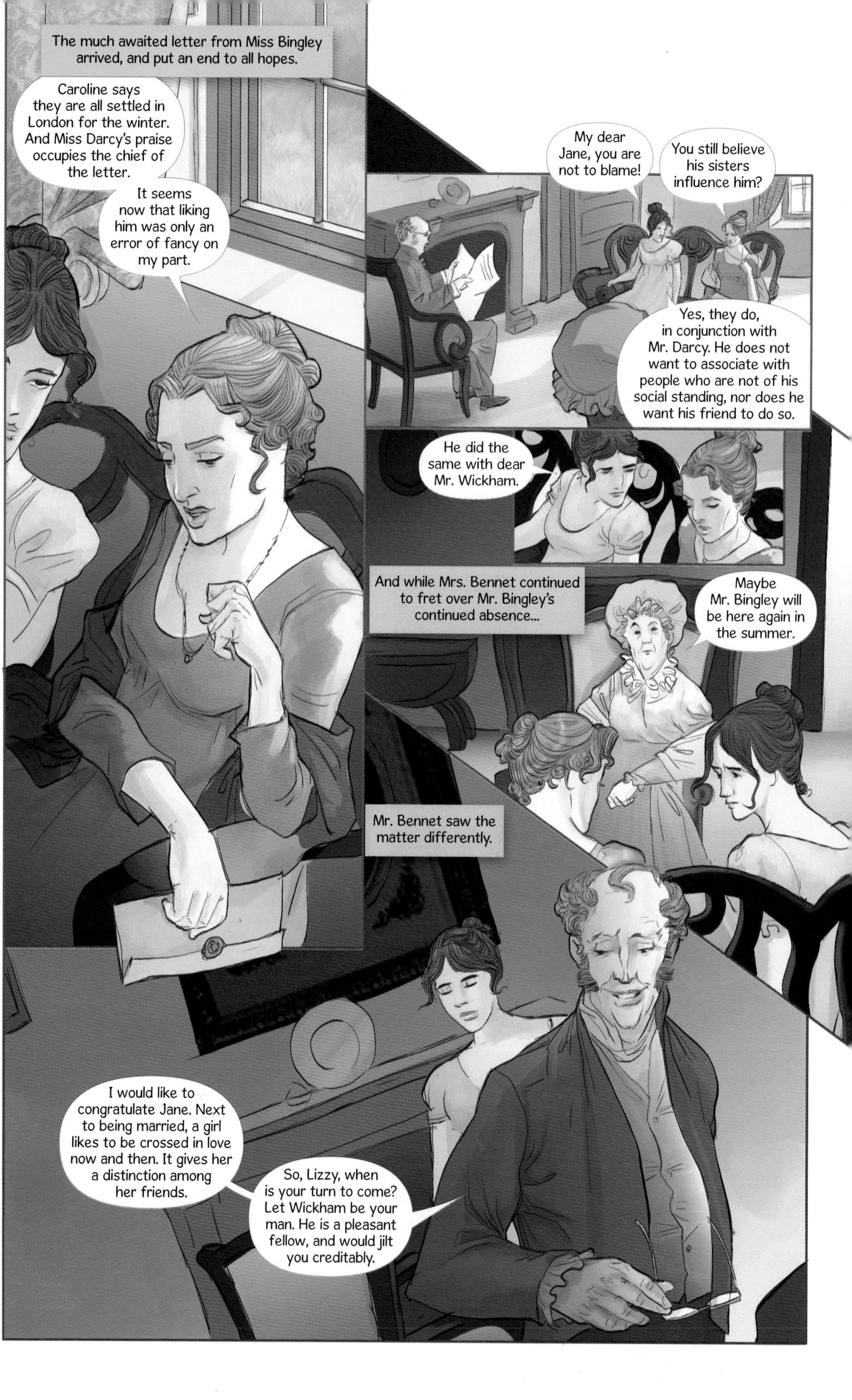

The much awaited letter from Miss Bingley arrived, and put an end to all hopes.
Caroline says they are all settled in London for the winter. And Miss Darcy's praise occupies the chief of the letter.
It seems now that liking him was only an error of fancy on my part.
My dear Jane, you are not to blame!
You still believe his sisters influence him?
Yes, they do, in conjunction with Mr. Darcy. He does not want to associate with people who are not of his social standing, nor does he want his friend to do so.
He did the same with dear Mr. Wickham.
And while Mrs. Bennet continued to fret over Mr. Bingley's continued absence...
Maybe Mr. Bingley will be here again in the summer.
Mr. Bennet saw the matter differently.
I would like to congratulate Jane. Next to being married, a girl likes to be crossed in love now and then. It gives her a distinction among her friends.
So, Lizzy, when is your turn to come? Let Wickham be your man. He is a pleasant fellow, and would jilt you creditably.

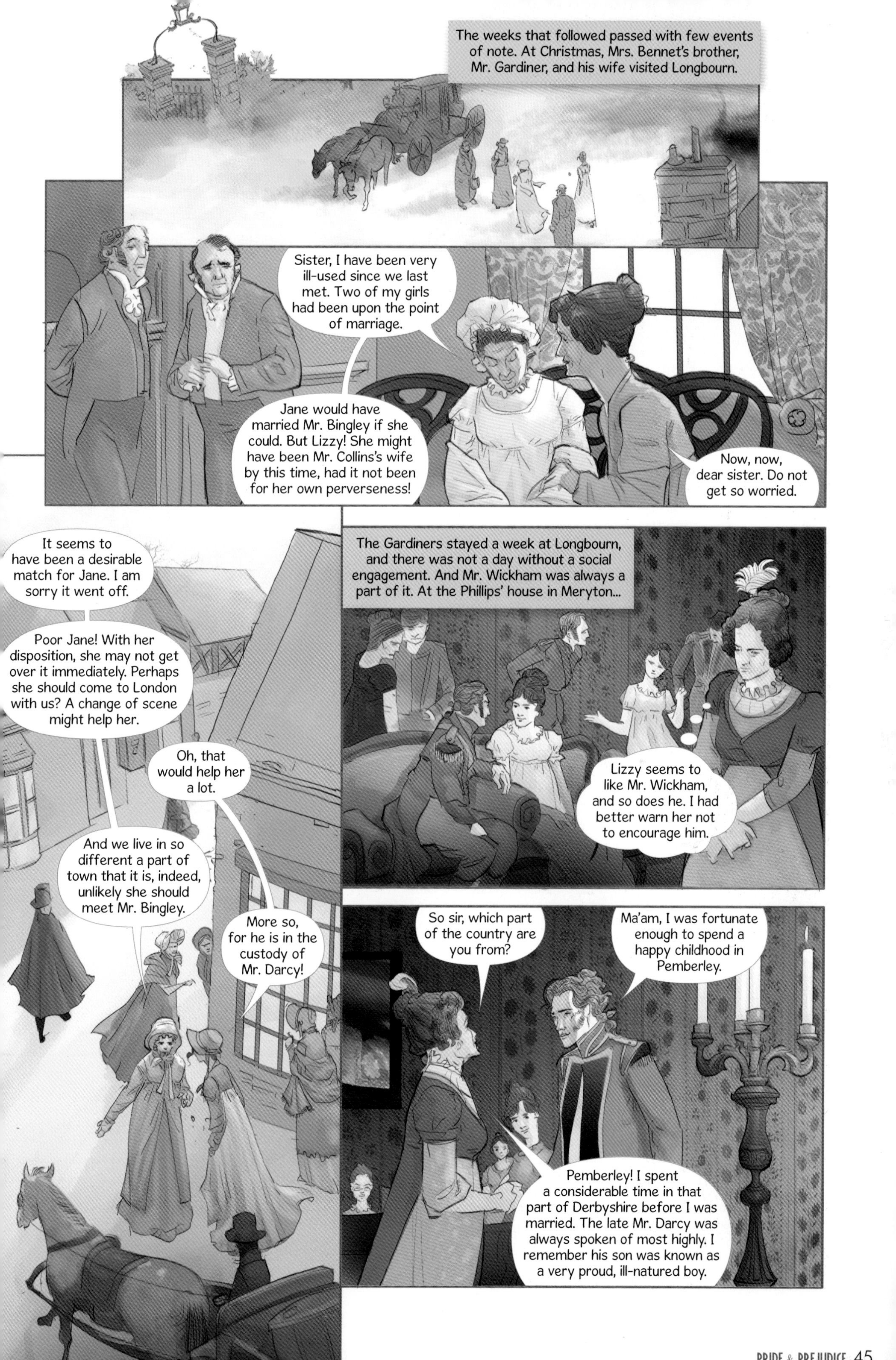
The weeks that followed passed with few events of note. At Christmas, Mrs. Bennet's brother, Mr. Gardiner, and his wife visited Longbourn.
Sister, I have been very ill-used since we last met. Two of my girls had been upon the point of marriage.
Jane would have married Mr. Bingley if she could. But Lizzy! She might have been Mr. Collins's wife by this time, had it not been for her own perverseness!
Now, now, dear sister. Do not get so worried.
It seems to have been a desirable match for Jane. I am sorry it went off.
Poor Jane! With her disposition, she may not get over it immediately. Perhaps she should come to London with us? A change of scene might help her.
Oh, that would help her a lot.
And we live in so different a part of town that it is, indeed, unlikely she should meet Mr. Bingley.
More so, for he is in the custody of Mr. Darcy!
The Gardiners stayed a week at Longbourn, and there was not a day without a social engagement. And Mr. Wickham was always a part of it. At the Phillips' house in Meryton...
Lizzy seems to like Mr. Wickham, and so does he. I had better warn her not to encourage him.
So sir, which part of the country are you from?
Ma'am, I was fortunate enough to spend a happy childhood in Pemberley.
Pemberley! I spent a considerable time in that part of Derbyshire before I was married. The late Mr. Darcy was always spoken of most highly. I remember his son was known as a very proud, ill-natured boy.

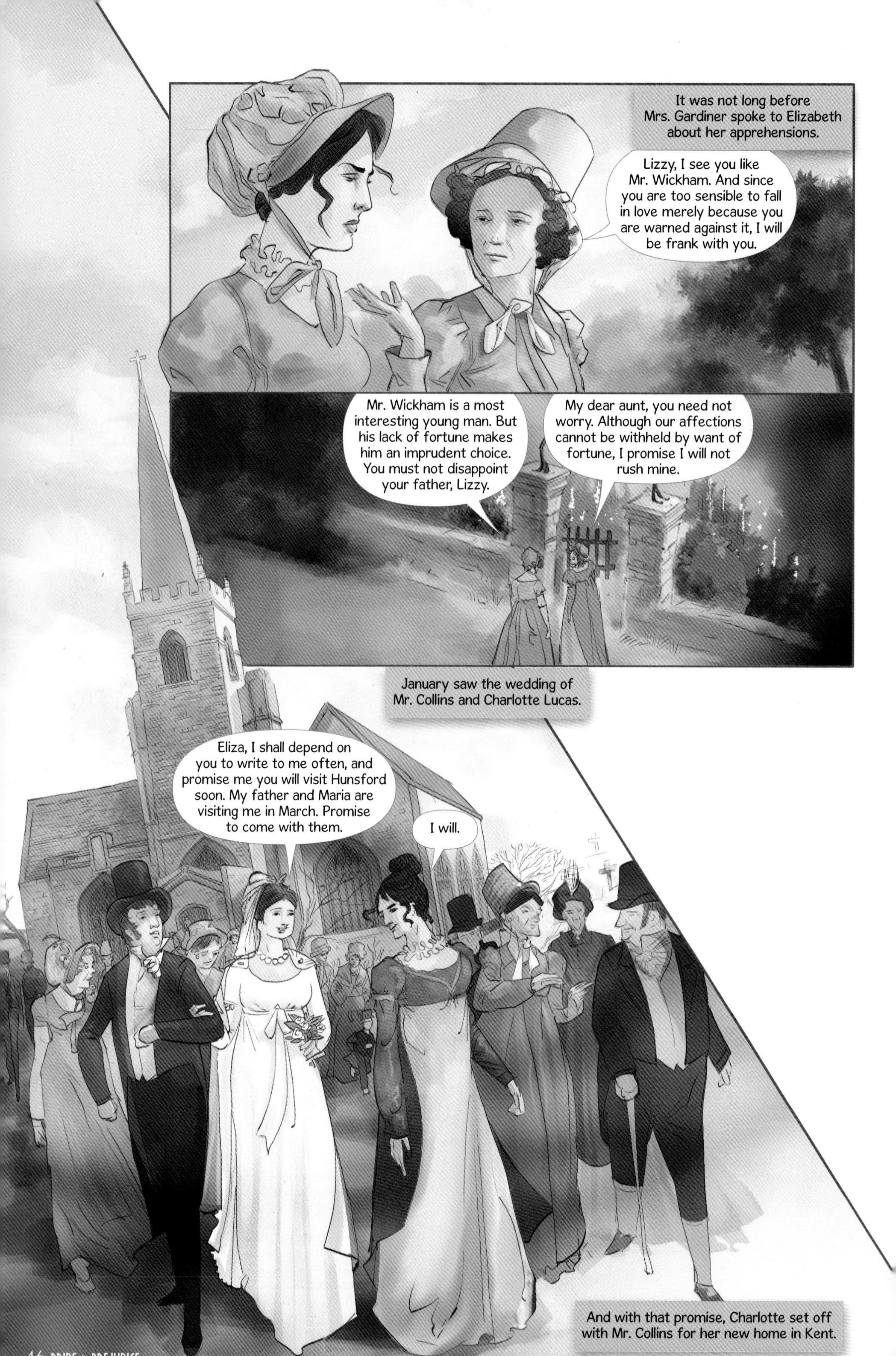
It was not long before Mrs. Gardiner spoke to Elizabeth about her apprehensions.
Lizzy, I see you like Mr. Wickham. And since you are too sensible to fall in love merely because you are warned against it, I will be frank with you.
Mr. Wickham is a most interesting young man. But his lack of fortune makes him an imprudent choice. You must not disappoint your father, Lizzy.
My dear aunt, you need not worry. Although our affections cannot be withheld by want of fortune, I promise I will not rush mine.
January saw the wedding of Mr. Collins and Charlotte Lucas.
Eliza, I shall depend on you to write to me often, and promise me you will visit Hunsford soon. My father and Maria are visiting me in March. Promise to come with them.
I will.
And with that promise, Charlotte set off with Mr. Collins for her new home in Kent.

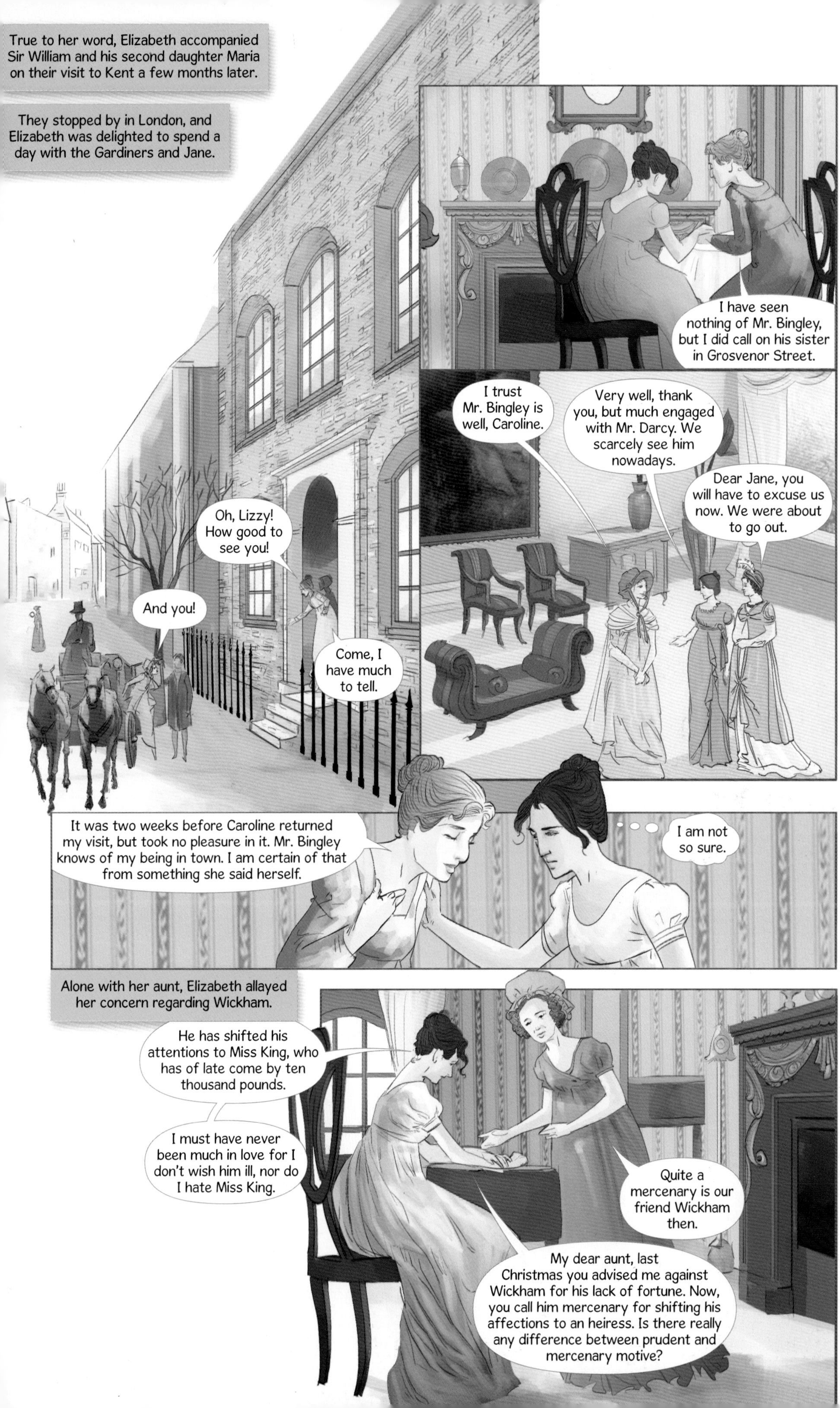
True to her word, Elizabeth accompanied Sir William and his second daughter Maria on their visit to Kent a few months later.
They stopped by in London, and Elizabeth was delighted to spend a day with the Gardiners and Jane.
Oh, Lizzy! How good to see you!
And you!
Come, I have much to tell.
I have seen nothing of Mr. Bingley, but I did call on his sister in Grosvenor Street.
I trust Mr. Bingley is well, Caroline.
Very well, thank you, but much engaged with Mr. Darcy. We scarcely see him nowadays.
Dear Jane, you will have to excuse us now. We were about to go out.
It was two weeks before Caroline returned my visit, but took no pleasure in it. Mr. Bingley knows of my being in town. I am certain of that from something she said herself.
I am not so sure.
Alone with her aunt, Elizabeth allayed her concern regarding Wickham.
He has shifted his attentions to Miss King, who has of late come by ten thousand pounds.
I must have never been much in love for I don't wish him ill, nor do I hate Miss King.
Quite a mercenary is our friend Wickham then.
My dear aunt, last Christmas you advised me against Wickham for his lack of fortune. Now, you call him mercenary for shifting his affections to an heiress. Is there really any difference between prudent and mercenary motive?

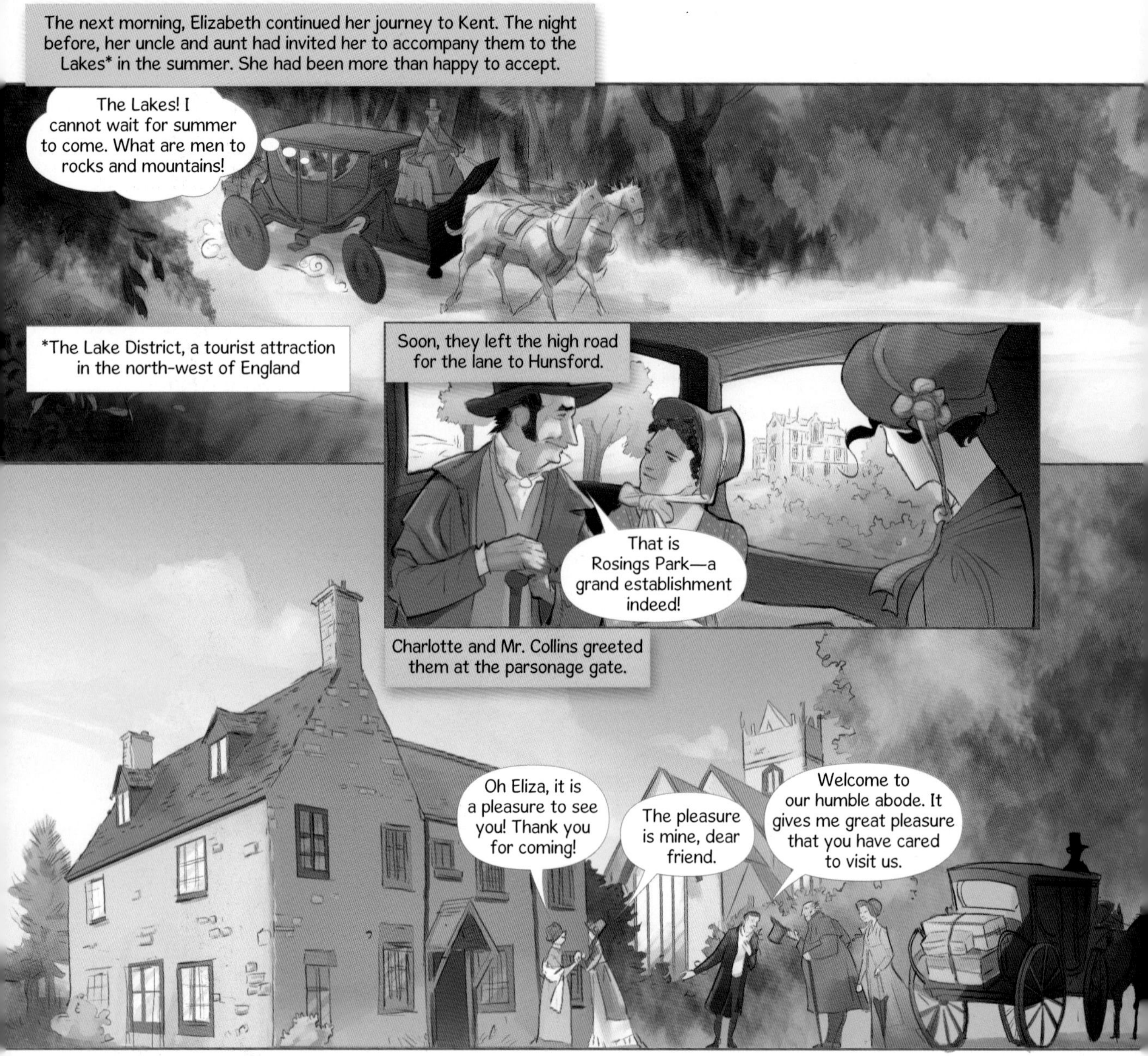
The next morning, Elizabeth continued her journey to Kent. The night before, her uncle and aunt had invited her to accompany them to the Lakes* in the summer. She had been more than happy to accept.
The Lakes! I cannot wait for summer to come. What are men to rocks and mountains!
*The Lake District, a tourist attraction in the north-west of England
Soon, they left the high road for the lane to Hunsford.
That is Rosings Park—a grand establishment indeed!
Charlotte and Mr. Collins greeted them at the parsonage gate.
Oh Eliza, it is a pleasure to see you! Thank you for coming!
The pleasure is mine, dear friend.
Welcome to our humble abode. It gives me great pleasure that you have cared to visit us.

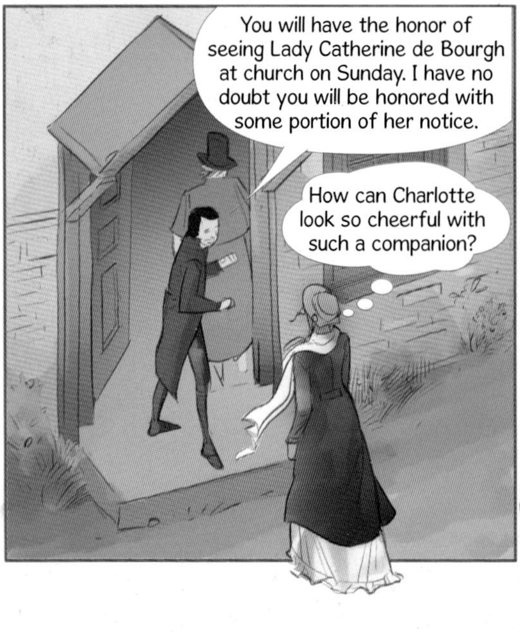
You will have the honor of seeing Lady Catherine de Bourgh at church on Sunday. I have no doubt you will be honored with some portion of her notice.
How can Charlotte look so cheerful with such a companion?

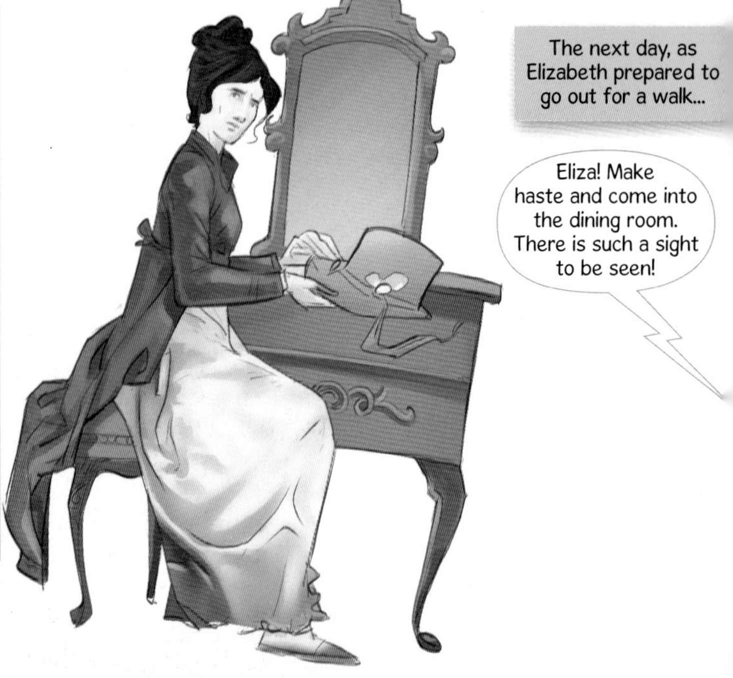
The next day, as Elizabeth prepared to go out for a walk...
Eliza! Make haste and come into the dining room. There is such a sight to be seen!

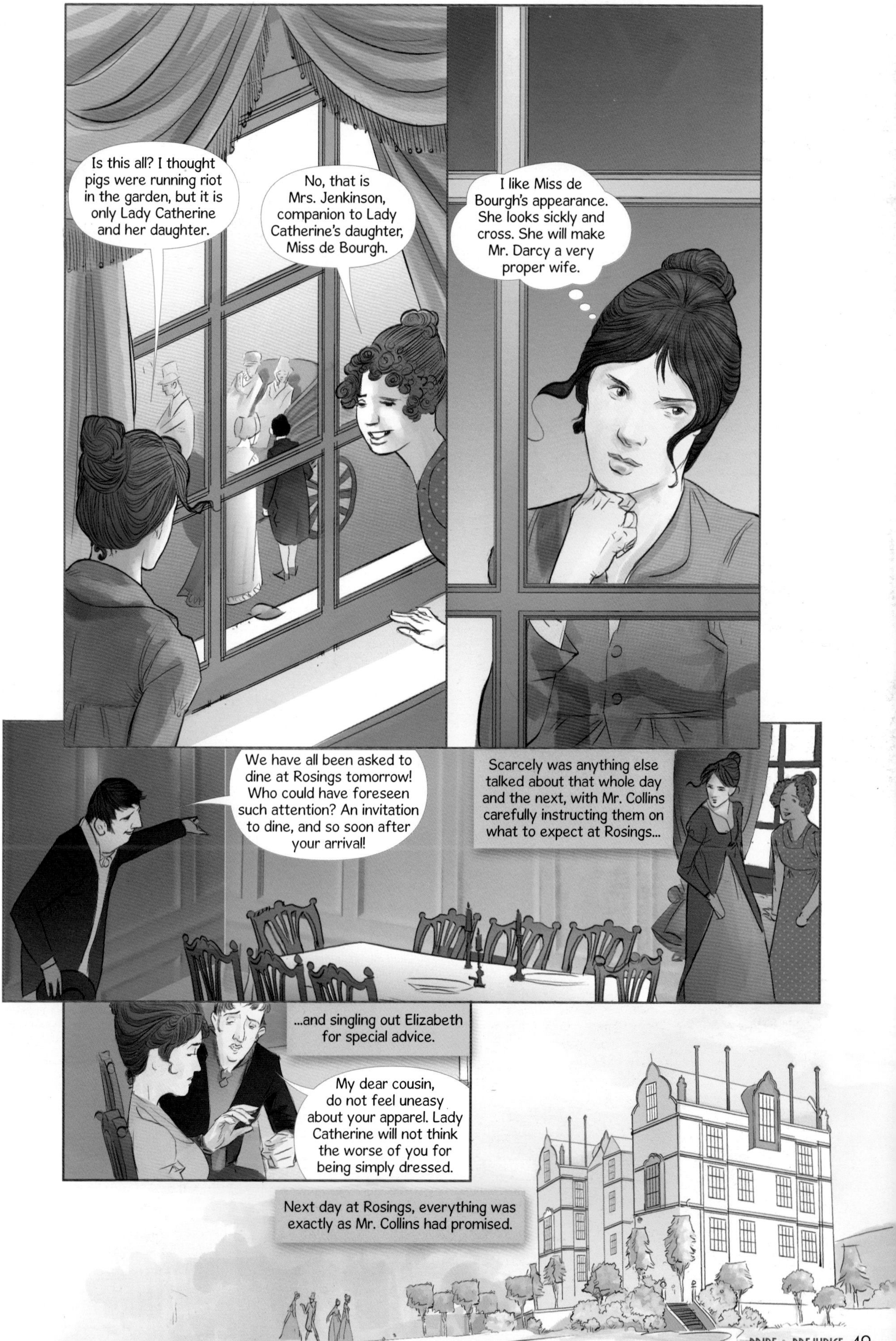
Is this all? I thought pigs were running riot in the garden, but it is only Lady Catherine and her daughter.
No, that is Mrs. Jenkinson, companion to Lady Catherine's daughter, Miss de Bourgh.
I like Miss de Bourgh's appearance. She looks sickly and cross. She will make Mr. Darcy a very proper wife.
We have all been asked to dine at Rosings tomorrow! Who could have foreseen such attention? An invitation to dine, and so soon after your arrival!
Scarcely was anything else talked about that whole day and the next, with Mr. Collins carefully instructing them on what to expect at Rosings...
...and singling out Elizabeth for special advice.
My dear cousin, do not feel uneasy about your apparel. Lady Catherine will not think the worse of you for being simply dressed.
Next day at Rosings, everything was exactly as Mr. Collins had promised.

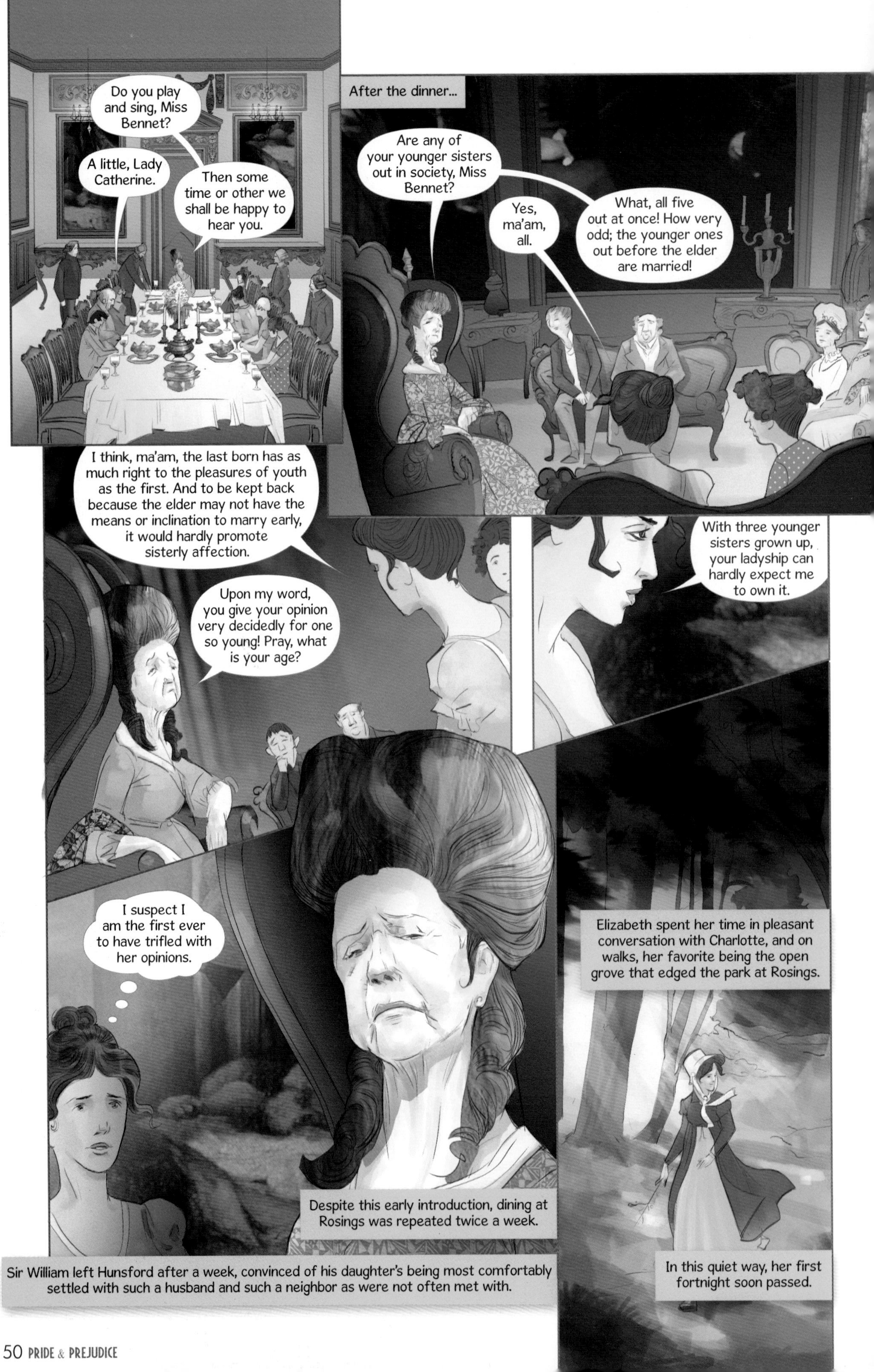
Do you play and sing, Miss Bennet?
A little, Lady Catherine.
Then some time or other we shall be happy to hear you.
After the dinner...
Are any of your younger sisters out in society, Miss Bennet?
Yes, ma'am, all.
What, all five out at once! How very odd; the younger ones out before the elder are married!
I think, ma'am, the last born has as much right to the pleasures of youth as the first. And to be kept back because the elder may not have the means or inclination to marry early, it would hardly promote sisterly affection.
Upon my word, you give your opinion very decidedly for one so young! Pray, what is your age?
With three younger sisters grown up, your ladyship can hardly expect me to own it.
I suspect I am the first ever to have trifled with her opinions.
Despite this early introduction, dining at Rosings was repeated twice a week.
Sir William left Hunsford after a week, convinced of his daughter's being most comfortably settled with such a husband and such a neighbor as were not often met with.
Elizabeth spent her time in pleasant conversation with Charlotte, and on walks, her favorite being the open grove that edged the park at Rosings.
In this quiet way, her first fortnight soon passed.

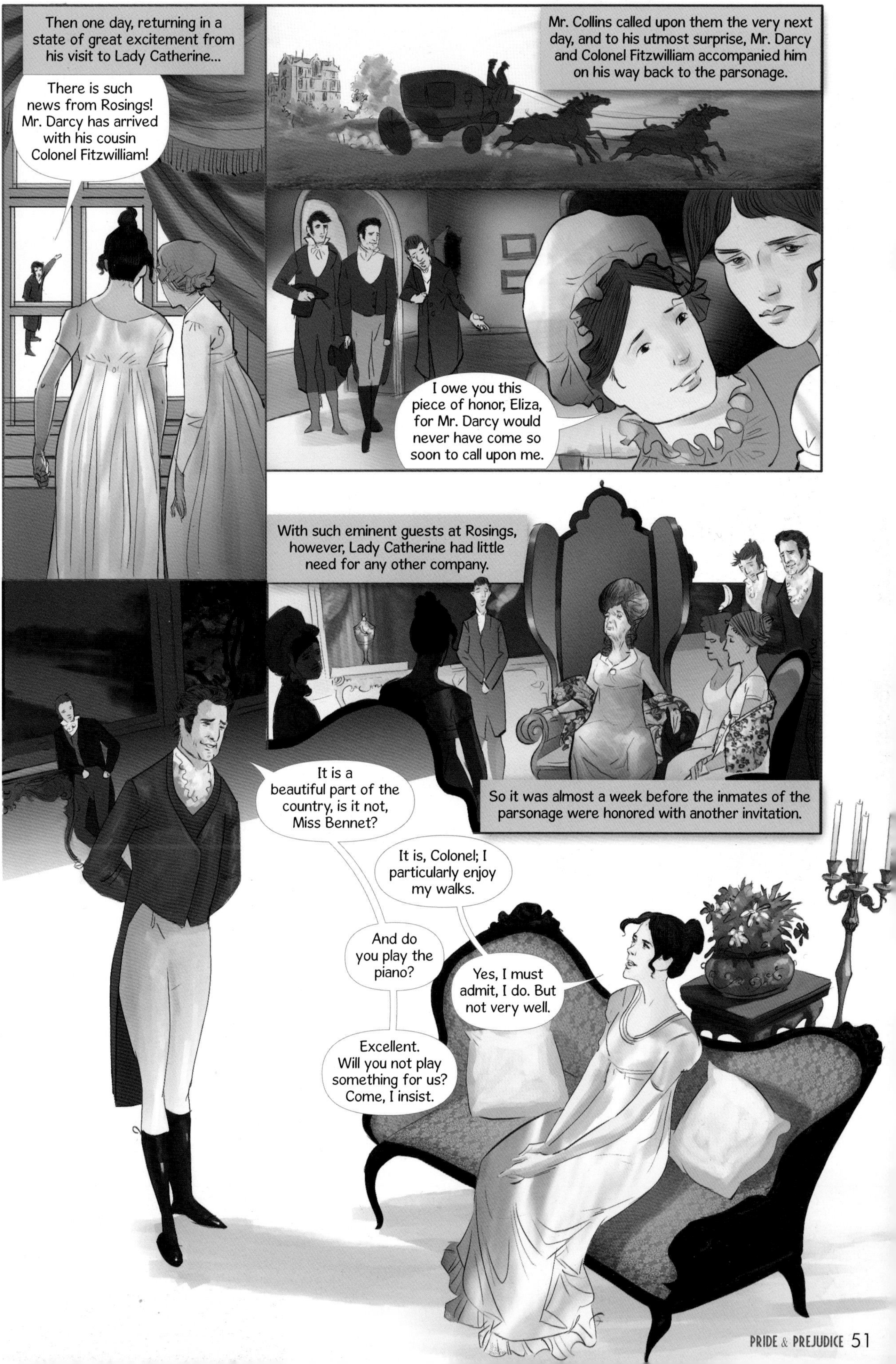

Then one day, returning in a state of great excitement from his visit to Lady Catherine...
There is such news from Rosings! Mr. Darcy has arrived with his cousin Colonel Fitzwilliam!
Mr. Collins called upon them the very next day, and to his utmost surprise, Mr. Darcy and Colonel Fitzwilliam accompanied him on his way back to the parsonage.
I owe you this piece of honor, Eliza, for Mr. Darcy would never have come so soon to call upon me.
With such eminent guests at Rosings, however, Lady Catherine had little need for any other company.
So it was almost a week before the inmates of the parsonage were honored with another invitation.
It is a beautiful part of the country, is it not, Miss Bennet?
It is, Colonel; I particularly enjoy my walks.
And do you play the piano?
Yes, I must admit, I do. But not very well.
Excellent. Will you not play something for us? Come, I insist.

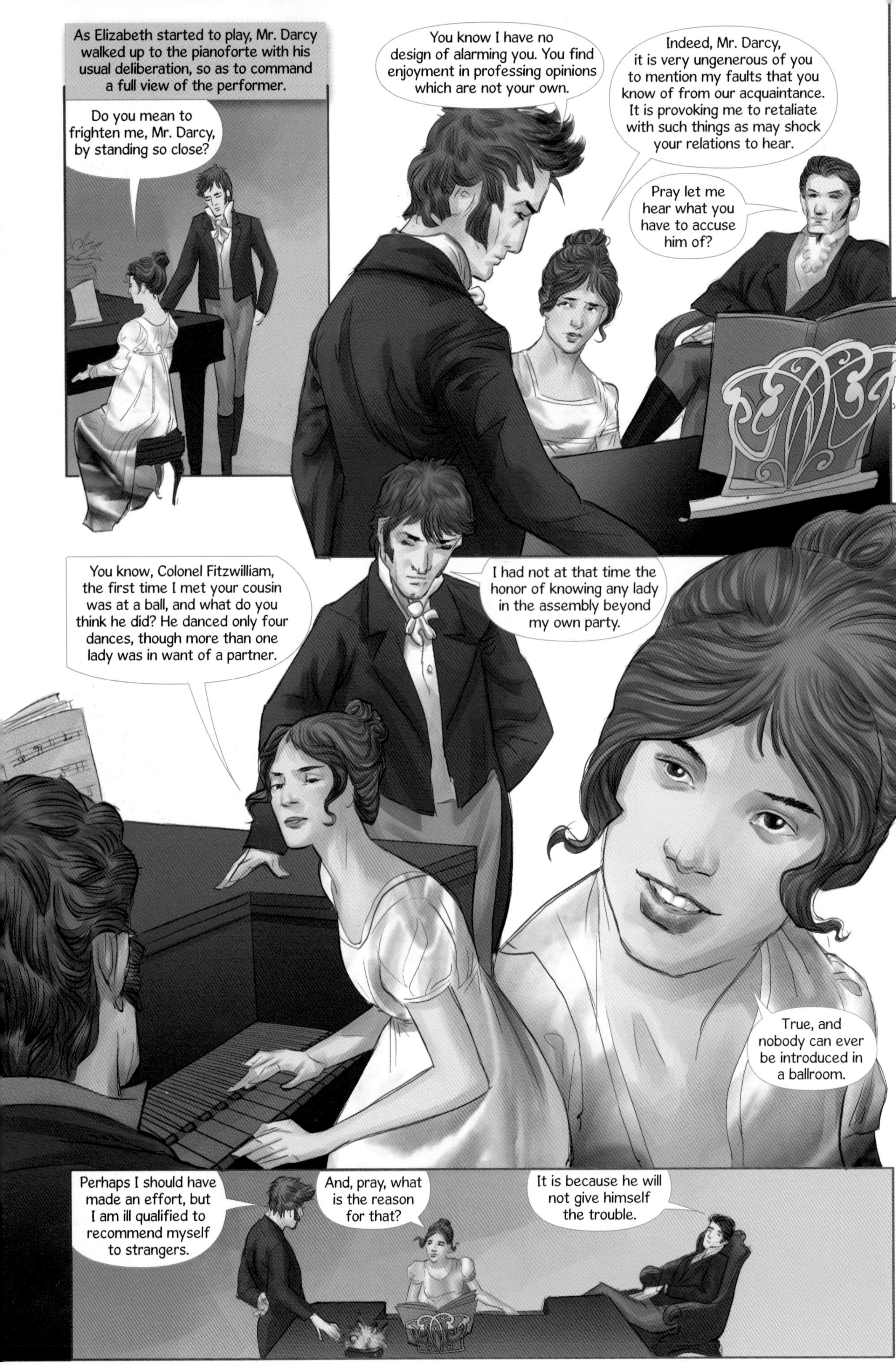

As Elizabeth started to play, Mr. Darcy walked up to the pianoforte with his usual deliberation, so as to command a full view of the performer.
Do you mean to frighten me, Mr. Darcy, by standing so close?
You know I have no design of alarming you. You find enjoyment in professing opinions which are not your own.
Indeed, Mr. Darcy, it is very ungenerous of you to mention my faults that you know of from our acquaintance. It is provoking me to retaliate with such things as may shock your relations to hear.
Pray let me hear what you have to accuse him of?
You know, Colonel Fitzwilliam, the first time I met your cousin was at a ball, and what do you think he did? He danced only four dances, though more than one lady was in want of a partner.
I had not at that time the honor of knowing any lady in the assembly beyond my own party.
True, and nobody can ever be introduced in a ballroom.
Perhaps I should have made an effort, but I am ill qualified to recommend myself to strangers.
And, pray, what is the reason for that?
It is because he will not give himself the trouble.

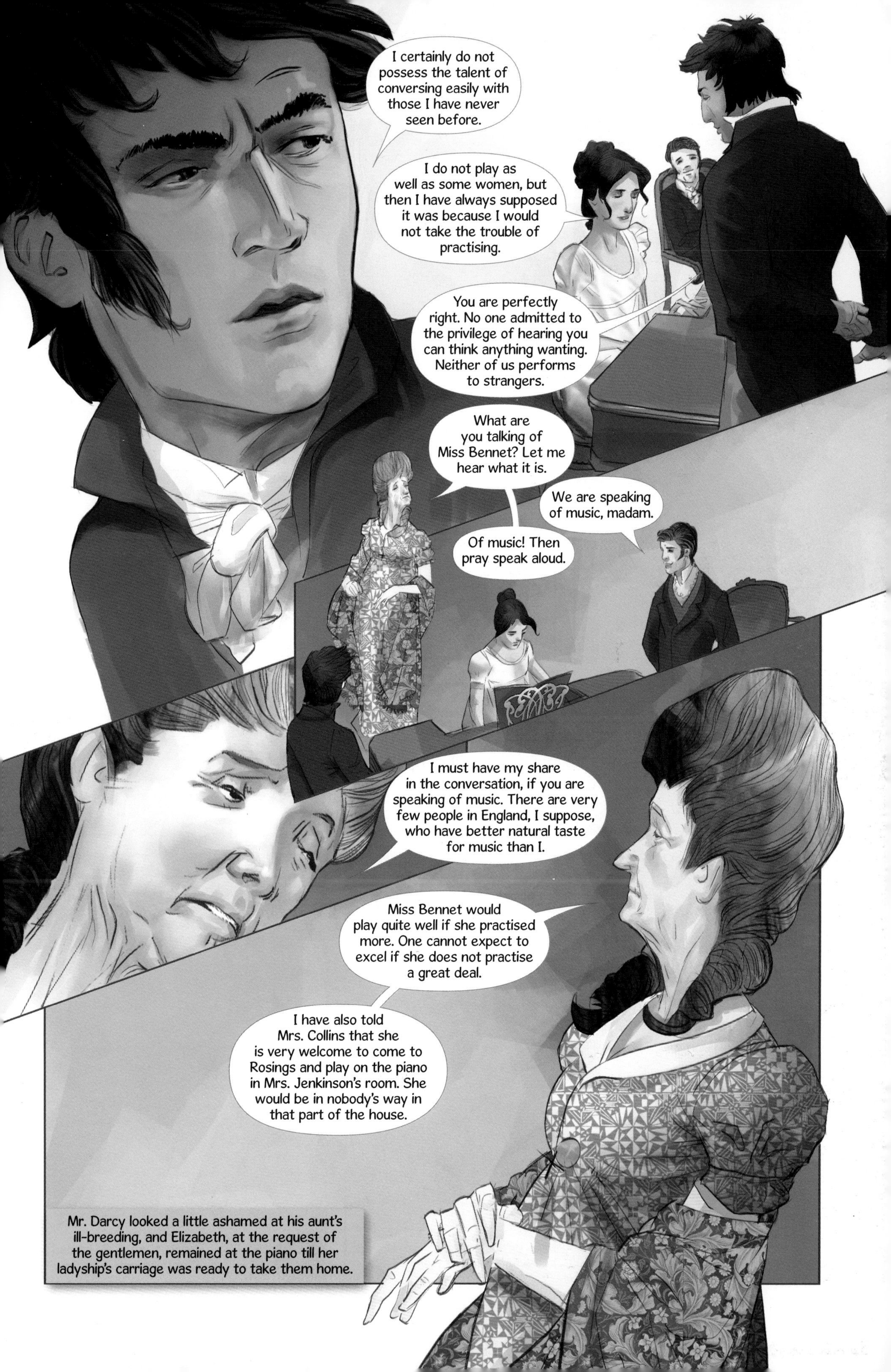
I certainly do not possess the talent of conversing easily with those I have never seen before.
I do not play as well as some women, but then I have always supposed it was because I would not take the trouble of practising.
You are perfectly right. No one admitted to the privilege of hearing you can think anything wanting. Neither of us performs to strangers.
What are you talking of Miss Bennet? Let me hear what it is.
We are speaking of music, madam.
Of music! Then pray speak aloud.
I must have my share in the conversation, if you are speaking of music. There are very few people in England, I suppose, who have better natural taste for music than I.
Miss Bennet would play quite well if she practised more. One cannot expect to excel if she does not practise a great deal.
I have also told Mrs. Collins that she is very welcome to come to Rosings and play on the piano in Mrs. Jenkinson's room. She would be in nobody's way in that part of the house.
Mr. Darcy looked a little ashamed at his aunt's ill-breeding, and Elizabeth, at the request of the gentlemen, remained at the piano till her ladyship's carriage was ready to take them home.

The next morning, the parsonage had an unexpected visitor...

Mr. Darcy!   Mrs. Collins and Maria have gone into the village but will soon return.

My apologies, ma'am, I did not know you were alone.

They sat down, and after Elizabeth's enquiries after Rosings, their conversation seemed in danger of sinking into total silence. So she tried to keep it alive.

Mr. Bingley and his sisters are well, I hope?

Perfectly well, thank you.

I understand that Mr. Bingley may not return to Netherfield.

I should not be surprised if that were so.

Mr. Collins seems very fortunate in his choice of a wife.

Yes, though I am not certain that my friend's choice of marrying Mr. Collins was the wisest she ever made.

At last, Charlotte and Maria returned from their walk.

I apologize for having intruded on Miss Bennet. I mistakenly believed you were at home.

No, no, Mr. Darcy, it is an honor.

Mr. Darcy stayed a few minutes longer, and then went away.

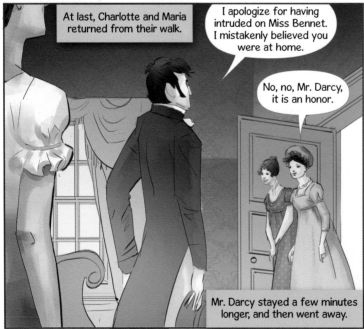

How very strange! My dear Eliza, he must be in love with you, or he would never have called in this familiar way.

You make me laugh! More likely he had nothing better to do.

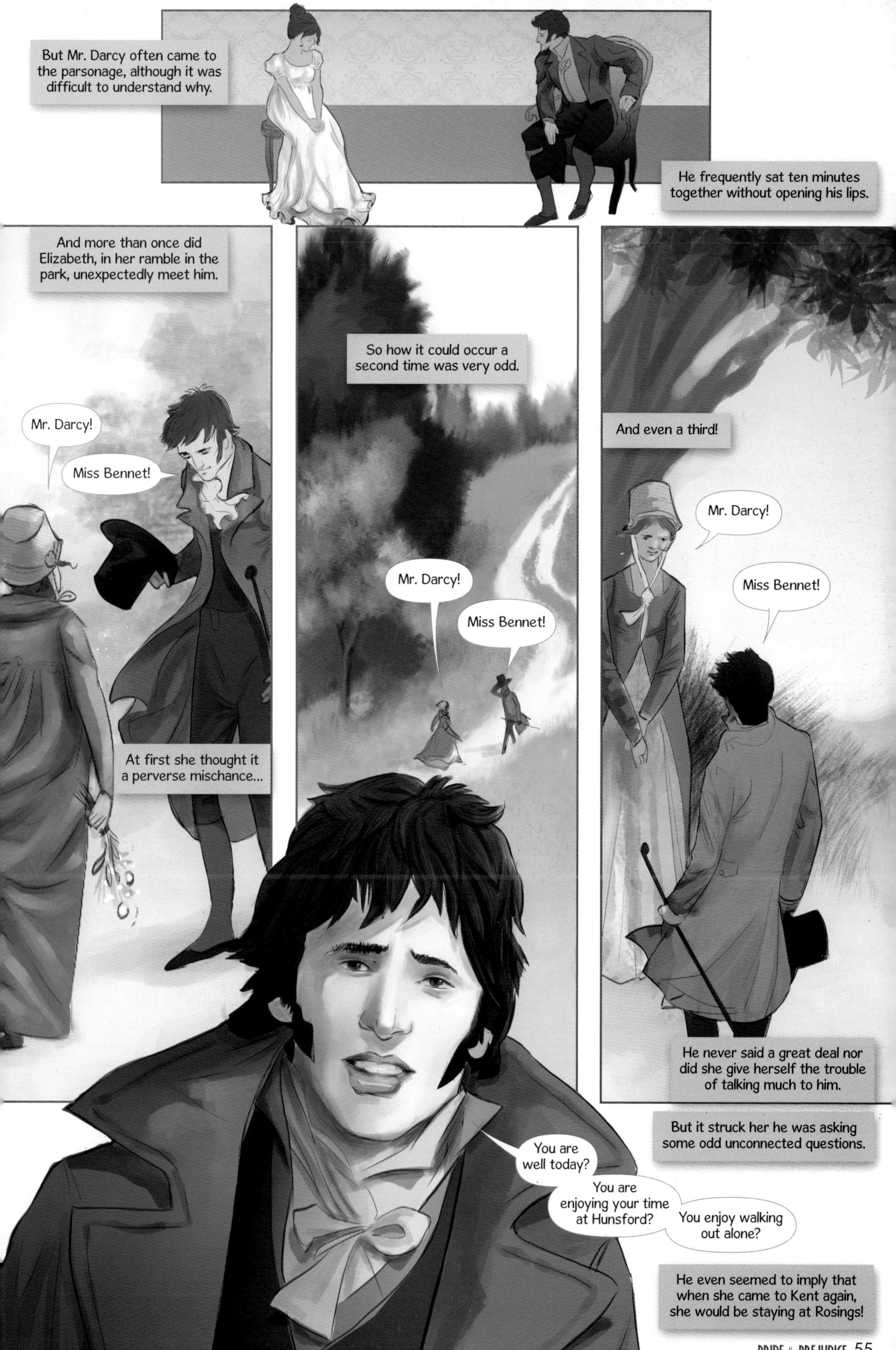
But Mr. Darcy often came to the parsonage, although it was difficult to understand why.
He frequently sat ten minutes together without opening his lips.
And more than once did Elizabeth, in her ramble in the park, unexpectedly meet him.
Mr. Darcy!
Miss Bennet!
At first she thought it a perverse mischance...
So how it could occur a second time was very odd.
Mr. Darcy!
Miss Bennet!
And even a third!
Mr. Darcy!
Miss Bennet!
He never said a great deal nor did she give herself the trouble of talking much to him.
But it struck her he was asking some odd unconnected questions.
You are well today?
You are enjoying your time at Hunsford?
You enjoy walking out alone?
He even seemed to imply that when she came to Kent again, she would be staying at Rosings!

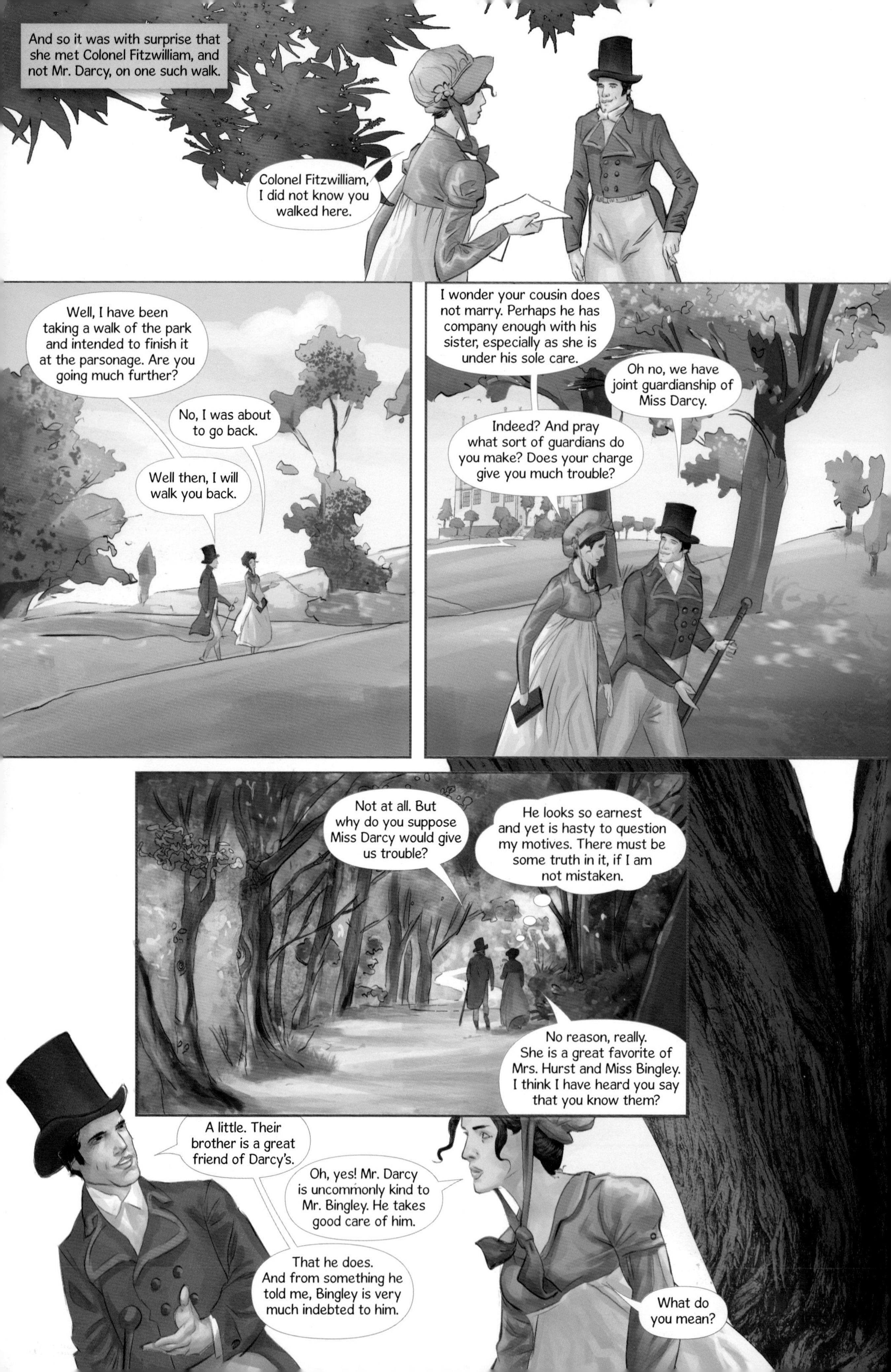
And so it was with surprise that she met Colonel Fitzwilliam, and not Mr. Darcy, on one such walk.
Colonel Fitzwilliam, I did not know you walked here.
Well, I have been taking a walk of the park and intended to finish it at the parsonage. Are you going much further?
No, I was about to go back.
Well then, I will walk you back.
I wonder your cousin does not marry. Perhaps he has company enough with his sister, especially as she is under his sole care.
Oh no, we have joint guardianship of Miss Darcy.
Indeed? And pray what sort of guardians do you make? Does your charge give you much trouble?
Not at all. But why do you suppose Miss Darcy would give us trouble?
He looks so earnest and yet is hasty to question my motives. There must be some truth in it, if I am not mistaken.
No reason, really. She is a great favorite of Mrs. Hurst and Miss Bingley. I think I have heard you say that you know them?
A little. Their brother is a great friend of Darcy's.
Oh, yes! Mr. Darcy is uncommonly kind to Mr. Bingley. He takes good care of him.
That he does. And from something he told me, Bingley is very much indebted to him.
What do you mean?

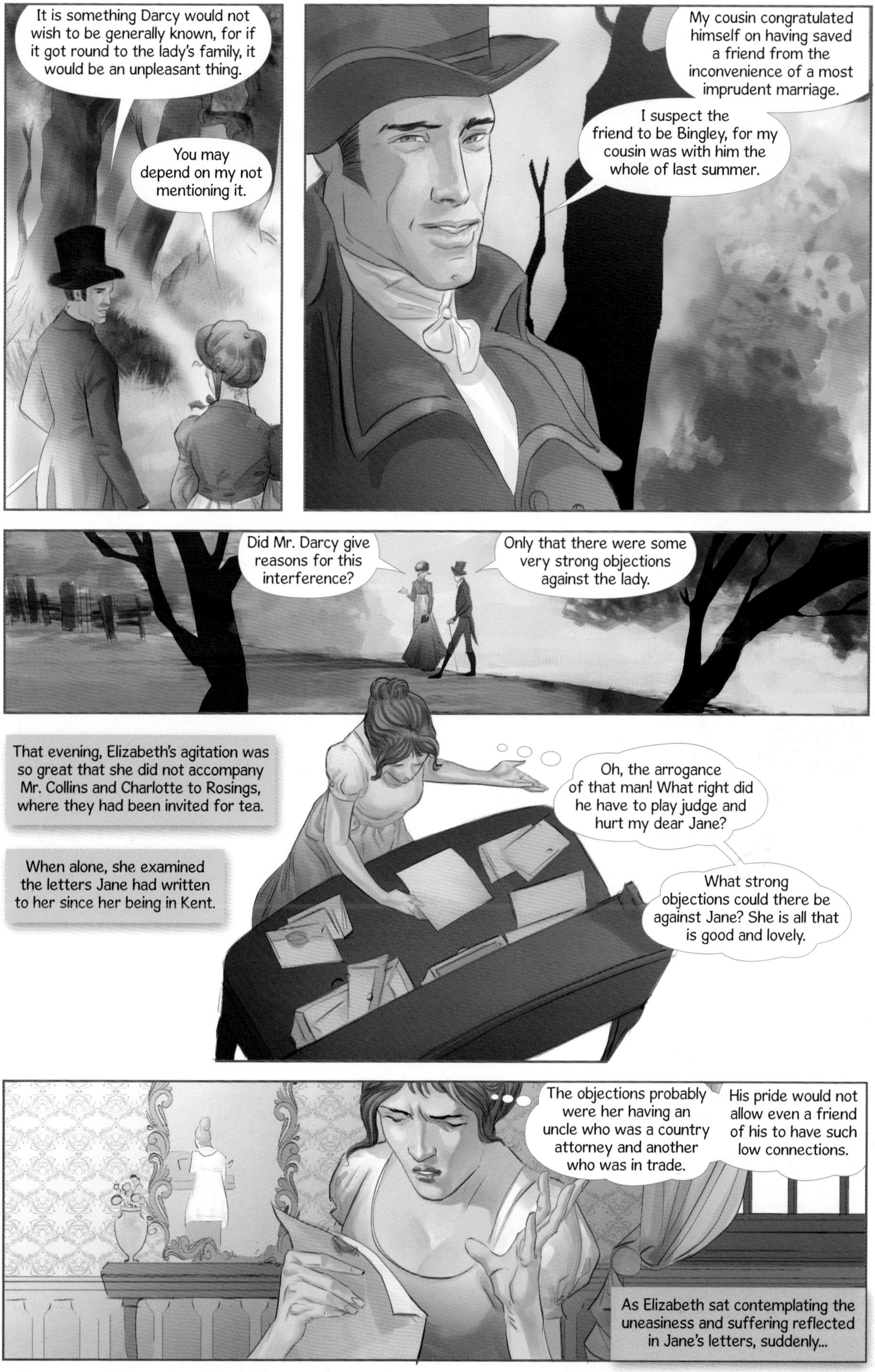

It is something Darcy would not wish to be generally known, for if it got round to the lady's family, it would be an unpleasant thing.
You may depend on my not mentioning it.
My cousin congratulated himself on having saved a friend from the inconvenience of a most imprudent marriage.
I suspect the friend to be Bingley, for my cousin was with him the whole of last summer.
Did Mr. Darcy give reasons for this interference?
Only that there were some very strong objections against the lady.
That evening, Elizabeth's agitation was so great that she did not accompany Mr. Collins and Charlotte to Rosings, where they had been invited for tea.
When alone, she examined the letters Jane had written to her since her being in Kent.
Oh, the arrogance of that man! What right did he have to play judge and hurt my dear Jane?
What strong objections could there be against Jane? She is all that is good and lovely.
The objections probably were her having an uncle who was a country attorney and another who was in trade.
His pride would not allow even a friend of his to have such low connections.
As Elizabeth sat contemplating the uneasiness and suffering reflected in Jane's letters, suddenly...

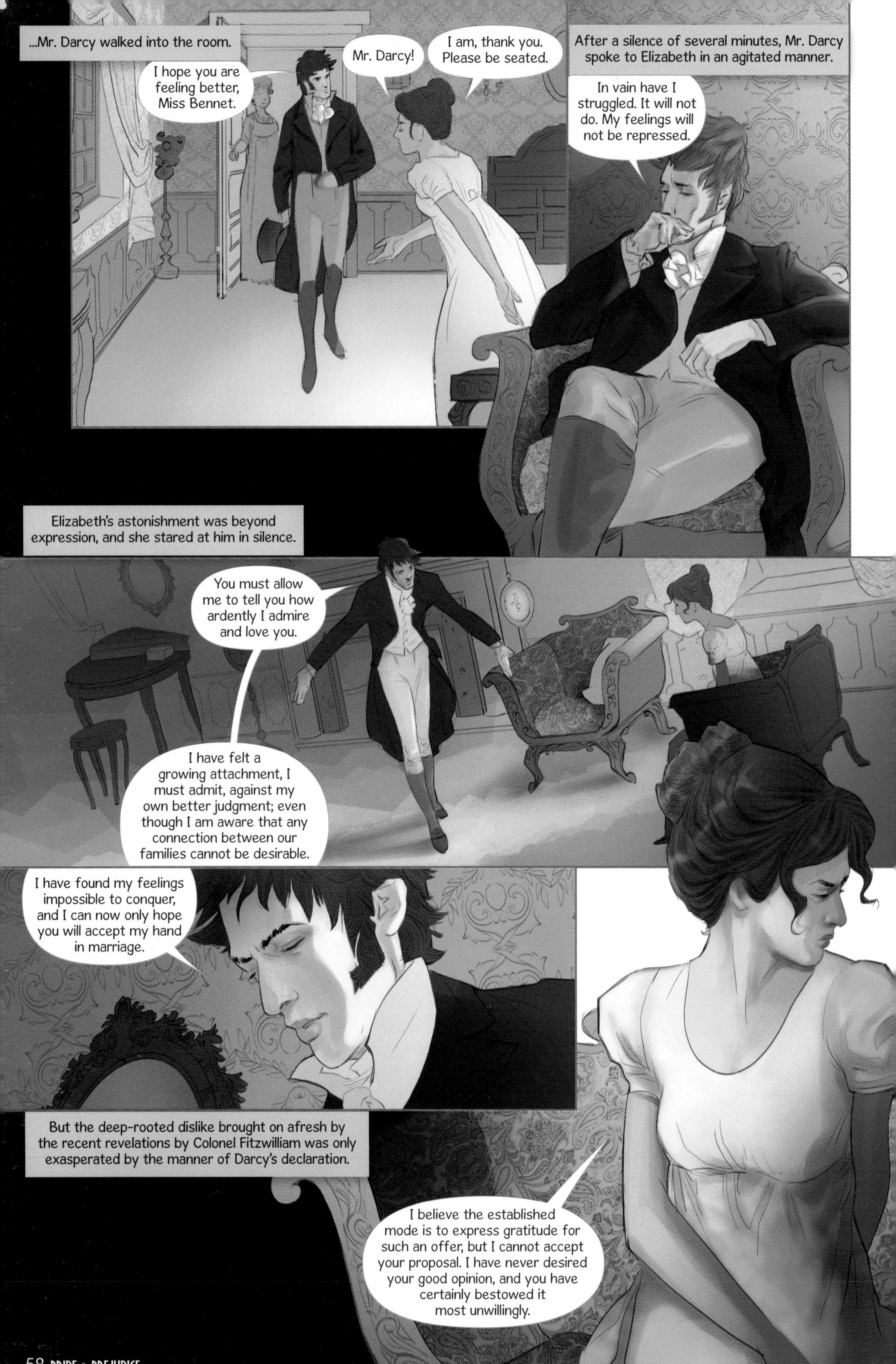
...Mr. Darcy walked into the room.
I hope you are feeling better, Miss Bennet.
Mr. Darcy!
I am, thank you. Please be seated.
After a silence of several minutes, Mr. Darcy spoke to Elizabeth in an agitated manner.
In vain have I struggled. It will not do. My feelings will not be repressed.
Elizabeth's astonishment was beyond expression, and she stared at him in silence.
You must allow me to tell you how ardently I admire and love you.
I have felt a growing attachment, I must admit, against my own better judgment; even though I am aware that any connection between our families cannot be desirable.
I have found my feelings impossible to conquer, and I can now only hope you will accept my hand in marriage.
But the deep-rooted dislike brought on afresh by the recent revelations by Colonel Fitzwilliam was only exasperated by the manner of Darcy's declaration.
I believe the established mode is to express gratitude for such an offer, but I cannot accept your proposal. I have never desired your good opinion, and you have certainly bestowed it most unwillingly.

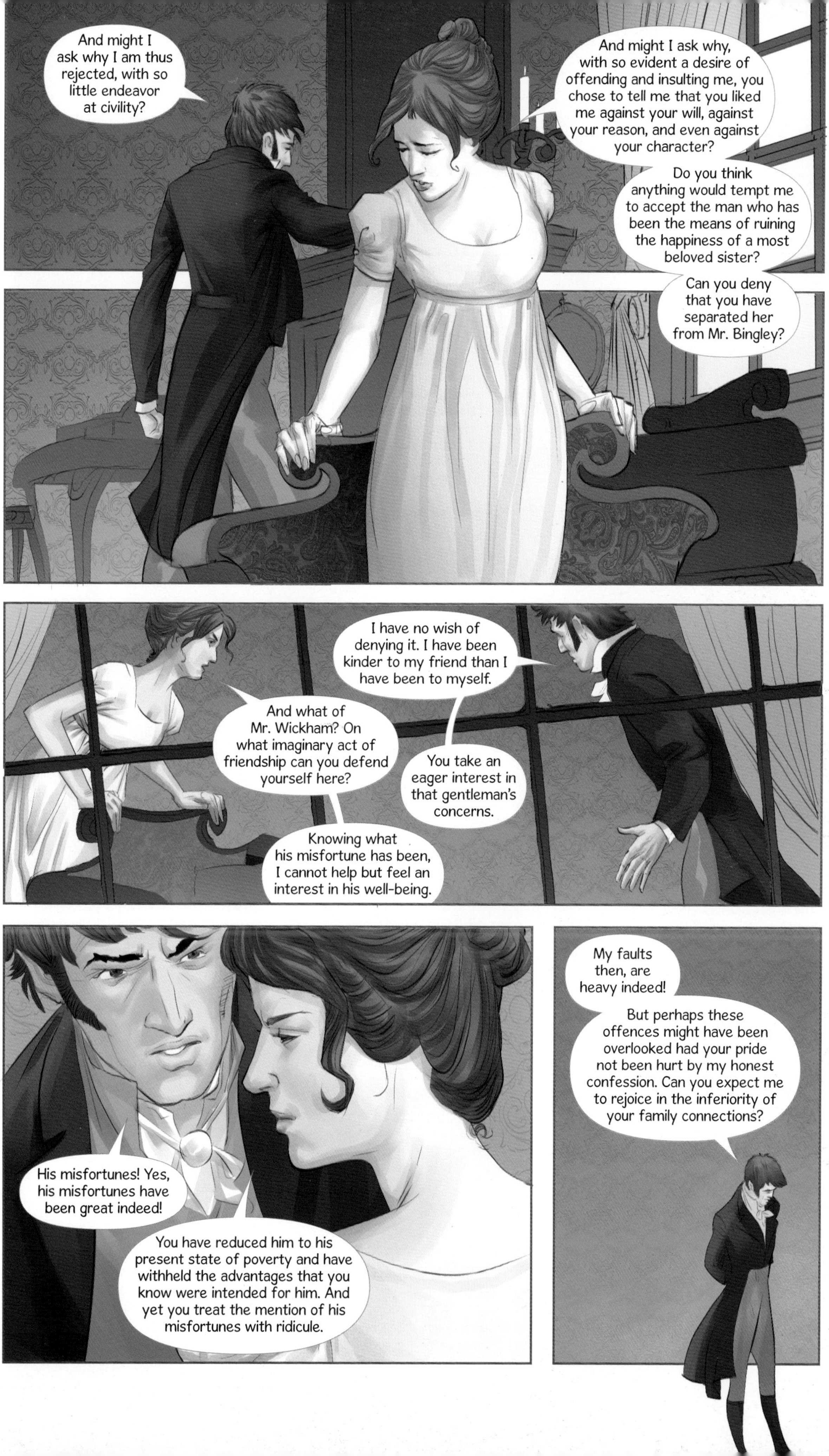
And might I ask why I am thus rejected, with so little endeavor at civility?
And might I ask why, with so evident a desire of offending and insulting me, you chose to tell me that you liked me against your will, against your reason, and even against your character?
Do you think anything would tempt me to accept the man who has been the means of ruining the happiness of a most beloved sister?
Can you deny that you have separated her from Mr. Bingley?
I have no wish of denying it. I have been kinder to my friend than I have been to myself.
And what of Mr. Wickham? On what imaginary act of friendship can you defend yourself here?
You take an eager interest in that gentleman's concerns.
Knowing what his misfortune has been, I cannot help but feel an interest in his well-being.
His misfortunes! Yes, his misfortunes have been great indeed!
You have reduced him to his present state of poverty and have withheld the advantages that you know were intended for him. And yet you treat the mention of his misfortunes with ridicule.
My faults then, are heavy indeed!
But perhaps these offences might have been overlooked had your pride not been hurt by my honest confession. Can you expect me to rejoice in the inferiority of your family connections?

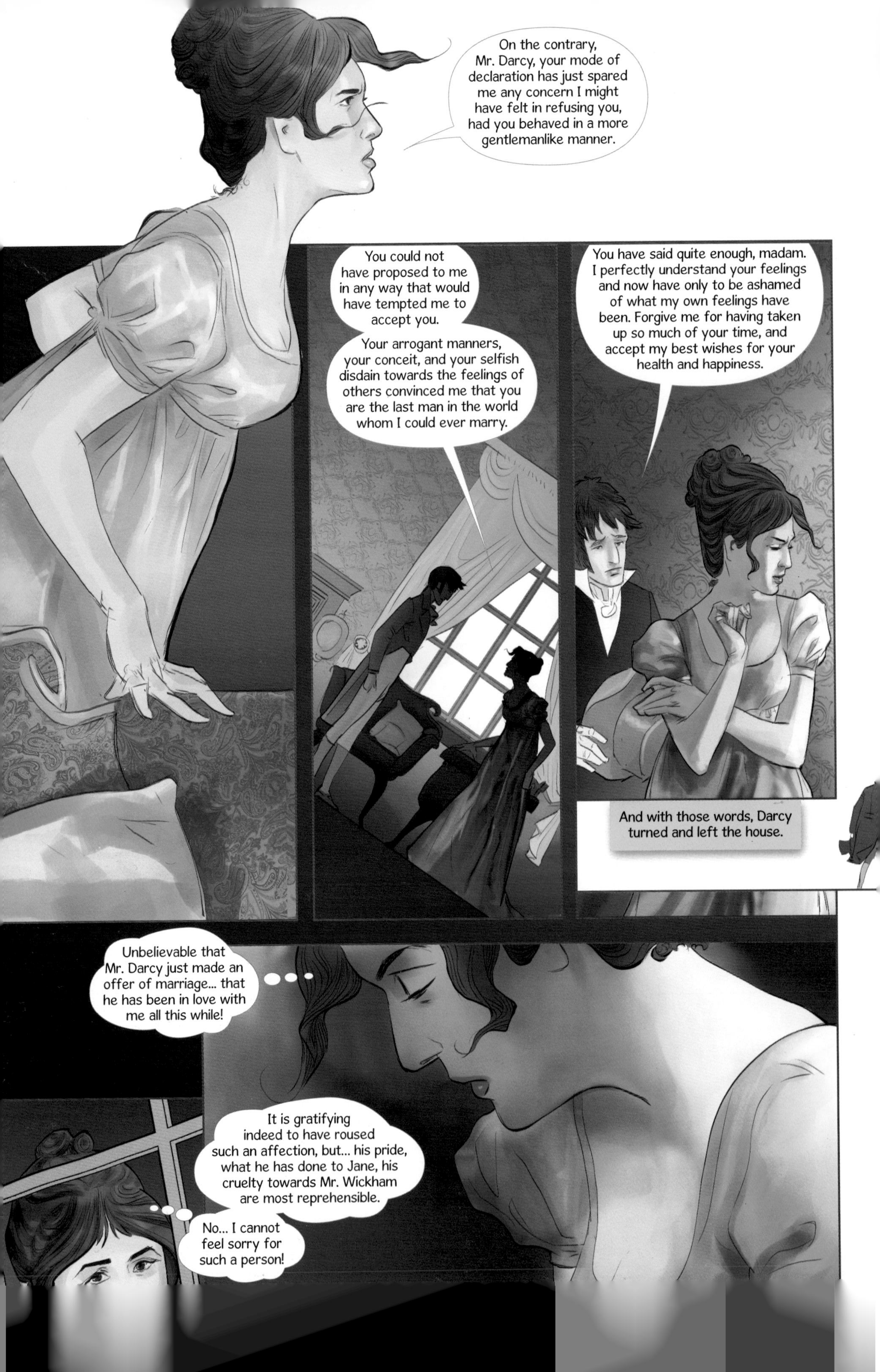
On the contrary, Mr. Darcy, your mode of declaration has just spared me any concern I might have felt in refusing you, had you behaved in a more gentlemanlike manner.
You could not have proposed to me in any way that would have tempted me to accept you.
Your arrogant manners, your conceit, and your selfish disdain towards the feelings of others convinced me that you are the last man in the world whom I could ever marry.
You have said quite enough, madam. I perfectly understand your feelings and now have only to be ashamed of what my own feelings have been. Forgive me for having taken up so much of your time, and accept my best wishes for your health and happiness.
And with those words, Darcy turned and left the house.
Unbelievable that Mr. Darcy just made an offer of marriage... that he has been in love with me all this while!
It is gratifying indeed to have roused such an affection, but... his pride, what he has done to Jane, his cruelty towards Mr. Wickham are most reprehensible.
No... I cannot feel sorry for such a person!

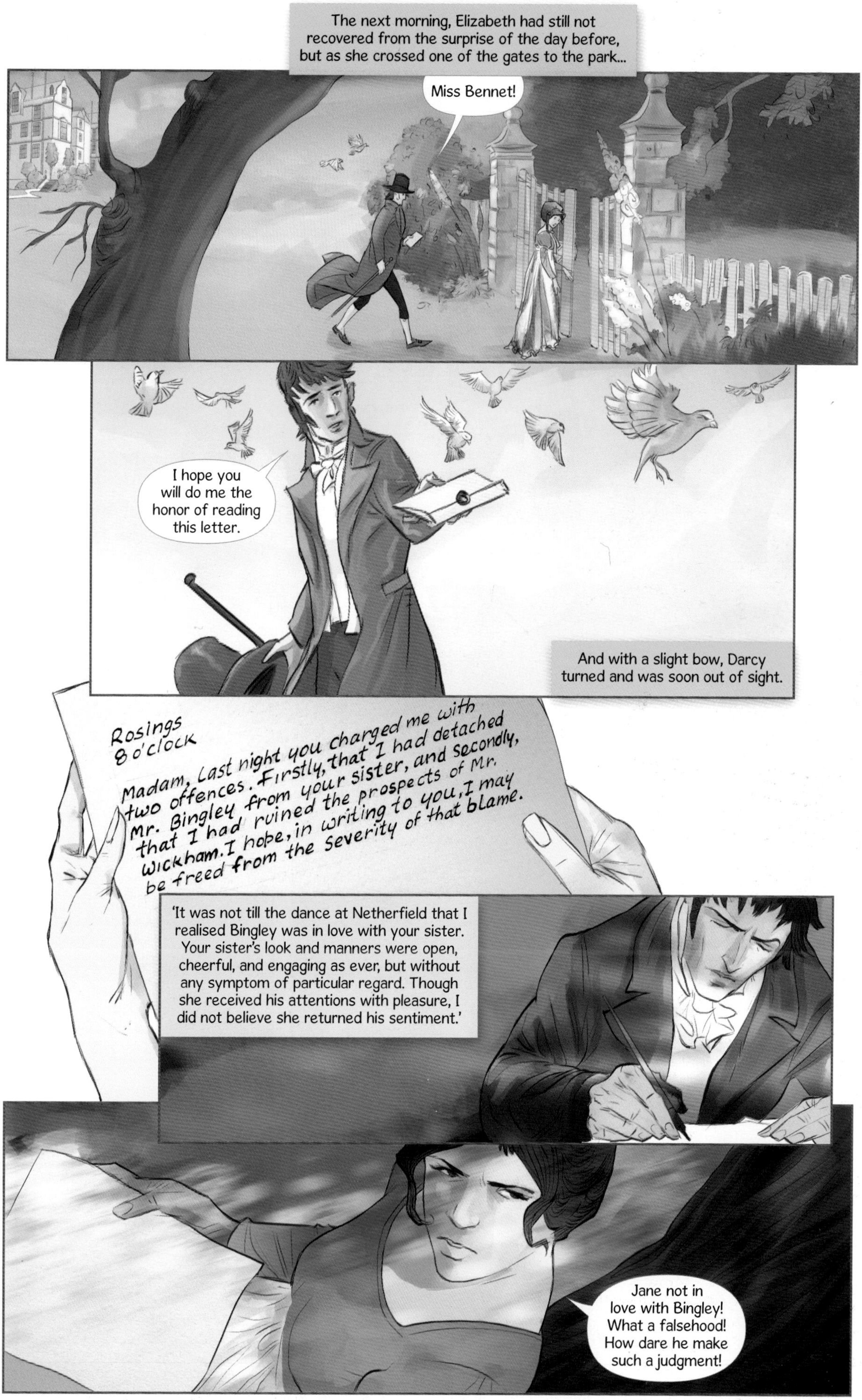
The next morning, Elizabeth had still not recovered from the surprise of the day before, but as she crossed one of the gates to the park...
Miss Bennet!
I hope you will do me the honor of reading this letter.
And with a slight bow, Darcy turned and was soon out of sight.
Rosings
8 o'clock
Madam, Last night you charged me with two offences. Firstly, that I had detached Mr. Bingley from your sister, and Secondly, that I had ruined the prospects of Mr. Wickham. I hope, in writing to you, I may be freed from the Severity of that blame.
'It was not till the dance at Netherfield that I realised Bingley was in love with your sister. Your sister's look and manners were open, cheerful, and engaging as ever, but without any symptom of particular regard. Though she received his attentions with pleasure, I did not believe she returned his sentiment.'
Jane not in love with Bingley! What a falsehood! How dare he make such a judgment!

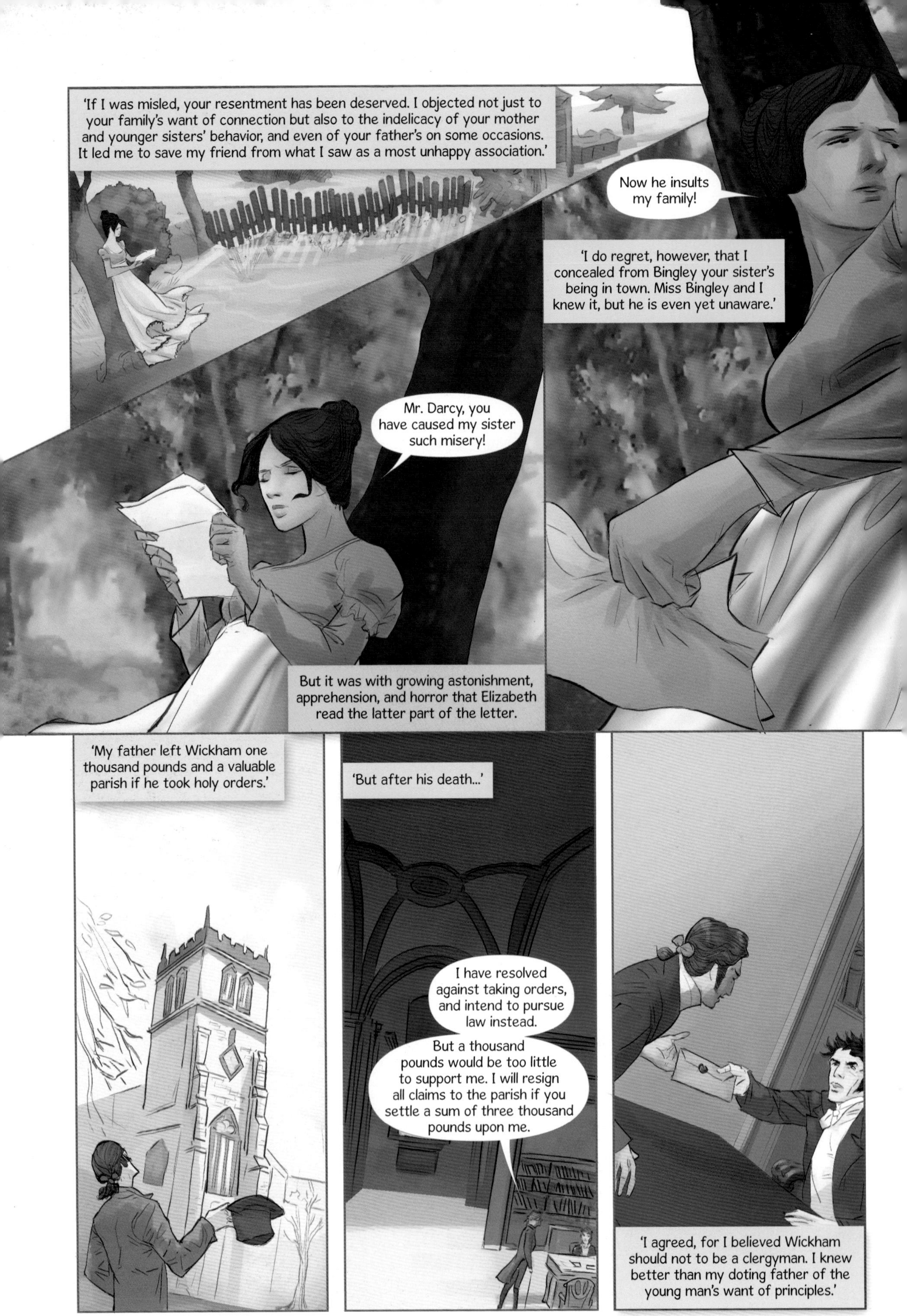
'If I was misled, your resentment has been deserved. I objected not just to your family's want of connection but also to the indelicacy of your mother and younger sisters' behavior, and even of your father's on some occasions. It led me to save my friend from what I saw as a most unhappy association.'
Now he insults my family!
'I do regret, however, that I concealed from Bingley your sister's being in town. Miss Bingley and I knew it, but he is even yet unaware.'
Mr. Darcy, you have caused my sister such misery!
But it was with growing astonishment, apprehension, and horror that Elizabeth read the latter part of the letter.
'My father left Wickham one thousand pounds and a valuable parish if he took holy orders.'
'But after his death...'
I have resolved against taking orders, and intend to pursue law instead.
But a thousand pounds would be too little to support me. I will resign all claims to the parish if you settle a sum of three thousand pounds upon me.
'I agreed, for I believed Wickham should not to be a clergyman. I knew better than my doting father of the young man's want of principles.'

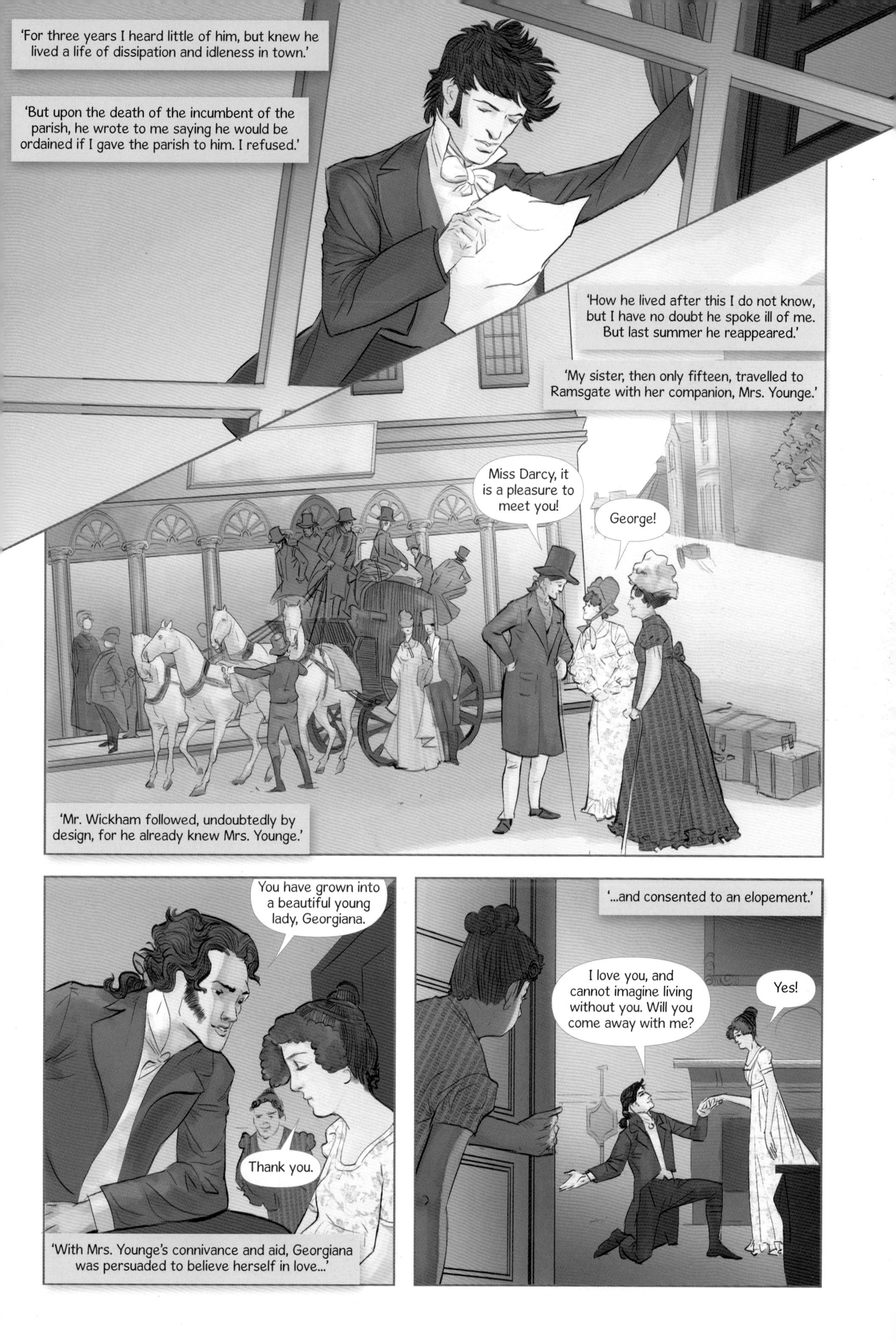
'For three years I heard little of him, but knew he lived a life of dissipation and idleness in town.'
'But upon the death of the incumbent of the parish, he wrote to me saying he would be ordained if I gave the parish to him. I refused.'
'How he lived after this I do not know, but I have no doubt he spoke ill of me. But last summer he reappeared.'
'My sister, then only fifteen, travelled to Ramsgate with her companion, Mrs. Younge.'
Miss Darcy, it is a pleasure to meet you!
George!
'Mr. Wickham followed, undoubtedly by design, for he already knew Mrs. Younge.'
You have grown into a beautiful young lady, Georgiana.
Thank you.
'With Mrs. Younge's connivance and aid, Georgiana was persuaded to believe herself in love...'
'...and consented to an elopement.'
I love you, and cannot imagine living without you. Will you come away with me?
Yes!

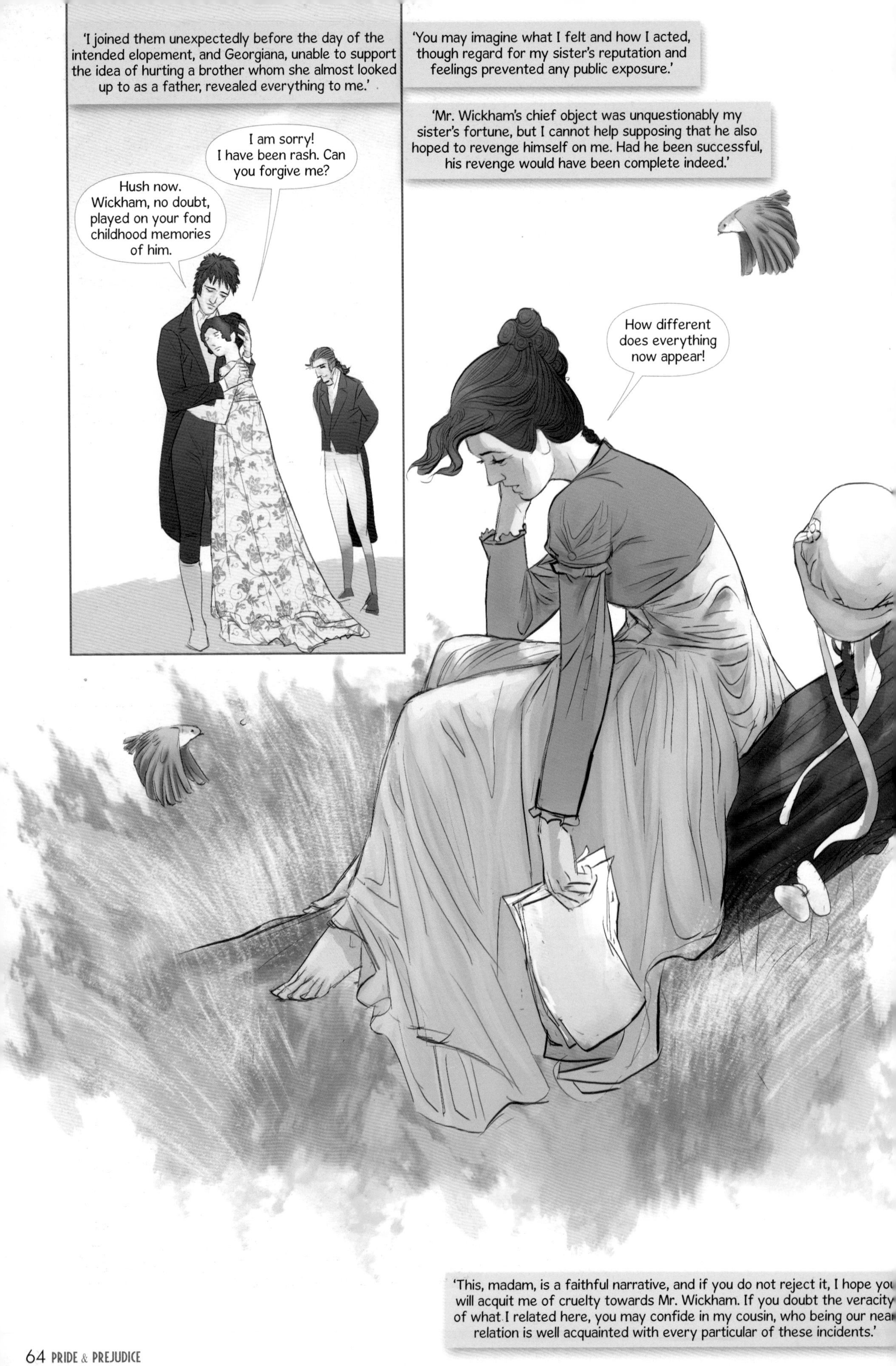
'I joined them unexpectedly before the day of the intended elopement, and Georgiana, unable to support the idea of hurting a brother whom she almost looked up to as a father, revealed everything to me.'
I am sorry! I have been rash. Can you forgive me?
Hush now. Wickham, no doubt, played on your fond childhood memories of him.
'You may imagine what I felt and how I acted, though regard for my sister's reputation and feelings prevented any public exposure.'
'Mr. Wickham's chief object was unquestionably my sister's fortune, but I cannot help supposing that he also hoped to revenge himself on me. Had he been successful, his revenge would have been complete indeed.'
How different does everything now appear!
'This, madam, is a faithful narrative, and if you do not reject it, I hope you will acquit me of cruelty towards Mr. Wickham. If you doubt the veracity of what I related here, you may confide in my cousin, who being our near relation is well acquainted with every particular of these incidents.'

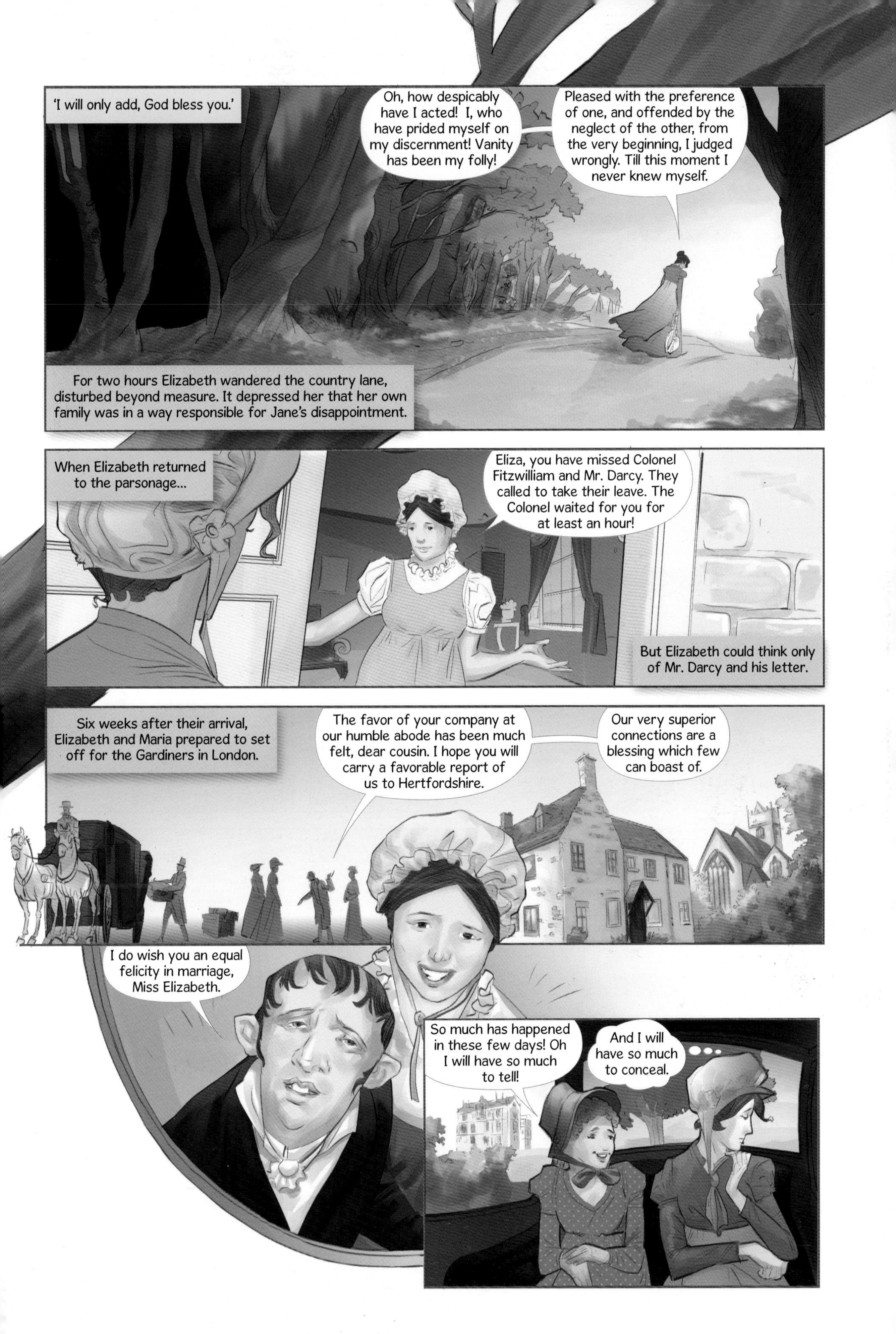
'I will only add, God bless you.'
Oh, how despicably have I acted! I, who have prided myself on my discernment! Vanity has been my folly!
Pleased with the preference of one, and offended by the neglect of the other, from the very beginning, I judged wrongly. Till this moment I never knew myself.
For two hours Elizabeth wandered the country lane, disturbed beyond measure. It depressed her that her own family was in a way responsible for Jane's disappointment.
When Elizabeth returned to the parsonage...
Eliza, you have missed Colonel Fitzwilliam and Mr. Darcy. They called to take their leave. The Colonel waited for you for at least an hour!
But Elizabeth could think only of Mr. Darcy and his letter.
Six weeks after their arrival, Elizabeth and Maria prepared to set off for the Gardiners in London.
The favor of your company at our humble abode has been much felt, dear cousin. I hope you will carry a favorable report of us to Hertfordshire.
Our very superior connections are a blessing which few can boast of.
I do wish you an equal felicity in marriage, Miss Elizabeth.
So much has happened in these few days! Oh I will have so much to tell!
And I will have so much to conceal.

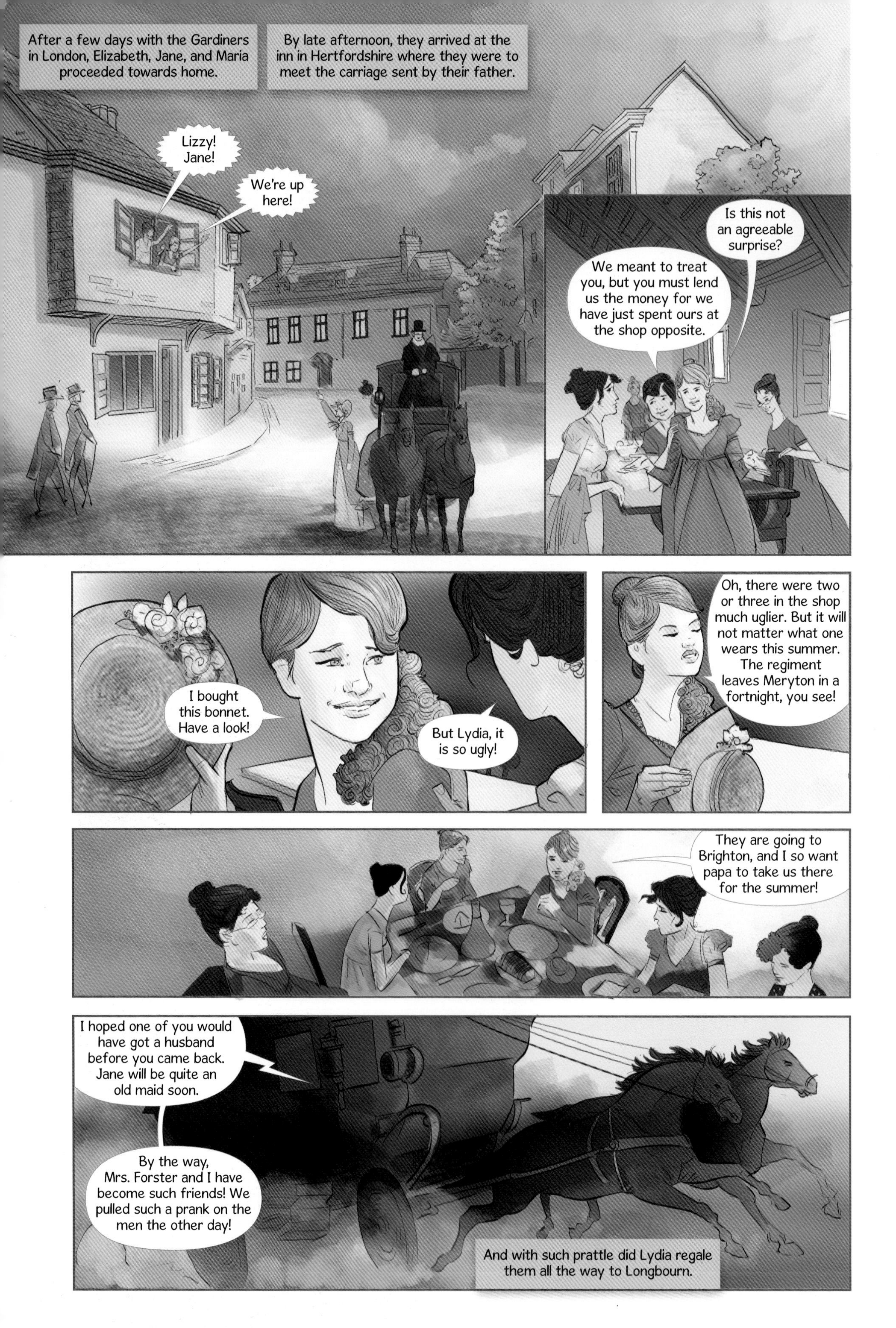
After a few days with the Gardiners in London, Elizabeth, Jane, and Maria proceeded towards home.
By late afternoon, they arrived at the inn in Hertfordshire where they were to meet the carriage sent by their father.
Lizzy! Jane!
We're up here!
We meant to treat you, but you must lend us the money for we have just spent ours at the shop opposite.
Is this not an agreeable surprise?
I bought this bonnet. Have a look!
But Lydia, it is so ugly!
Oh, there were two or three in the shop much uglier. But it will not matter what one wears this summer. The regiment leaves Meryton in a fortnight, you see!
They are going to Brighton, and I so want papa to take us there for the summer!
I hoped one of you would have got a husband before you came back. Jane will be quite an old maid soon.
By the way, Mrs. Forster and I have become such friends! We pulled such a prank on the men the other day!
And with such prattle did Lydia regale them all the way to Longbourn.

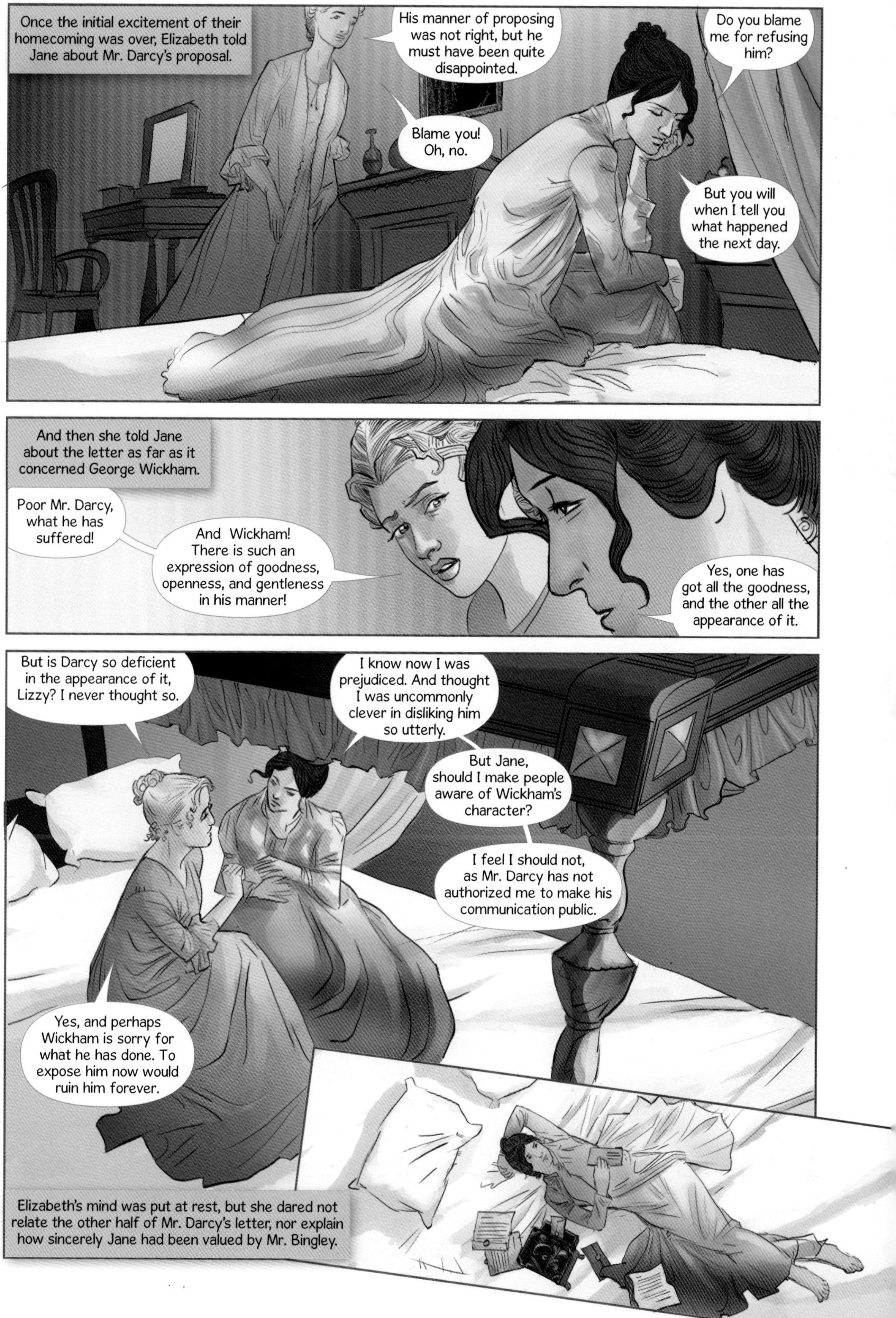
Once the initial excitement of their homecoming was over, Elizabeth told Jane about Mr. Darcy's proposal.
His manner of proposing was not right, but he must have been quite disappointed.
Do you blame me for refusing him?
Blame you! Oh, no.
But you will when I tell you what happened the next day.
And then she told Jane about the letter as far as it concerned George Wickham.
Poor Mr. Darcy, what he has suffered!
And Wickham! There is such an expression of goodness, openness, and gentleness in his manner!
Yes, one has got all the goodness, and the other all the appearance of it.
But is Darcy so deficient in the appearance of it, Lizzy? I never thought so.
I know now I was prejudiced. And thought I was uncommonly clever in disliking him so utterly.
But Jane, should I make people aware of Wickham's character?
I feel I should not, as Mr. Darcy has not authorized me to make his communication public.
Yes, and perhaps Wickham is sorry for what he has done. To expose him now would ruin him forever.
Elizabeth's mind was put at rest, but she dared not relate the other half of Mr. Darcy's letter, nor explain how sincerely Jane had been valued by Mr. Bingley.

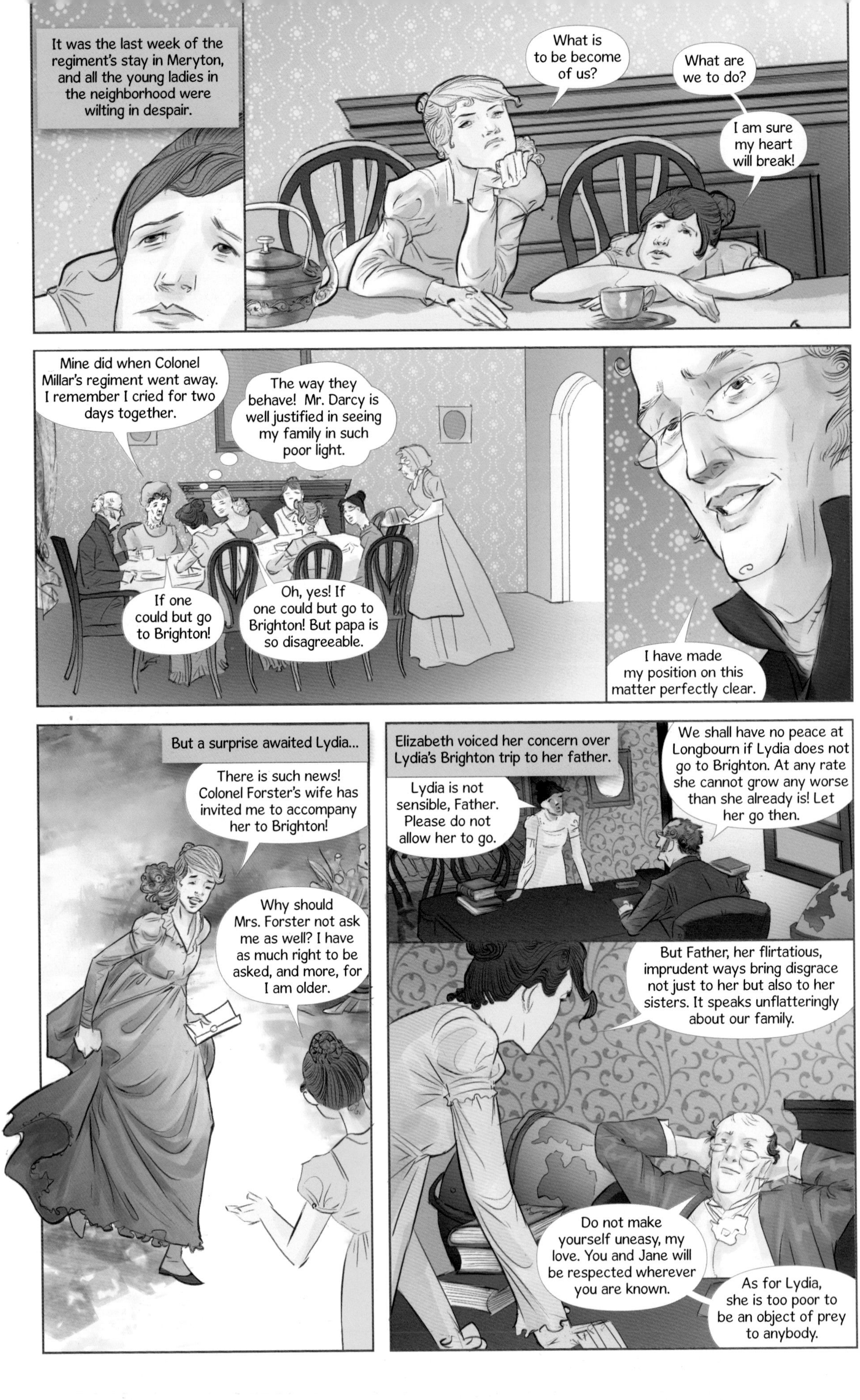
It was the last week of the regiment's stay in Meryton, and all the young ladies in the neighborhood were wilting in despair.
What is to be become of us?
What are we to do?
I am sure my heart will break!
Mine did when Colonel Millar's regiment went away. I remember I cried for two days together.
The way they behave! Mr. Darcy is well justified in seeing my family in such poor light.
If one could but go to Brighton!
Oh, yes! If one could but go to Brighton! But papa is so disagreeable.
I have made my position on this matter perfectly clear.
But a surprise awaited Lydia...
There is such news! Colonel Forster's wife has invited me to accompany her to Brighton!
Why should Mrs. Forster not ask me as well? I have as much right to be asked, and more, for I am older.
Elizabeth voiced her concern over Lydia's Brighton trip to her father.
Lydia is not sensible, Father. Please do not allow her to go.
We shall have no peace at Longbourn if Lydia does not go to Brighton. At any rate she cannot grow any worse than she already is! Let her go then.
But Father, her flirtatious, imprudent ways bring disgrace not just to her but also to her sisters. It speaks unflatteringly about our family.
Do not make yourself uneasy, my love. You and Jane will be respected wherever you are known.
As for Lydia, she is too poor to be an object of prey to anybody.

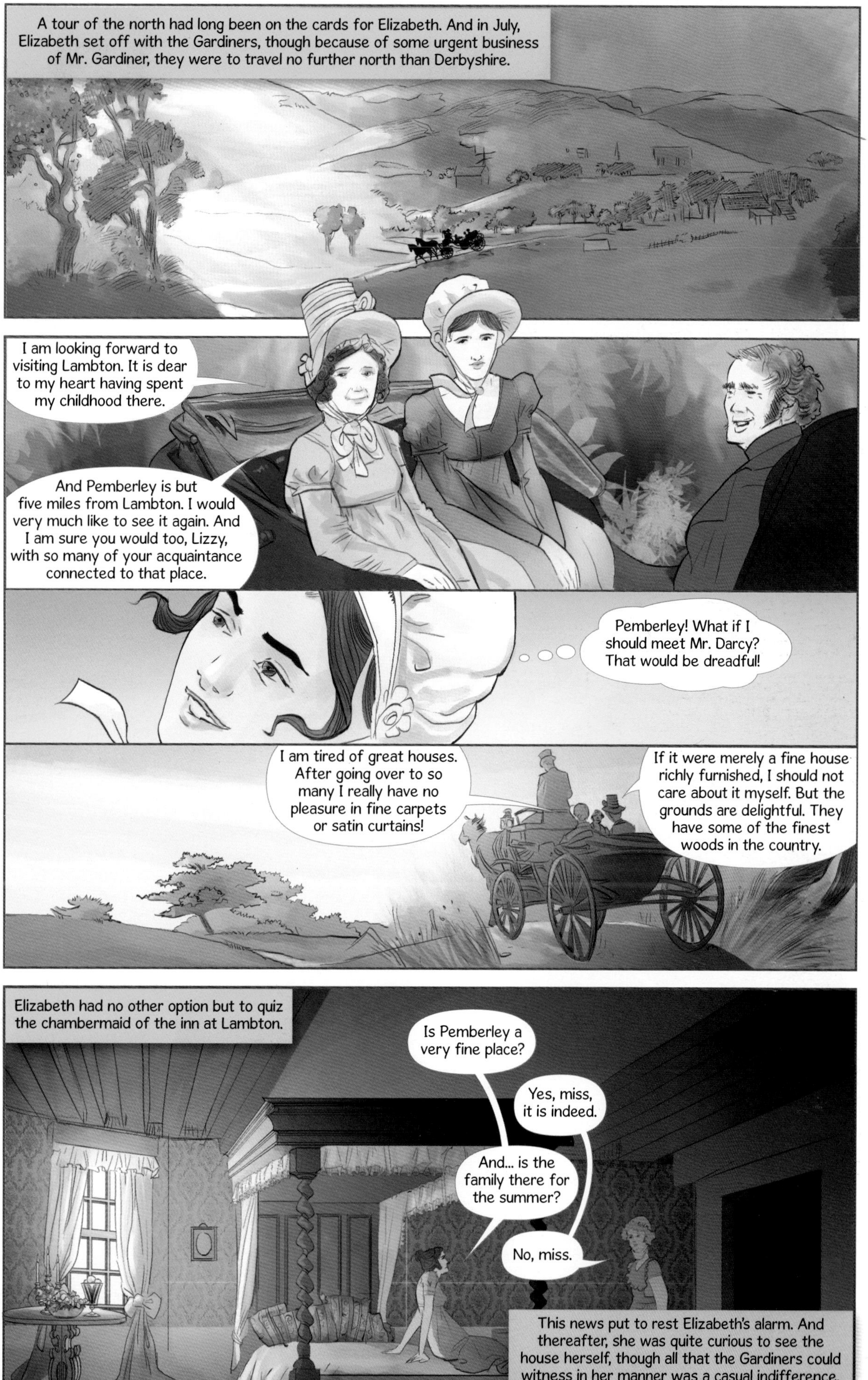
A tour of the north had long been on the cards for Elizabeth. And in July, Elizabeth set off with the Gardiners, though because of some urgent business of Mr. Gardiner, they were to travel no further north than Derbyshire.
I am looking forward to visiting Lambton. It is dear to my heart having spent my childhood there.
And Pemberley is but five miles from Lambton. I would very much like to see it again. And I am sure you would too, Lizzy, with so many of your acquaintance connected to that place.
Pemberley! What if I should meet Mr. Darcy? That would be dreadful!
I am tired of great houses. After going over to so many I really have no pleasure in fine carpets or satin curtains!
If it were merely a fine house richly furnished, I should not care about it myself. But the grounds are delightful. They have some of the finest woods in the country.
Elizabeth had no other option but to quiz the chambermaid of the inn at Lambton.
Is Pemberley a very fine place?
Yes, miss, it is indeed.
And... is the family there for the summer?
No, miss.
This news put to rest Elizabeth's alarm. And thereafter, she was quite curious to see the house herself, though all that the Gardiners could witness in her manner was a casual indifference.

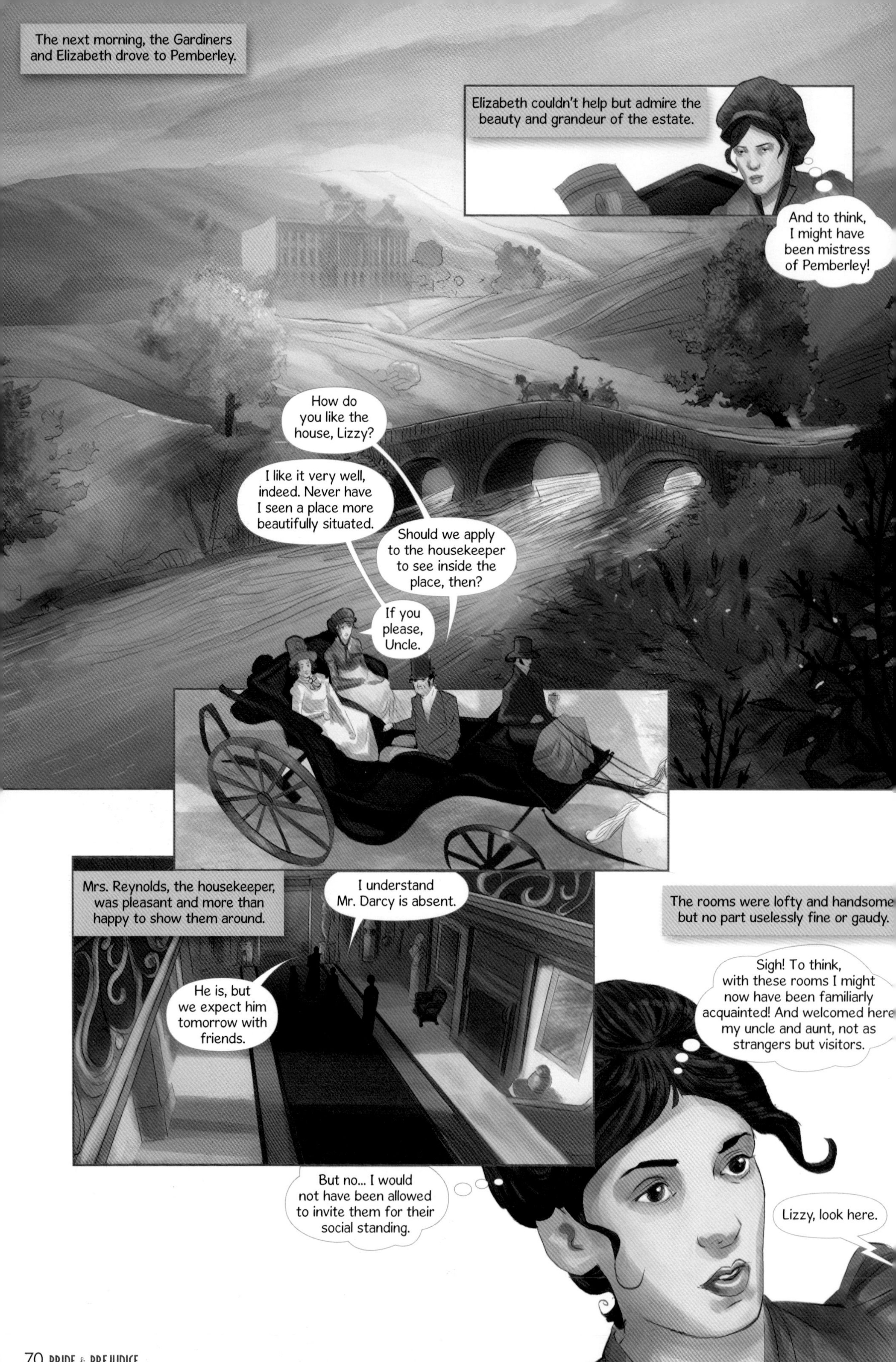
The next morning, the Gardiners and Elizabeth drove to Pemberley.
Elizabeth couldn't help but admire the beauty and grandeur of the estate.
And to think, I might have been mistress of Pemberley!
How do you like the house, Lizzy?
I like it very well, indeed. Never have I seen a place more beautifully situated.
Should we apply to the housekeeper to see inside the place, then?
If you please, Uncle.
Mrs. Reynolds, the housekeeper, was pleasant and more than happy to show them around.
I understand Mr. Darcy is absent.
He is, but we expect him tomorrow with friends.
The rooms were lofty and handsome but no part uselessly fine or gaudy.
Sigh! To think, with these rooms I might now have been familiarly acquainted! And welcomed here my uncle and aunt, not as strangers but visitors.
But no... I would not have been allowed to invite them for their social standing.
Lizzy, look here.

That is Mr. Wickham, son of the late master's steward. He is now in the army. But I am afraid he has turned out very wild.

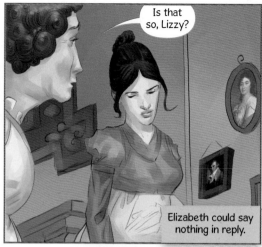

Is that so, Lizzy?

Elizabeth could say nothing in reply.

And this is my master.

What a handsome face! But, Lizzy, you can tell us whether it is a good likeness or not.

Does the young lady know Mr. Darcy?

A little.

And do you not think him a very handsome gentleman, ma'am?

Yes, very handsome.

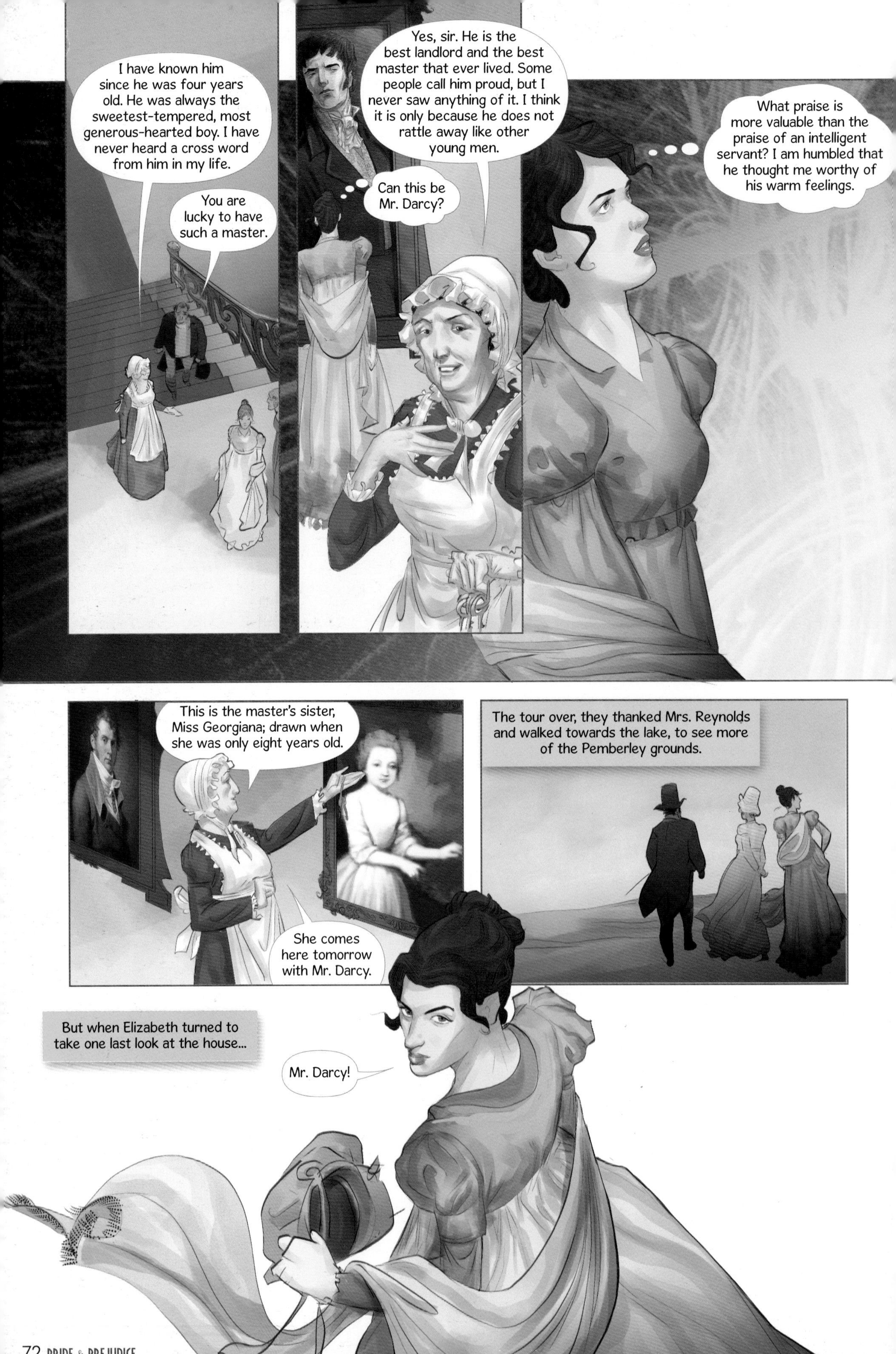
I have known him since he was four years old. He was always the sweetest-tempered, most generous-hearted boy. I have never heard a cross word from him in my life.
You are lucky to have such a master.
Yes, sir. He is the best landlord and the best master that ever lived. Some people call him proud, but I never saw anything of it. I think it is only because he does not rattle away like other young men.
Can this be Mr. Darcy?
What praise is more valuable than the praise of an intelligent servant? I am humbled that he thought me worthy of his warm feelings.
This is the master's sister, Miss Georgiana; drawn when she was only eight years old.
She comes here tomorrow with Mr. Darcy.
The tour over, they thanked Mrs. Reynolds and walked towards the lake, to see more of the Pemberley grounds.
But when Elizabeth turned to take one last look at the house...
Mr. Darcy!

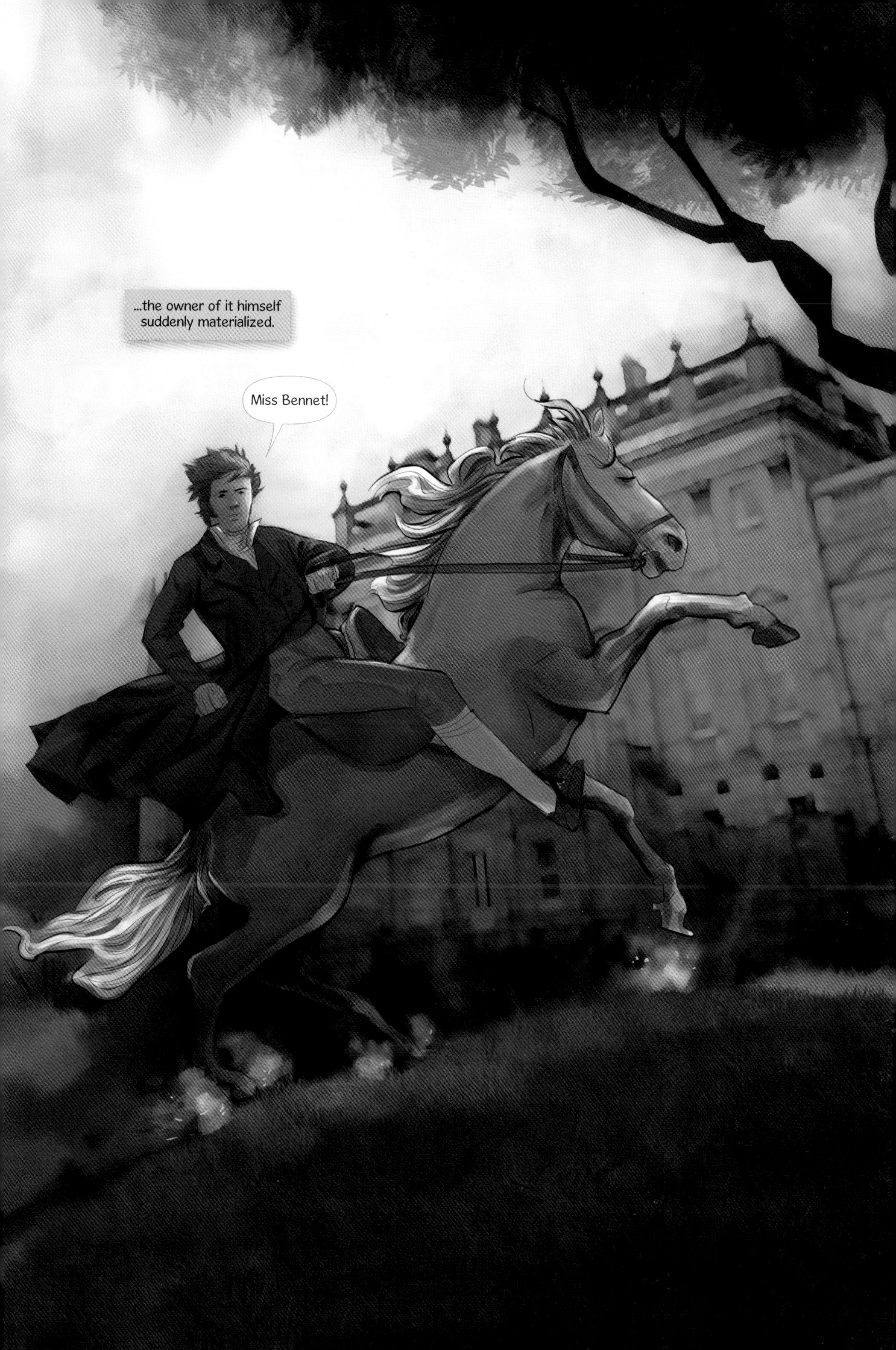
...the owner of it himself suddenly materialized.
Miss Bennet!

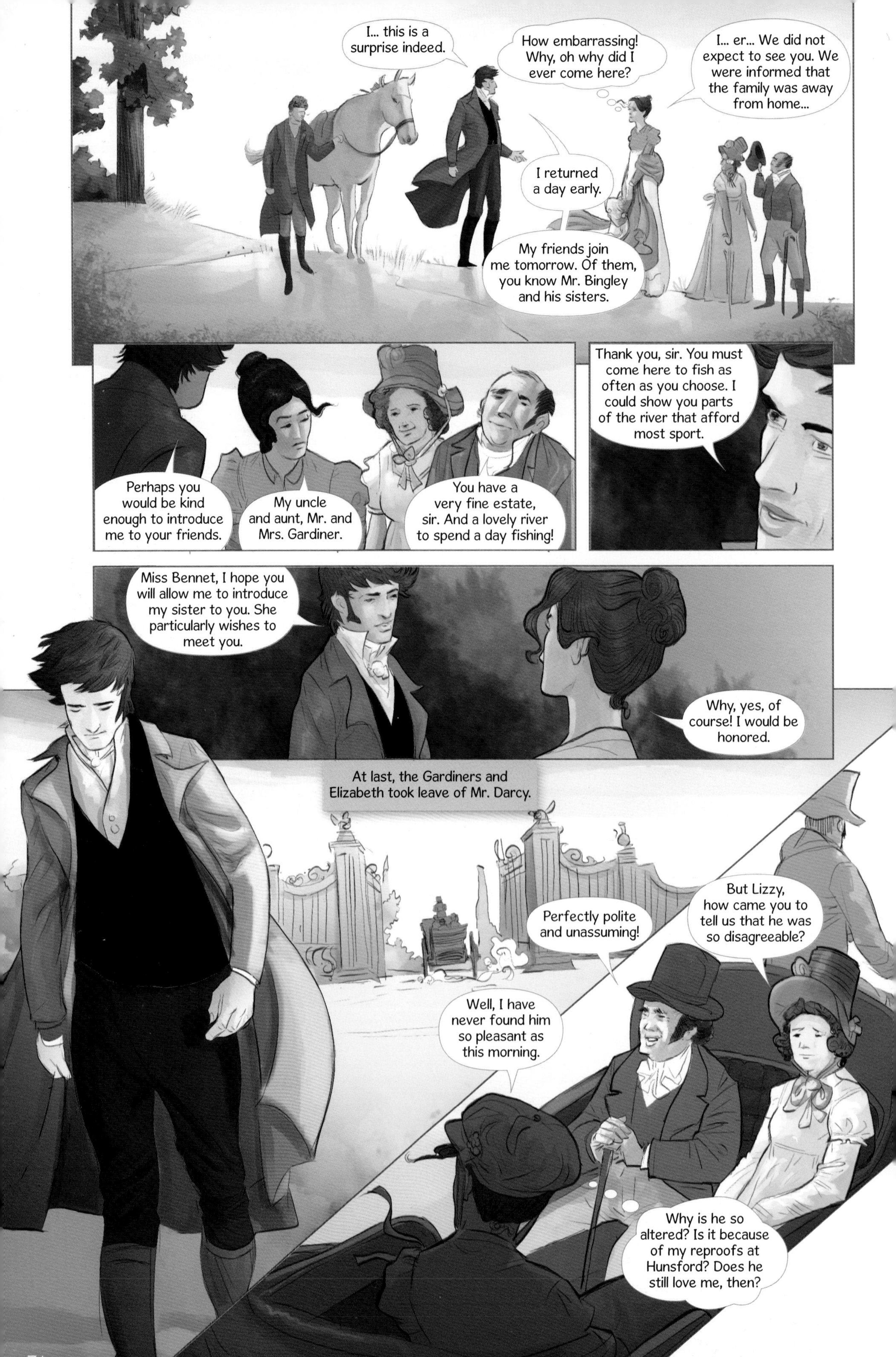
I... this is a surprise indeed.
How embarrassing! Why, oh why did I ever come here?
I... er... We did not expect to see you. We were informed that the family was away from home...
I returned a day early.
My friends join me tomorrow. Of them, you know Mr. Bingley and his sisters.
Perhaps you would be kind enough to introduce me to your friends.
My uncle and aunt, Mr. and Mrs. Gardiner.
You have a very fine estate, sir. And a lovely river to spend a day fishing!
Thank you, sir. You must come here to fish as often as you choose. I could show you parts of the river that afford most sport.
Miss Bennet, I hope you will allow me to introduce my sister to you. She particularly wishes to meet you.
Why, yes, of course! I would be honored.
At last, the Gardiners and Elizabeth took leave of Mr. Darcy.
Perfectly polite and unassuming!
But Lizzy, how came you to tell us that he was so disagreeable?
Well, I have never found him so pleasant as this morning.
Why is he so altered? Is it because of my reproofs at Hunsford? Does he still love me, then?

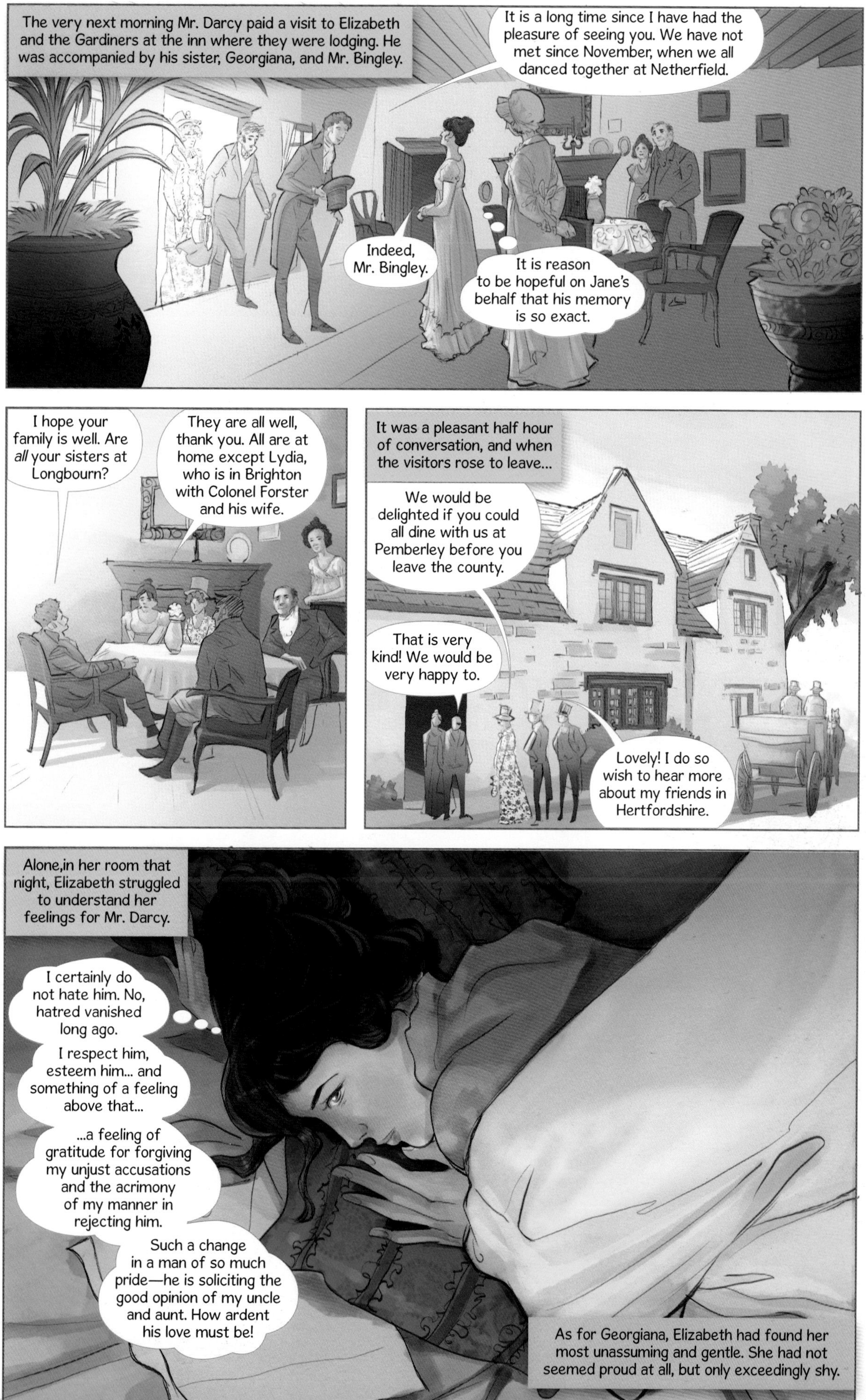
The very next morning Mr. Darcy paid a visit to Elizabeth and the Gardiners at the inn where they were lodging. He was accompanied by his sister, Georgiana, and Mr. Bingley.
It is a long time since I have had the pleasure of seeing you. We have not met since November, when we all danced together at Netherfield.
Indeed, Mr. Bingley.
It is reason to be hopeful on Jane's behalf that his memory is so exact.
I hope your family is well. Are *all* your sisters at Longbourn?
They are all well, thank you. All are at home except Lydia, who is in Brighton with Colonel Forster and his wife.
It was a pleasant half hour of conversation, and when the visitors rose to leave...
We would be delighted if you could all dine with us at Pemberley before you leave the county.
That is very kind! We would be very happy to.
Lovely! I do so wish to hear more about my friends in Hertfordshire.
Alone,in her room that night, Elizabeth struggled to understand her feelings for Mr. Darcy.
I certainly do not hate him. No, hatred vanished long ago.
I respect him, esteem him... and something of a feeling above that...
...a feeling of gratitude for forgiving my unjust accusations and the acrimony of my manner in rejecting him.
Such a change in a man of so much pride—he is soliciting the good opinion of my uncle and aunt. How ardent his love must be!
As for Georgiana, Elizabeth had found her most unassuming and gentle. She had not seemed proud at all, but only exceedingly shy.

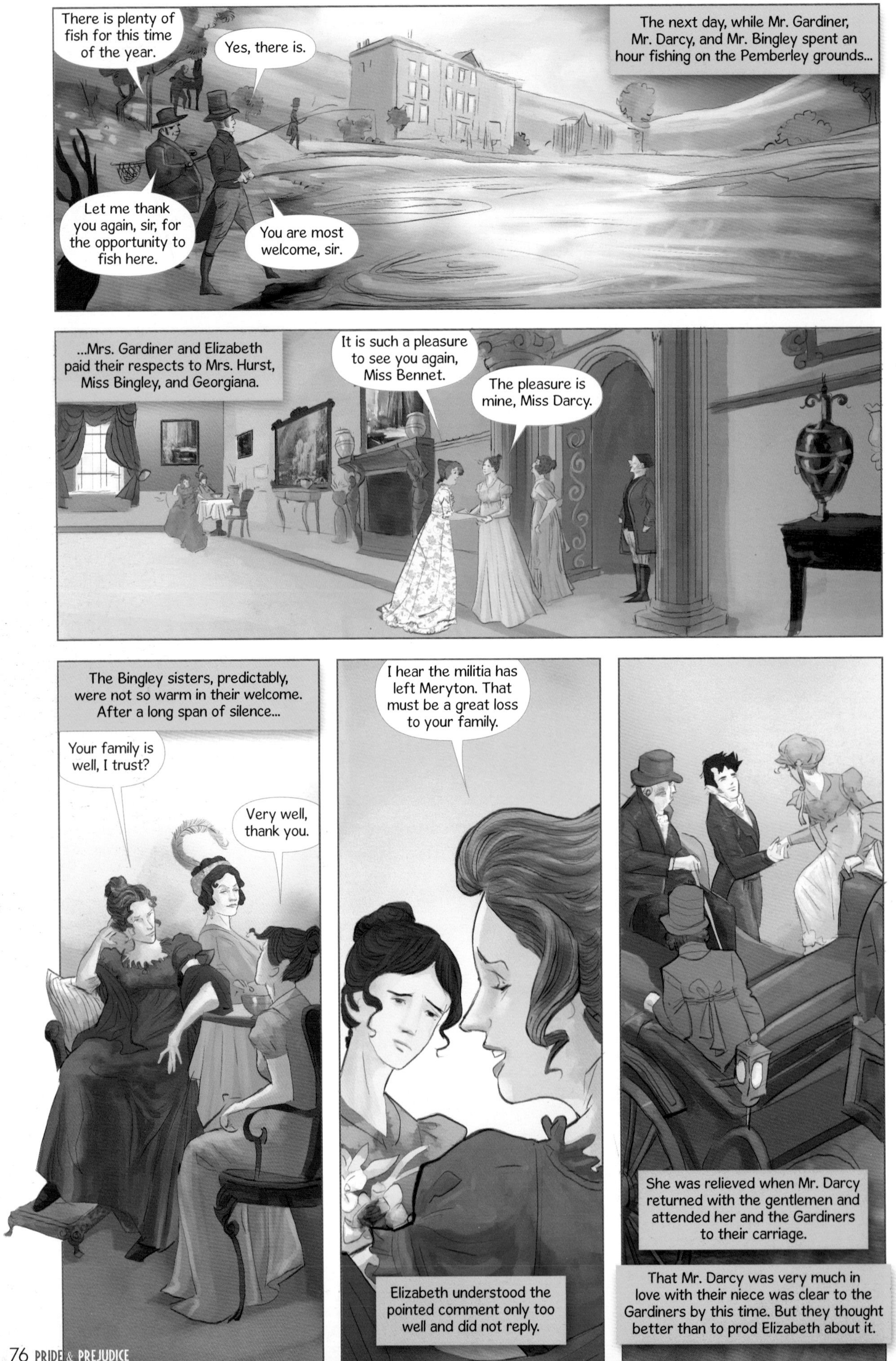
The next day, while Mr. Gardiner, Mr. Darcy, and Mr. Bingley spent an hour fishing on the Pemberley grounds...
There is plenty of fish for this time of the year.
Yes, there is.
Let me thank you again, sir, for the opportunity to fish here.
You are most welcome, sir.
...Mrs. Gardiner and Elizabeth paid their respects to Mrs. Hurst, Miss Bingley, and Georgiana.
It is such a pleasure to see you again, Miss Bennet.
The pleasure is mine, Miss Darcy.
The Bingley sisters, predictably, were not so warm in their welcome. After a long span of silence...
Your family is well, I trust?
Very well, thank you.
I hear the militia has left Meryton. That must be a great loss to your family.
Elizabeth understood the pointed comment only too well and did not reply.
She was relieved when Mr. Darcy returned with the gentlemen and attended her and the Gardiners to their carriage.
That Mr. Darcy was very much in love with their niece was clear to the Gardiners by this time. But they thought better than to prod Elizabeth about it.

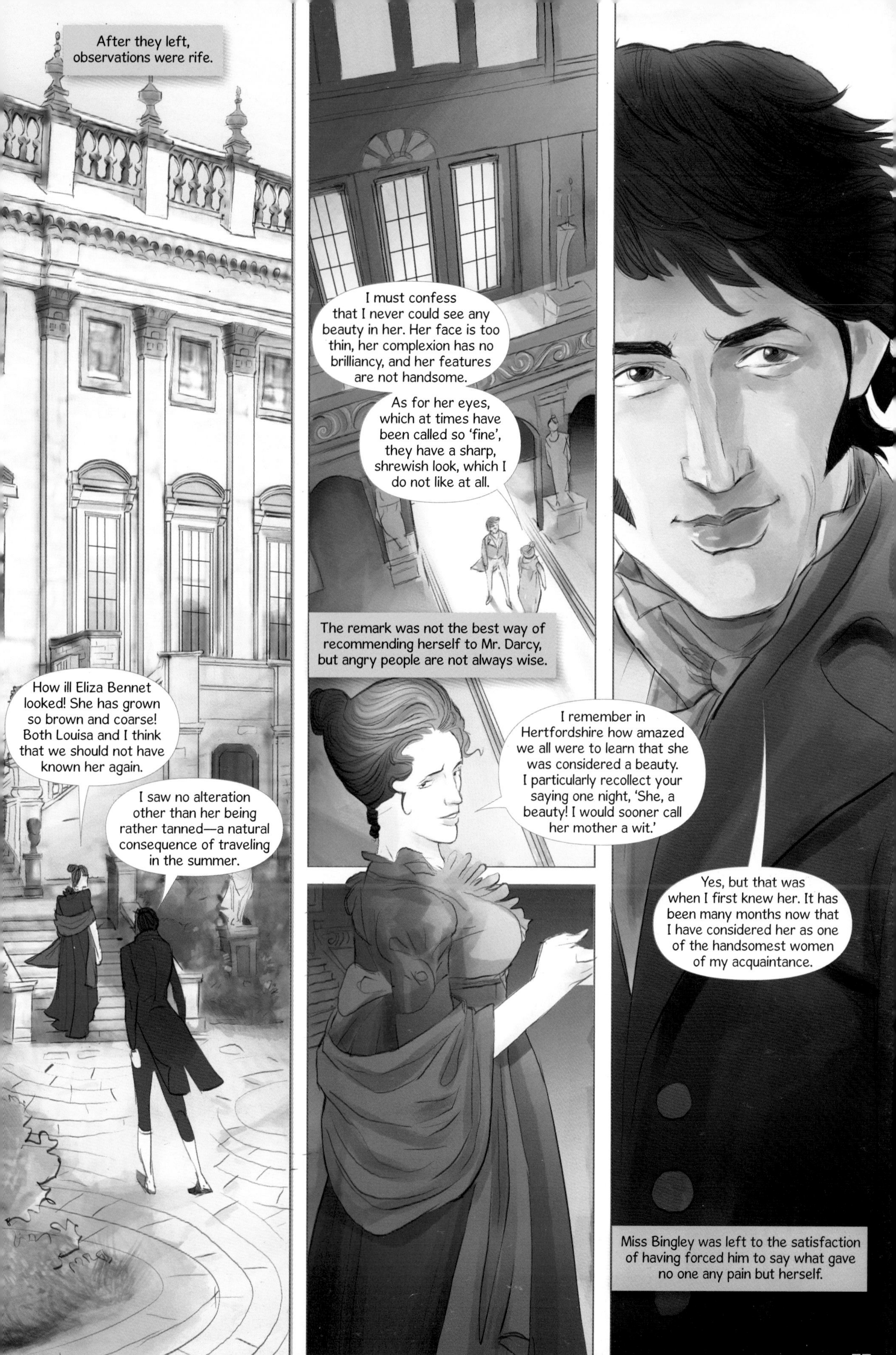
After they left, observations were rife.
How ill Eliza Bennet looked! She has grown so brown and coarse! Both Louisa and I think that we should not have known her again.
I saw no alteration other than her being rather tanned—a natural consequence of traveling in the summer.
I must confess that I never could see any beauty in her. Her face is too thin, her complexion has no brilliancy, and her features are not handsome.
As for her eyes, which at times have been called so 'fine', they have a sharp, shrewish look, which I do not like at all.
The remark was not the best way of recommending herself to Mr. Darcy, but angry people are not always wise.
I remember in Hertfordshire how amazed we all were to learn that she was considered a beauty. I particularly recollect your saying one night, 'She, a beauty! I would sooner call her mother a wit.'
Yes, but that was when I first knew her. It has been many months now that I have considered her as one of the handsomest women of my acquaintance.
Miss Bingley was left to the satisfaction of having forced him to say what gave no one any pain but herself.

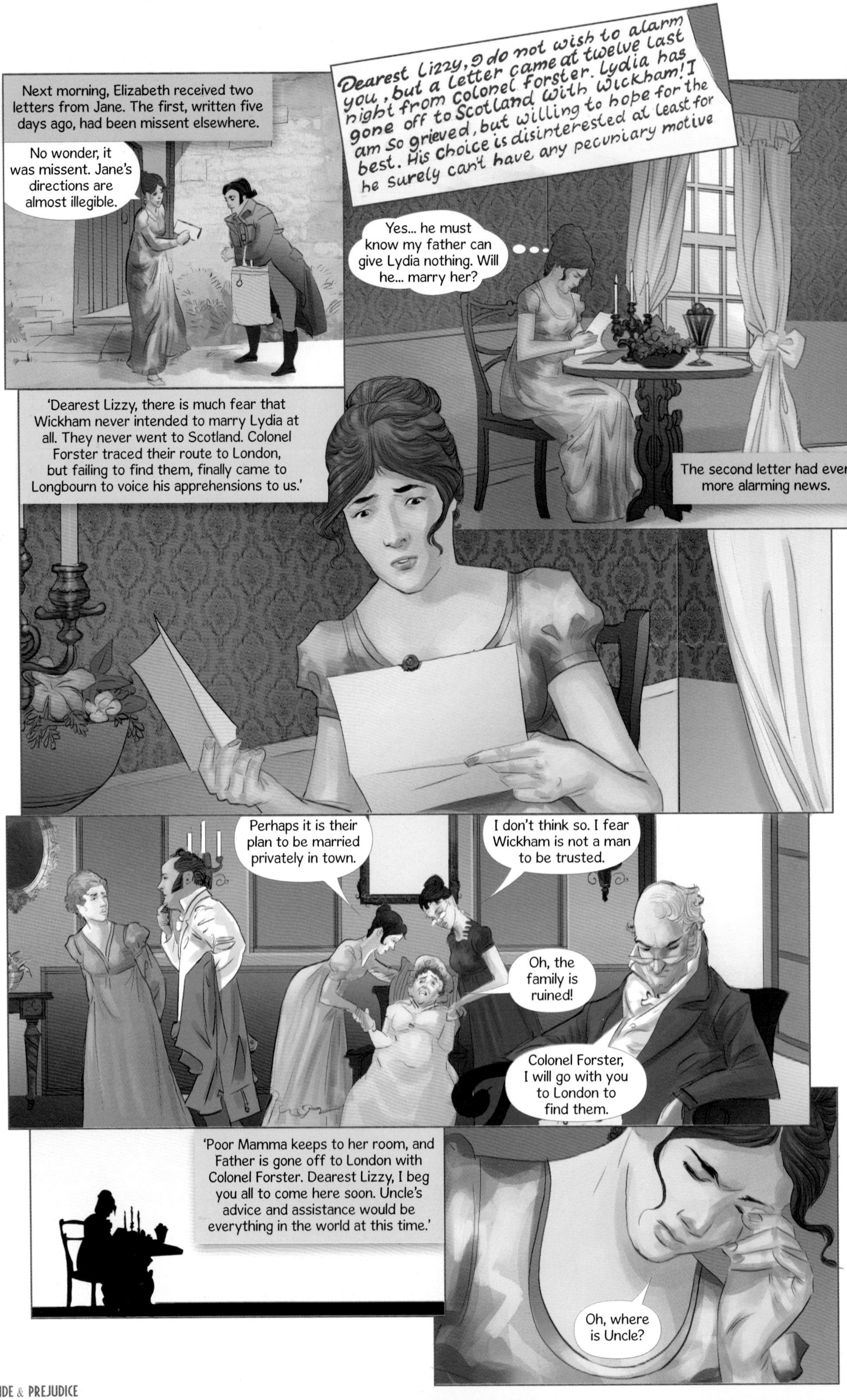
Next morning, Elizabeth received two letters from Jane. The first, written five days ago, had been missent elsewhere.
No wonder, it was missent. Jane's directions are almost illegible.
Dearest Lizzy, I do not wish to alarm you, but a letter came at twelve last night from Colonel Forster. Lydia has gone off to Scotland with Wickham! I am so grieved, but willing to hope for the best. His choice is disinterested at least for he surely can't have any pecuniary motive
Yes... he must know my father can give Lydia nothing. Will he... marry her?
'Dearest Lizzy, there is much fear that Wickham never intended to marry Lydia at all. They never went to Scotland. Colonel Forster traced their route to London, but failing to find them, finally came to Longbourn to voice his apprehensions to us.'
The second letter had even more alarming news.
Perhaps it is their plan to be married privately in town.
I don't think so. I fear Wickham is not a man to be trusted.
Oh, the family is ruined!
Colonel Forster, I will go with you to London to find them.
'Poor Mamma keeps to her room, and Father is gone off to London with Colonel Forster. Dearest Lizzy, I beg you all to come here soon. Uncle's advice and assistance would be everything in the world at this time.'
Oh, where is Uncle?

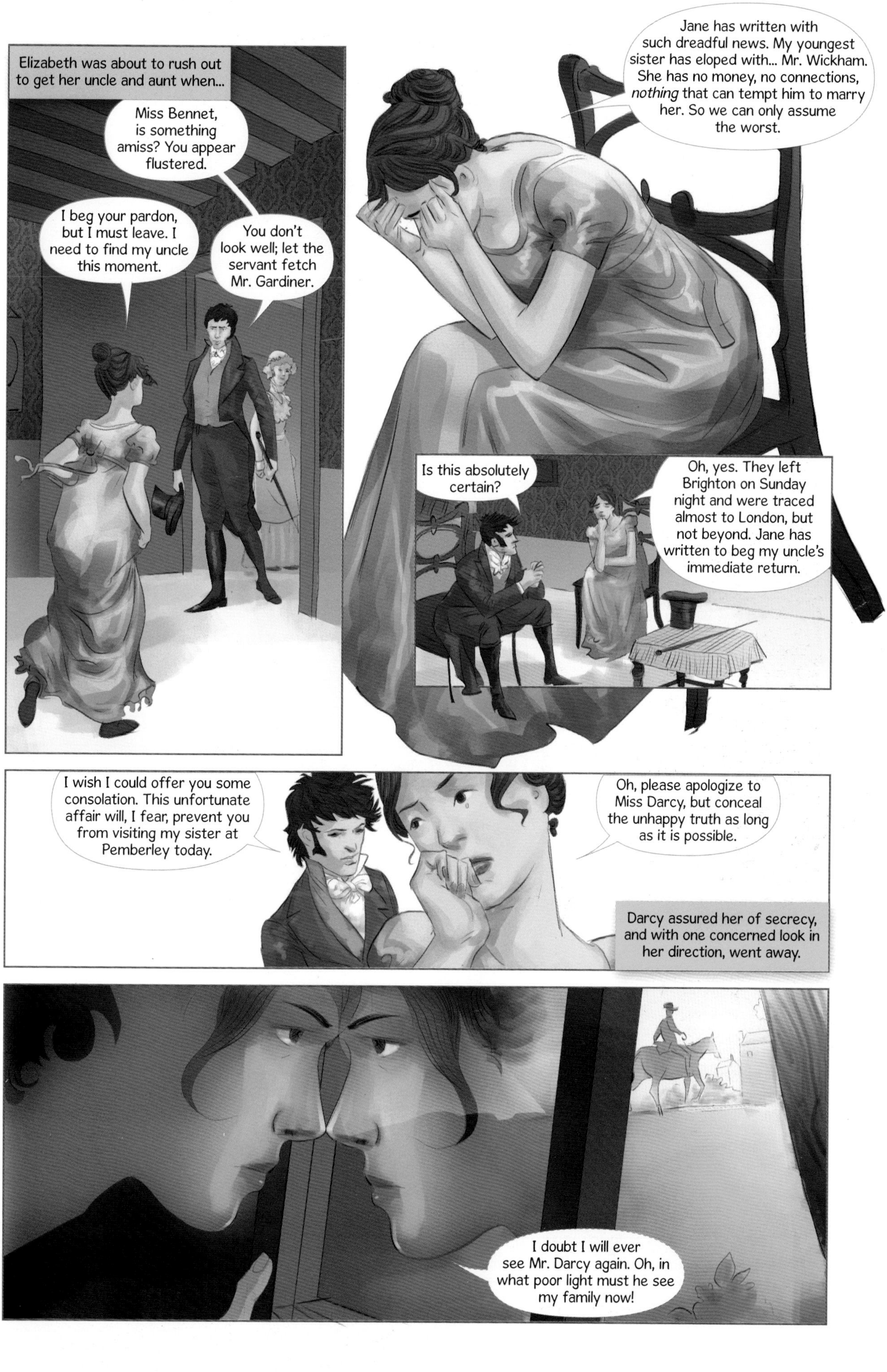
Elizabeth was about to rush out to get her uncle and aunt when...
Miss Bennet, is something amiss? You appear flustered.
I beg your pardon, but I must leave. I need to find my uncle this moment.
You don't look well; let the servant fetch Mr. Gardiner.
Jane has written with such dreadful news. My youngest sister has eloped with... Mr. Wickham. She has no money, no connections, *nothing* that can tempt him to marry her. So we can only assume the worst.
Is this absolutely certain?
Oh, yes. They left Brighton on Sunday night and were traced almost to London, but not beyond. Jane has written to beg my uncle's immediate return.
I wish I could offer you some consolation. This unfortunate affair will, I fear, prevent you from visiting my sister at Pemberley today.
Oh, please apologize to Miss Darcy, but conceal the unhappy truth as long as it is possible.
Darcy assured her of secrecy, and with one concerned look in her direction, went away.
I doubt I will ever see Mr. Darcy again. Oh, in what poor light must he see my family now!

The very next day, Elizabeth and Mr. and Mrs. Gardiner were returned to Longbourn.

I am so pleased to see you all! Now everything will be well!

Oh, Jane, you look so pale. How much you must have gone through!

Is Father in London?

Yes, he went on Tuesday.

Have you heard from him?

Once, and he informed that he will not write again till there is something of importance to mention.

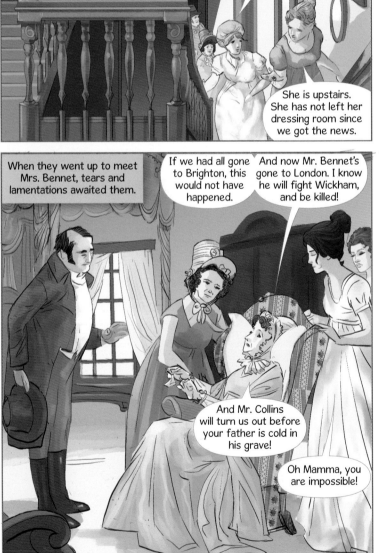

And Mamma? How is she?

She is upstairs. She has not left her dressing room since we got the news.

When they went up to meet Mrs. Bennet, tears and lamentations awaited them.

If we had all gone to Brighton, this would not have happened.

And now Mr. Bennet's gone to London. I know he will fight Wickham, and be killed!

And Mr. Collins will turn us out before your father is cold in his grave!

Oh Mamma, you are impossible!

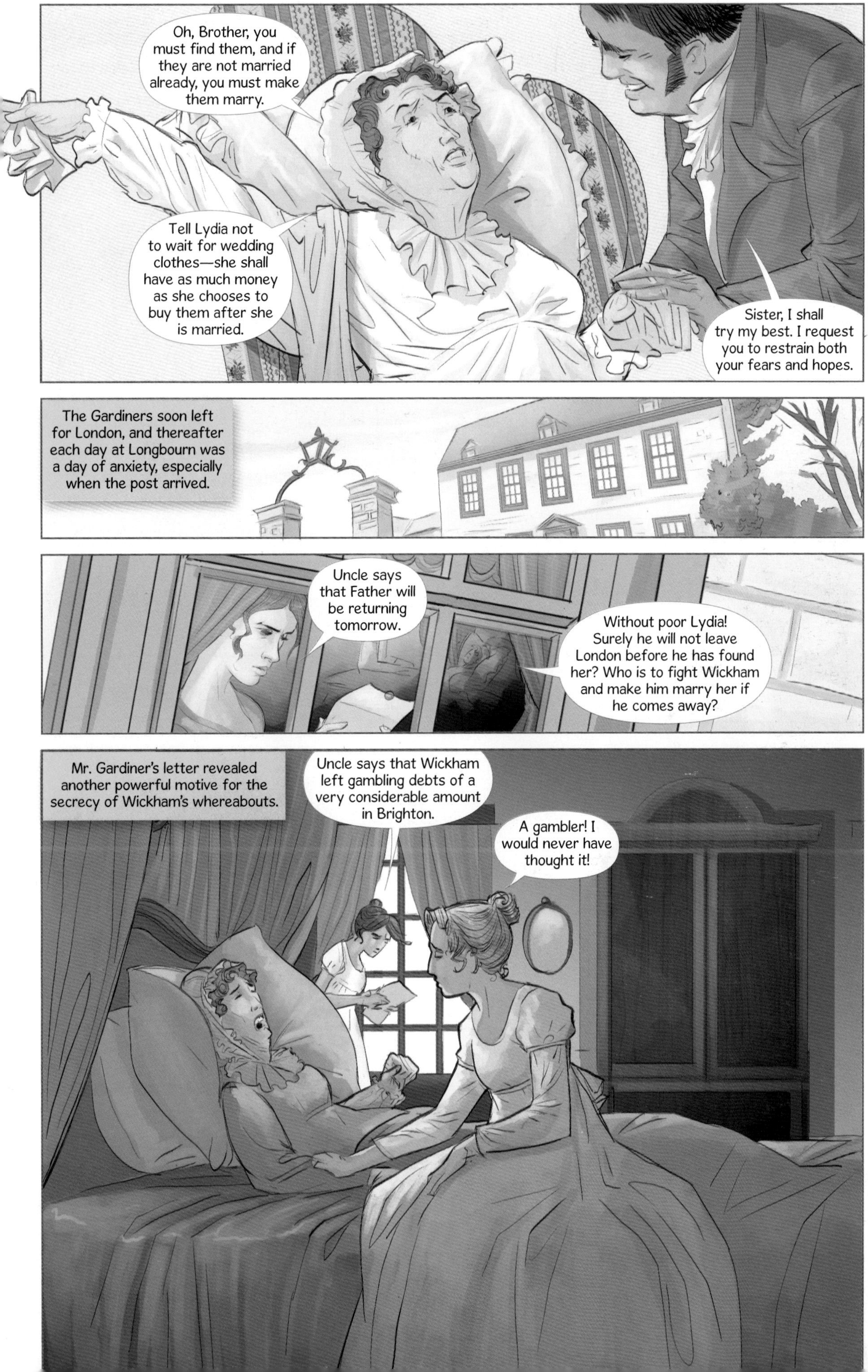
Oh, Brother, you must find them, and if they are not married already, you must make them marry.
Tell Lydia not to wait for wedding clothes—she shall have as much money as she chooses to buy them after she is married.
Sister, I shall try my best. I request you to restrain both your fears and hopes.
The Gardiners soon left for London, and thereafter each day at Longbourn was a day of anxiety, especially when the post arrived.
Uncle says that Father will be returning tomorrow.
Without poor Lydia! Surely he will not leave London before he has found her? Who is to fight Wickham and make him marry her if he comes away?
Mr. Gardiner's letter revealed another powerful motive for the secrecy of Wickham's whereabouts.
Uncle says that Wickham left gambling debts of a very considerable amount in Brighton.
A gambler! I would never have thought it!

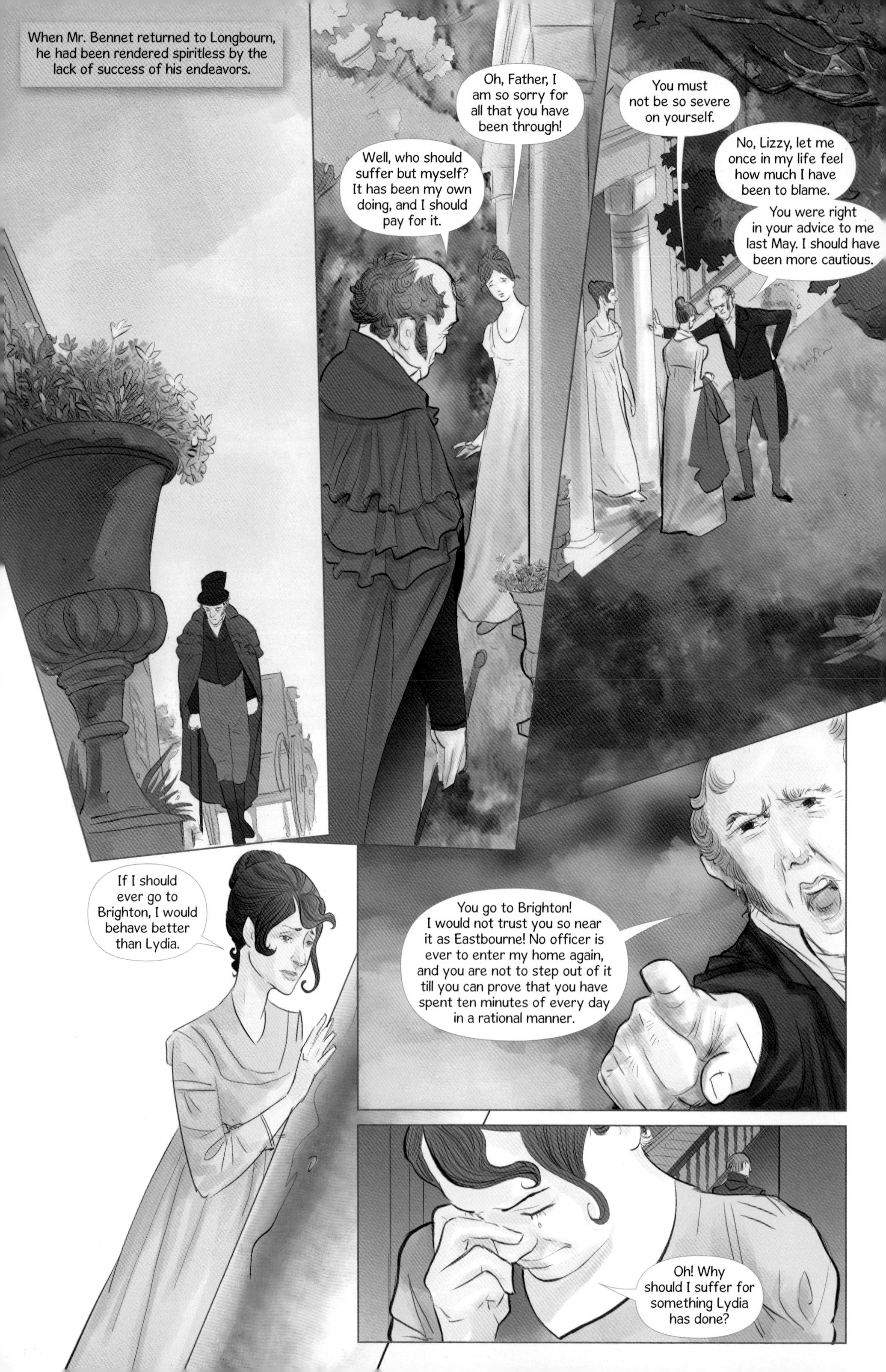
When Mr. Bennet returned to Longbourn, he had been rendered spiritless by the lack of success of his endeavors.
Oh, Father, I am so sorry for all that you have been through!
Well, who should suffer but myself? It has been my own doing, and I should pay for it.
You must not be so severe on yourself.
No, Lizzy, let me once in my life feel how much I have been to blame.
You were right in your advice to me last May. I should have been more cautious.
If I should ever go to Brighton, I would behave better than Lydia.
You go to Brighton! I would not trust you so near it as Eastbourne! No officer is ever to enter my home again, and you are not to step out of it till you can prove that you have spent ten minutes of every day in a rational manner.
Oh! Why should I suffer for something Lydia has done?

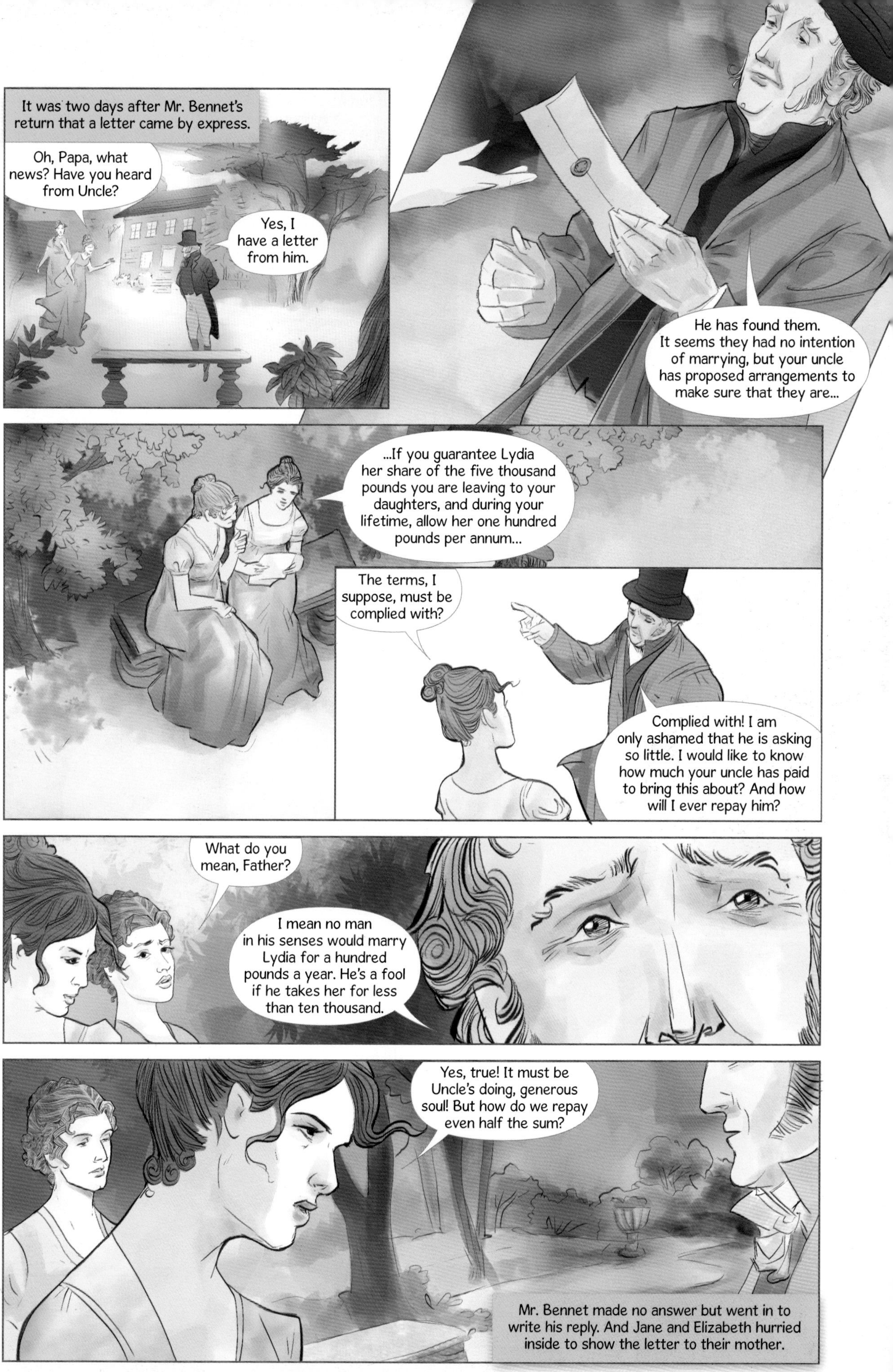
It was two days after Mr. Bennet's return that a letter came by express.
Oh, Papa, what news? Have you heard from Uncle?
Yes, I have a letter from him.
He has found them. It seems they had no intention of marrying, but your uncle has proposed arrangements to make sure that they are...
...If you guarantee Lydia her share of the five thousand pounds you are leaving to your daughters, and during your lifetime, allow her one hundred pounds per annum...
The terms, I suppose, must be complied with?
Complied with! I am only ashamed that he is asking so little. I would like to know how much your uncle has paid to bring this about? And how will I ever repay him?
What do you mean, Father?
I mean no man in his senses would marry Lydia for a hundred pounds a year. He's a fool if he takes her for less than ten thousand.
Yes, true! It must be Uncle's doing, generous soul! But how do we repay even half the sum?
Mr. Bennet made no answer but went in to write his reply. And Jane and Elizabeth hurried inside to show the letter to their mother.

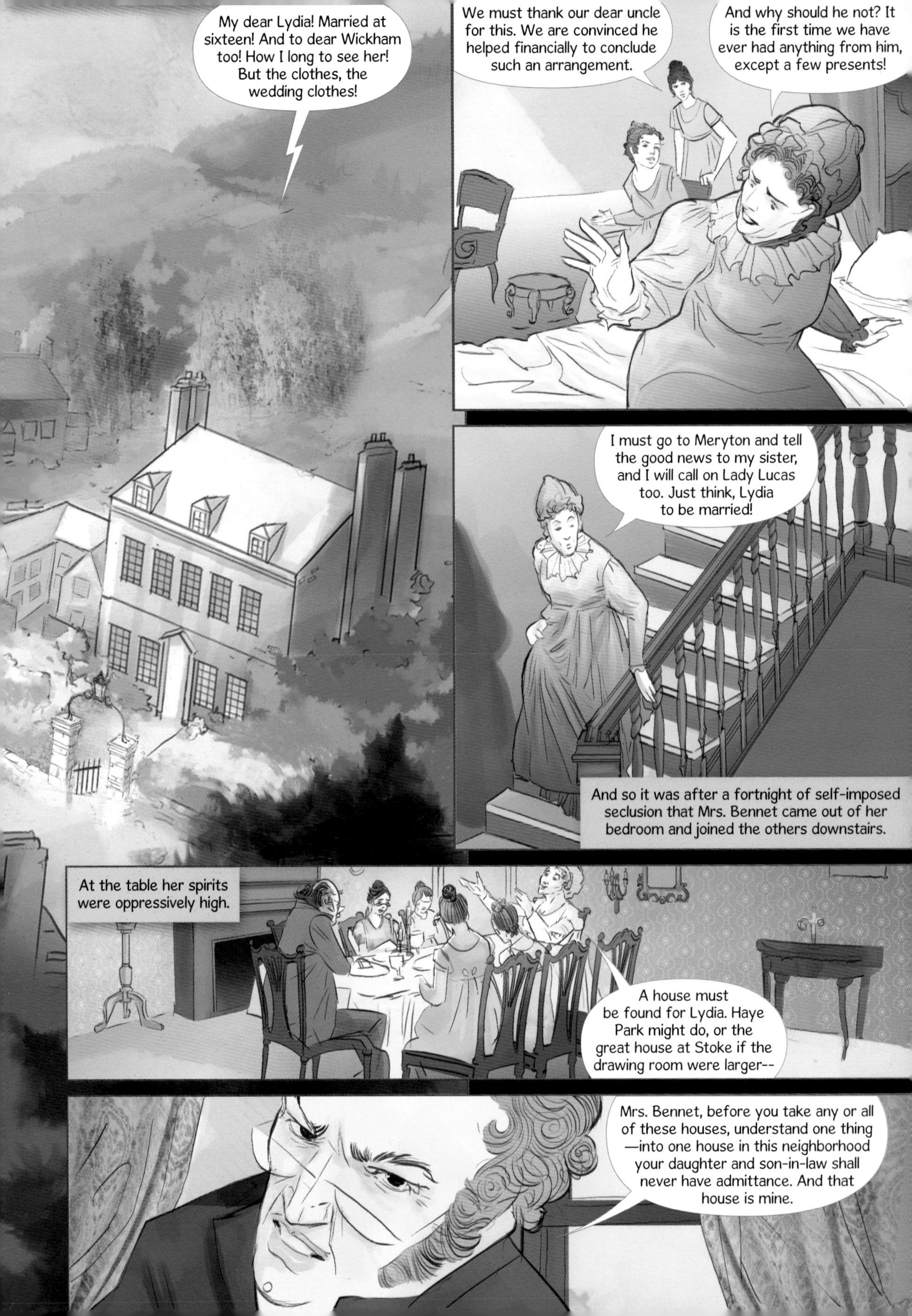
My dear Lydia! Married at sixteen! And to dear Wickham too! How I long to see her! But the clothes, the wedding clothes!
We must thank our dear uncle for this. We are convinced he helped financially to conclude such an arrangement.
And why should he not? It is the first time we have ever had anything from him, except a few presents!
I must go to Meryton and tell the good news to my sister, and I will call on Lady Lucas too. Just think, Lydia to be married!
And so it was after a fortnight of self-imposed seclusion that Mrs. Bennet came out of her bedroom and joined the others downstairs.
At the table her spirits were oppressively high.
A house must be found for Lydia. Haye Park might do, or the great house at Stoke if the drawing room were larger--
Mrs. Bennet, before you take any or all of these houses, understand one thing—into one house in this neighborhood your daughter and son-in-law shall never have admittance. And that house is mine.

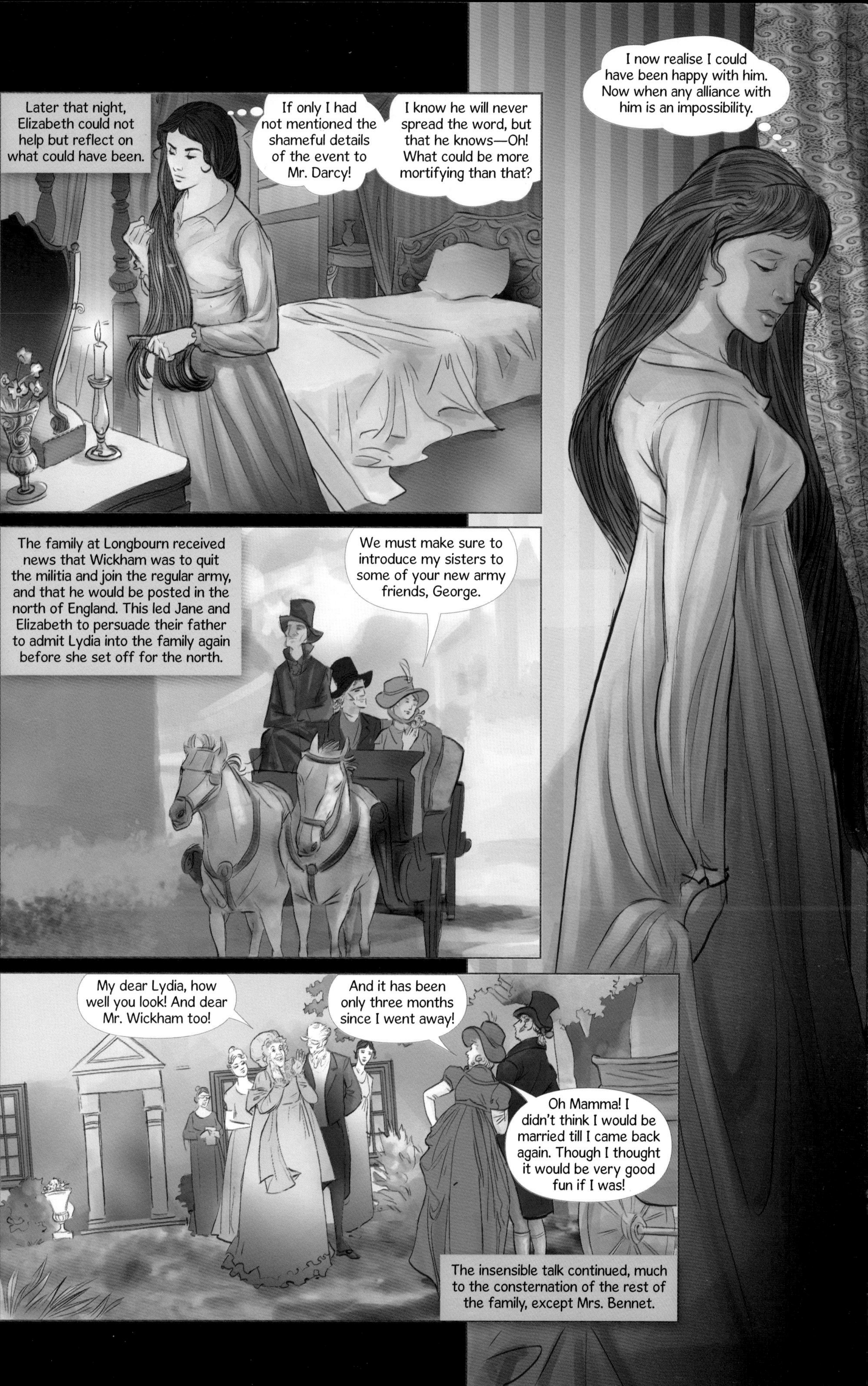

Later that night, Elizabeth could not help but reflect on what could have been.
If only I had not mentioned the shameful details of the event to Mr. Darcy!
I know he will never spread the word, but that he knows—Oh! What could be more mortifying than that?
I now realise I could have been happy with him. Now when any alliance with him is an impossibility.
The family at Longbourn received news that Wickham was to quit the militia and join the regular army, and that he would be posted in the north of England. This led Jane and Elizabeth to persuade their father to admit Lydia into the family again before she set off for the north.
We must make sure to introduce my sisters to some of your new army friends, George.
My dear Lydia, how well you look! And dear Mr. Wickham too!
And it has been only three months since I went away!
Oh Mamma! I didn't think I would be married till I came back again. Though I thought it would be very good fun if I was!
The insensible talk continued, much to the consternation of the rest of the family, except Mrs. Bennet.

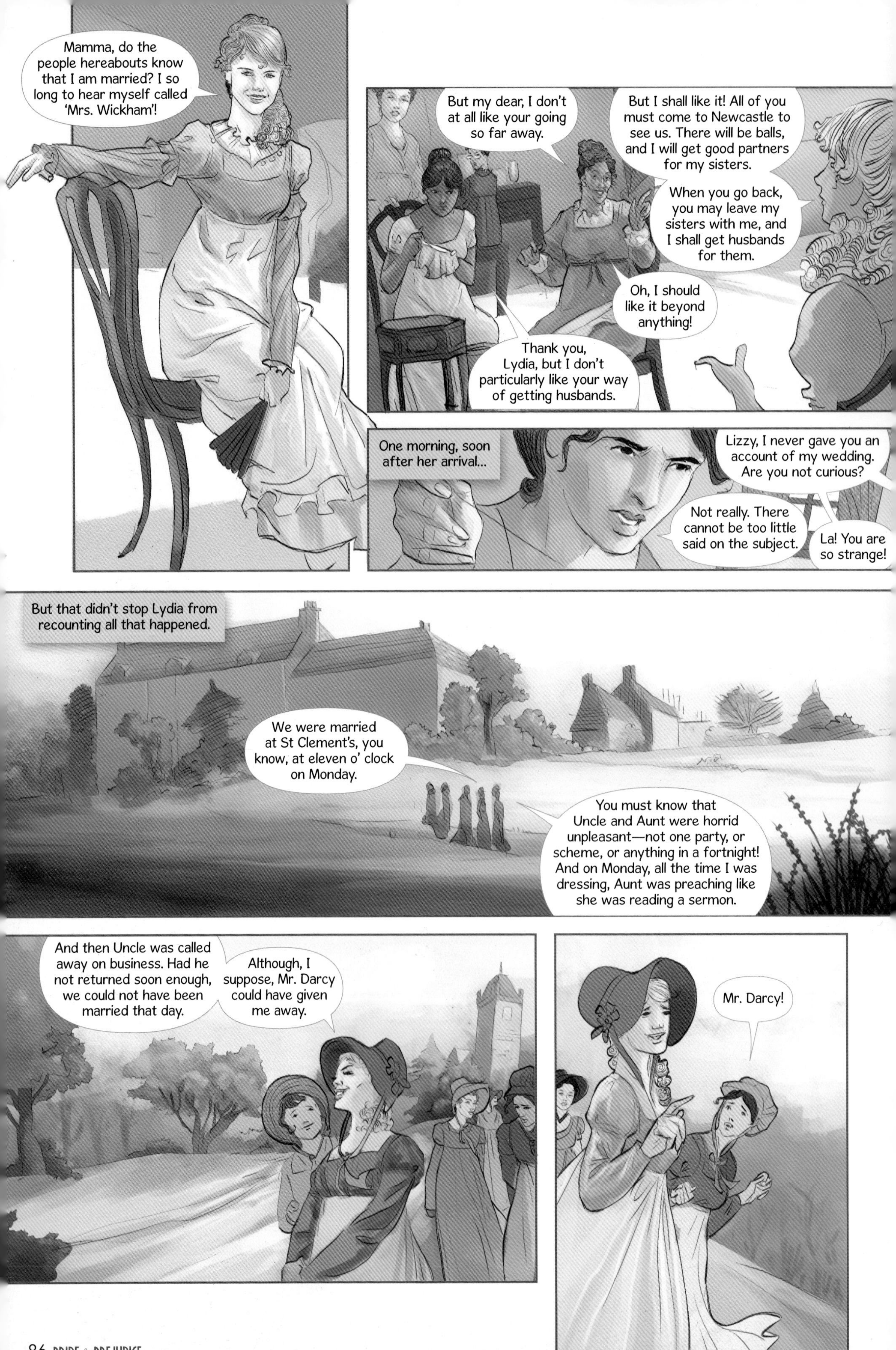
Mamma, do the people hereabouts know that I am married? I so long to hear myself called 'Mrs. Wickham'!
But my dear, I don't at all like your going so far away.
But I shall like it! All of you must come to Newcastle to see us. There will be balls, and I will get good partners for my sisters.
When you go back, you may leave my sisters with me, and I shall get husbands for them.
Oh, I should like it beyond anything!
Thank you, Lydia, but I don't particularly like your way of getting husbands.
One morning, soon after her arrival...
Lizzy, I never gave you an account of my wedding. Are you not curious?
Not really. There cannot be too little said on the subject.
La! You are so strange!
But that didn't stop Lydia from recounting all that happened.
We were married at St Clement's, you know, at eleven o' clock on Monday.
You must know that Uncle and Aunt were horrid unpleasant—not one party, or scheme, or anything in a fortnight! And on Monday, all the time I was dressing, Aunt was preaching like she was reading a sermon.
And then Uncle was called away on business. Had he not returned soon enough, we could not have been married that day.
Although, I suppose, Mr. Darcy could have given me away.
Mr. Darcy!

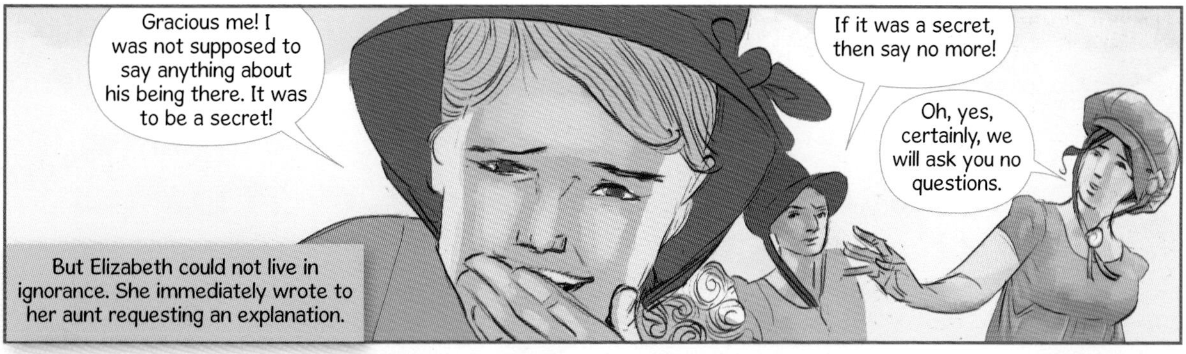
Gracious me! I was not supposed to say anything about his being there. It was to be a secret!
If it was a secret, then say no more!
Oh, yes, certainly, we will ask you no questions.
But Elizabeth could not live in ignorance. She immediately wrote to her aunt requesting an explanation.

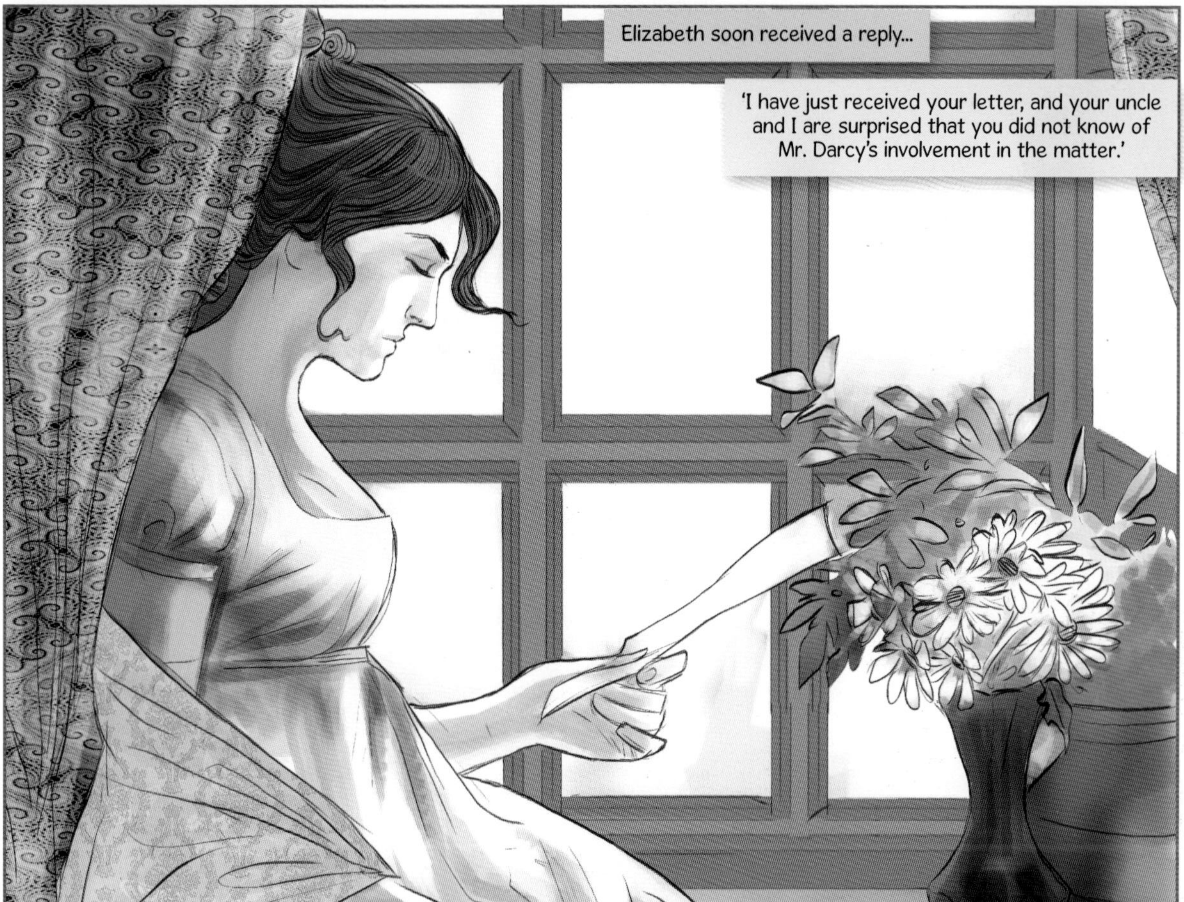
Elizabeth soon received a reply...
'I have just received your letter, and your uncle and I are surprised that you did not know of Mr. Darcy's involvement in the matter.'

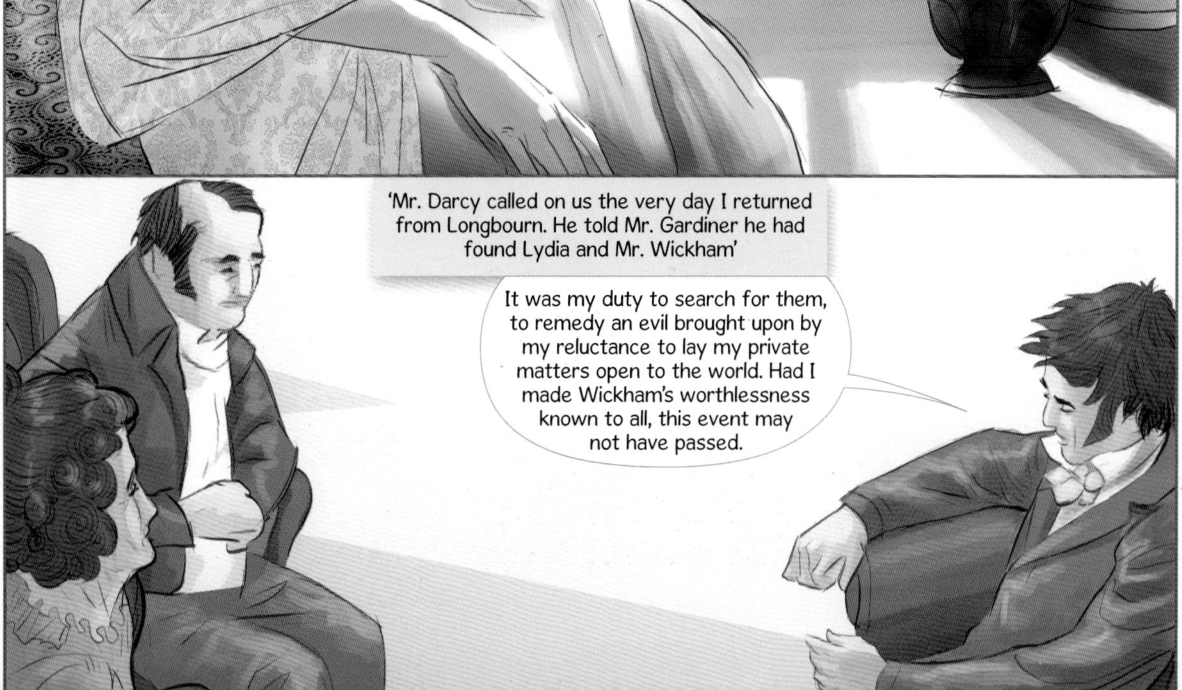
'Mr. Darcy called on us the very day I returned from Longbourn. He told Mr. Gardiner he had found Lydia and Mr. Wickham'
It was my duty to search for them, to remedy an evil brought upon by my reluctance to lay my private matters open to the world. Had I made Wickham's worthlessness known to all, this event may not have passed.

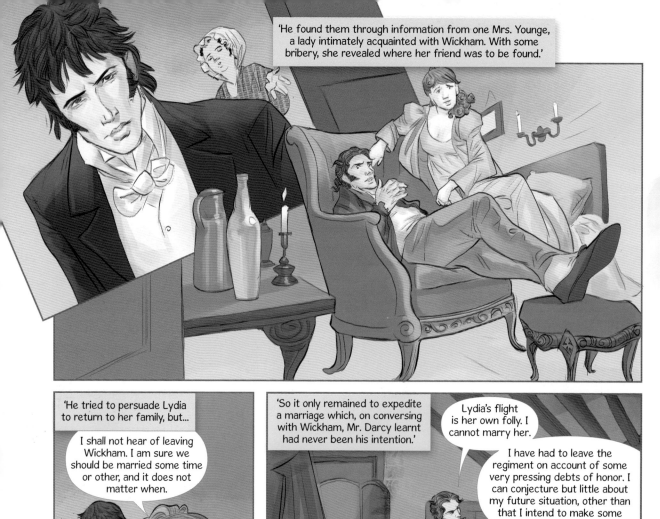

'He found them through information from one Mrs. Younge, a lady intimately acquainted with Wickham. With some bribery, she revealed where her friend was to be found.'

'He tried to persuade Lydia to return to her family, but...

I shall not hear of leaving Wickham. I am sure we should be married some time or other, and it does not matter when.

'So it only remained to expedite a marriage which, on conversing with Wickham, Mr. Darcy learnt had never been his intention.'

Lydia's flight is her own folly. I cannot marry her.

I have had to leave the regiment on account of some very pressing debts of honor. I can conjecture but little about my future situation, other than that I intend to make some fortune by marriage.

But I believe, under your circumstances, you would not reject a reasonable offer of immediate relief.

'Mr. Darcy paid Wickham's debts, amounting to more than a thousand pounds, and purchased his commission in the army. Your uncle was most ready to pay for these, but Mr. Darcy was very obstinate. Nothing was to be done that he did not do himself.

'Mr. Darcy was also present at the wedding to ensure that all went well. He made us promise to keep his role in bringing about this marriage a secret, and so your uncle was forced to take credit much against his own wishes.'

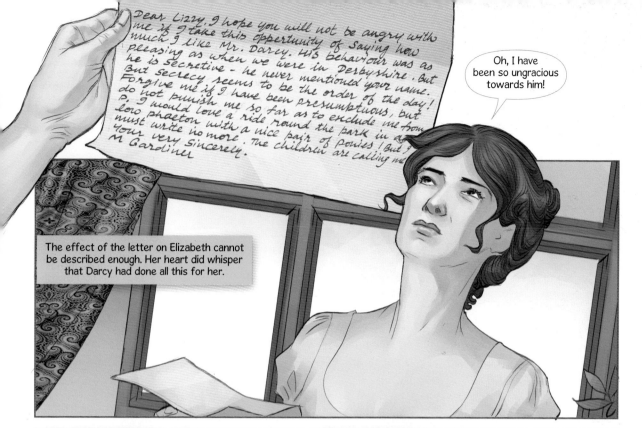

Dear Lizzy, I hope you will not be angry with me if I take this opportunity of saying how much I like Mr. Darcy. His behaviour was as pleasing as when we were in Derbyshire. But he is secretive - he never mentioned your name. But secrecy seems to be the order of the day! Forgive me if I have been presumptuous, but do not punish me so far as to exclude me from P. I would love a ride, round the park in a low phaeton with a nice pair of ponies! But I must write no more. The children are calling me.
Your very sincerely,
M Gardiner

Oh, I have been so ungracious towards him!

The effect of the letter on Elizabeth cannot be described enough. Her heart did whisper that Darcy had done all this for her.

Wickham and Lydia remained for about ten days at Longbourn. On the day of their departure...

Oh, my dear! When shall we meet again?

Oh Mamma, I don't know! Not these two or three years perhaps.

Write to me very often, won't you?

As often as I can, but married women never have much time for writing.

My sisters may write to me. They will have nothing else to do.

What a fine fellow! He simpers, smirks, and gives his love to all!

There is nothing so bad as parting with dear ones. One is so forlorn without them.

This is what happens when you marry a daughter off. So you should be happy that your other four are single!

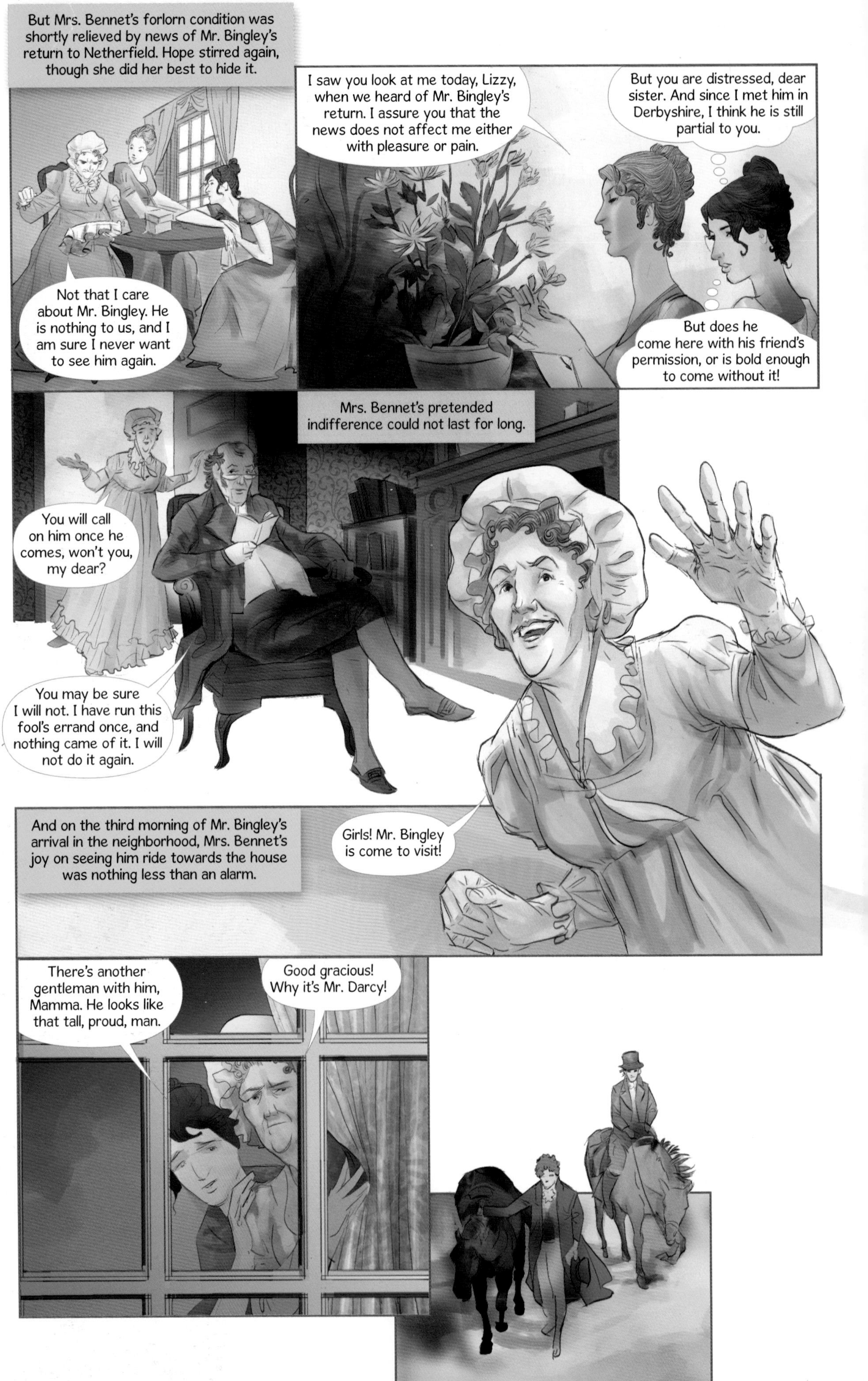

But Mrs. Bennet's forlorn condition was shortly relieved by news of Mr. Bingley's return to Netherfield. Hope stirred again, though she did her best to hide it.
Not that I care about Mr. Bingley. He is nothing to us, and I am sure I never want to see him again.
I saw you look at me today, Lizzy, when we heard of Mr. Bingley's return. I assure you that the news does not affect me either with pleasure or pain.
But you are distressed, dear sister. And since I met him in Derbyshire, I think he is still partial to you.
But does he come here with his friend's permission, or is bold enough to come without it!
Mrs. Bennet's pretended indifference could not last for long.
You will call on him once he comes, won't you, my dear?
You may be sure I will not. I have run this fool's errand once, and nothing came of it. I will not do it again.
And on the third morning of Mr. Bingley's arrival in the neighborhood, Mrs. Bennet's joy on seeing him ride towards the house was nothing less than an alarm.
Girls! Mr. Bingley is come to visit!
There's another gentleman with him, Mamma. He looks like that tall, proud, man.
Good gracious! Why it's Mr. Darcy!

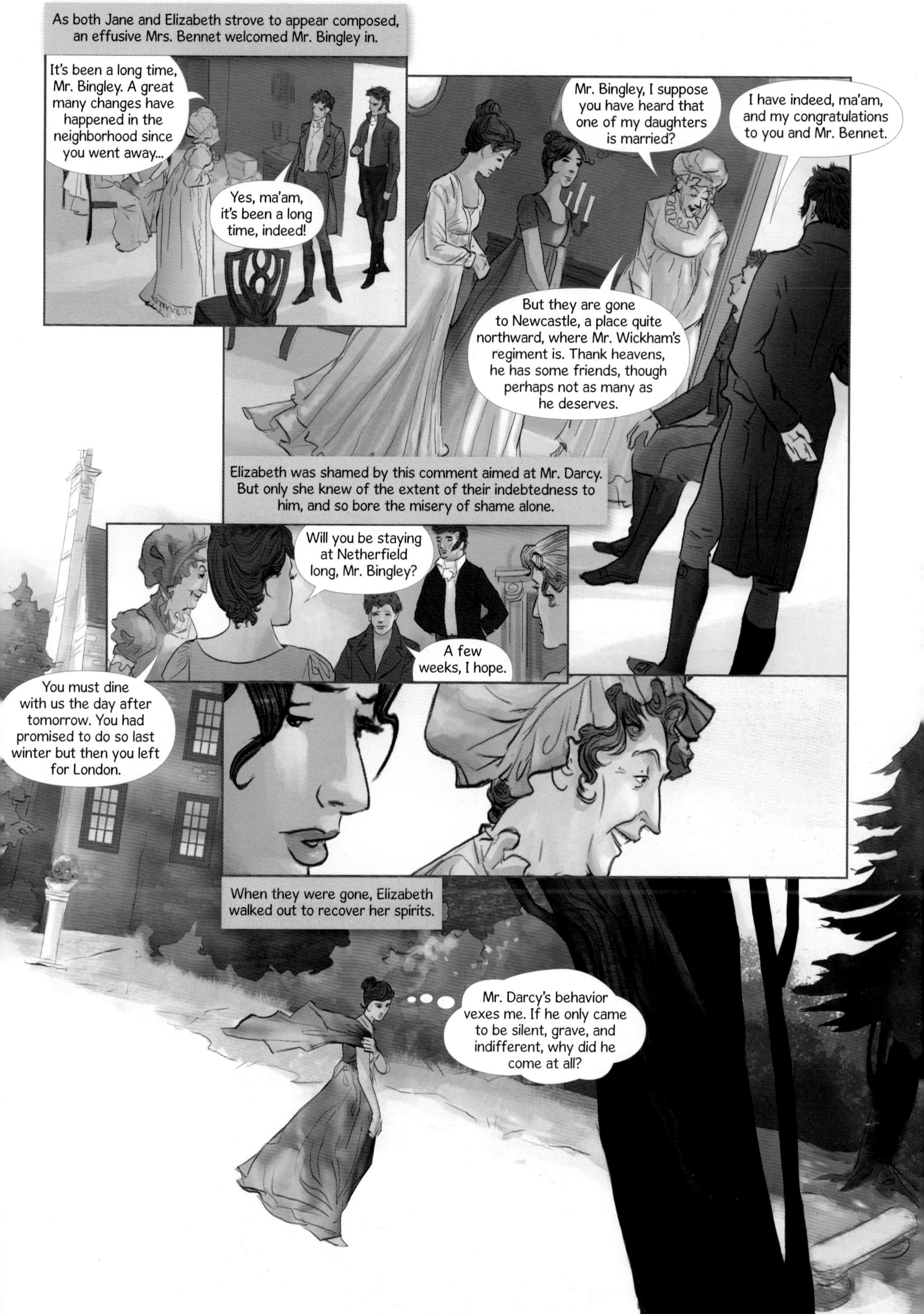

As both Jane and Elizabeth strove to appear composed, an effusive Mrs. Bennet welcomed Mr. Bingley in.
It's been a long time, Mr. Bingley. A great many changes have happened in the neighborhood since you went away...
Yes, ma'am, it's been a long time, indeed!
Mr. Bingley, I suppose you have heard that one of my daughters is married?
I have indeed, ma'am, and my congratulations to you and Mr. Bennet.
But they are gone to Newcastle, a place quite northward, where Mr. Wickham's regiment is. Thank heavens, he has some friends, though perhaps not as many as he deserves.
Elizabeth was shamed by this comment aimed at Mr. Darcy. But only she knew of the extent of their indebtedness to him, and so bore the misery of shame alone.
Will you be staying at Netherfield long, Mr. Bingley?
A few weeks, I hope.
You must dine with us the day after tomorrow. You had promised to do so last winter but then you left for London.
When they were gone, Elizabeth walked out to recover her spirits.
Mr. Darcy's behavior vexes me. If he only came to be silent, grave, and indifferent, why did he come at all?

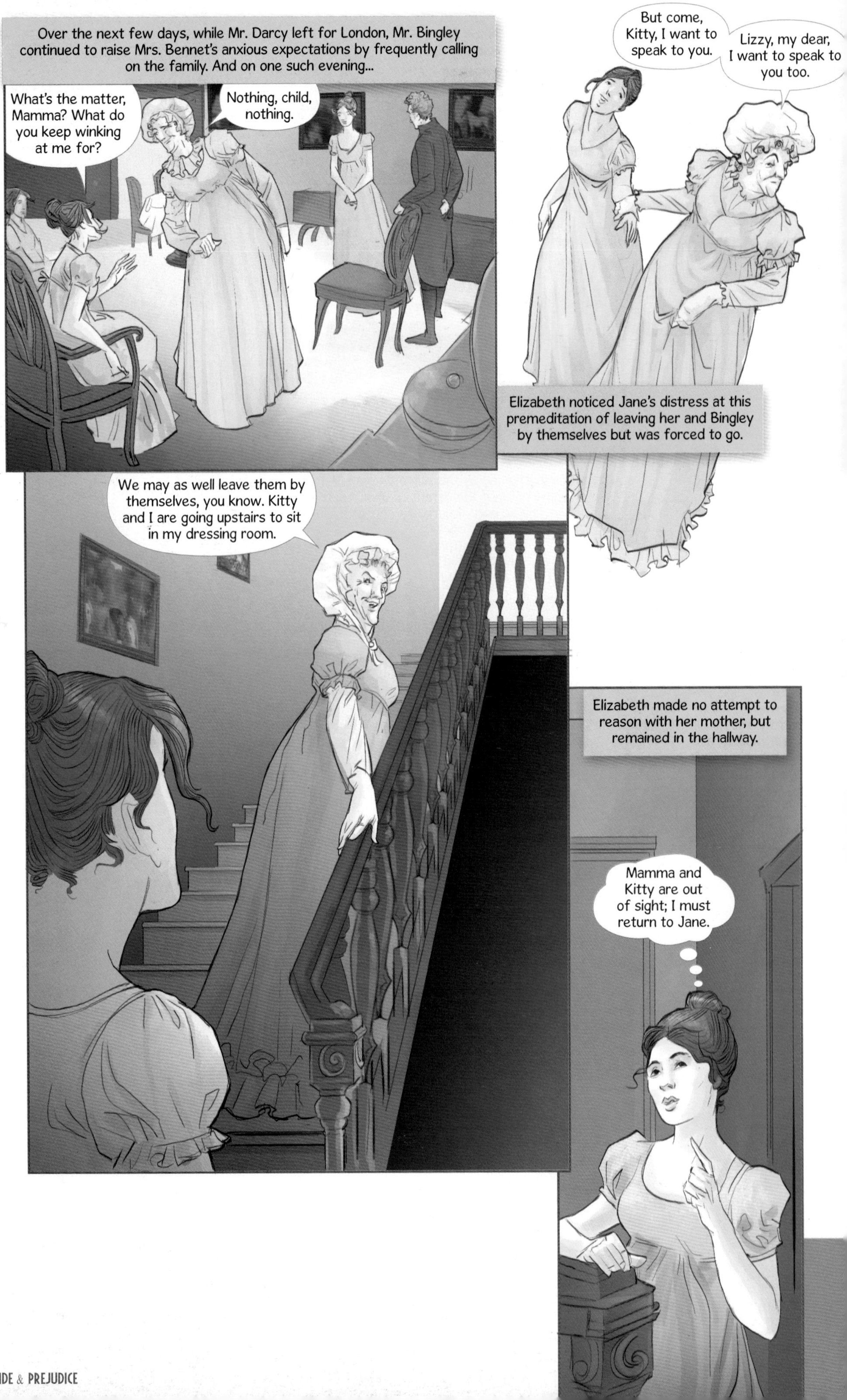

Over the next few days, while Mr. Darcy left for London, Mr. Bingley continued to raise Mrs. Bennet's anxious expectations by frequently calling on the family. And on one such evening...
What's the matter, Mamma? What do you keep winking at me for?
Nothing, child, nothing.
But come, Kitty, I want to speak to you.
Lizzy, my dear, I want to speak to you too.
Elizabeth noticed Jane's distress at this premeditation of leaving her and Bingley by themselves but was forced to go.
We may as well leave them by themselves, you know. Kitty and I are going upstairs to sit in my dressing room.
Elizabeth made no attempt to reason with her mother, but remained in the hallway.
Mamma and Kitty are out of sight; I must return to Jane.

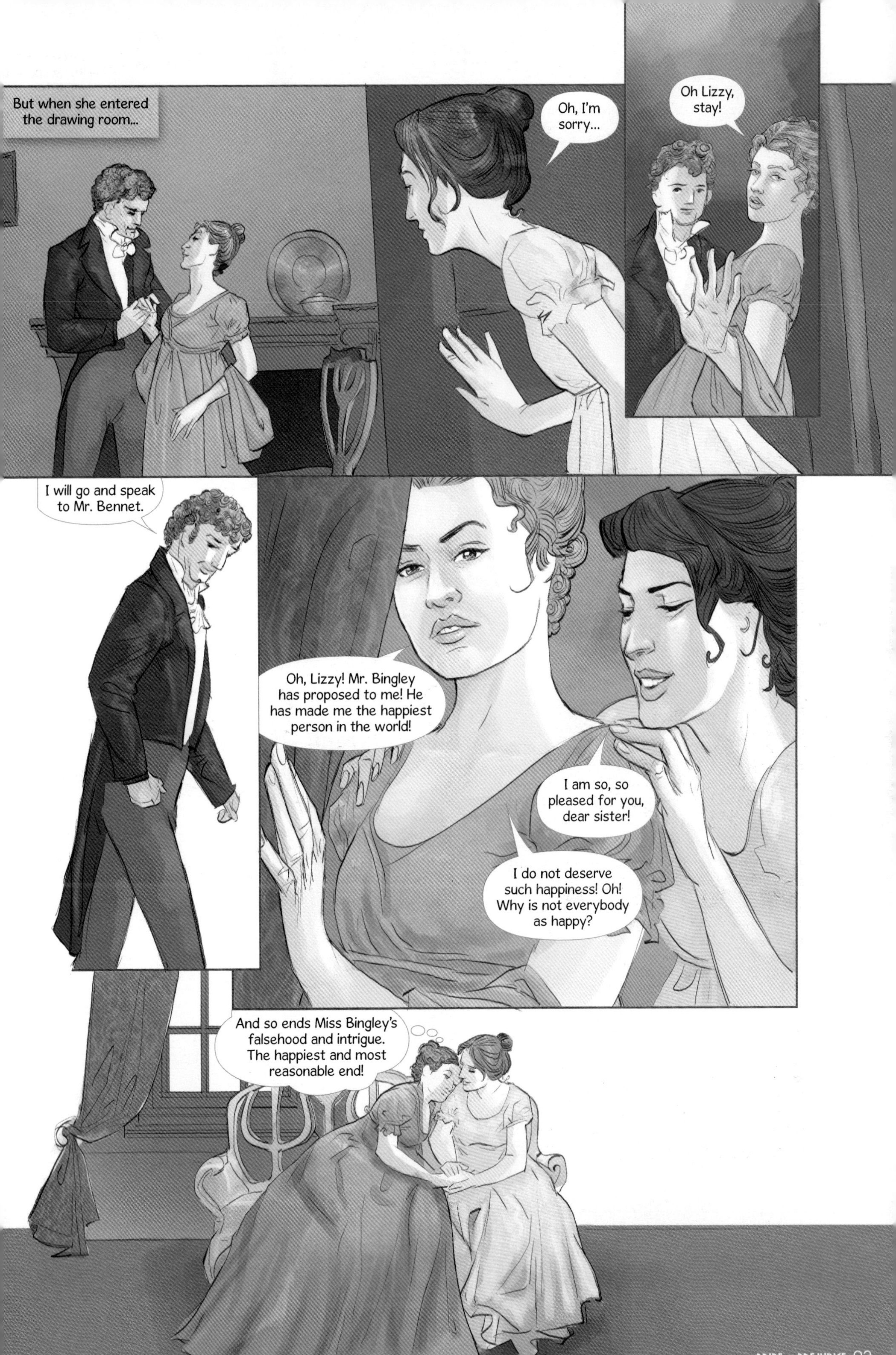
But when she entered the drawing room...
Oh, I'm sorry...
Oh Lizzy, stay!
I will go and speak to Mr. Bennet.
Oh, Lizzy! Mr. Bingley has proposed to me! He has made me the happiest person in the world!
I am so, so pleased for you, dear sister!
I do not deserve such happiness! Oh! Why is not everybody as happy?
And so ends Miss Bingley's falsehood and intrigue. The happiest and most reasonable end!

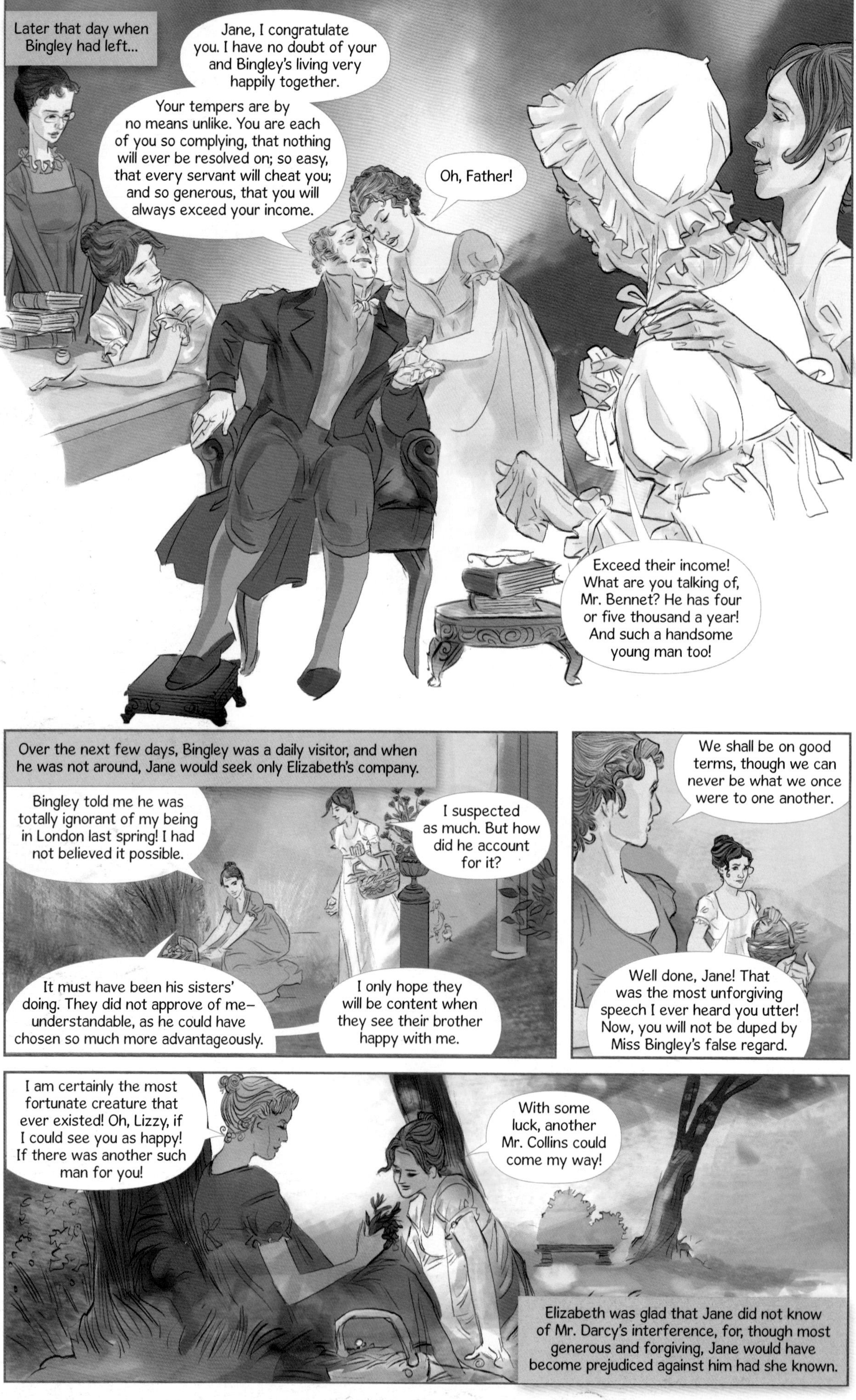

Later that day when Bingley had left...
Jane, I congratulate you. I have no doubt of your and Bingley's living very happily together.
Your tempers are by no means unlike. You are each of you so complying, that nothing will ever be resolved on; so easy, that every servant will cheat you; and so generous, that you will always exceed your income.
Oh, Father!
Exceed their income! What are you talking of, Mr. Bennet? He has four or five thousand a year! And such a handsome young man too!
Over the next few days, Bingley was a daily visitor, and when he was not around, Jane would seek only Elizabeth's company.
Bingley told me he was totally ignorant of my being in London last spring! I had not believed it possible.
I suspected as much. But how did he account for it?
It must have been his sisters' doing. They did not approve of me—understandable, as he could have chosen so much more advantageously.
I only hope they will be content when they see their brother happy with me.
We shall be on good terms, though we can never be what we once were to one another.
Well done, Jane! That was the most unforgiving speech I ever heard you utter! Now, you will not be duped by Miss Bingley's false regard.
I am certainly the most fortunate creature that ever existed! Oh, Lizzy, if I could see you as happy! If there was another such man for you!
With some luck, another Mr. Collins could come my way!
Elizabeth was glad that Jane did not know of Mr. Darcy's interference, for, though most generous and forgiving, Jane would have become prejudiced against him had she known.

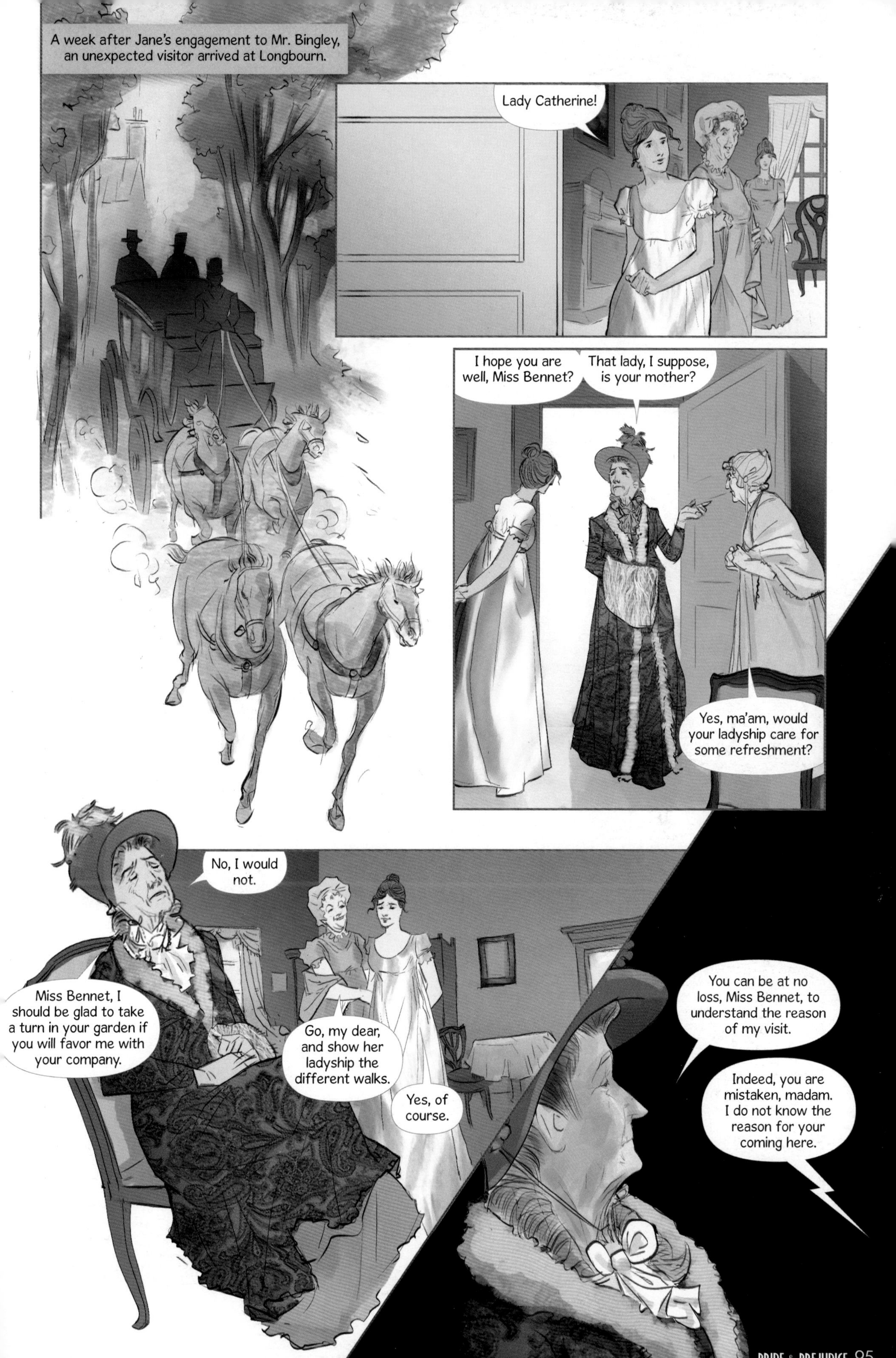
A week after Jane's engagement to Mr. Bingley, an unexpected visitor arrived at Longbourn.
Lady Catherine!
I hope you are well, Miss Bennet?
That lady, I suppose, is your mother?
Yes, ma'am, would your ladyship care for some refreshment?
No, I would not.
Miss Bennet, I should be glad to take a turn in your garden if you will favor me with your company.
Go, my dear, and show her ladyship the different walks.
Yes, of course.
You can be at no loss, Miss Bennet, to understand the reason of my visit.
Indeed, you are mistaken, madam. I do not know the reason for your coming here.

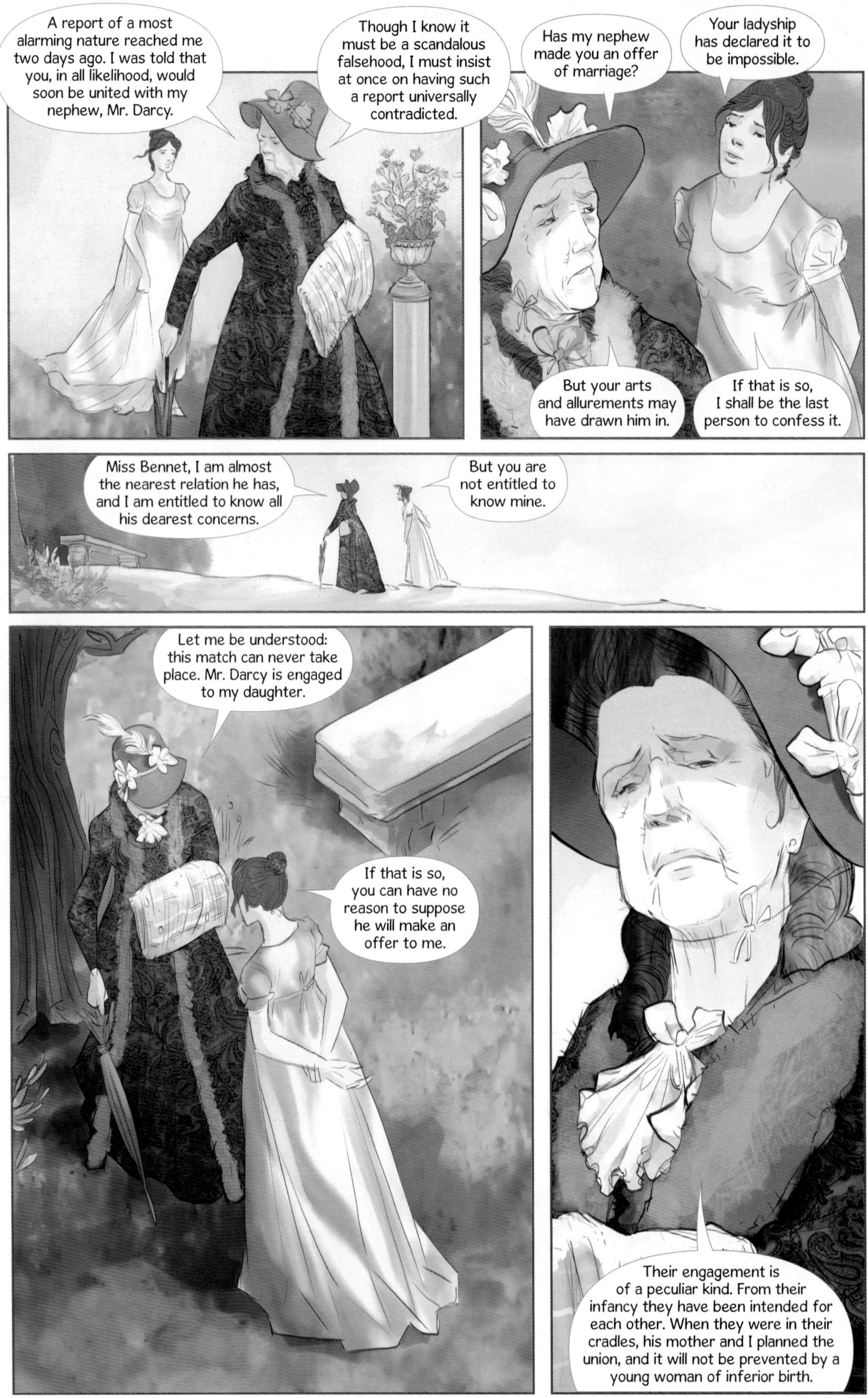
A report of a most alarming nature reached me two days ago. I was told that you, in all likelihood, would soon be united with my nephew, Mr. Darcy.
Though I know it must be a scandalous falsehood, I must insist at once on having such a report universally contradicted.
Has my nephew made you an offer of marriage?
Your ladyship has declared it to be impossible.
But your arts and allurements may have drawn him in.
If that is so, I shall be the last person to confess it.
Miss Bennet, I am almost the nearest relation he has, and I am entitled to know all his dearest concerns.
But you are not entitled to know mine.
Let me be understood: this match can never take place. Mr. Darcy is engaged to my daughter.
If that is so, you can have no reason to suppose he will make an offer to me.
Their engagement is of a peculiar kind. From their infancy they have been intended for each other. When they were in their cradles, his mother and I planned the union, and it will not be prevented by a young woman of inferior birth.

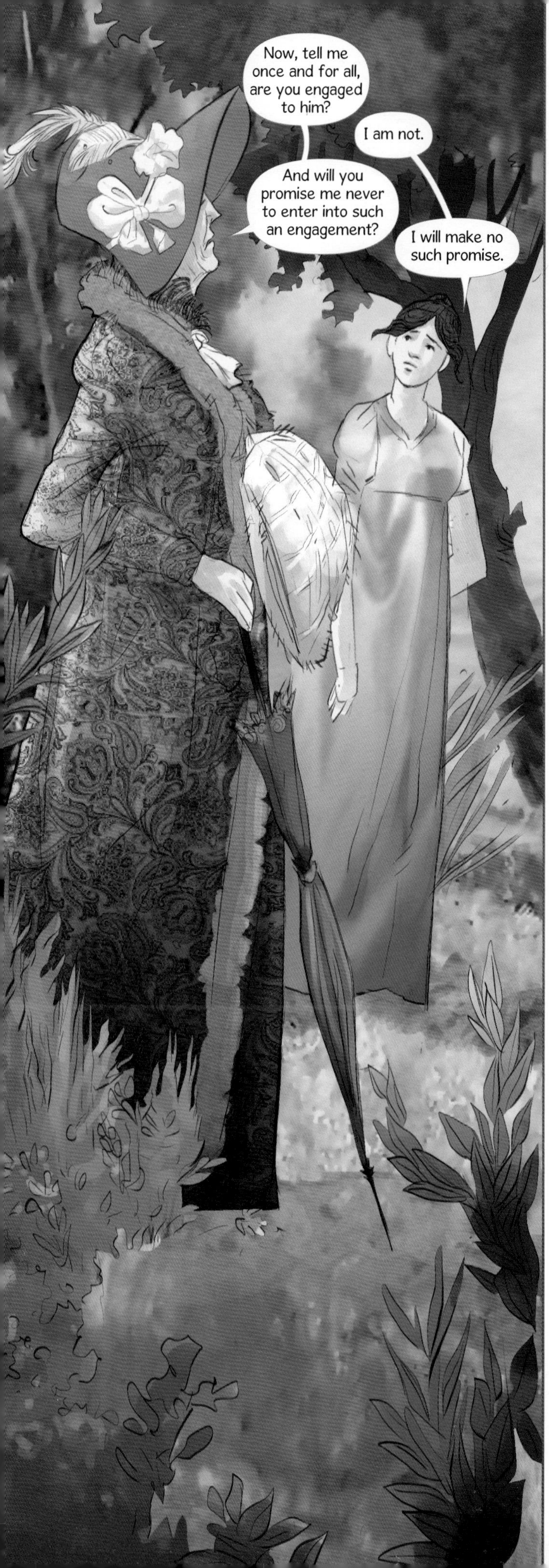
Now, tell me once and for all, are you engaged to him?
I am not.
And will you promise me never to enter into such an engagement?
I will make no such promise.

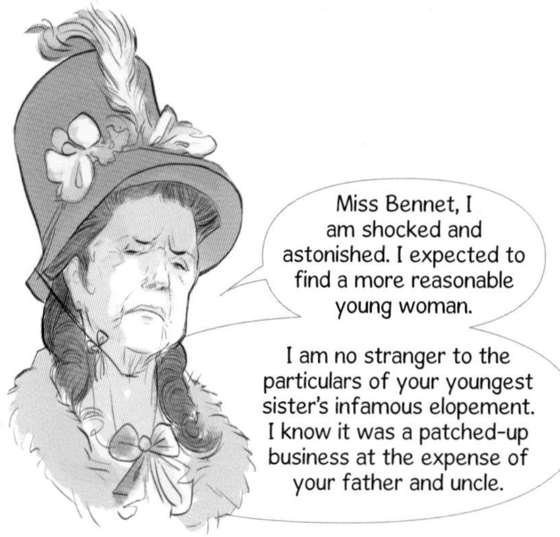
Miss Bennet, I am shocked and astonished. I expected to find a more reasonable young woman.
I am no stranger to the particulars of your youngest sister's infamous elopement. I know it was a patched-up business at the expense of your father and uncle.

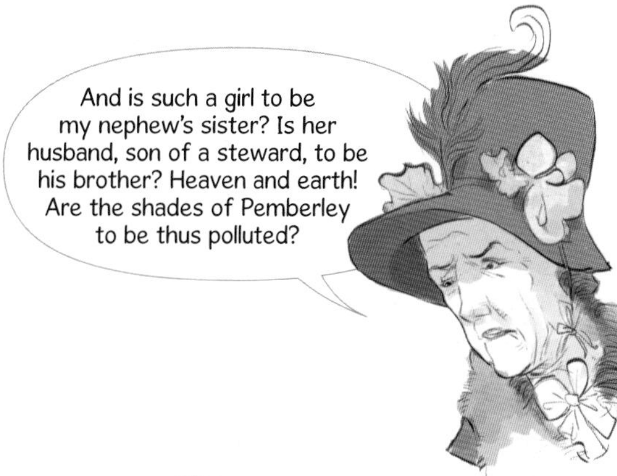
And is such a girl to be my nephew's sister? Is her husband, son of a steward, to be his brother? Heaven and earth! Are the shades of Pemberley to be thus polluted?

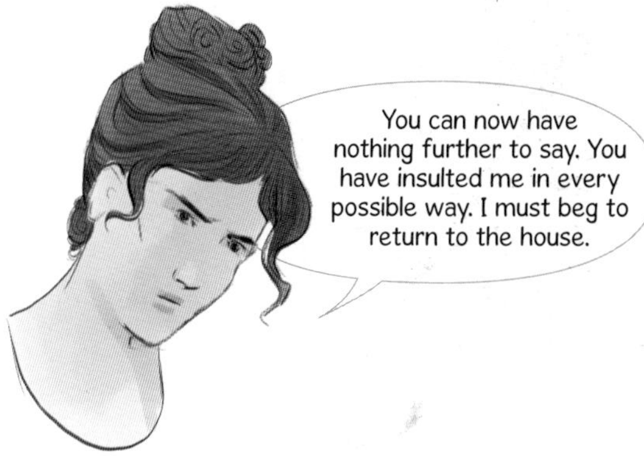
You can now have nothing further to say. You have insulted me in every possible way. I must beg to return to the house.

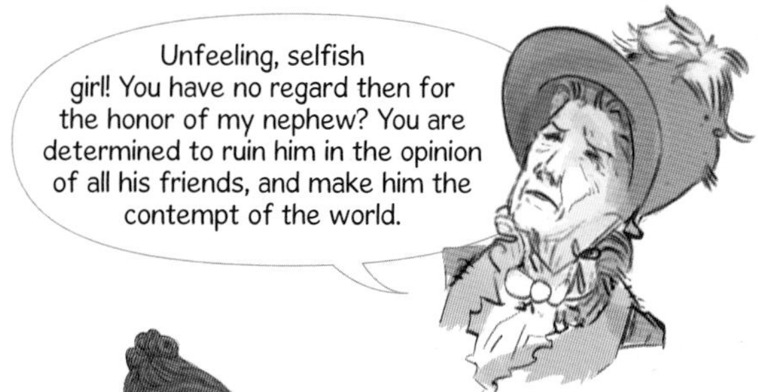
Unfeeling, selfish girl! You have no regard then for the honor of my nephew? You are determined to ruin him in the opinion of all his friends, and make him the contempt of the world.

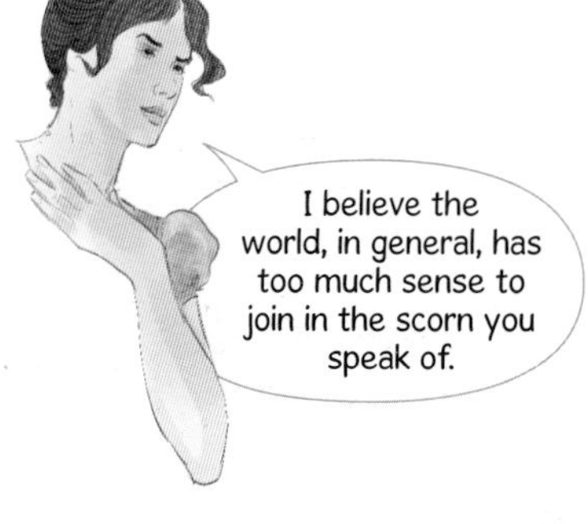
I believe the world, in general, has too much sense to join in the scorn you speak of.

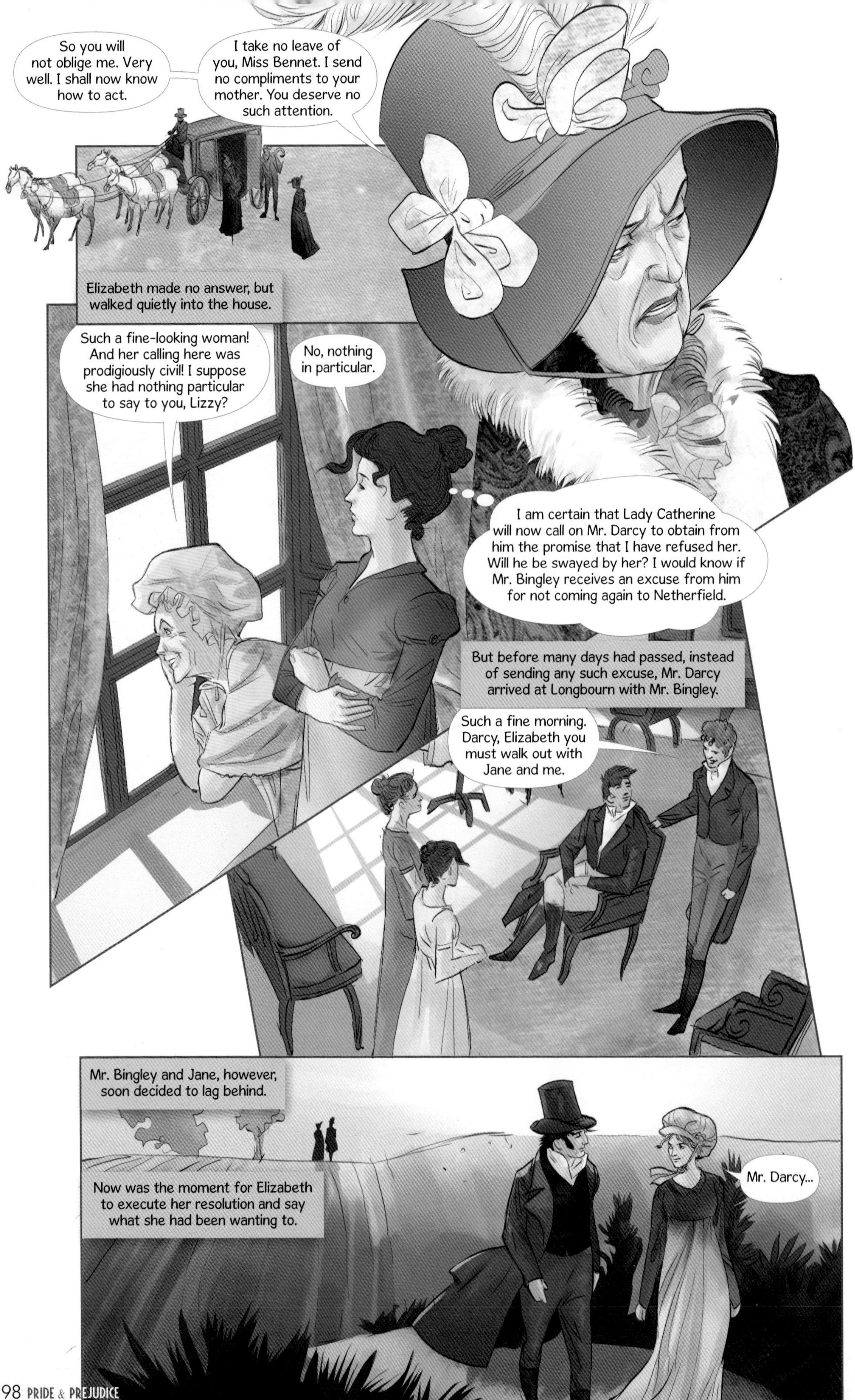
So you will not oblige me. Very well. I shall now know how to act.
I take no leave of you, Miss Bennet. I send no compliments to your mother. You deserve no such attention.
Elizabeth made no answer, but walked quietly into the house.
Such a fine-looking woman! And her calling here was prodigiously civil! I suppose she had nothing particular to say to you, Lizzy?
No, nothing in particular.
I am certain that Lady Catherine will now call on Mr. Darcy to obtain from him the promise that I have refused her. Will he be swayed by her? I would know if Mr. Bingley receives an excuse from him for not coming again to Netherfield.
But before many days had passed, instead of sending any such excuse, Mr. Darcy arrived at Longbourn with Mr. Bingley.
Such a fine morning. Darcy, Elizabeth you must walk out with Jane and me.
Mr. Bingley and Jane, however, soon decided to lag behind.
Now was the moment for Elizabeth to execute her resolution and say what she had been wanting to.
Mr. Darcy...

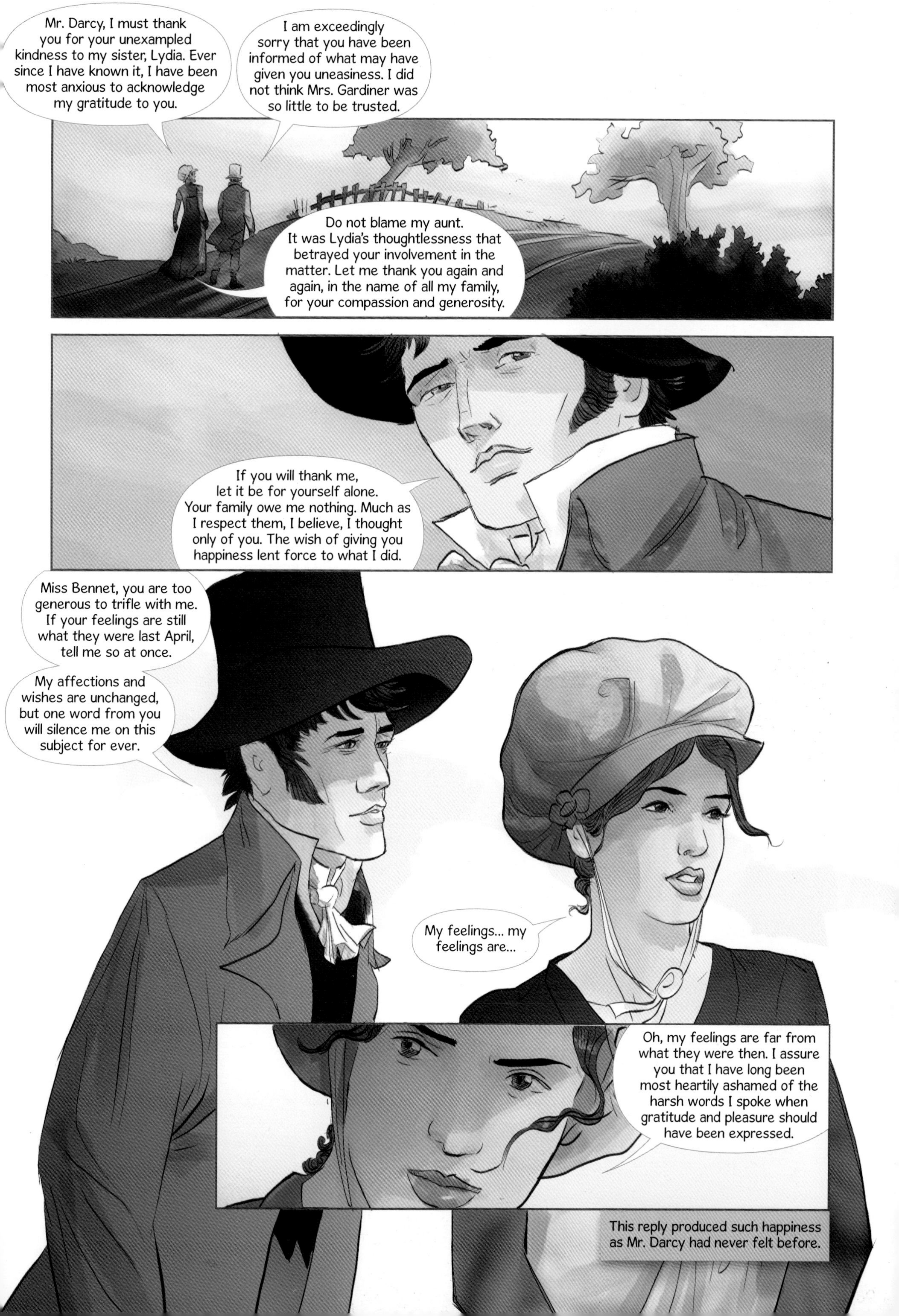
Mr. Darcy, I must thank you for your unexampled kindness to my sister, Lydia. Ever since I have known it, I have been most anxious to acknowledge my gratitude to you.
I am exceedingly sorry that you have been informed of what may have given you uneasiness. I did not think Mrs. Gardiner was so little to be trusted.
Do not blame my aunt. It was Lydia's thoughtlessness that betrayed your involvement in the matter. Let me thank you again and again, in the name of all my family, for your compassion and generosity.
If you will thank me, let it be for yourself alone. Your family owe me nothing. Much as I respect them, I believe, I thought only of you. The wish of giving you happiness lent force to what I did.
Miss Bennet, you are too generous to trifle with me. If your feelings are still what they were last April, tell me so at once.
My affections and wishes are unchanged, but one word from you will silence me on this subject for ever.
My feelings... my feelings are...
Oh, my feelings are far from what they were then. I assure you that I have long been most heartily ashamed of the harsh words I spoke when gratitude and pleasure should have been expressed.
This reply produced such happiness as Mr. Darcy had never felt before.

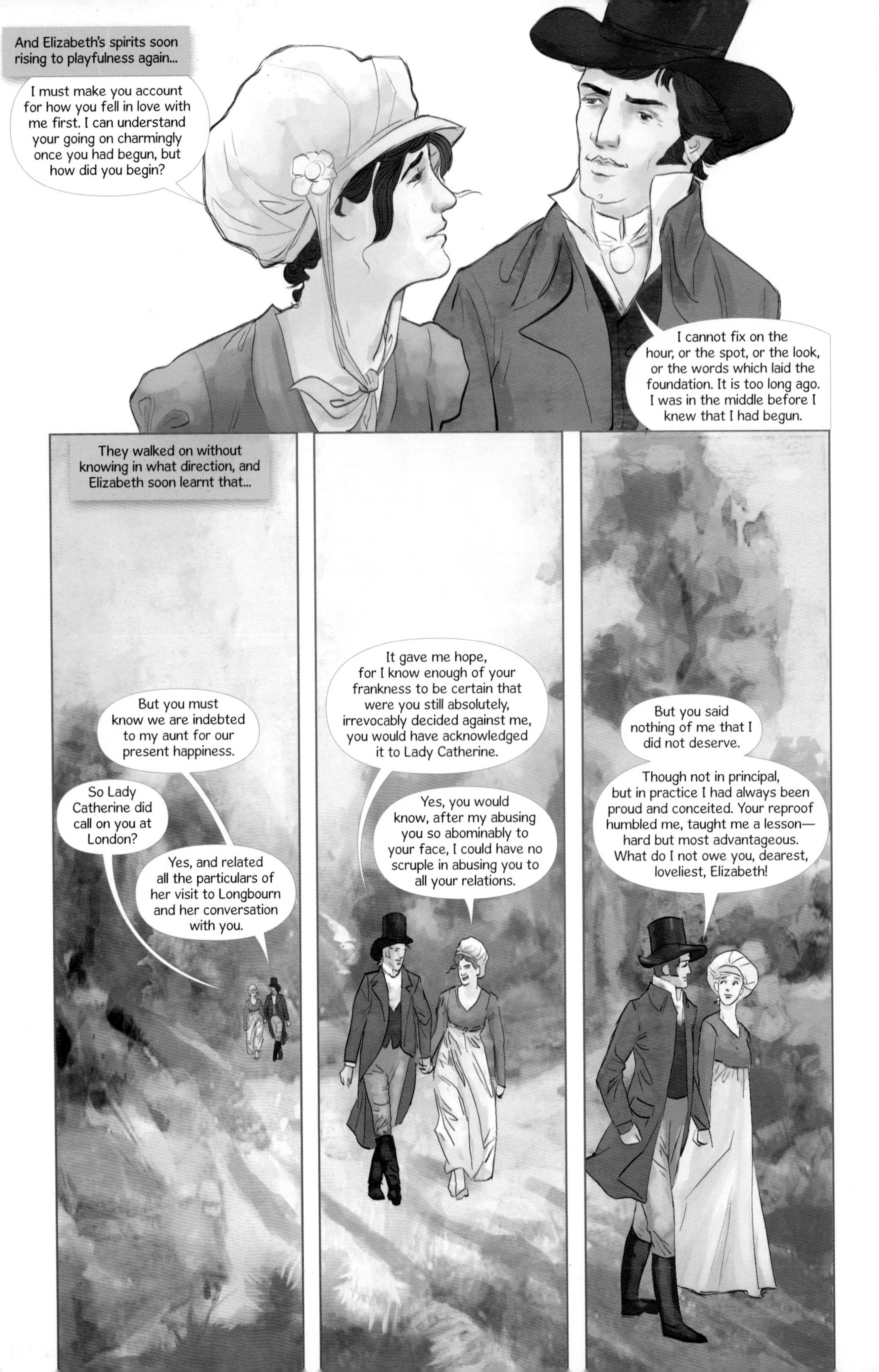

And Elizabeth's spirits soon rising to playfulness again...
I must make you account for how you fell in love with me first. I can understand your going on charmingly once you had begun, but how did you begin?
I cannot fix on the hour, or the spot, or the look, or the words which laid the foundation. It is too long ago. I was in the middle before I knew that I had begun.
They walked on without knowing in what direction, and Elizabeth soon learnt that...
But you must know we are indebted to my aunt for our present happiness.
So Lady Catherine did call on you at London?
Yes, and related all the particulars of her visit to Longbourn and her conversation with you.
It gave me hope, for I know enough of your frankness to be certain that were you still absolutely, irrevocably decided against me, you would have acknowledged it to Lady Catherine.
Yes, you would know, after my abusing you so abominably to your face, I could have no scruple in abusing you to all your relations.
But you said nothing of me that I did not deserve.
Though not in principal, but in practice I had always been proud and conceited. Your reproof humbled me, taught me a lesson—hard but most advantageous. What do I not owe you, dearest, loveliest, Elizabeth!

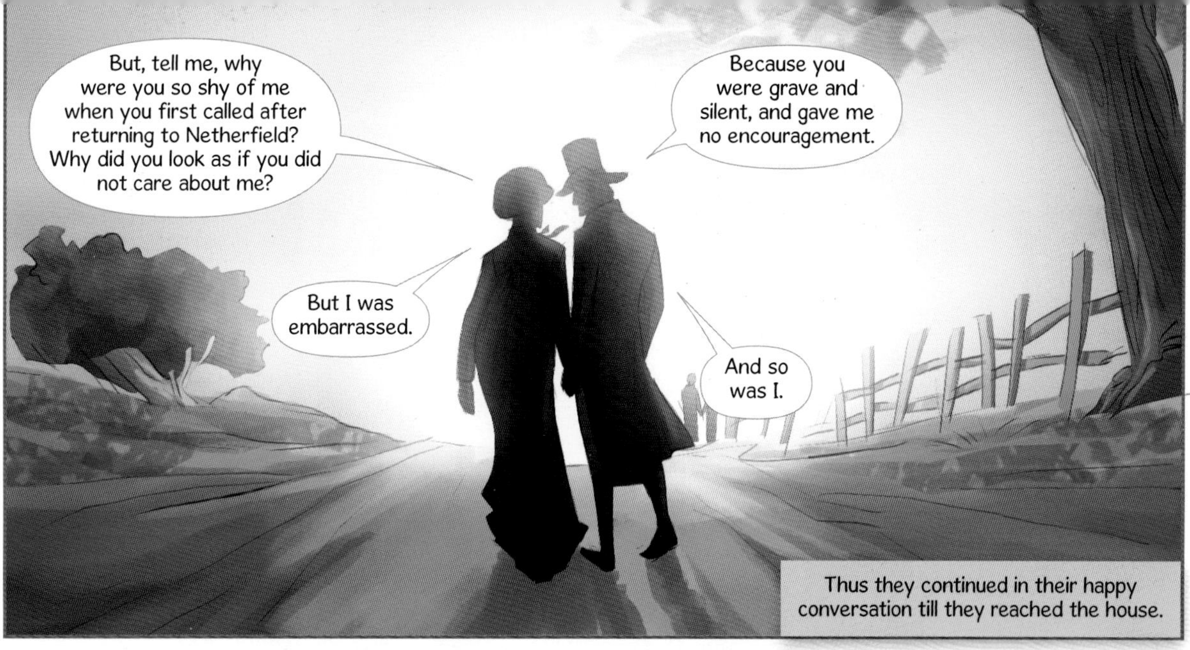
But, tell me, why were you so shy of me when you first called after returning to Netherfield? Why did you look as if you did not care about me?
Because you were grave and silent, and gave me no encouragement.
But I was embarrassed.
And so was I.
Thus they continued in their happy conversation till they reached the house.

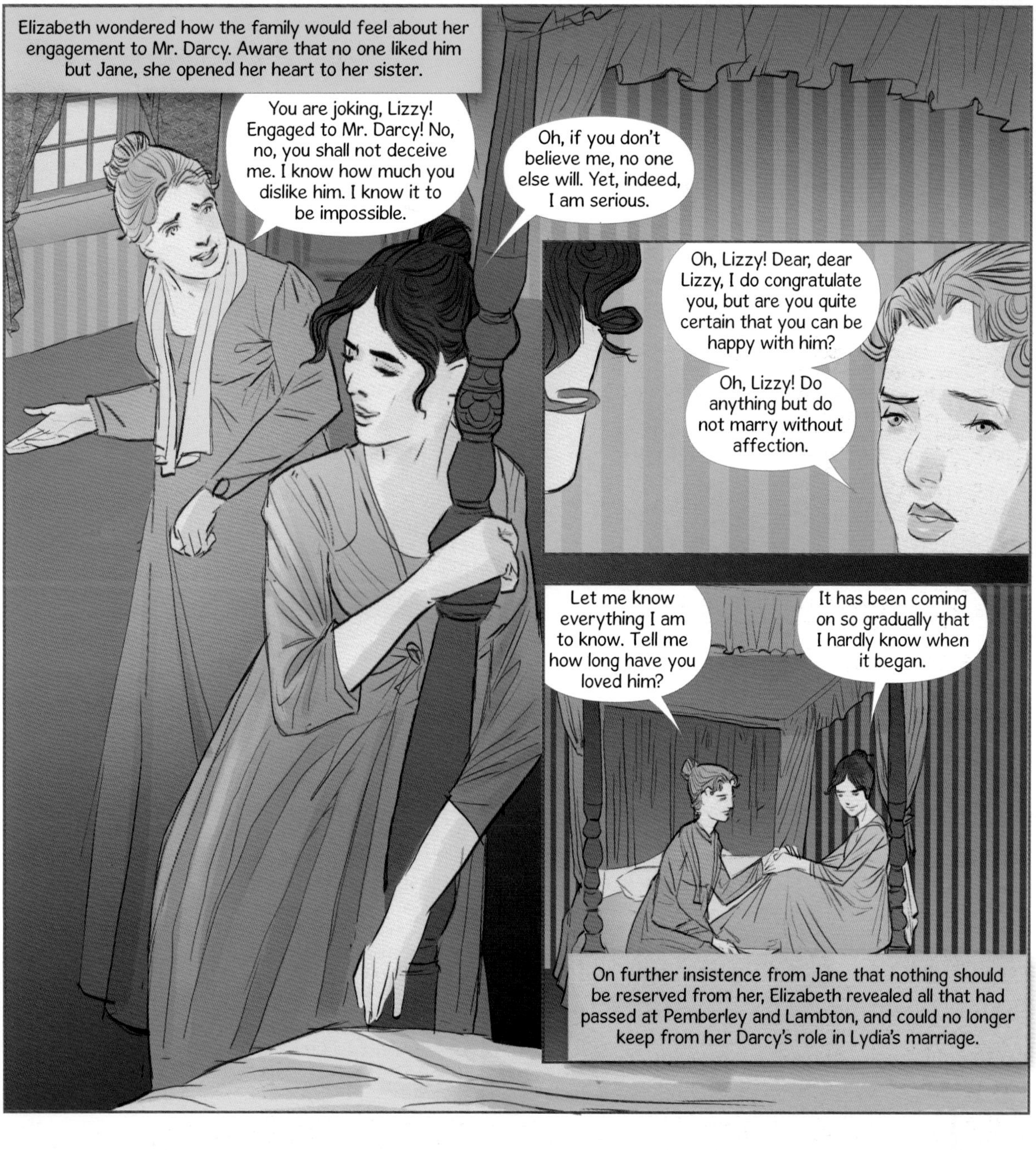
Elizabeth wondered how the family would feel about her engagement to Mr. Darcy. Aware that no one liked him but Jane, she opened her heart to her sister.
You are joking, Lizzy! Engaged to Mr. Darcy! No, no, you shall not deceive me. I know how much you dislike him. I know it to be impossible.
Oh, if you don't believe me, no one else will. Yet, indeed, I am serious.
Oh, Lizzy! Dear, dear Lizzy, I do congratulate you, but are you quite certain that you can be happy with him?
Oh, Lizzy! Do anything but do not marry without affection.
Let me know everything I am to know. Tell me how long have you loved him?
It has been coming on so gradually that I hardly know when it began.
On further insistence from Jane that nothing should be reserved from her, Elizabeth revealed all that had passed at Pemberley and Lambton, and could no longer keep from her Darcy's role in Lydia's marriage.

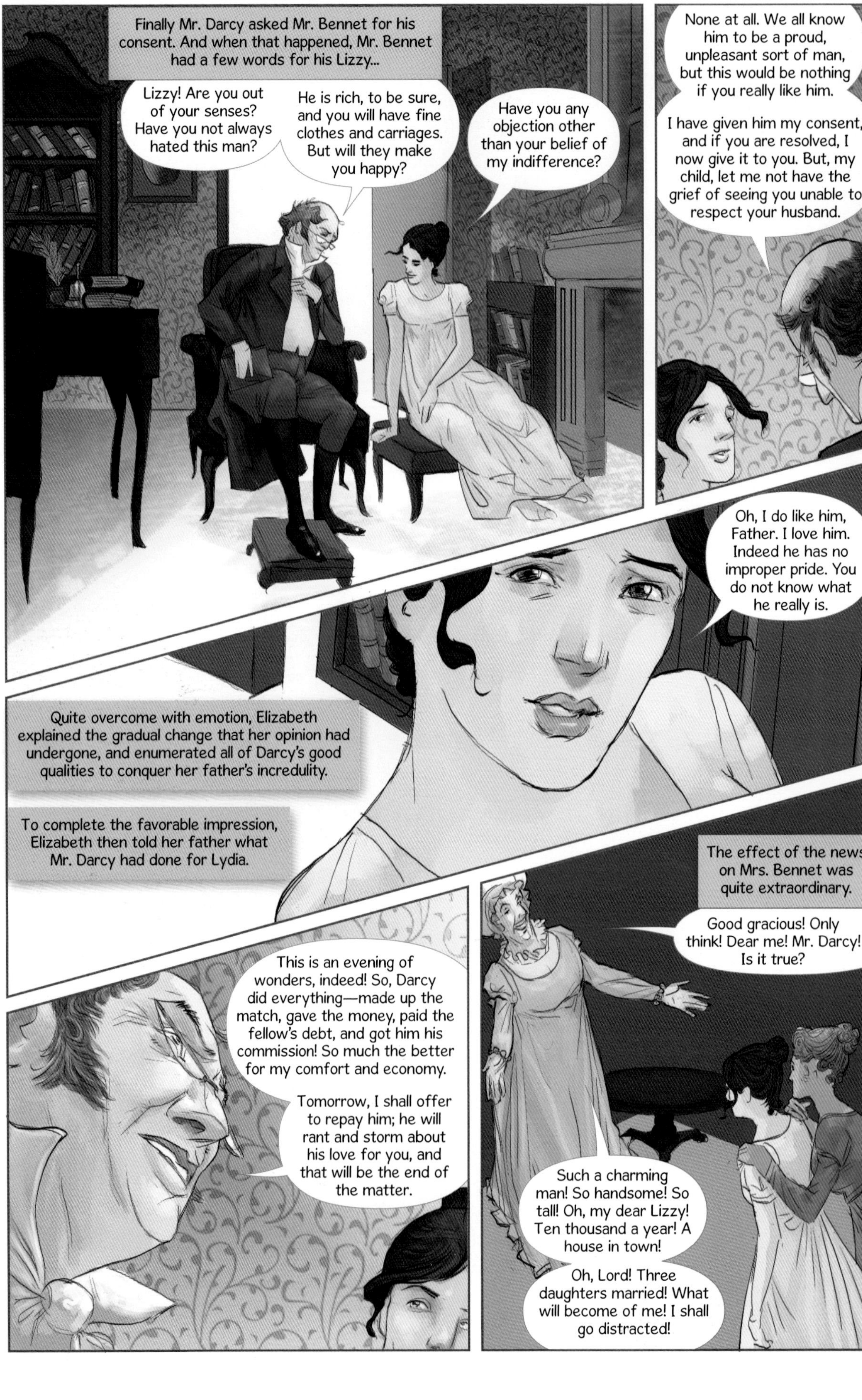
Finally Mr. Darcy asked Mr. Bennet for his consent. And when that happened, Mr. Bennet had a few words for his Lizzy...
Lizzy! Are you out of your senses? Have you not always hated this man?
He is rich, to be sure, and you will have fine clothes and carriages. But will they make you happy?
Have you any objection other than your belief of my indifference?
None at all. We all know him to be a proud, unpleasant sort of man, but this would be nothing if you really like him.
I have given him my consent, and if you are resolved, I now give it to you. But, my child, let me not have the grief of seeing you unable to respect your husband.
Oh, I do like him, Father. I love him. Indeed he has no improper pride. You do not know what he really is.
Quite overcome with emotion, Elizabeth explained the gradual change that her opinion had undergone, and enumerated all of Darcy's good qualities to conquer her father's incredulity.
To complete the favorable impression, Elizabeth then told her father what Mr. Darcy had done for Lydia.
This is an evening of wonders, indeed! So, Darcy did everything—made up the match, gave the money, paid the fellow's debt, and got him his commission! So much the better for my comfort and economy.
Tomorrow, I shall offer to repay him; he will rant and storm about his love for you, and that will be the end of the matter.
The effect of the news on Mrs. Bennet was quite extraordinary.
Good gracious! Only think! Dear me! Mr. Darcy! Is it true?
Such a charming man! So handsome! So tall! Oh, my dear Lizzy! Ten thousand a year! A house in town!
Oh, Lord! Three daughters married! What will become of me! I shall go distracted!

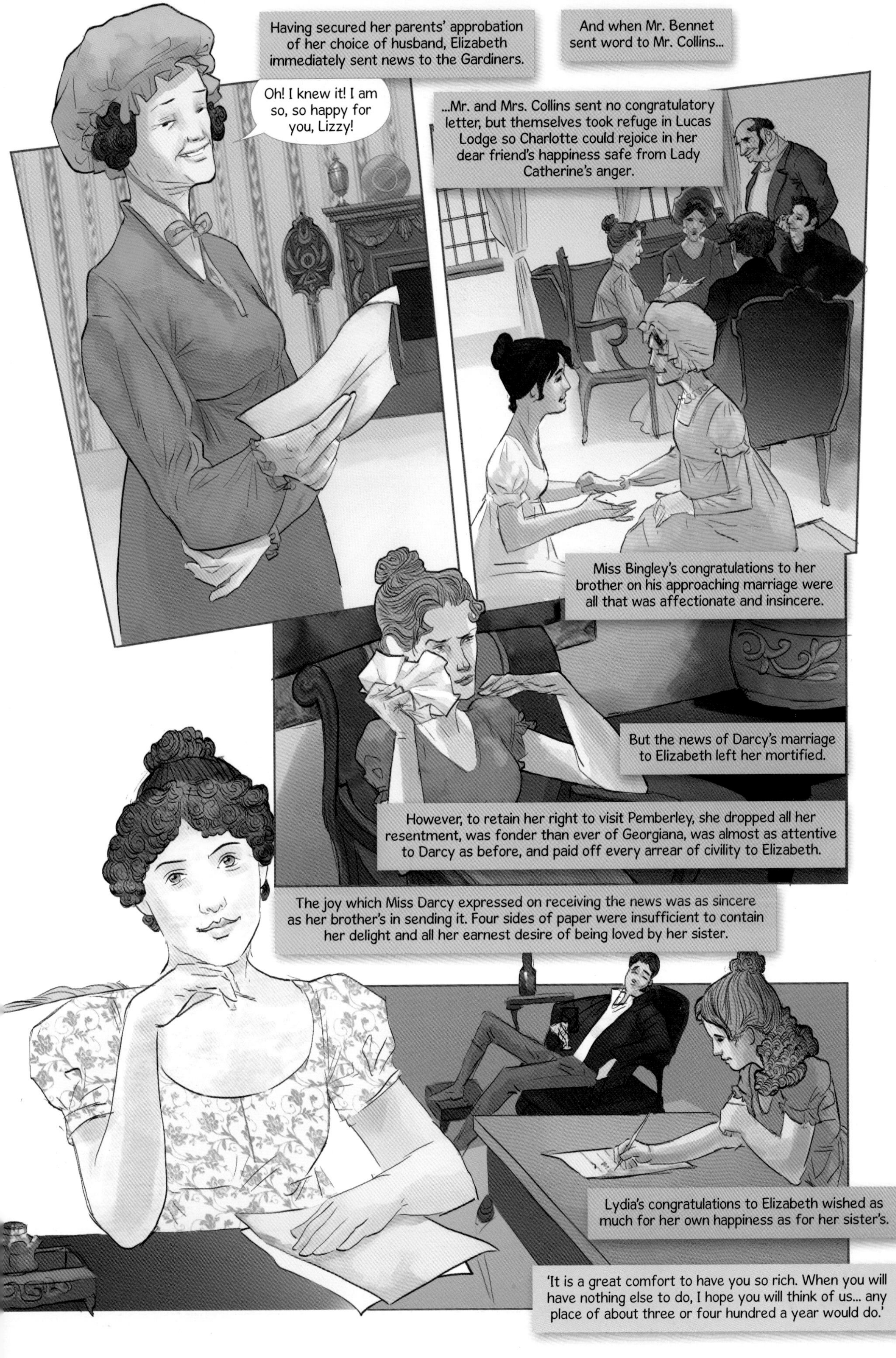
Having secured her parents' approbation of her choice of husband, Elizabeth immediately sent news to the Gardiners.
Oh! I knew it! I am so, so happy for you, Lizzy!
And when Mr. Bennet sent word to Mr. Collins...
...Mr. and Mrs. Collins sent no congratulatory letter, but themselves took refuge in Lucas Lodge so Charlotte could rejoice in her dear friend's happiness safe from Lady Catherine's anger.
Miss Bingley's congratulations to her brother on his approaching marriage were all that was affectionate and insincere.
But the news of Darcy's marriage to Elizabeth left her mortified.
However, to retain her right to visit Pemberley, she dropped all her resentment, was fonder than ever of Georgiana, was almost as attentive to Darcy as before, and paid off every arrear of civility to Elizabeth.
The joy which Miss Darcy expressed on receiving the news was as sincere as her brother's in sending it. Four sides of paper were insufficient to contain her delight and all her earnest desire of being loved by her sister.
Lydia's congratulations to Elizabeth wished as much for her own happiness as for her sister's.
'It is a great comfort to have you so rich. When you will have nothing else to do, I hope you will think of us... any place of about three or four hundred a year would do.'

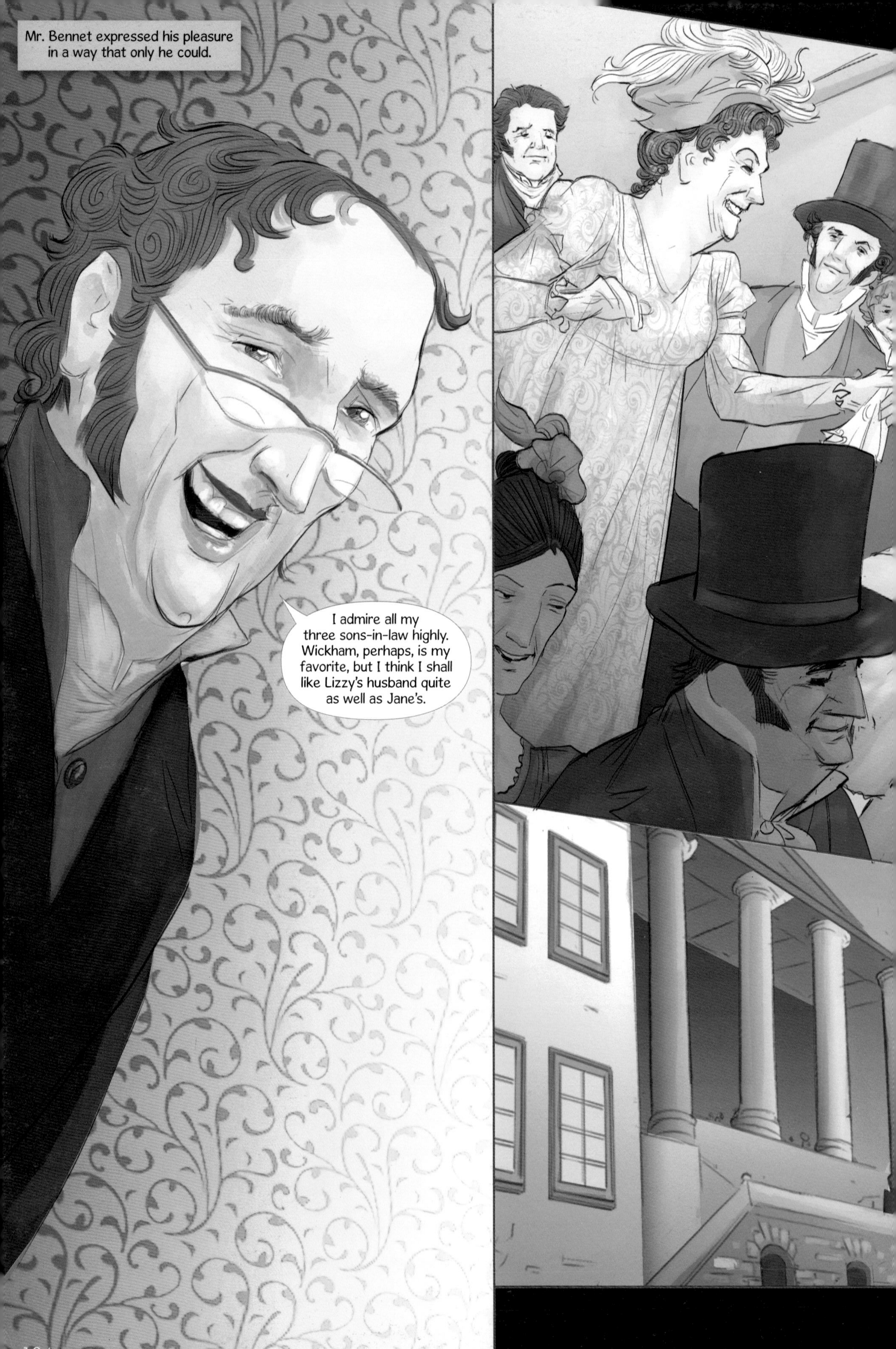

Mr. Bennet expressed his pleasure in a way that only he could.
I admire all my three sons-in-law highly. Wickham, perhaps, is my favorite, but I think I shall like Lizzy's husband quite as well as Jane's.

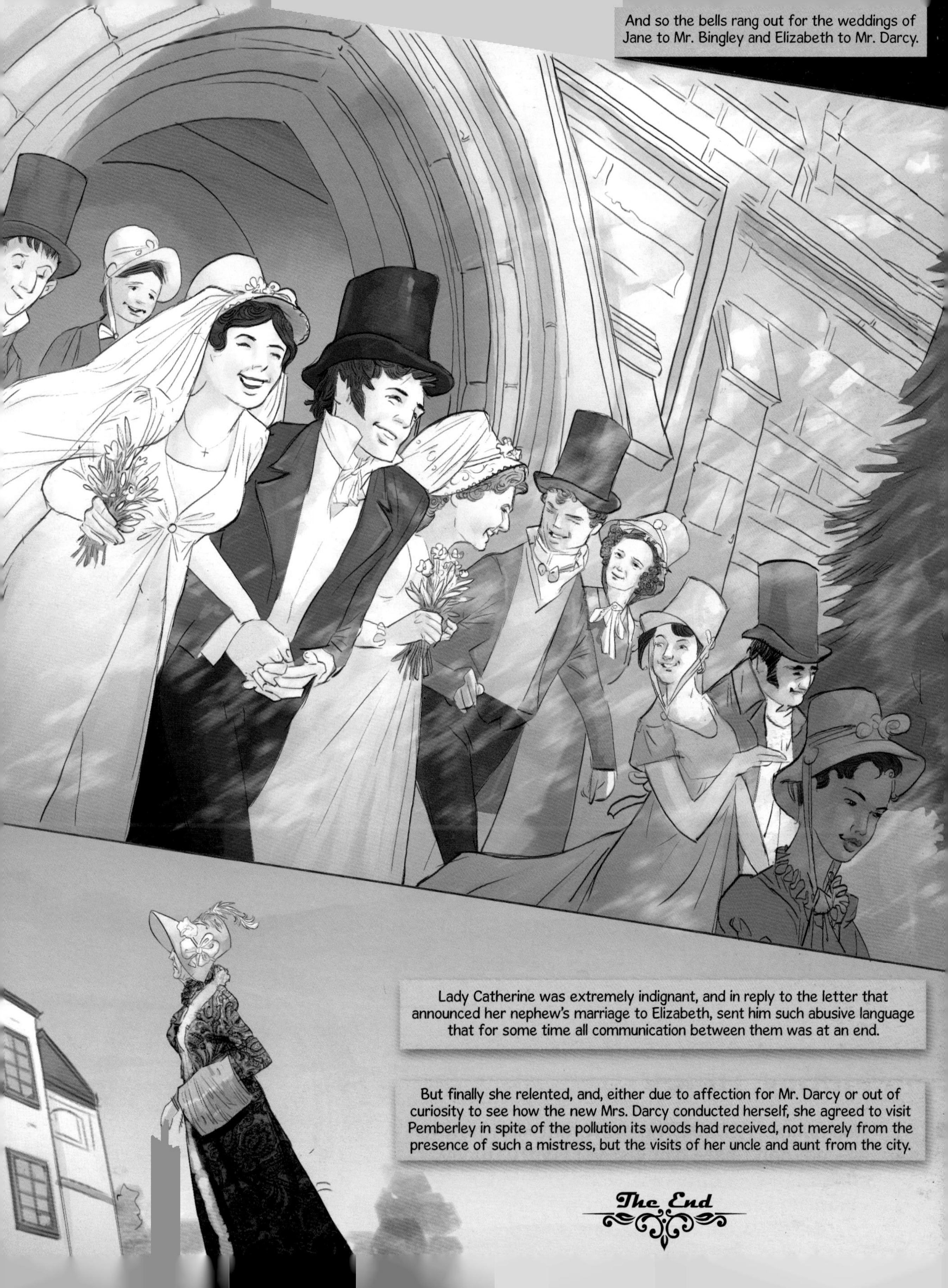

And so the bells rang out for the weddings of Jane to Mr. Bingley and Elizabeth to Mr. Darcy.
Lady Catherine was extremely indignant, and in reply to the letter that announced her nephew's marriage to Elizabeth, sent him such abusive language that for some time all communication between them was at an end.
But finally she relented, and, either due to affection for Mr. Darcy or out of curiosity to see how the new Mrs. Darcy conducted herself, she agreed to visit Pemberley in spite of the pollution its woods had received, not merely from the presence of such a mistress, but the visits of her uncle and aunt from the city.
The End

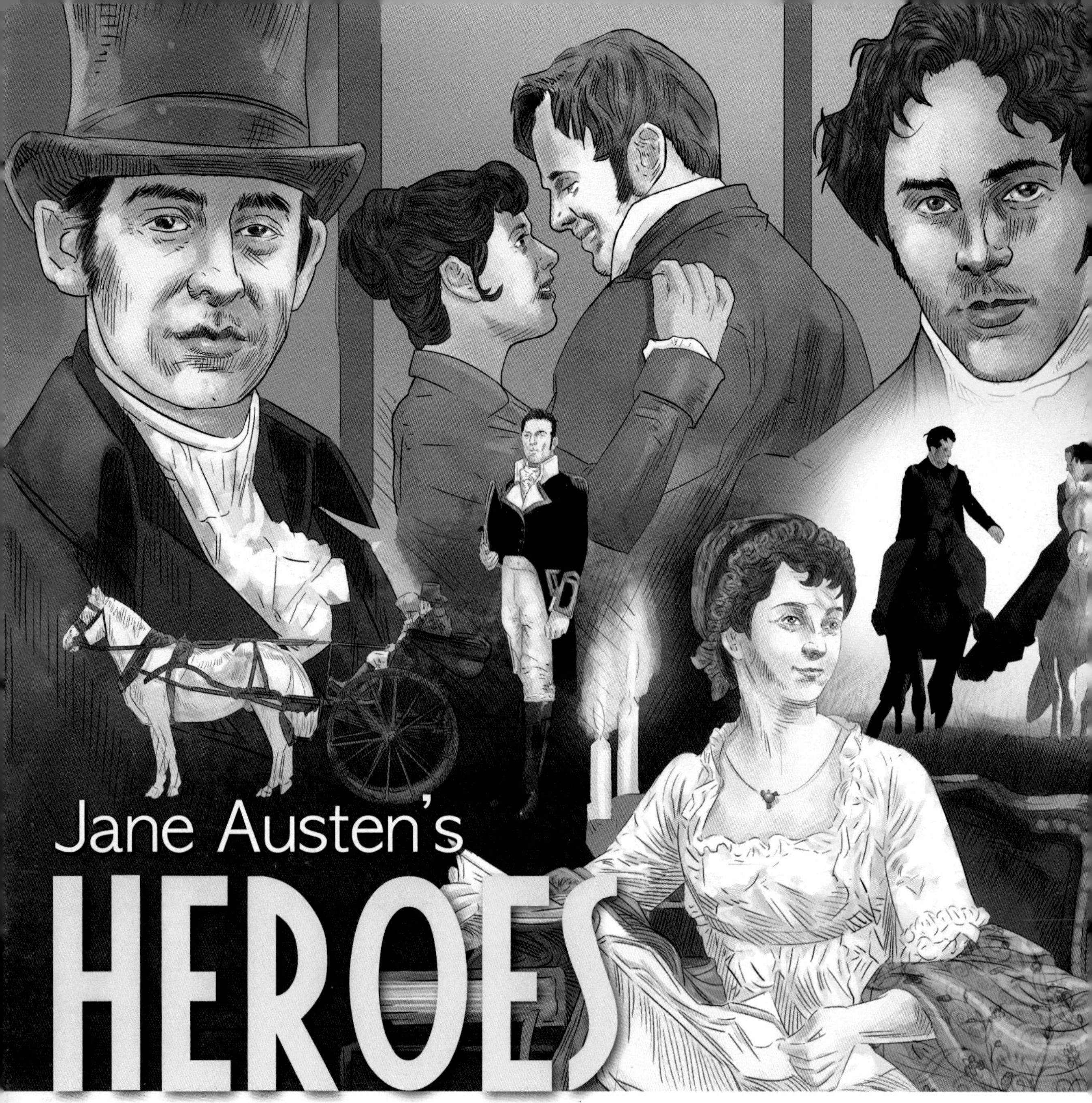

Jane Austen's HEROES

Everyone loves Jane Austen's heroines, but what makes an Austen heroine fall in love? Here's our pick of Austen's perfect men.

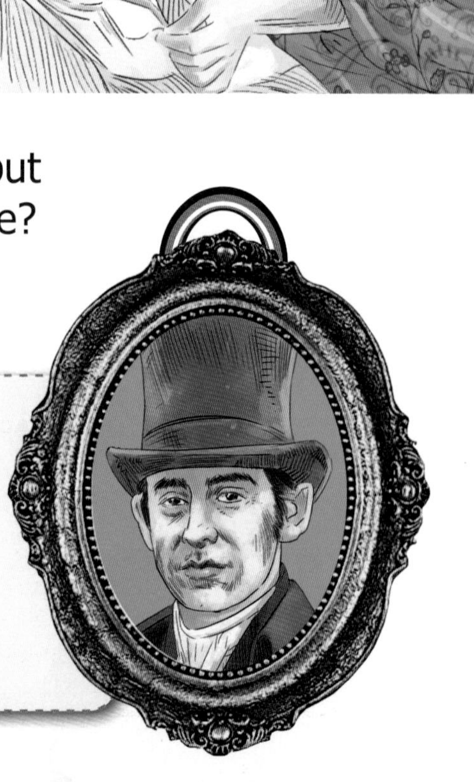

Henry Tilney

Northanger Abbey : The irreverent Mr. Know-it-all—no, don't hate him just yet. Witty, funny, and easygoing, Catherine Morland's Prince Charming is also the most entertaining, and of course most charming, of Jane's heroes.

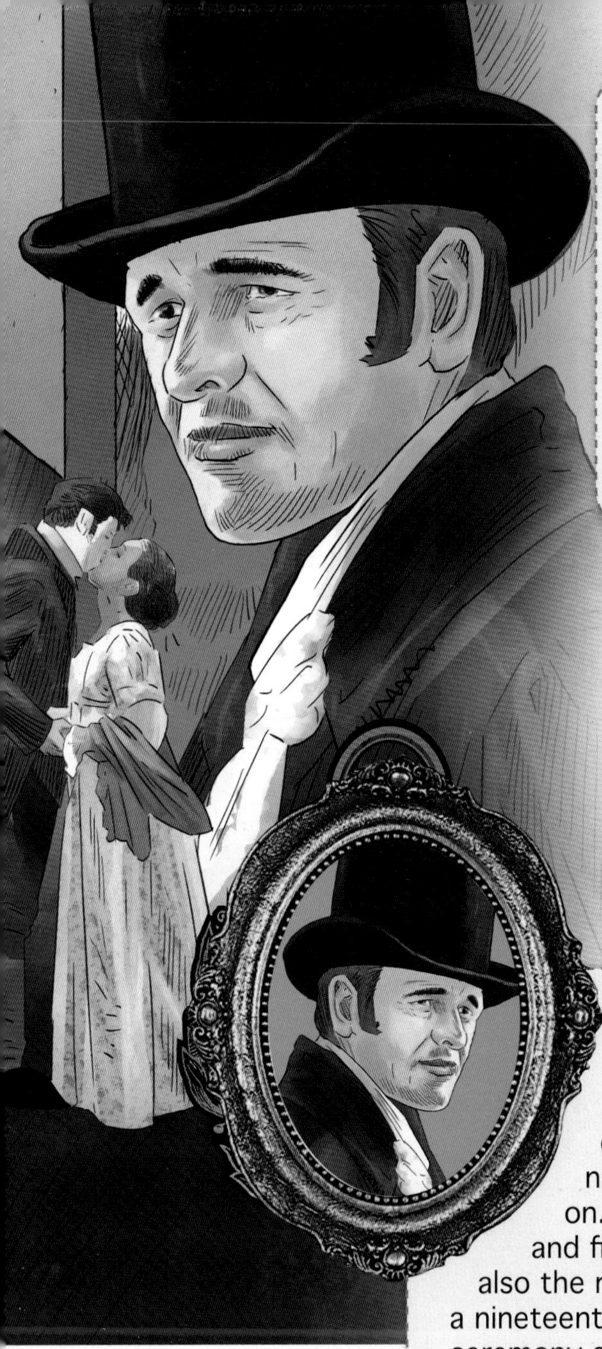

Henry Crawford

Mansfield Park : Alright, so what if he's more of a villain? Isn't he just so handsome, romantic, and fascinating? Besides, he really does love Fanny Price and is mostly good to her. A little less vanity, arrogance, and flirtation, and he would almost be a hero.

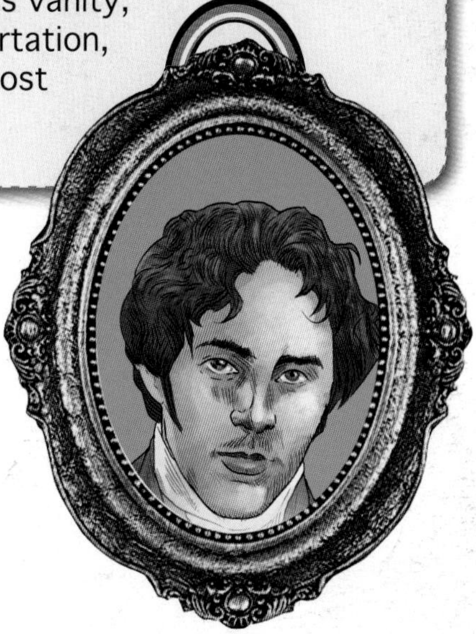

George Knightley

Emma : Rich, suave, intelligent, compassionate, generous, humorous—you name it, the list of manly virtues goes on and on. Emma Woodhouse's best friend forever and finally the love of her life, Mr. Knightley is also the most modern of Austen's heroes—Imagine, a nineteenth century landlord who has 'nothing of ceremony about him'!

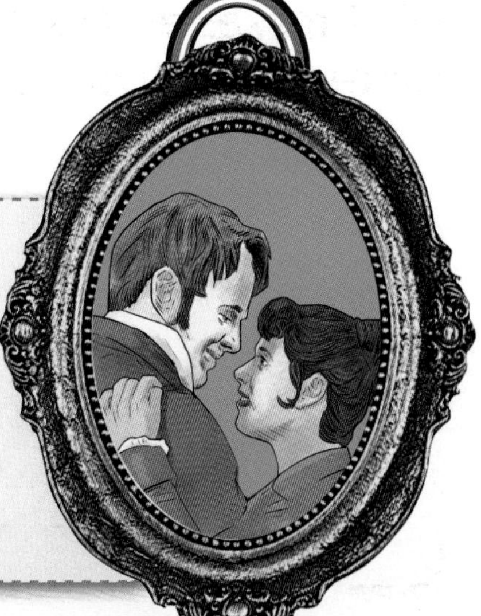

Frederick Wentworth

Persuasion : An officer and a gentleman, Captain Wentworth is brave enough to make a fortune with his sword and romantic enough to stay constant to Anne Elliot through nine long years of separation.

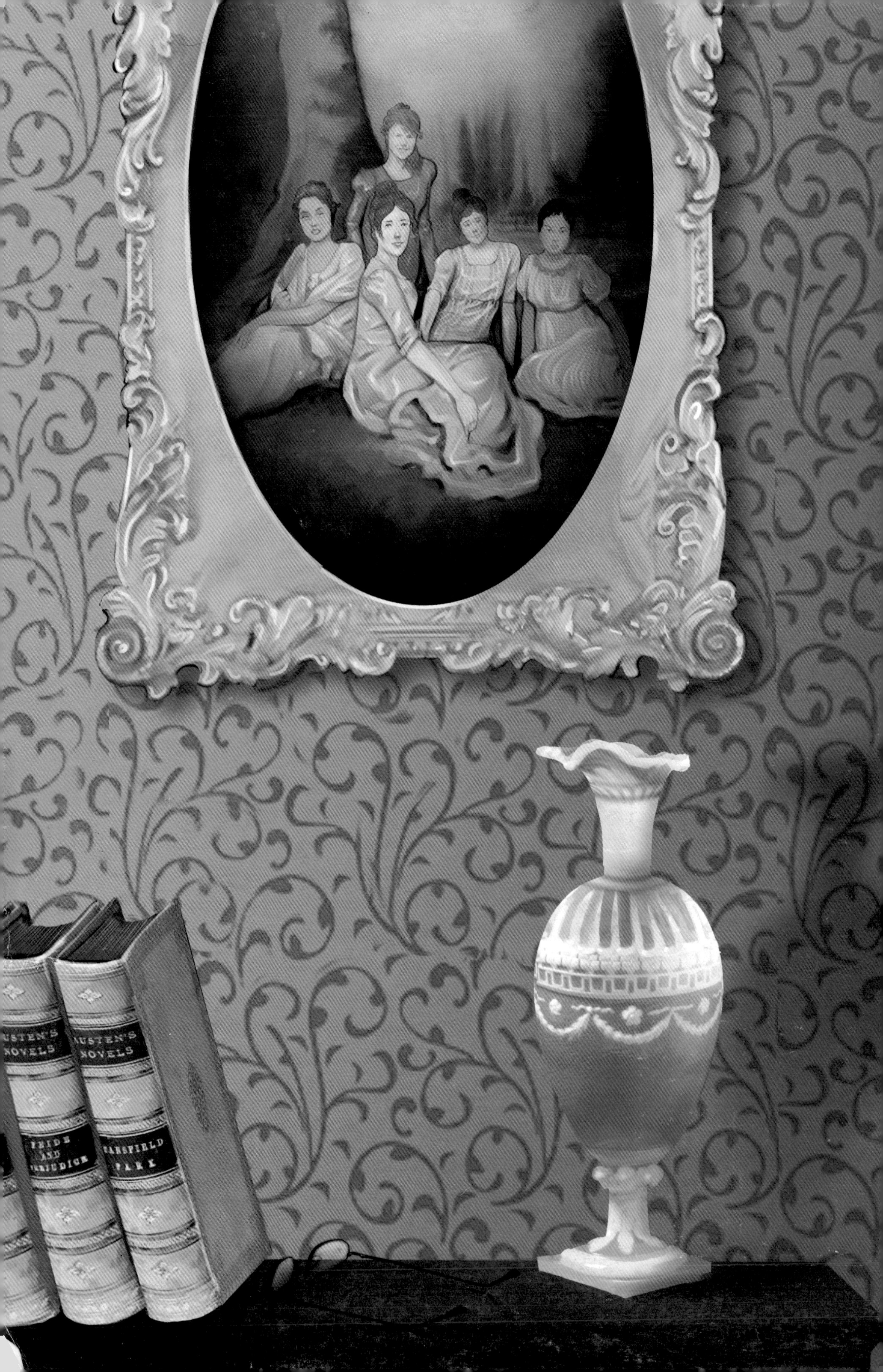
AUSTEN'S
NOVELS
ANSFIELD
PARK

HEDGEHOG'S
HOME FOR
WINTER

by
ELENA ULYEVA

illustrated by
DARIA PARKHAEVA

Most hedgehogs sleep through the winter, but this one is still awake! He's very curious and wants to learn all about **nature**.

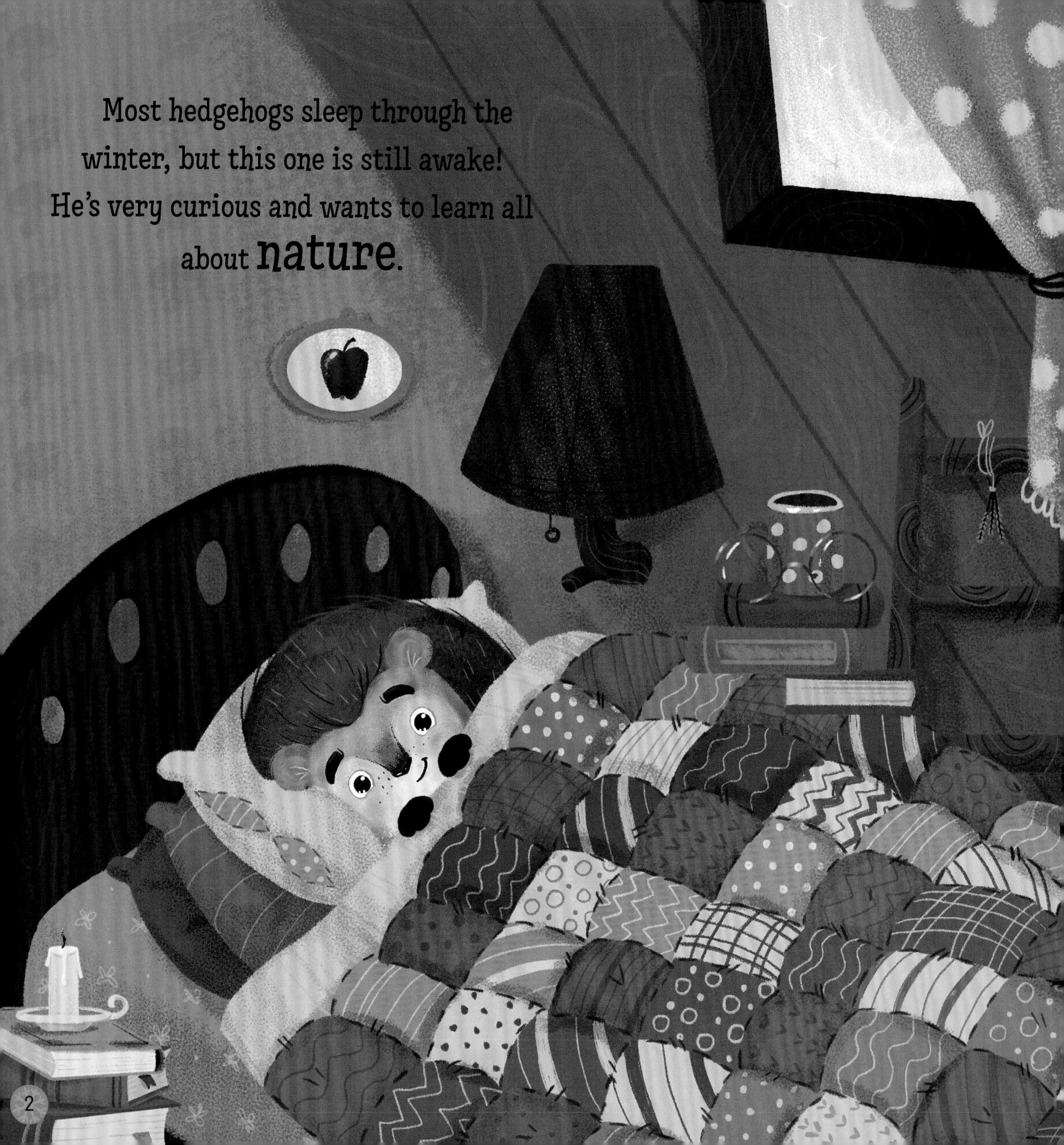

One **chilly** morning, Hedgehog looked out his window.

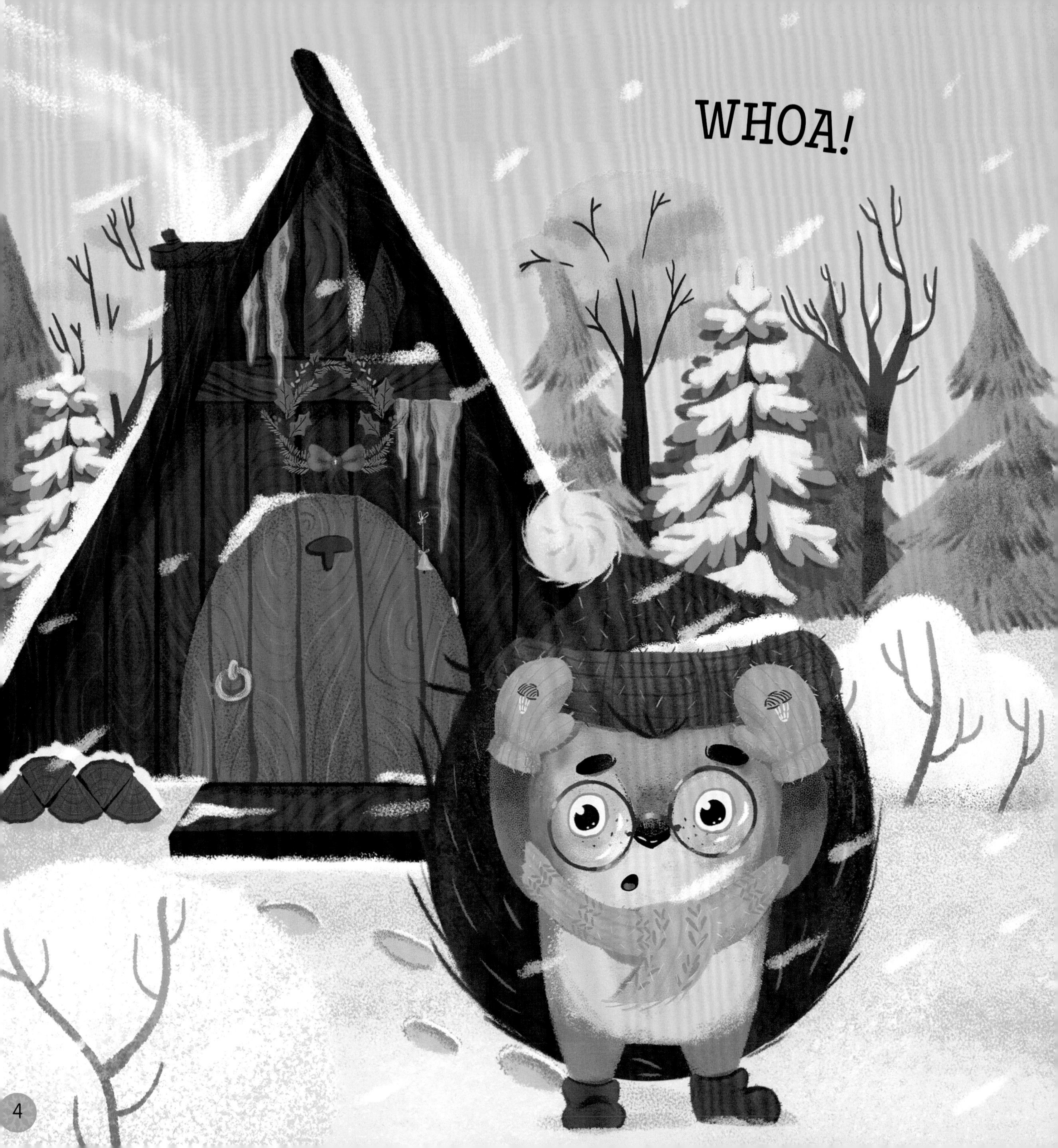
WHOA!

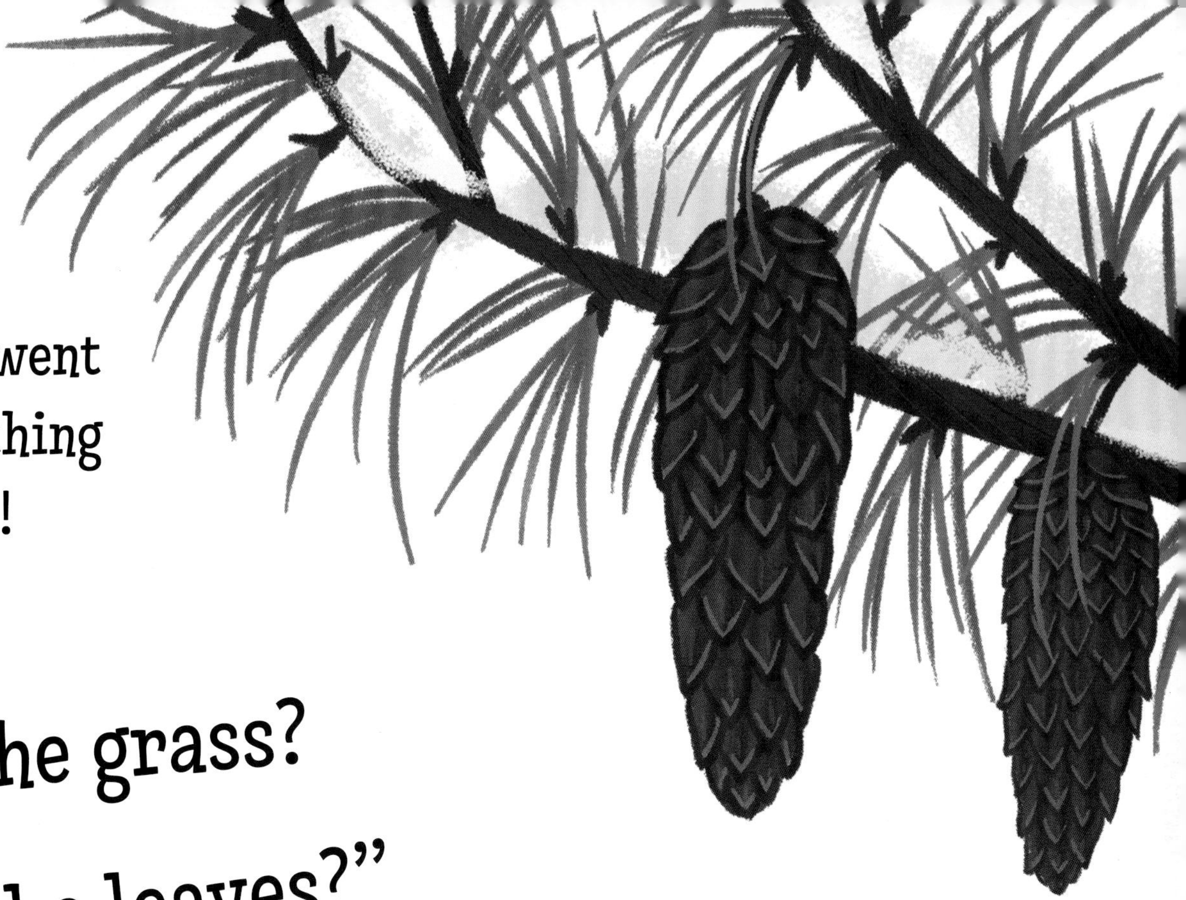

He got dressed and went outside—but everything looked different!

"Where's the grass? And the leaves?" he exclaimed.

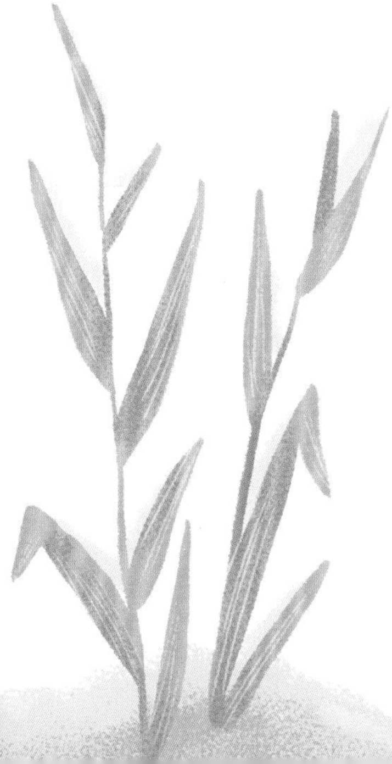

"And it's not **raining** anymore—it's snowing!"

Suddenly, a **fierce** wind blew, bringing with it cold air and **MORE** snow!

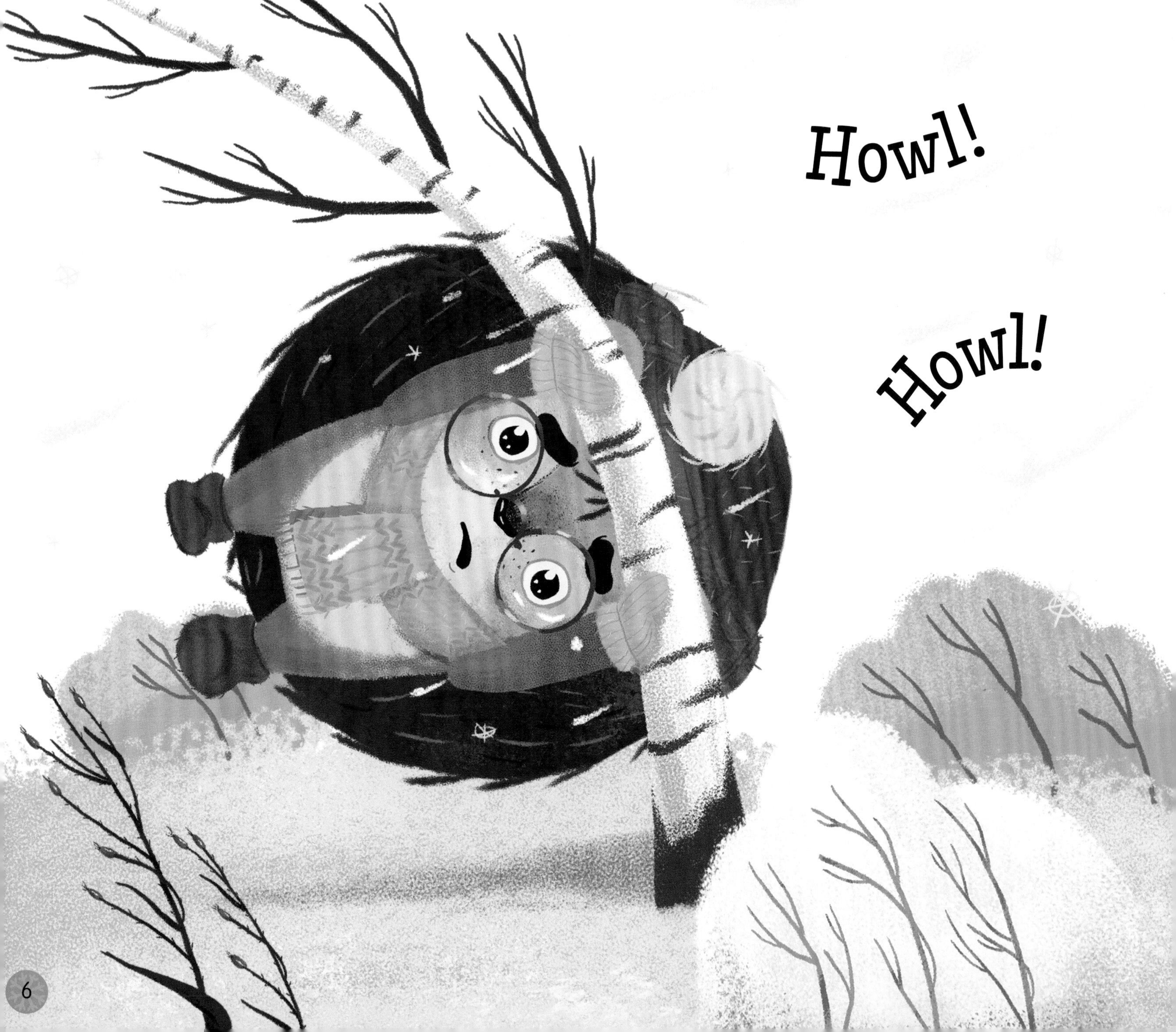
Howl!
Howl!

Hedgehog shivered.

"The other animals must be cold, too," he said.

"I'll bet they need my help!"

Brrr!

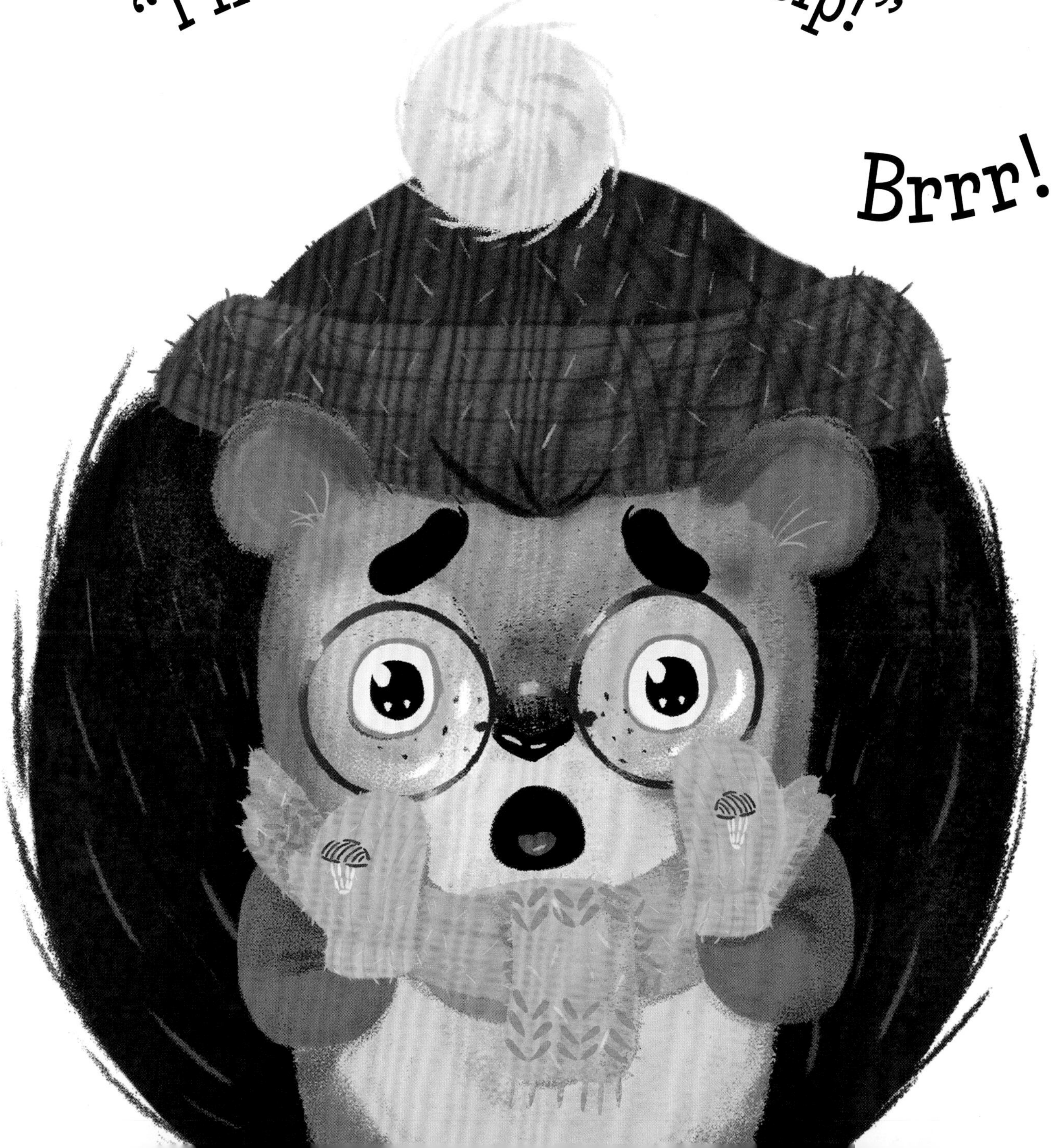

Hedgehog began to call to the insects.

"Butterflies?
Bumblebees?
Grasshoppers?
Ladybugs?'

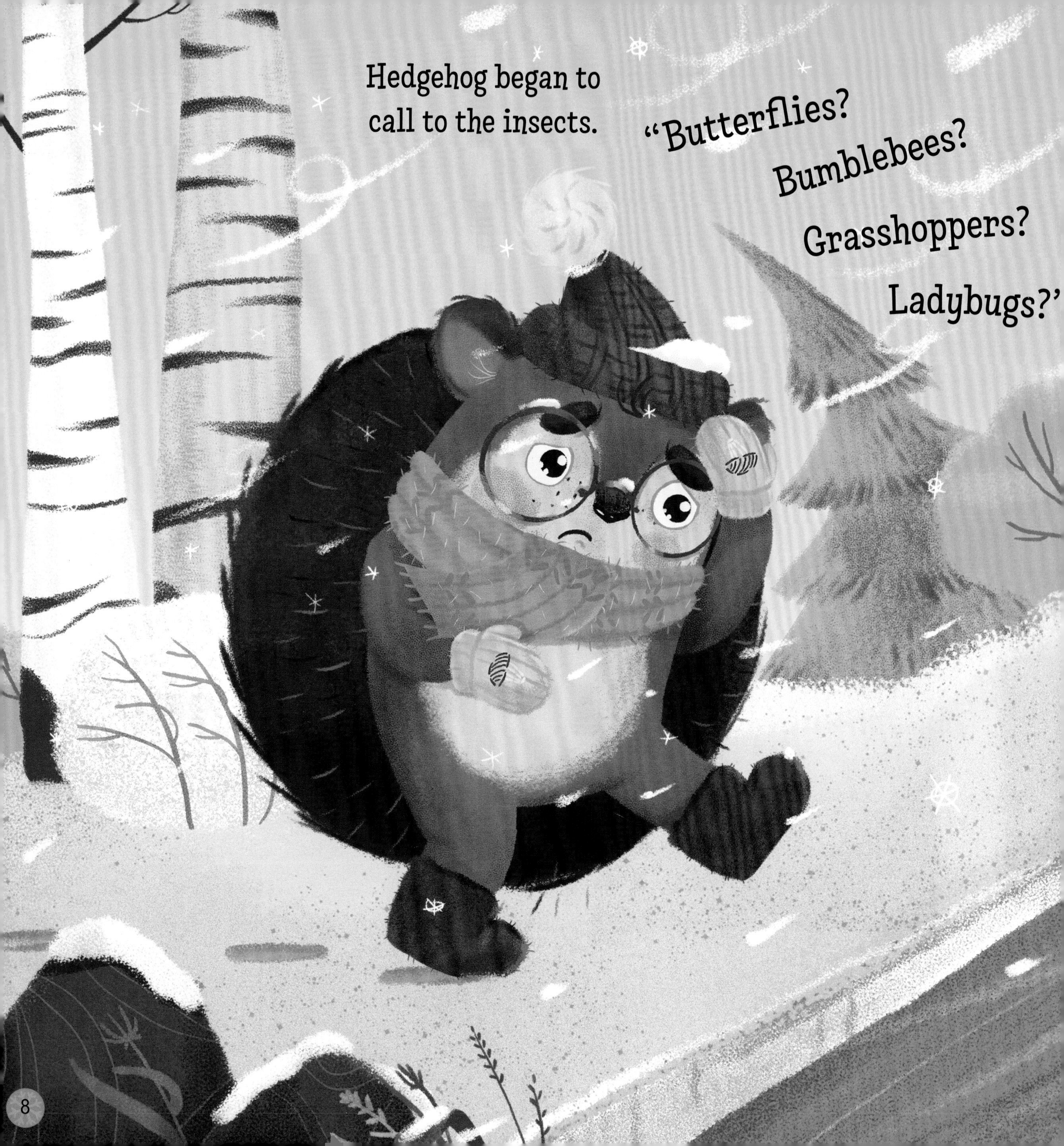

But then he saw an old log and peeked inside. His friends were covered up in leaves, sound asleep!

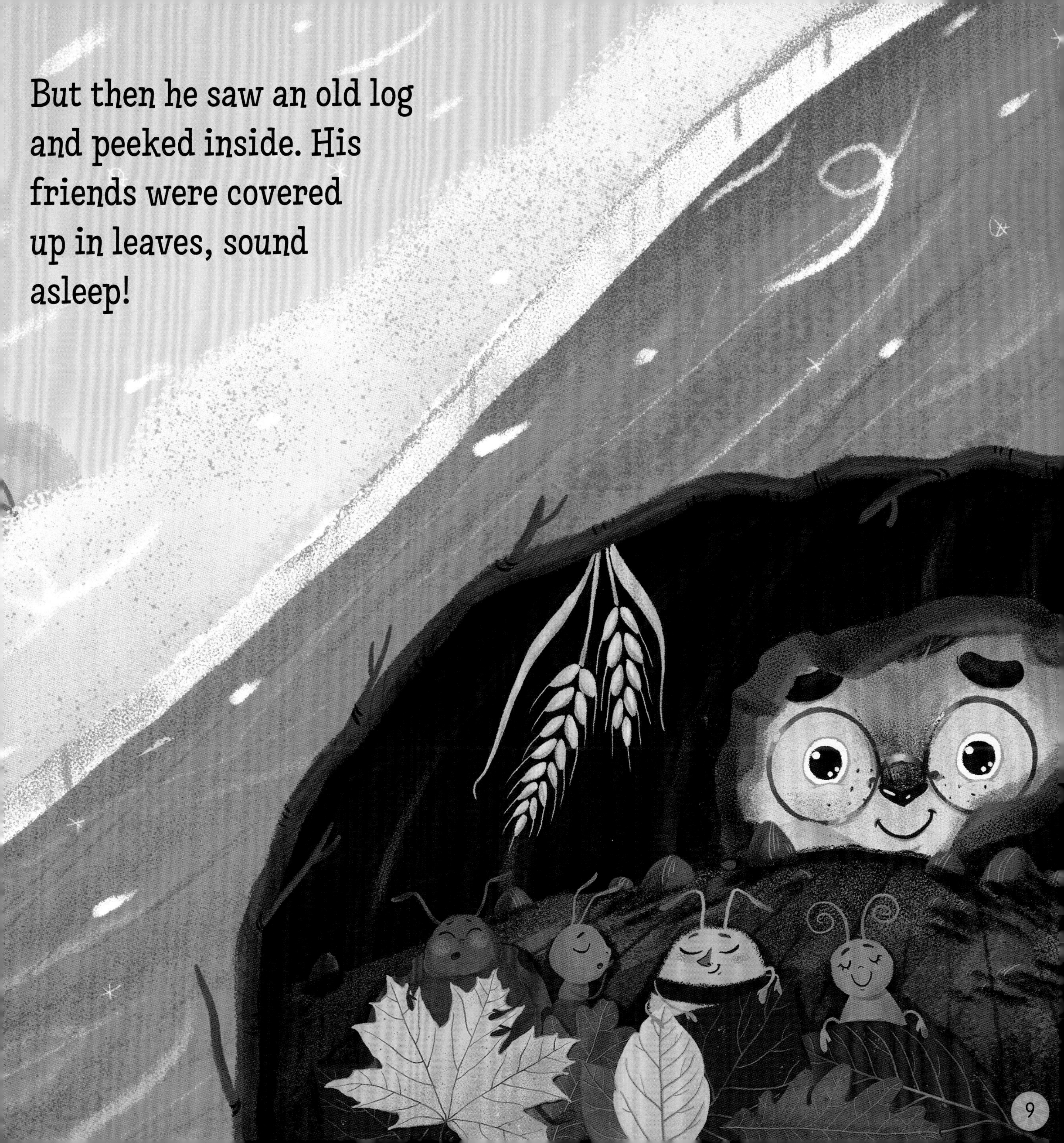

Hedgehog went down to the river.
But he didn't see water—he saw ice!

"Hello down there!" he called.
"Are you okay in the ice?"

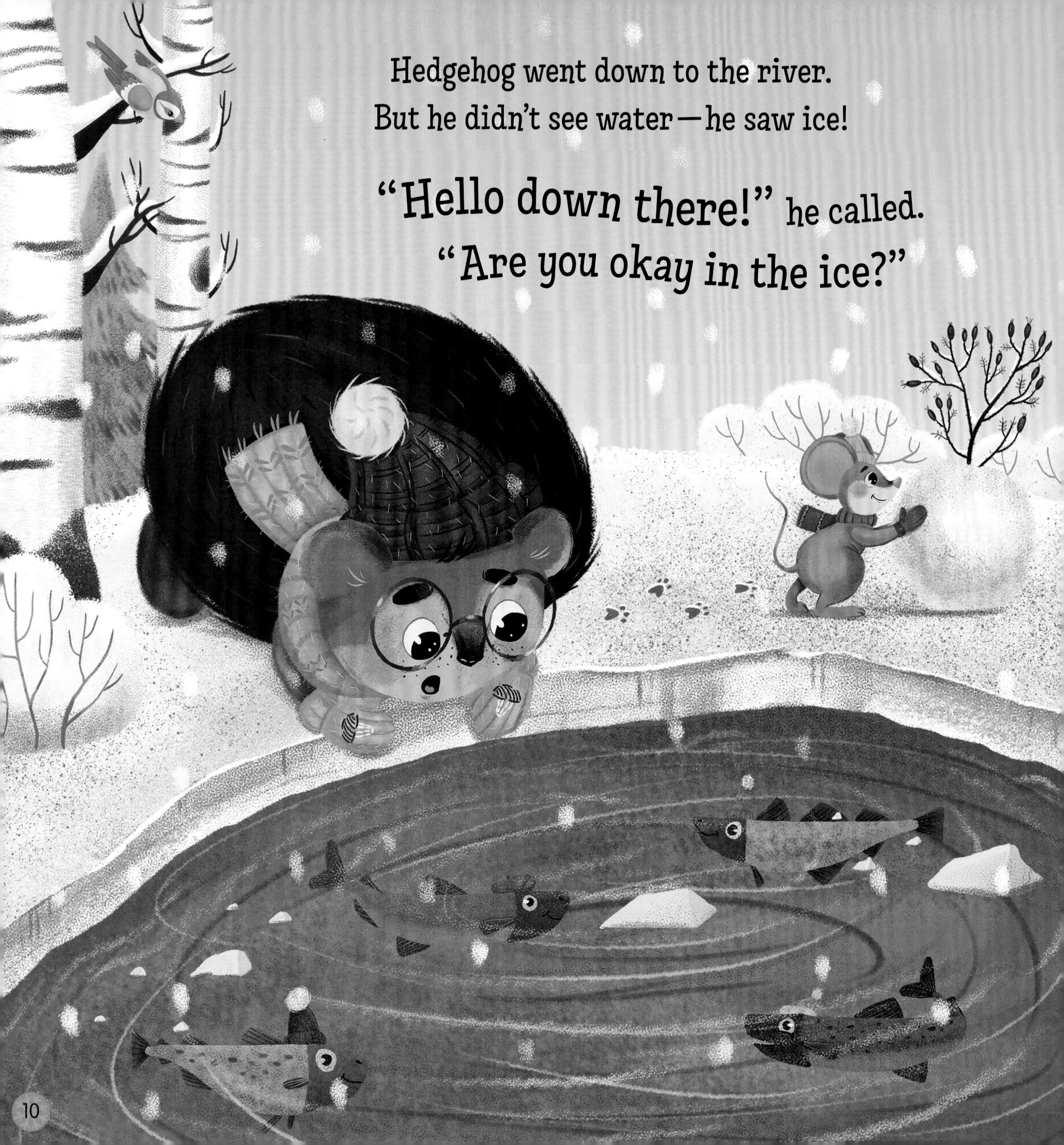

“We’re okay, Hedgehog,”

replied a crayfish.

“We’re snuggled up at the bottom of the river.”

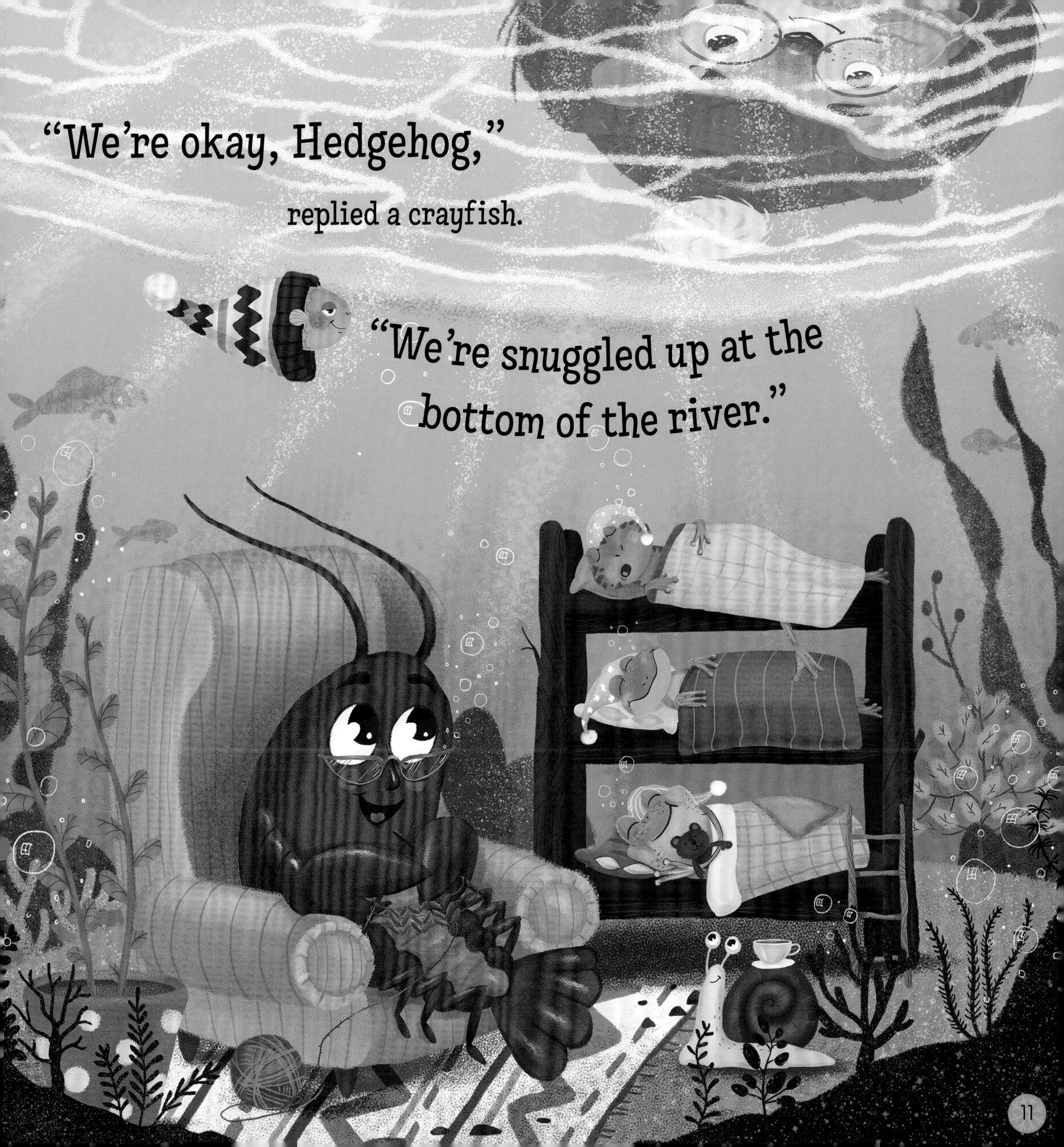

Hedgehog was leaving the river
when he heard noises coming
from underground.

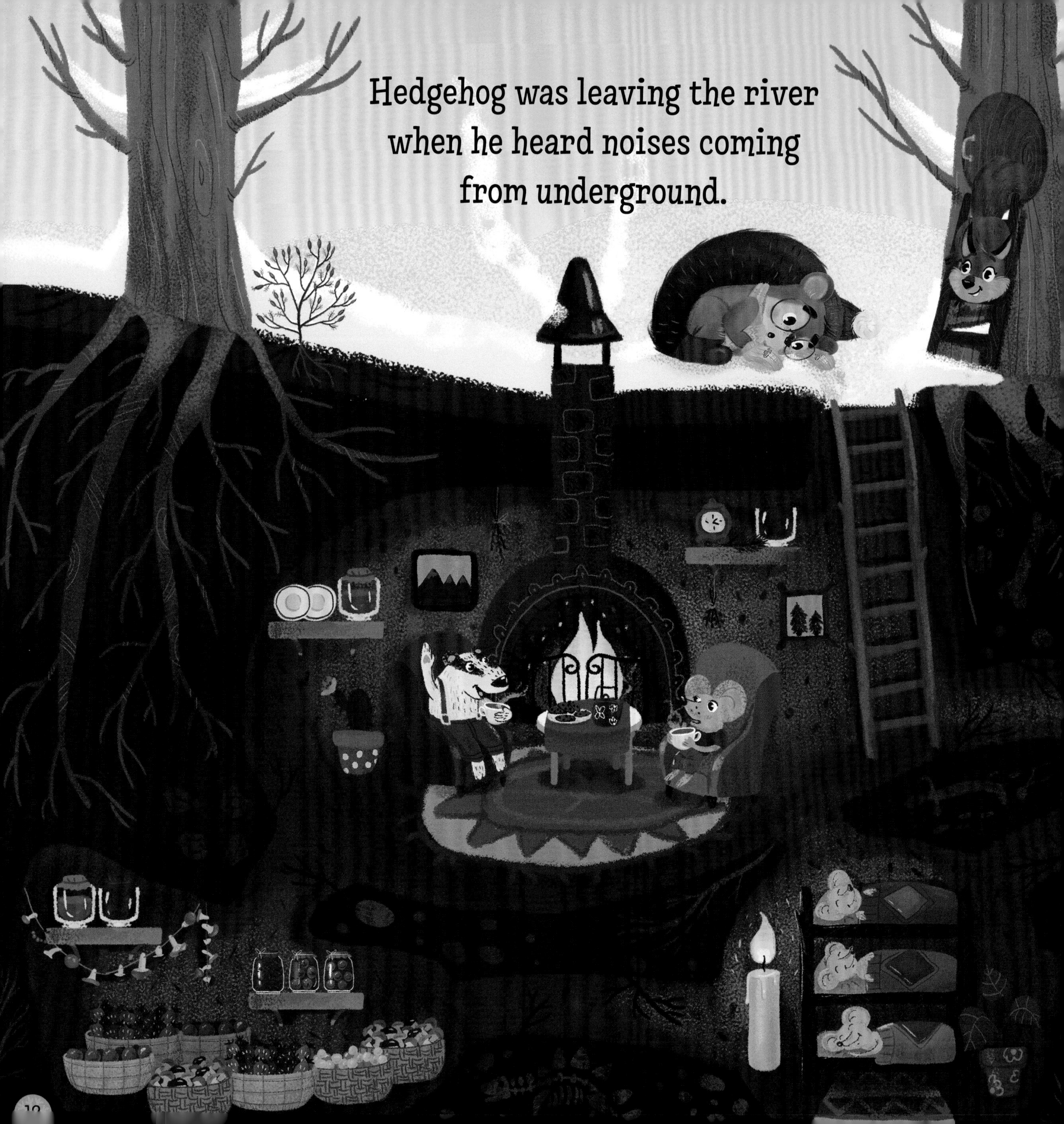

"Mice? Chipmunks? Moles?
Are you okay?" he called.

"Hi, Hedgehog!" replied a mouse. "We're having a great time! Our burrows are warm, and there's plenty of food."

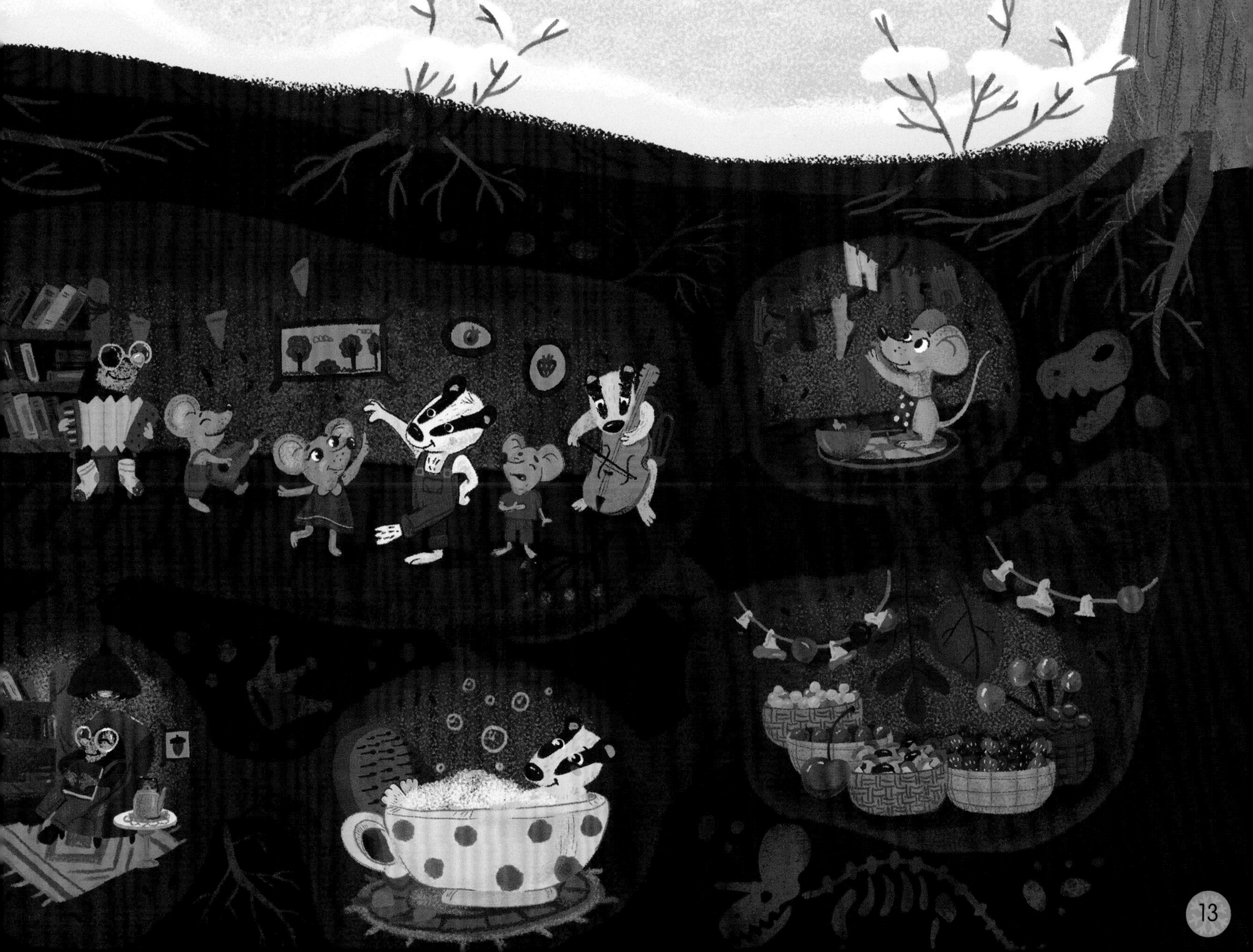

"We have a bunch of food to eat, too!"
called a squirrel from a nearby tree.

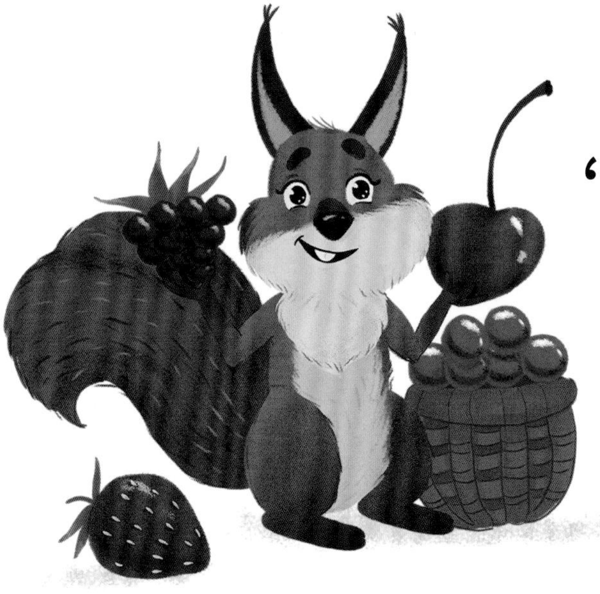

"We have berries,

mushrooms,

and nuts—

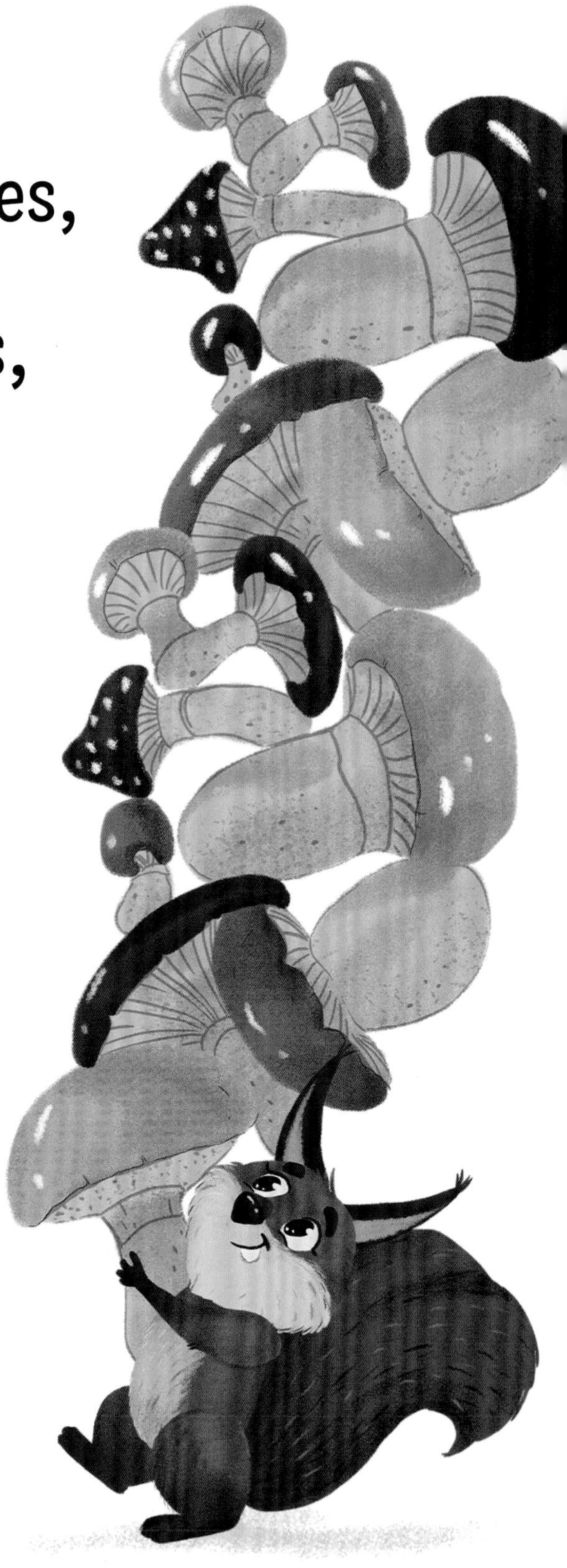

everything I collected during the fall."

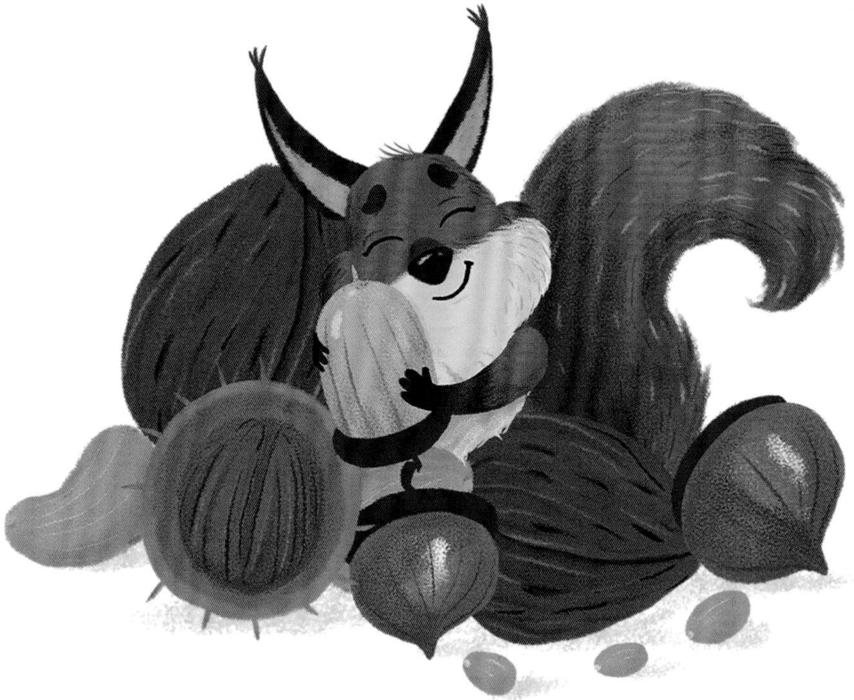

"Everyone seems
so **happy!**"
Hedgehog said.

"I'm going to see how the rest
of my friends are doing."

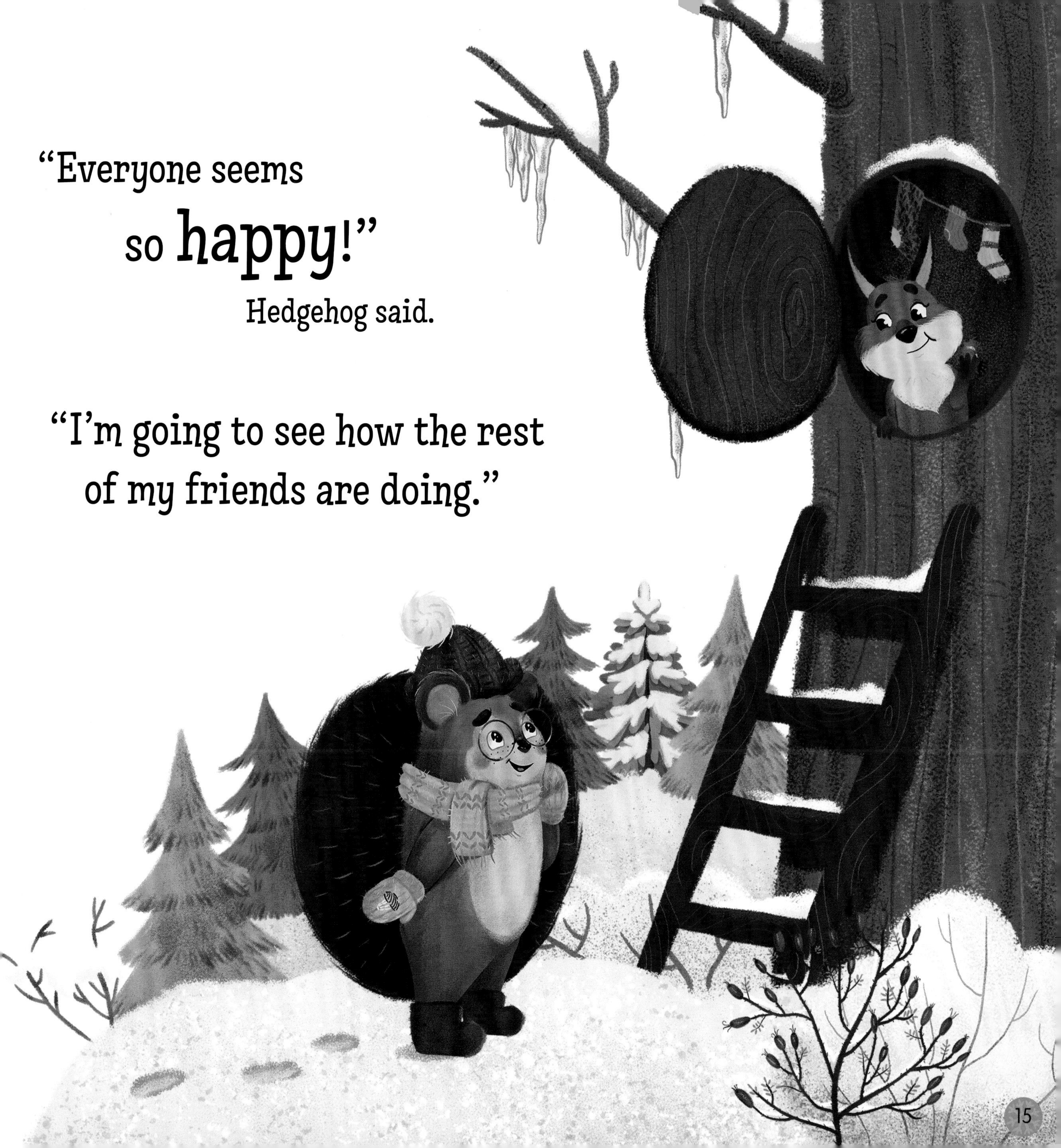

He saw Wolf and Fox in a clearing.

"Fox! Wolf! Are you okay in all of this snow?" he asked.

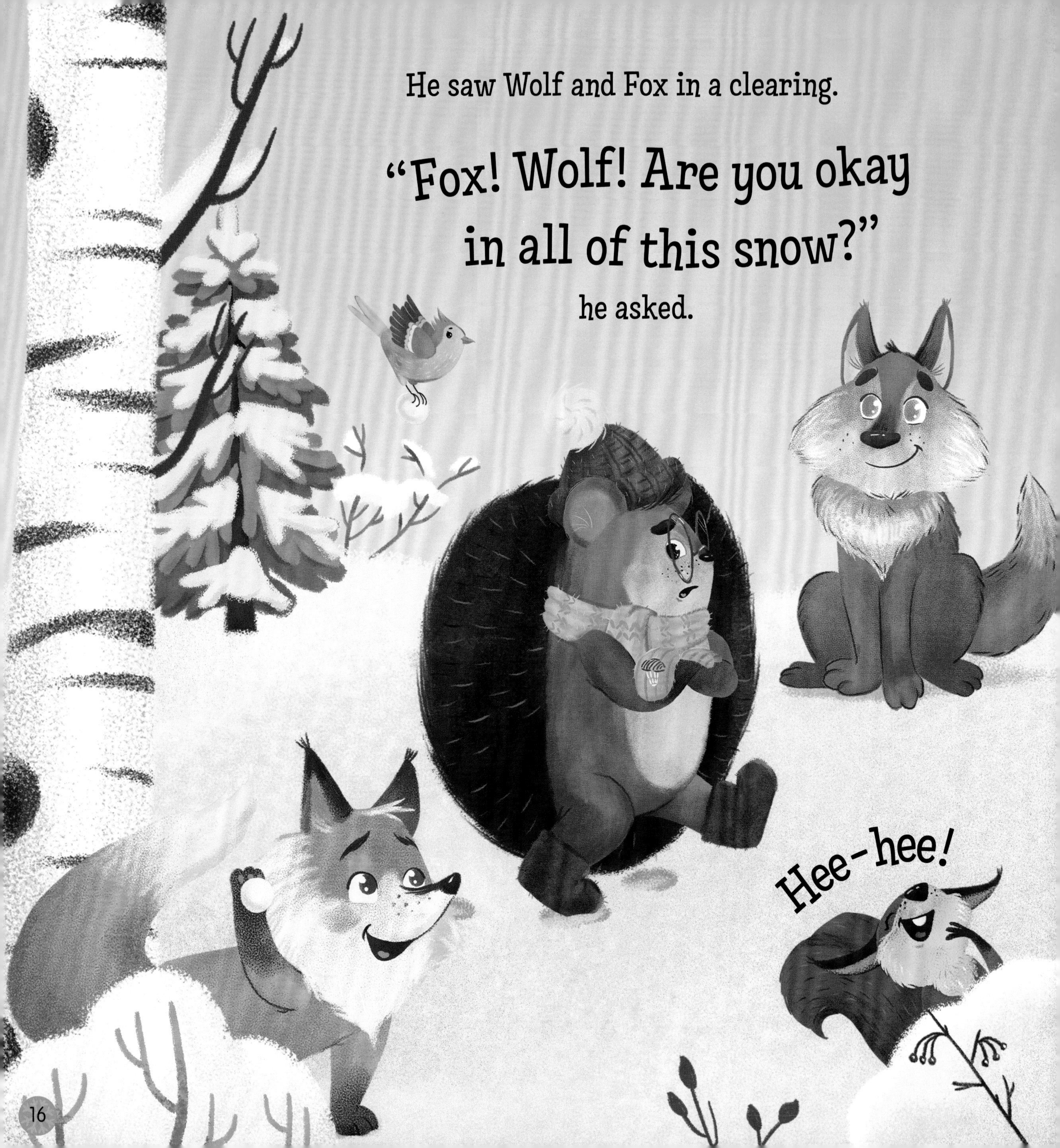
Hee-hee!

"We're fine!" Wolf replied.
"Our fur coats keep us warm."

"Play with us!" Fox called.

"I will later, Fox," Hedgehog replied.
"Right now, I need to check
on Hare."

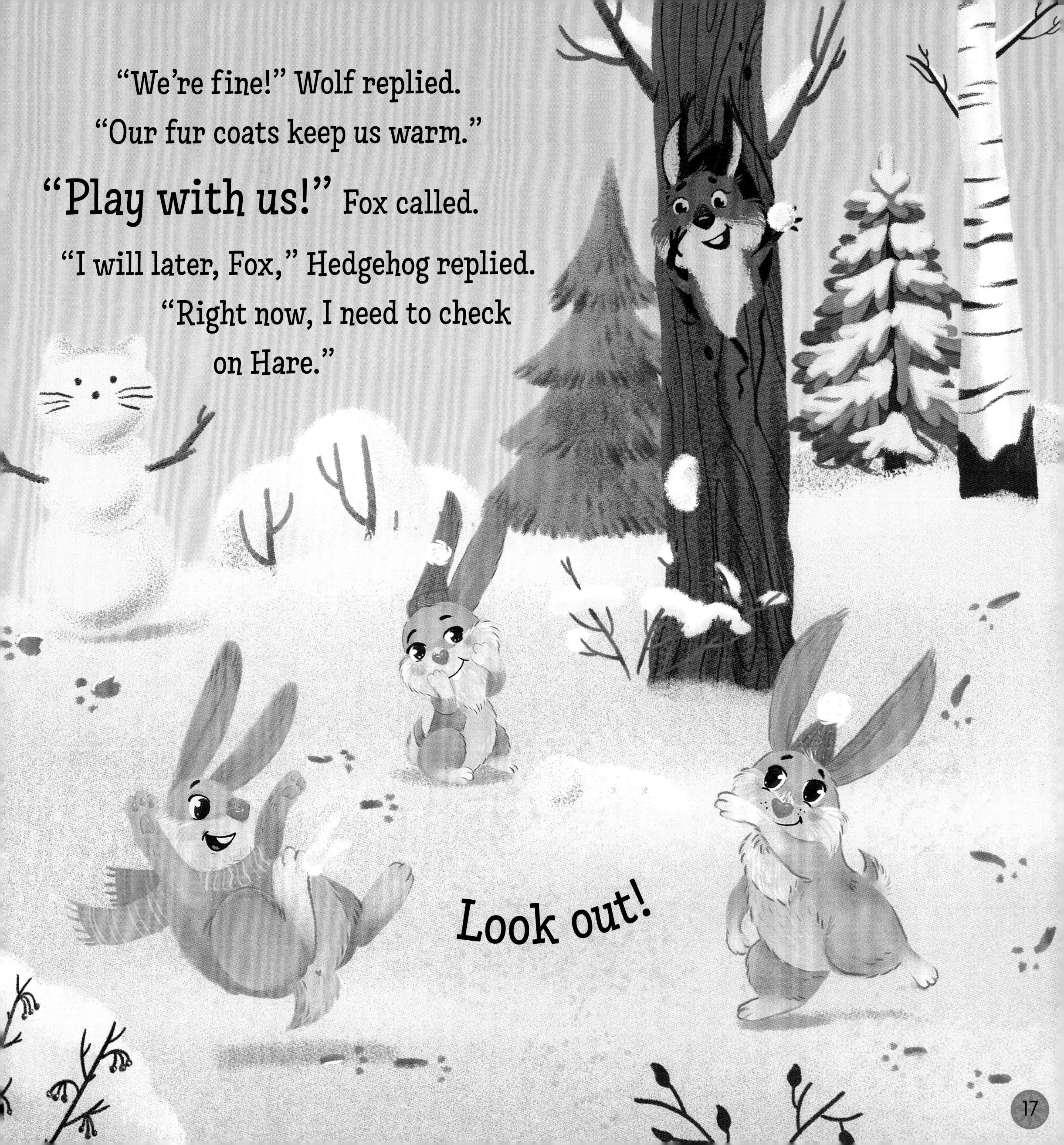

Look out!

"You look cozy in your fur coat, too, Hare," Hedgehog said.

"I am!" Hare replied.
"Just like your hat and scarf keep you warm and cozy!"

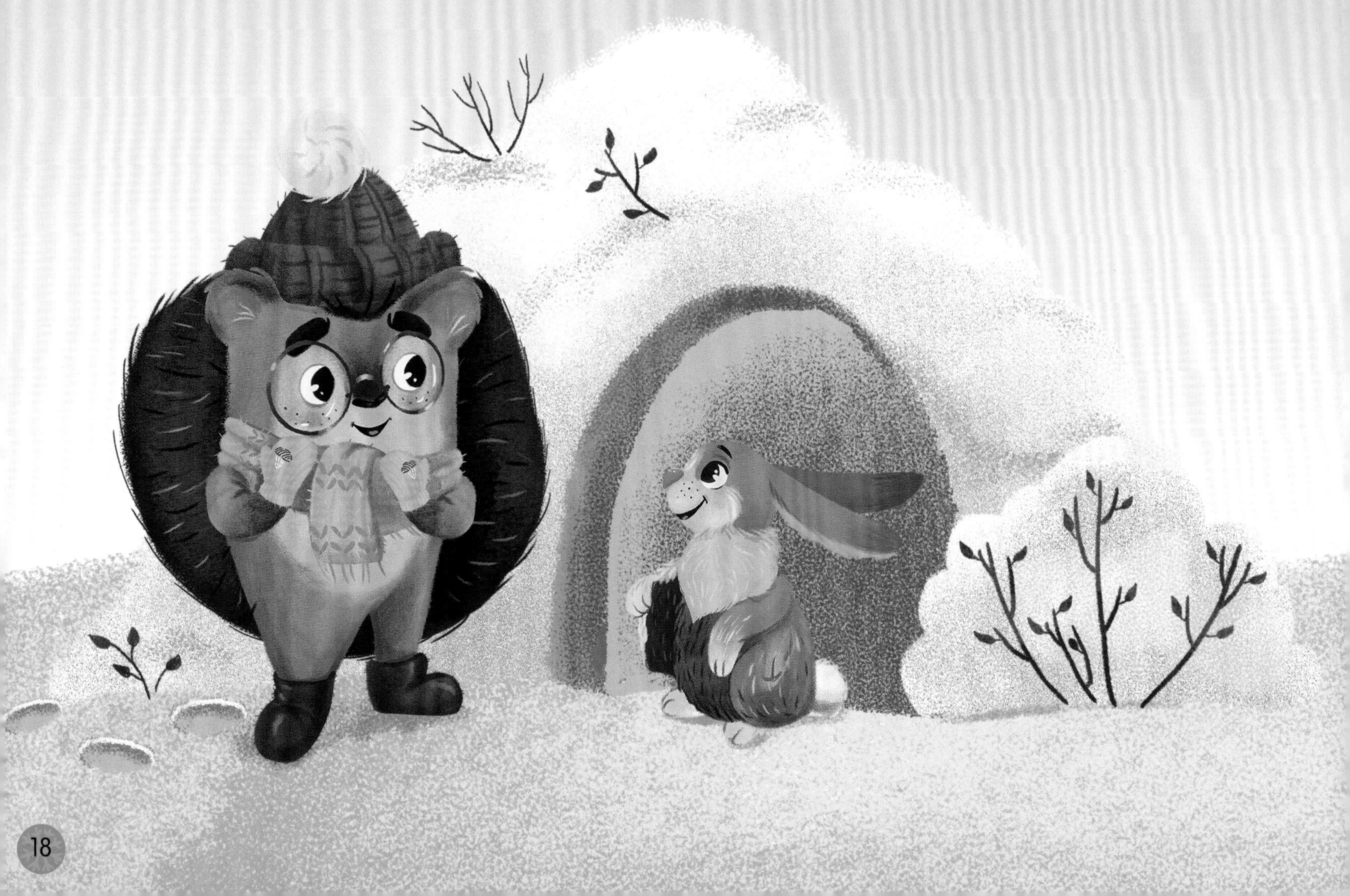

Hedgehog watched
Hare hop off into
the forest.

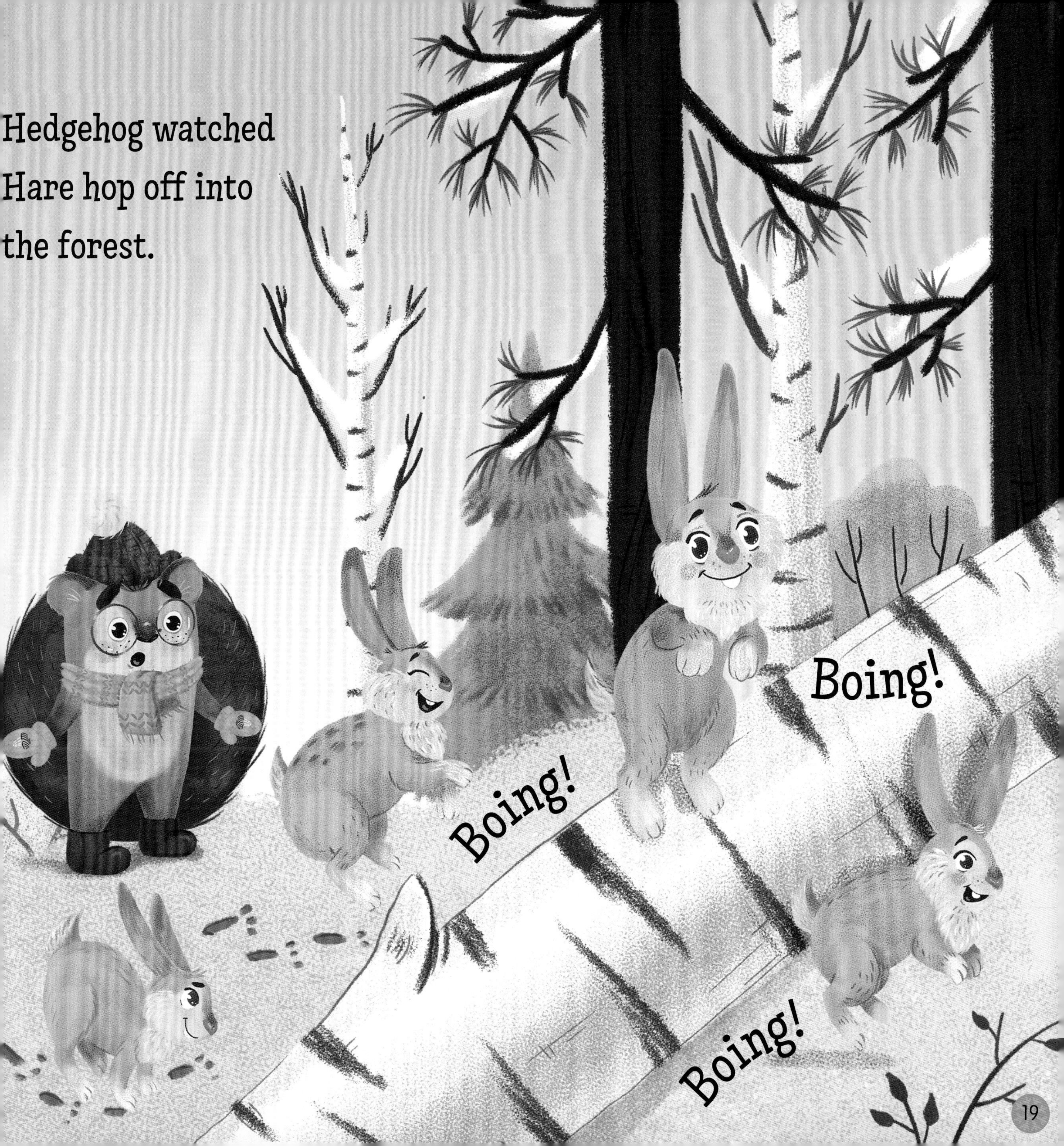
Boing!
Boing!
Boing!

After Hare left, Hedgehog thought about Bear.

"I'd better go see if she needs my help!" he said.

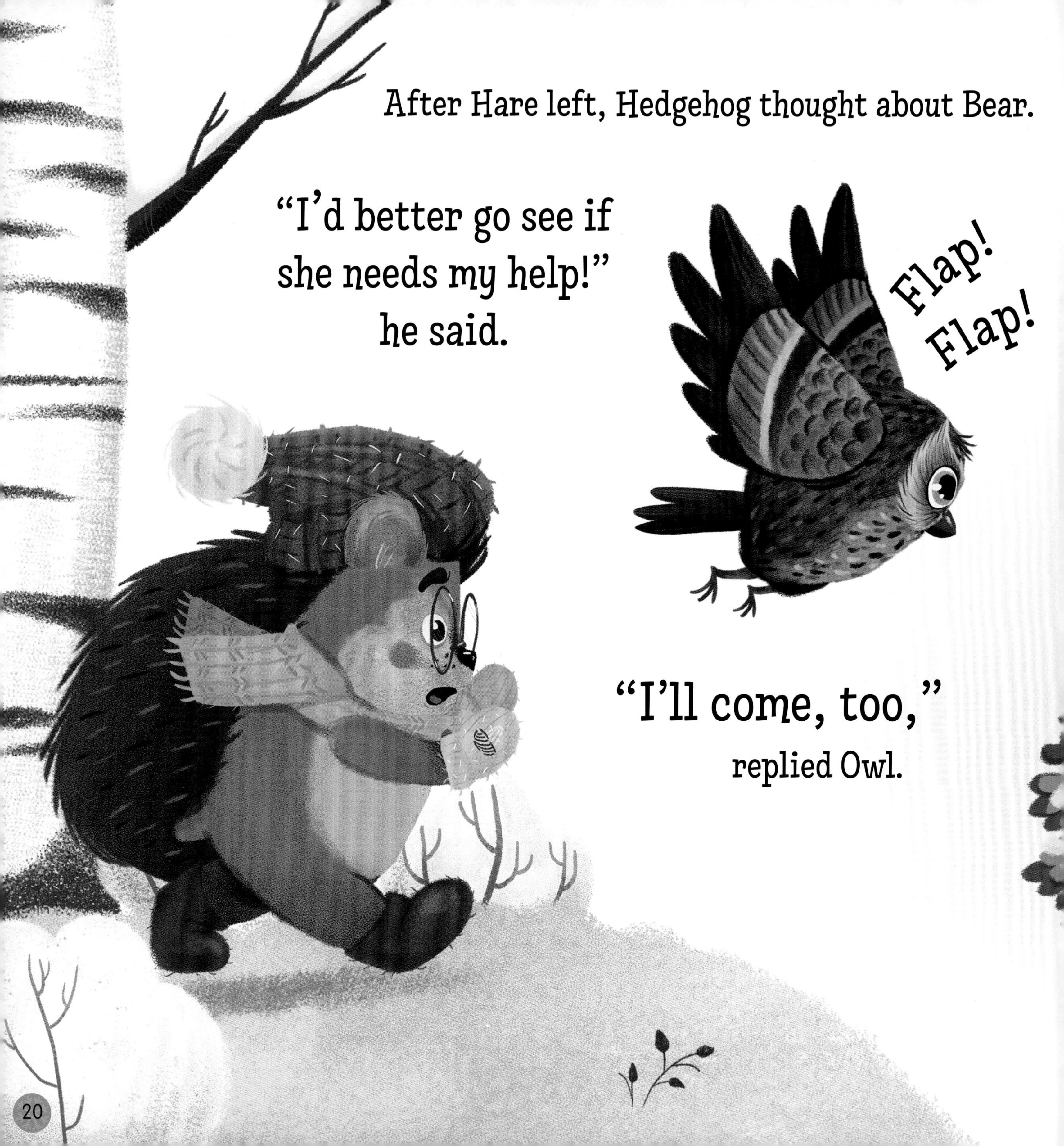
Flap!
Flap!

"I'll come, too," replied Owl.

"Shhh...don't wake her up,"
Owl whispered.
"She sleeps in her cave until spring."

Hedgehog smiled.
"She sleeps during the winter, just like me!"

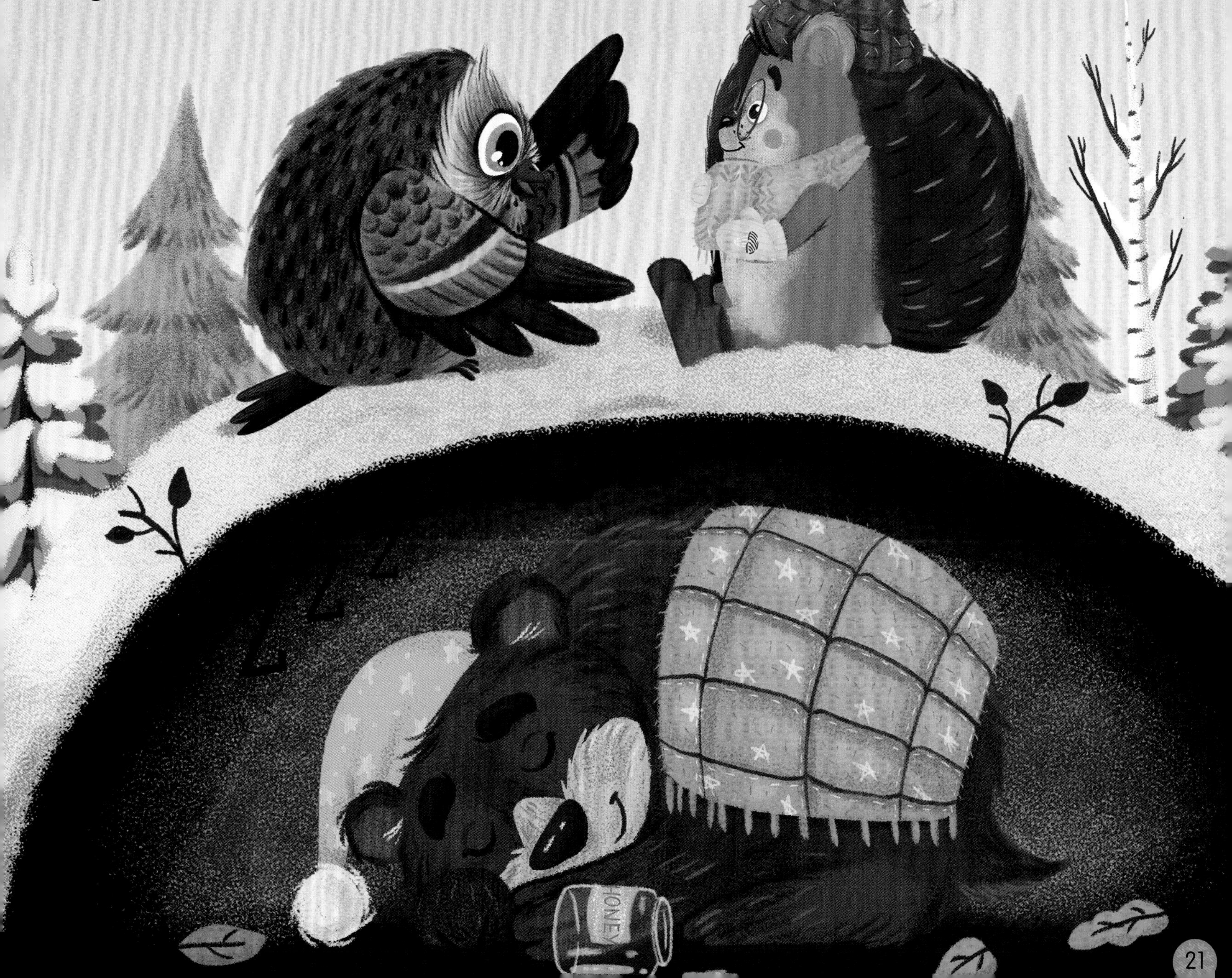
HONEY

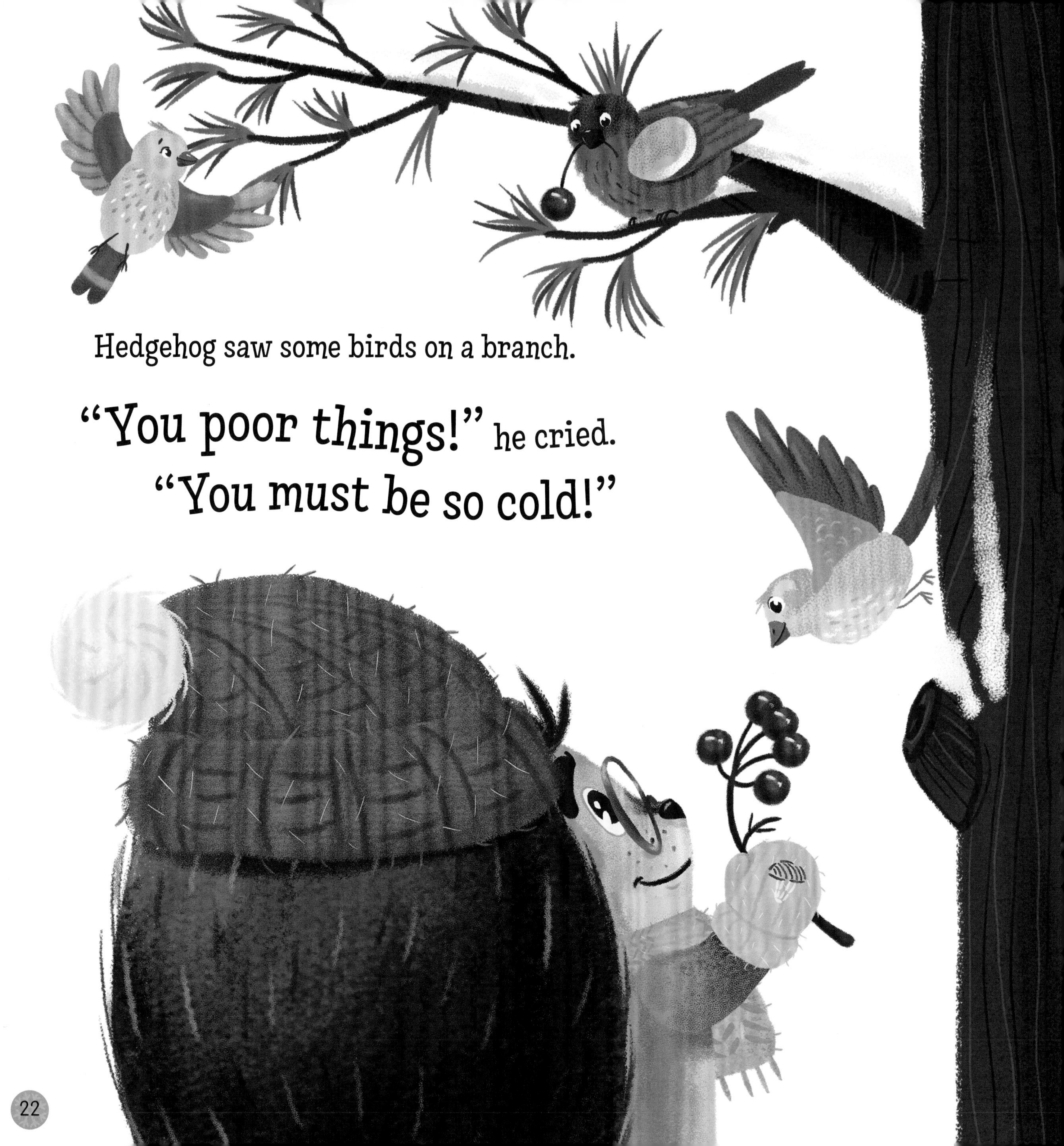

Hedgehog saw some birds on a branch.

"You poor things!" he cried.
"You must be so cold!"

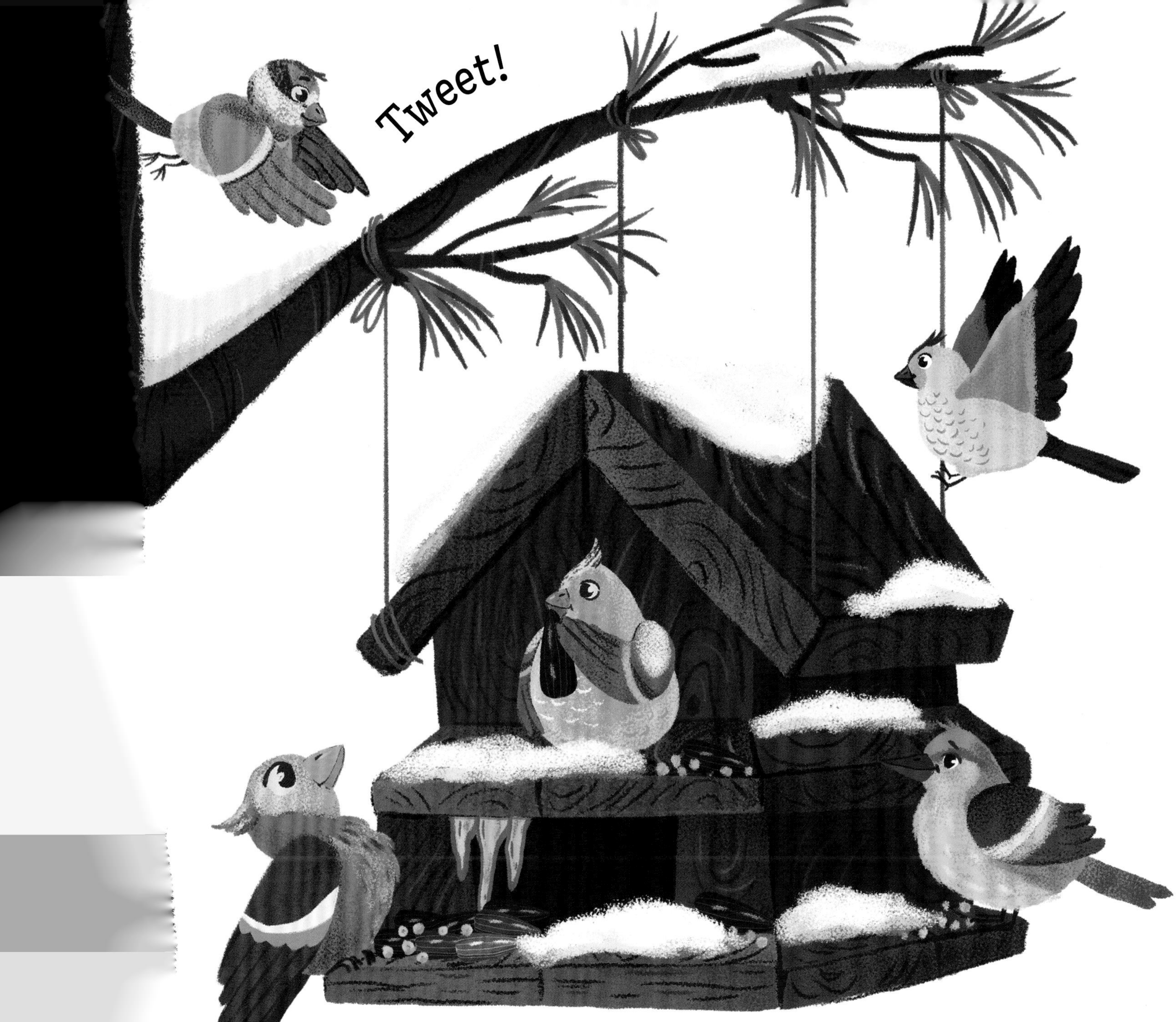
Tweet!

The busy birds smiled.

"We're okay, Hedgehog!" one bird answered. "Our other bird friends flew south for the winter, but we like to stay here."

Hedgehog was confused.

"But why didn't you **fly south** for the winter, too?" he asked them.

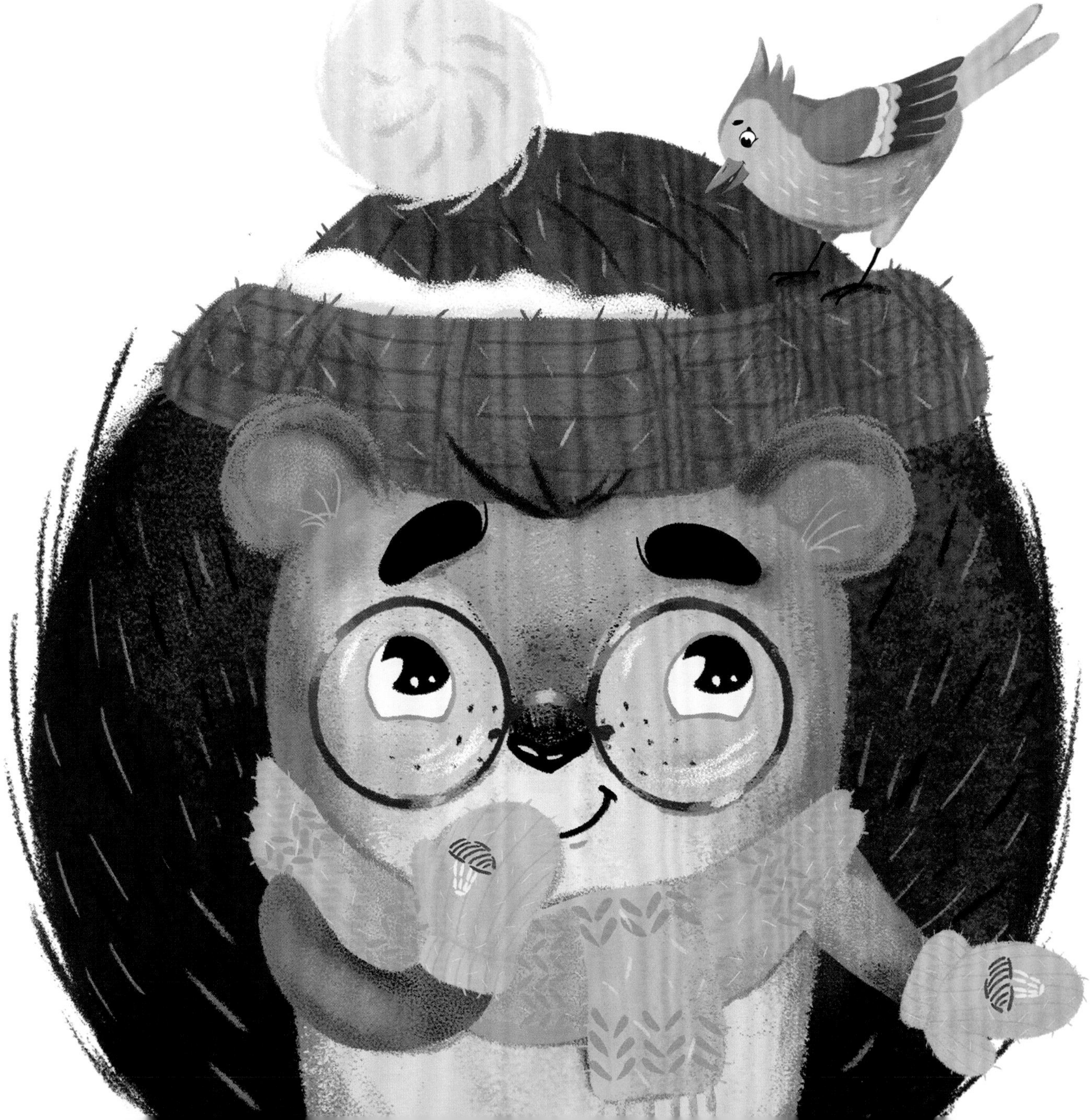

"We don't mind being where it's cold,"

replied another bird.

Tweet!

Tweet!

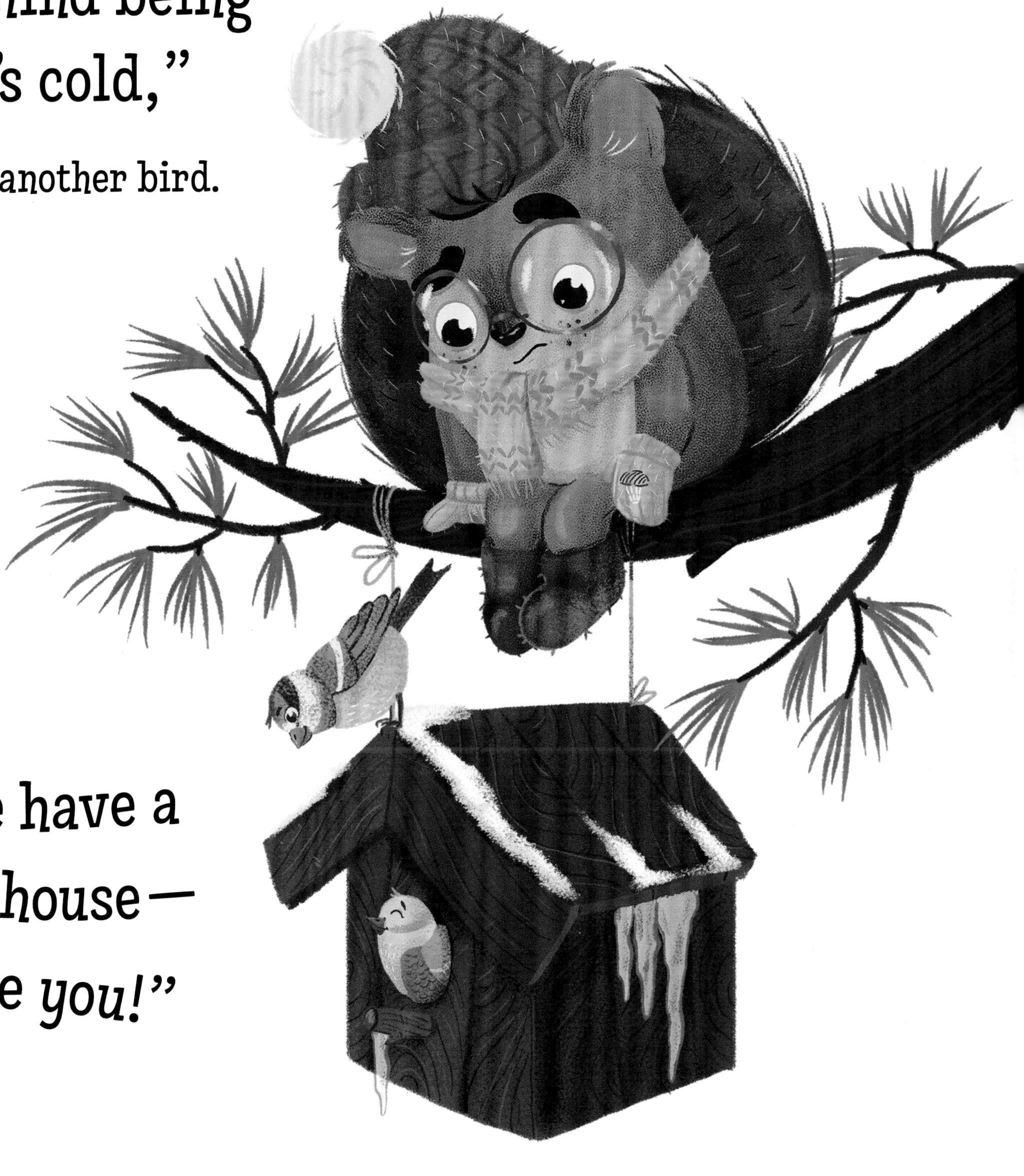

"And we have a warm house— just like *you!*"

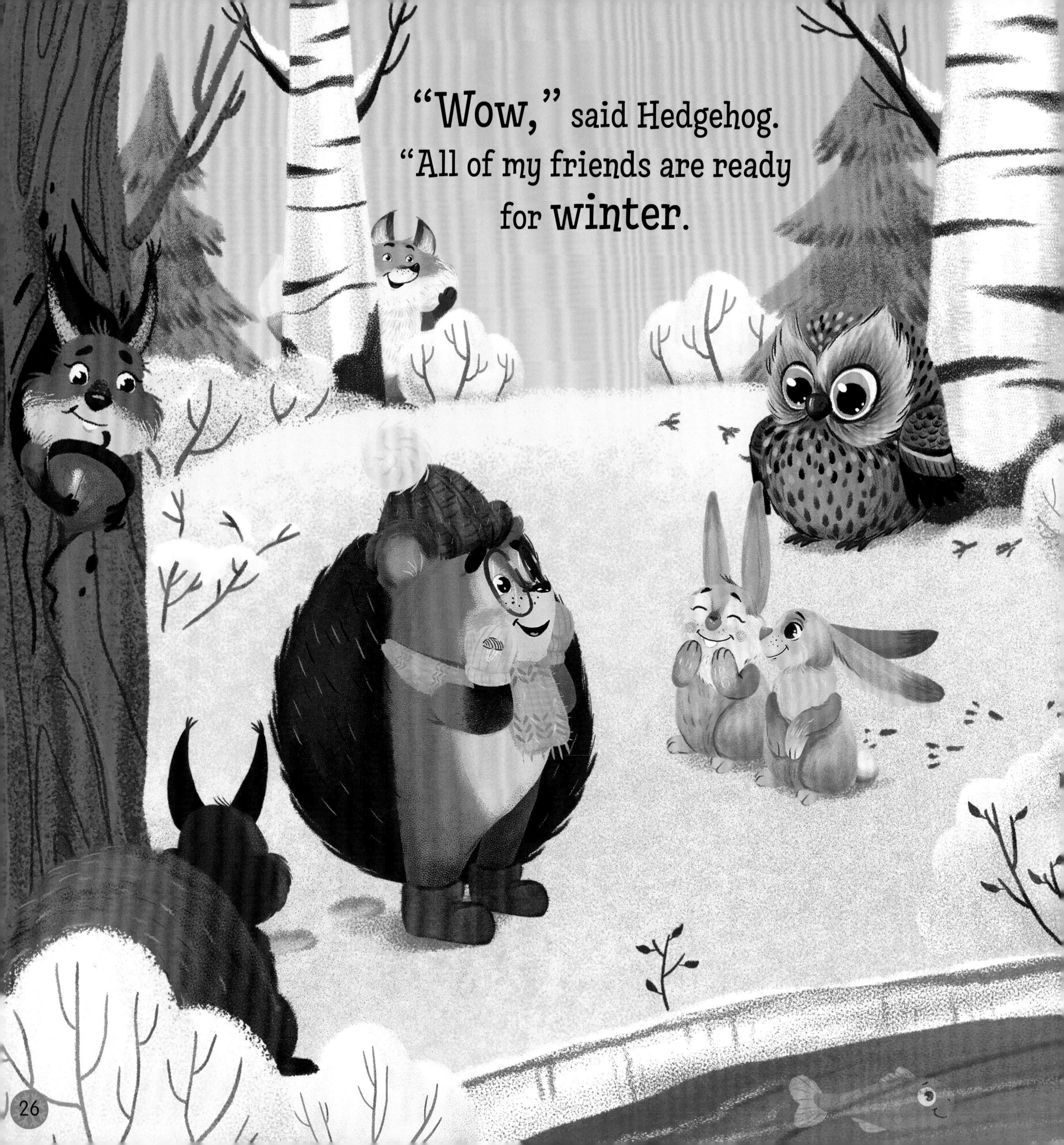

"Wow," said Hedgehog.
"All of my friends are ready
for **winter**.

Nature has taken care of everything for us!”

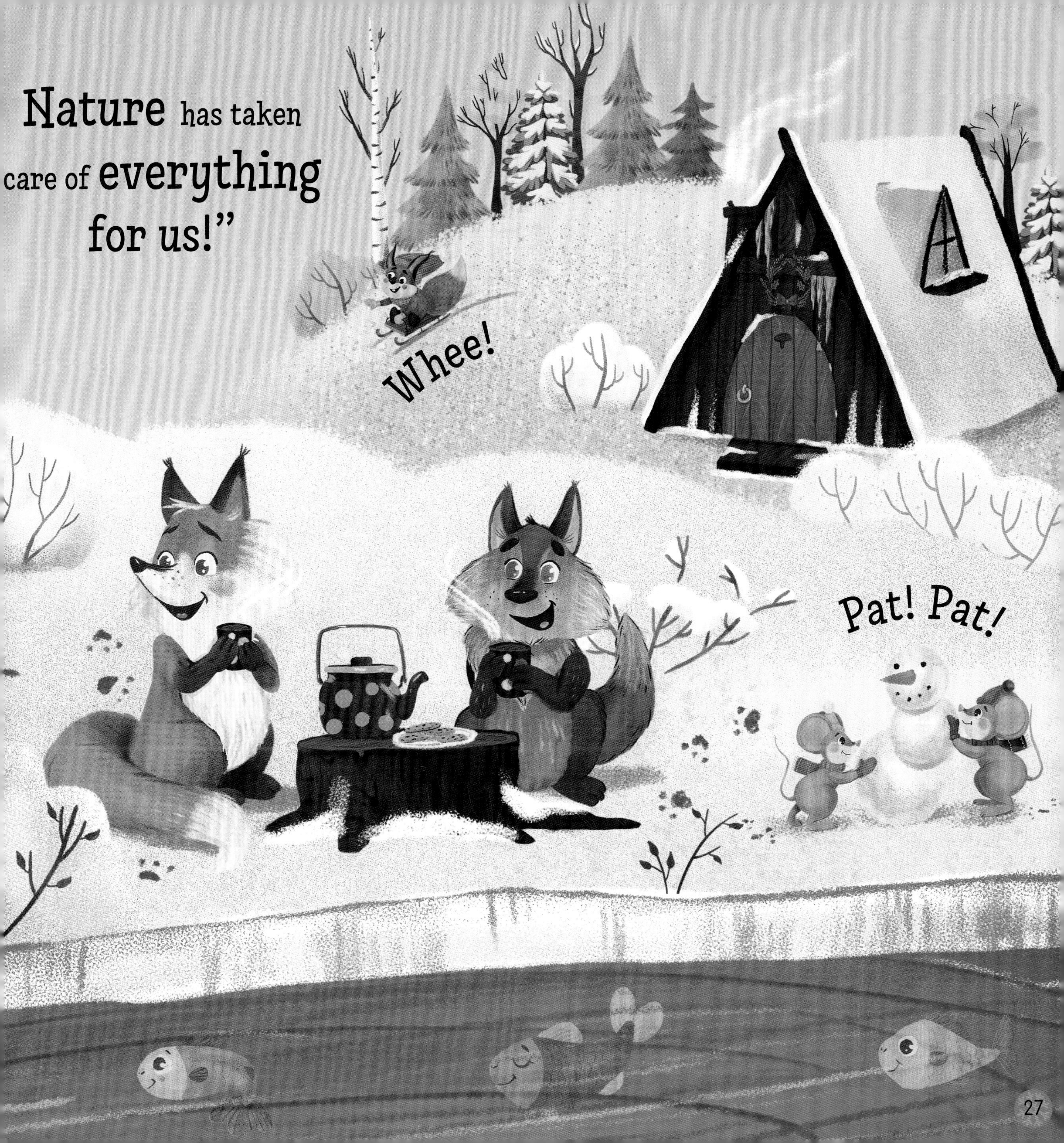
Whee!
Pat! Pat!

Back home, Hedgehog got into bed.
"My friends are safe," he said.
"Now I can take a nap."

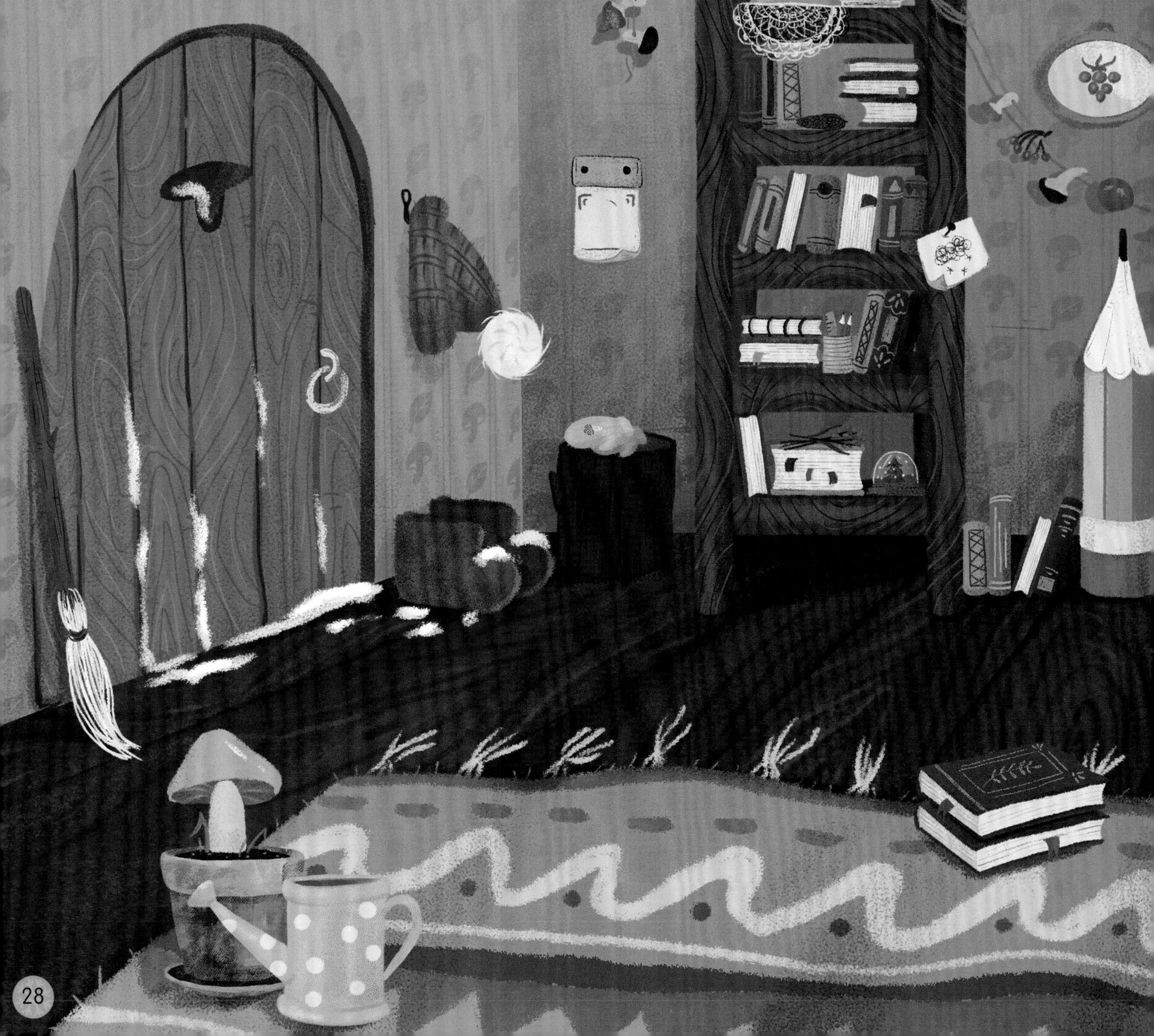

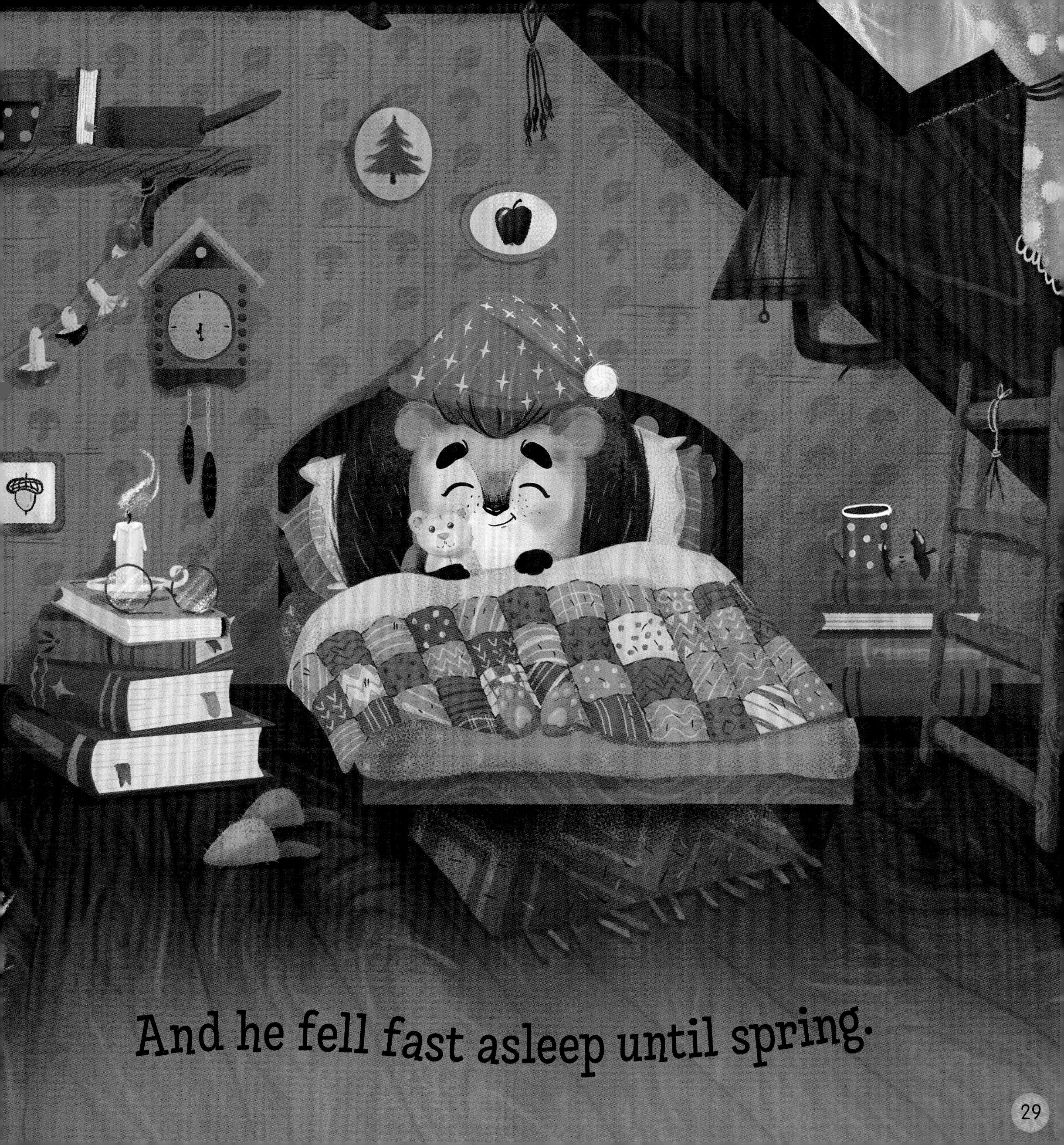

And he fell *fast* asleep until spring.

LET'S LEARN ABOUT WINTER WITH HEDGEHOG!

WINTER MONTHS

DECEMBER

Many animals **hibernate**, which means that they go into a deep sleep and wake up in the spring. Some birds fly south, where it's warmer.

JANUARY

In many parts of the world, you'll need to wear warm clothes when you go outside. Temperatures drop, and in some places, snow falls.

FEBRUARY

It's still cold and snowy in many places around the world. But spring is right around the corner!

WHAT HAPPENS IN WINTER?

SNOW FALLS

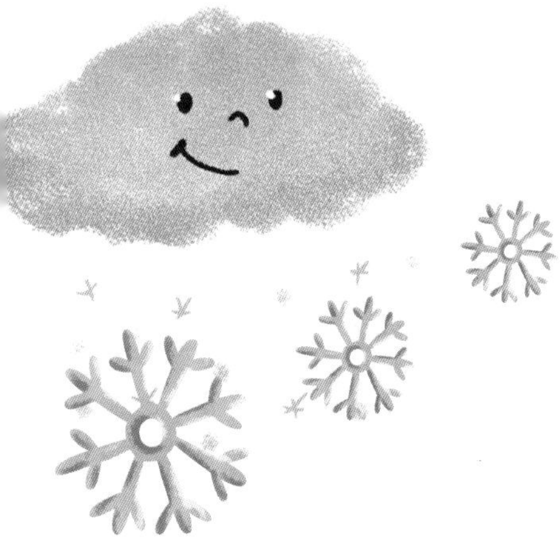

TEMPERATURES DROP

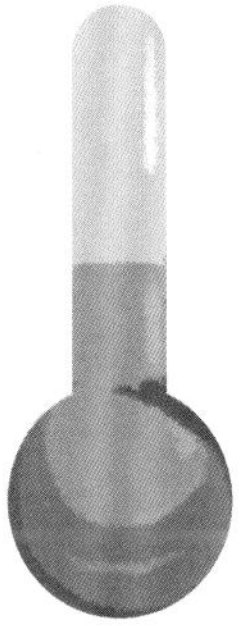

ICICLES FORM

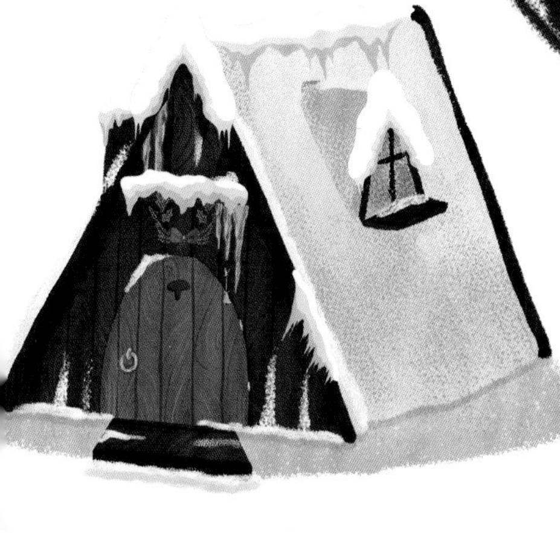

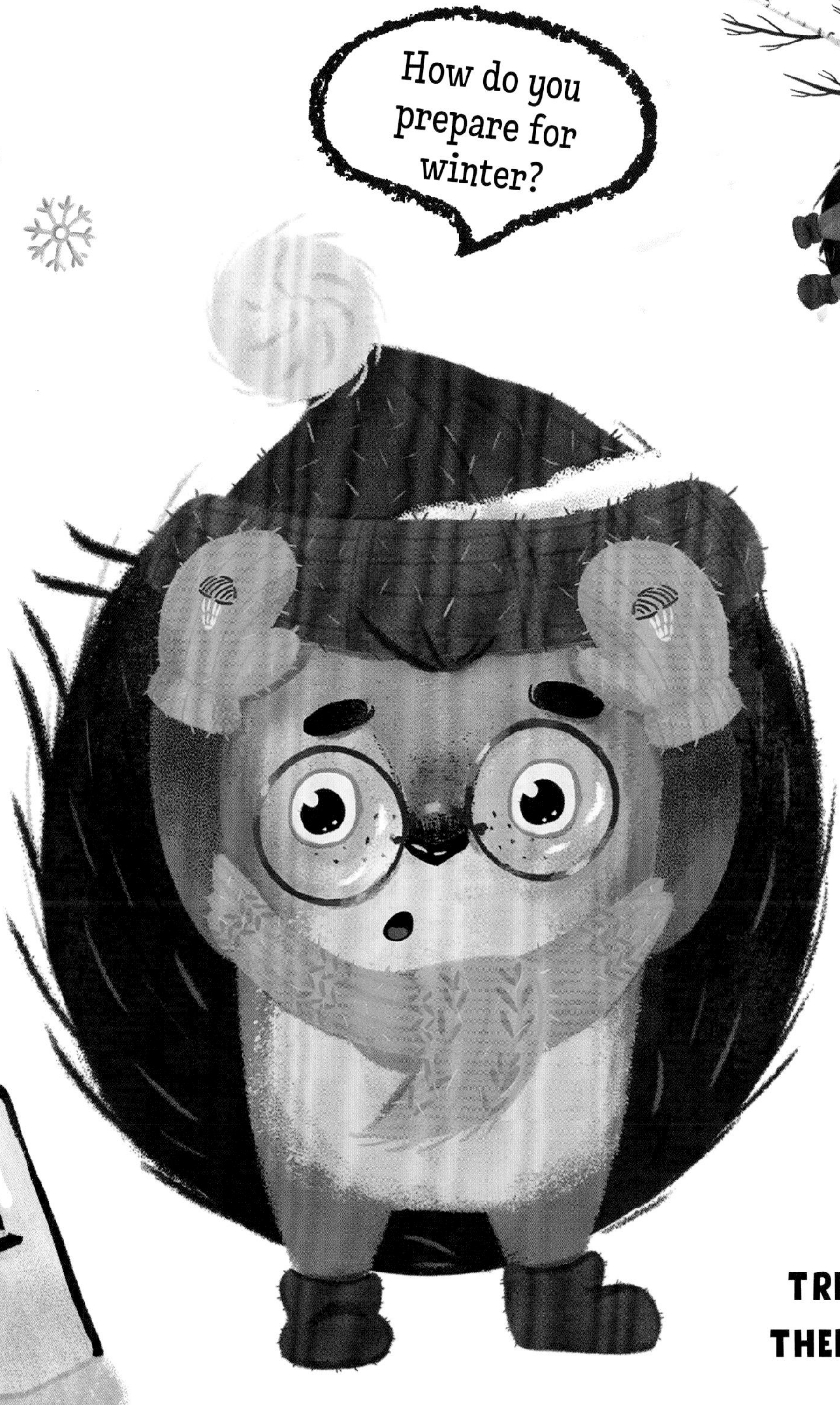
How do you prepare for winter?

WIND BLOWS

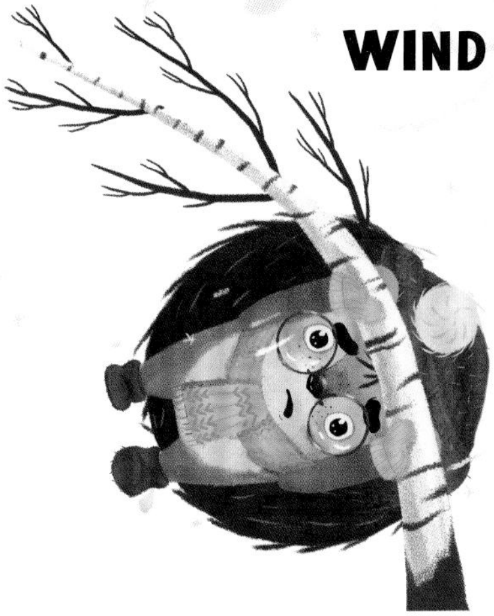

ANIMALS PREPARE

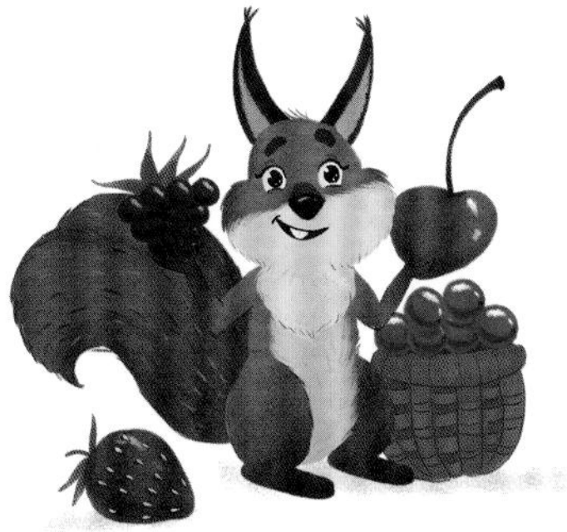

TREES LOSE THEIR LEAVES

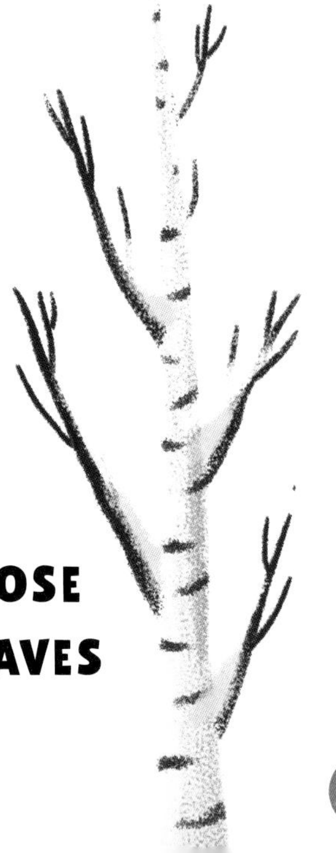

How to Make a SNOW VOLCANO

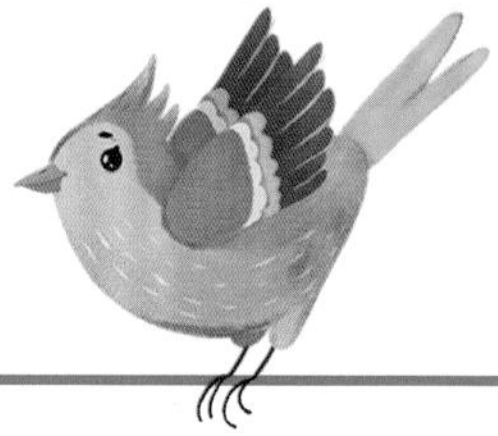

What You Need

* Plastic cup
* Water
* 4-6 tablespoons baking soda
  (This will be extra-foamy and do several eruptions.)
* 1 teaspoon liquid dish soap
* 2-4 tablespoons washable paint
  (depending on the intensity of the color desired)
* Spoon
* Snow
* 1 cup vinegar

If you don't have snow where you live, you can still do this experiment! Find an area with pea gravel, sand, or dirt, and use that material to form the volcano.

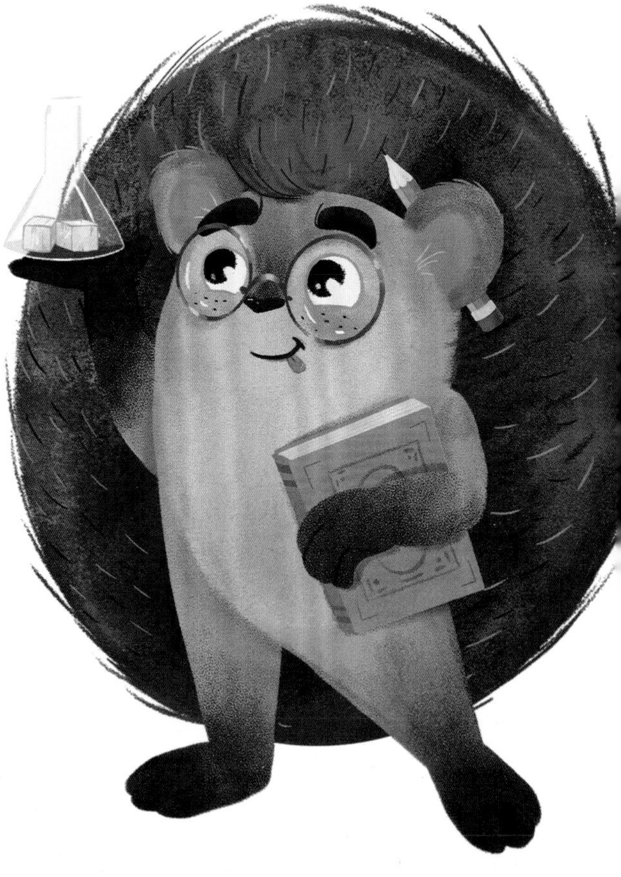

What You Do

Fill the cup with water about 2/3 of the way full. Add the baking soda, liquid dish soap, and washable paint to the cup. Stir with a spoon. Carefully form a volcano shape in the snow around the cup. You should be able to see just the top of the cup. Add the vinegar . . . and watch the eruption!